ABSOLUTE
FRIENDS

John le Carré

SCEPTRE

Copyright © David Cornwell 2003

First published in Great Britain in 2004 by
Hodder & Stoughton
An Hachette UK company

This Sceptre paperback edition 2011

12

The right of John le Carré to be identified as the Author
of the Work has been asserted by him in accordance
with the Copyright, Designs and Patents Act 1988.

A CIP catalogue record for this title is available from the British Library

ISBN 978 0 340 92369 6

Typeset in Fournier MT by Palimpsest Book Production Limited,
Falkirk, Stirlingshire

Printed and bound by Clays Ltd, St Ives plc

Hodder & Stoughton policy is to use papers that are natural, renewable and
recyclable products and made from wood grown in sustainable forests.
The logging and manufacturing processes are expected to conform to the
environmental regulations of the country of origin.

Hodder & Stoughton Ltd
338 Euston Road
London NW1 3BH

www.hodder.co.uk

ABSOLUTE
FRIENDS

1

On the day his destiny returned to claim him, Ted Mundy was sporting a bowler hat and balancing on a soapbox in one of Mad King Ludwig's castles in Bavaria. It wasn't a classic bowler, more your Laurel and Hardy than Savile Row. It wasn't an English hat, despite the Union Jack blazoned in Oriental silk on the handkerchief pocket of his elderly tweed jacket. The maker's grease-stained label on the inside of the crown proclaimed it to be the work of Messrs Steinmatzky & Sons, of Vienna.

And since it wasn't his own hat – as he hastened to explain to any luckless stranger, preferably female, who fell victim to his boundless accessibility – neither was it a piece of self-castigation. 'It's a hat of office, madam,' he would insist, garrulously begging her pardon in a set piece he had off perfectly. 'A gem of history, briefly entrusted to me by generations of previous incumbents of my post – wandering scholars, poets, dreamers, men of the cloth – and every man

jack of us a loyal servant of the late King Ludwig – hah!'
The *hah!* perhaps being some kind of involuntary throwback to his military childhood. 'Well, what's the alternative,
I mean to say? You can hardly ask a thoroughbred
Englishman to tote an *umbrella* like the Japanese guides, can
you? Not here in Bavaria, my goodness, no. Not fifty miles
from where our own dear Neville Chamberlain made his pact
with the devil. Well, *can* you, madam?'

And if his audience, as is often the case, turns out to be
too pretty to have heard of Neville Chamberlain or know
which devil is referred to, then in a rush of generosity the
thoroughbred Englishman will supply his beginners' version
of the shameful Munich Agreement of 1938, in which he
does not shy from remarking how even our beloved British
monarchy, not to mention our aristocracy and the Tory Party
here on earth, favoured practically *any* accommodation with
Hitler rather than a war.

'British establishment absolutely terrified of Bolshevism,
you see,' he blurts, in the elaborate telegramese that, like
hah!, overcomes him when he is in full cry. 'Powers-that-be
in America no different. All *any of 'em* ever wanted was to
turn Hitler loose on the Red Peril.' And how in German
eyes, therefore, Neville Chamberlain's rolled-up umbrella
remains *to this very day, madam*, the shameful emblem of
British appeasement of *Our Dear Führer*, his invariable name
for Adolf Hitler. 'I mean frankly, in this country, *as* an
Englishman, I'd rather stand in the rain without one. Still,
that's not what you came here for, is it? You came to see Mad
Ludwig's favourite castle, not listen to an old bore ranting
on about Neville Chamberlain. What? What? Been a
pleasure, madam' – doffing the clown's bowler in self-parody
and revealing an anarchic forelock of salt-and-pepper hair

that bounces out of its trap like a greyhound the moment it's released – 'Ted Mundy, jester to the Court of Ludwig, at your service.'

And who do they think they've met, these punters – or *Billies*, as the British tour operators prefer to call them – if they think at all? Who is this Ted Mundy to them as a fleeting memory? A bit of a comedian, obviously. A failure at something – a professional English bloody fool in a bowler and a Union Jack, all things to all men and nothing to himself, fifty in the shade, nice enough chap, wouldn't necessarily trust him with my daughter. And those vertical wrinkles above the eyebrows like fine slashes of a scalpel, could be anger, could be nightmares: Ted Mundy, tour guide.

It's three minutes short of five o'clock in the evening, late May, and the last tour of the day is about to begin. The air is turning chilly, a red spring sun is sinking in the young beech trees. Ted Mundy perches like a giant grasshopper on the balcony, knees up, bowler tipped against the dying rays. He is poring over a rumpled copy of the *Süddeutsche Zeitung* that he keeps rolled up like a dog-chew in an inner pocket of his jacket for these moments of respite between tours. The Iraqi war officially ended little more than a month ago. Mundy, its unabashed opponent, scrutinises the lesser head-lines: Prime Minister Tony Blair will travel to Kuwait to express his thanks to the Kuwaiti people for their cooperation in the successful conflict.

'Humph,' says Mundy aloud, brows furrowed.

During his tour, Mr Blair will make a brief stopover in Iraq. The emphasis will be on reconstruction rather than triumphalism.

3

'I should *bloody well* hope so,' Mundy growls, his glower intensifying.

Mr Blair has no doubt whatever that Iraq's weapons of mass destruction will shortly be found. US Defense Secretary Rumsfeld, on the other hand, speculates that the Iraqis may have destroyed them before the war began.

'Why don't you make up your stupid minds then?' Mundy harrumphs.

His day thus far has followed its usual complex and unlikely course. Prompt at six he rises from the bed he shares with his young Turkish partner Zara. Tiptoeing across the corridor he wakes her eleven-year-old son Mustafa in time for him to wash and clean his teeth, say his morning prayers, eat the breakfast of bread, olives, tea and chocolate spread that Mundy has meantime prepared for him. All this is done in an atmosphere of great stealth. Zara works late shift in a kebab café close to Munich's main railway station, and must not on any account be woken. Since starting her night job she has been arriving home around three in the morning, in the care of a friendly Kurdish taxi driver who lives in the same block. Muslim ritual should then permit her to say a quick prayer before sunrise and enjoy eight hours of good sleep, which is what she needs. But Mustafa's day begins at seven, and he too must pray. It took all Mundy's powers of persuasion, and Mustafa's also, to convince Zara that Mundy could preside over her son's devotions, and she could get her hours in. Mustafa is a quiet, cat-like child, with a cap of black hair, scared brown eyes and a raucous boing-boing voice.

From the apartment block − a shabby box of weeping concrete and external wiring − man and boy pick their way across wasteland to a bus shelter covered in graffiti, much of it abusive. The block is what these days is called an ethnic village: Kurds, Yemenis and Turks live packed together in it. Other children are already assembled here, some with mothers or fathers. It would be reasonable for Mundy to consign Mustafa to their care, but he prefers to ride with him to the school and shake his hand at the gates, sometimes formally kissing him on both cheeks. In the twilight time before Mundy appeared in his life, Mustafa suffered humiliation and fear. He needs rebuilding.

Returning from school to the apartment takes twenty minutes of Mundy's huge strides, and he arrives with one half of him hoping Zara is still asleep and the other half that she is just awake, in which case she will make at first drowsy, then increasingly passionate love with him before he leaps into his elderly Volkswagen Beetle and joins the southbound traffic for the seventy-minute drive to the Linderhof and work.

The journey is irksome but necessary. A year ago, all three members of the family were separately in despair. Today they are a fighting force bent upon improving their collective lives. The story of how this miracle came about is one that Mundy recounts to himself whenever the traffic threatens to drive him mad:

He is on his uppers.

Again.

He is practically on the run.

Egon, his business partner and co-principal of their struggling Academy of Professional English, has fled with the last of the assets. Mundy himself has been obliged to creep out of Heidelberg at dead of night with whatever he can cram into the Volkswagen, plus 704 euros of petty cash that Egon has carelessly left unstolen in the safe.

Arriving in Munich with the dawn, he leaves the Volkswagen with its Heidelberg registration in a discreet corner of a high-rise car park in case his creditors have served an order on it. Then he does what he always does when life is closing in on him: he walks.

And because all his life, for reasons far back in his childhood, he has had a natural leaning towards ethnic diversity, his feet lead him almost of their own accord to a street full of Turkish shops and cafés that are just beginning to wake up. The day is sunny, he is hungry, he selects a café at random, lowers his long body cautiously onto a plastic chair that refuses to sit still on the uneven pavement, and asks the waiter for a large medium-sweet Turkish coffee and two poppy-seed rolls with butter and jam. He has barely begun his breakfast when a young woman settles on the chair beside him and with her hand held half across her mouth asks him, in a faltering Turkish-Bavarian accent, whether he would like to go to bed with her for money.

Zara is in her late twenties and improbably, inconsolably beautiful. She wears a thin blue blouse and black brassière, and a black skirt skimpy enough to display her bare thighs. She is dangerously slim. Mundy wrongly assumes drugs. It is also to his later shame that, for longer than he cares to admit, he is half inclined to take her up on her offer. He is sleepless, jobless, womanless and near enough penniless.

But when he takes a closer look at the young woman he is proposing to sleep with, he is conscious of such desperation in her stare and such intelligence behind her eyes, and such a lack of confidence in her part, that he quickly takes a hold of himself, and instead offers her breakfast, which she warily accepts on condition she may take half of it home to her sick mother. Mundy, now hugely grateful to be in contact with a fellow human being in low water, has a better suggestion: she shall eat all the breakfast, and they will together buy food for her mother at one of the halal shops up and down the road.

She hears him without expression, eyes downcast. Desperately empathising with her, Mundy suspects she is asking herself whether he is just crazy or seriously weird. He strains to appear neither of these things to her, but patently fails. In a gesture that goes straight to his heart, she draws her food with both hands to her own side of the table in case he means to take it back.

In doing so, she reveals her mouth. Her four front teeth are sheared off at the root. While she eats, he scans the street for a pimp. She doesn't seem to have one. Perhaps the café owns her. He doesn't know, but his instincts are already protective. As they rise to leave, it becomes apparent to Zara that her head barely reaches up to Mundy's shoulder, for she starts away from him in alarm. He adopts his tall man's stoop, but she keeps her distance from him. She is by now his sole concern in life. His problems are negligible by comparison with hers. In the halal shop, under his urgent entreaty, she buys a piece of lamb, apple tea, couscous, fruit, honey, vegetables, halva and a giant triangular bar of Toblerone chocolate on special offer.

'How many mothers have you got, actually?' he asks her cheerfully, but it's not a joke she shares.

Shopping, she remains tense and tight-lipped, haggling in Turkish from behind her hand, then stabbing her finger at the fruit – not this one, that one. The speed and skill with which she calculates impress him deeply. He may be many kinds of man, but he is no sort of negotiator. When he tries to carry the shopping bags – there are two by now, both weighty – she fights them from him in fierce tugs.

'You want sleep with me?' she asks again impatiently, when she has them safely in her hands. Her message is clear: you've paid for me, so take me and leave me alone.

'No,' he replies.

'What you want?'

'To see you safely home.'

She shakes her head vigorously. 'Not home. Hotel.'

He tries to explain that his purposes are friendly rather than sexual but she is too tired to listen to him and begins weeping without changing her facial expression.

He chooses another café and they sit down. Her tears keep rolling but she ignores them. He presses her to talk about herself and she does so without any particular interest in her subject. She seems to have no barriers left. She is a country girl from the plains of Adana, the eldest daughter of a farming family, she tells him in her faltering Bavarian argot while she stares at the table. Her father promised her in marriage to the son of a neighbouring farmer. The boy was held up as a computer genius, earning good money in Germany. When he came home to visit the family in Adana, there was a traditional wedding feast, the two farms were declared to be joined, and Zara returned to Munich with her husband, only to discover he was not a computer genius at all, but a full-time, round-the-clock armed bandit. He was twenty-four, she was seventeen and expecting a child by him.

'It was gang,' she declares simply. 'All boys were bad crooks. They are crazy. Steal cars, sell drugs, make night-clubs, control prostitutes. They do all bad things. Now he is in prison. If he would not be in prison, my brothers will kill him.'

Her husband had been sent to prison nine months ago, but had found time to terrify the wits out of his son and smash his wife's face in before he went. A seven-year sentence, other charges pending. One of the gang turned police witness. Her story continues in a monotonous flow as they walk through the town, now in German, now in snatches of Turkish when her German fails her. Sometimes he wonders whether she knows he is still beside her. *Mustafa*, she says, when he asks the boy's name. She has asked him nothing about himself. She is carrying the shopping bags and he makes no further attempt to carry them for her. She is wearing blue beads, and he remembers from somewhere far back in his life that for superstitious Muslims blue beads ward off the evil eye. She is sniffing but the tears are no longer rolling down her cheeks. He guesses she has made herself cheer up before meeting someone who mustn't know she has been crying. They are in Munich's Westend, which hardly accords with its elegant London equivalent: drab, pre-war apartment houses in old greys and browns; washing hanging out to dry in the windows, kids playing on a patch of moulting grass. A boy sees their approach, breaks free of his friends, picks up a rock and advances on them menacingly. Zara calls to him in Turkish.

'What do you want?' the boy yells.

'A piece of your Toblerone please, Mustafa,' Mundy says.

The boy stares at him, talks again to his mother, then edges forward, keeping the rock in his right hand while he pokes in the bags with his left. Like his mother, he is gaunt, with shadowed eyes. Like his mother, he seems to have no emotions left.

'And a cup of apple tea,' Mundy adds. 'With you and all your friends.'

Led by Mustafa who is by now carrying the bags, and escorted by three stalwart dark-eyed boys, Mundy follows Zara up three flights of grimy stone stairs. They reach a steel-lined door, Mustafa delves inside his shirt and with a proprietorial air pulls out a front-door key on a chain. He steps into the house, accompanied by his friends. Zara steps after them. Mundy waits to be invited.

'You will please come in,' Mustafa announces in good Bavarian. 'You will be most welcome. But if you touch my mother, we shall kill you.'

For the next ten weeks Mundy sleeps on Mustafa's sofa bed in the living room with his legs hanging over the end while Mustafa sleeps with his mother, keeping a baseball bat beside him in case Mundy tries anything on. At first Mustafa refuses to go to school, so Mundy takes him to the zoo and plays ball games with him on the moulting grass while Zara stays home and lapses gradually into a state of convalescence, which is Mundy's hope. Bit by bit he assumes the rôle of secular father to a Muslim child and platonic guardian to a traumatised woman in a state of religious shame. The neighbours, initially suspicious of this gangling English intruder who laughs so much, begin to tolerate him, while Mundy for his part does everything he can to separate himself from his country's hated colonialist reputation. For money they use the rest of his seven hundred euros and the pittance that Zara receives from her Turkish family and German social security. In the evenings she likes to cook and Mundy plays kitchen boy to her. At first she objects to this, then grudgingly allows it. Cooking together becomes the main event of the day. Her rare laughter is like God's gift to him, broken teeth and all. Her life's ambition, he learns, is to qualify as a nurse.

A morning comes when Mustafa announces that he will go to school. Mundy escorts him, and is proudly introduced by Mustafa as his new father. The same week, all three make their first appearance together at the mosque. Expecting a gilded dome and a minaret, Mundy is startled to find himself in a tiled room on an upper floor of a down-at-heel house sandwiched between bridal costumiers, halal shops and stores selling used electrical goods. From his past he remembers that he mustn't point his feet at anyone, or shake hands with women, but place his right hand over his heart and drop his head in respect. With Zara consigned to the women's room, Mustafa takes his hand, guides him to the men's prayer-line and instructs him when to stand, when to make an obeisance, and when to kneel and press his brow to the strip of rush matting that does duty for the soil.

Mustafa's gratification in Mundy is immense. Until now, he has been obliged to sit upstairs with his mother and the younger kids. Thanks to Mundy he is now downstairs with the men. When prayers are over, Mustafa and Mundy may now shake hands with all the men around them, while each expresses the hope that the other's prayers have found a good reception in Heaven.

'Study and God will make you wise,' the enlightened young imam advises Mundy as he leaves. 'If you do not study, you will become the victim of dangerous ideologies. You are married to Zara, I believe?'

Mundy has the grace to blush, and mutters something about, well, hope to one day.

'The formality is not important,' the young imam assures him. 'Responsibility is all. Be responsible and God will reward you.'

A week later Zara gets herself a night job at the kebab

café by the station. The manager, having failed to go to bed with her, decides instead to depend on her. She wears the scarf and becomes his star employee, allowed to handle cash and protected by a very tall Englishman. A couple more weeks and Mundy too finds himself a place in the world: as English tour guide at the Linderhof. Next day, Zara pays a solitary visit to the enlightened young imam and his wife. Returning, she closets herself for an hour alone with Mustafa. The same night Mustafa and Mundy exchange beds.

Mundy has known stranger passages in his life, but none, he is convinced, has filled him with such satisfaction. His love for Zara knows no bounds. He loves Mustafa no less, and loves him best for loving his mother.

The English-Spoken cattle pen is opening, the usual multicultural gaggle of sightseers shuffles forward. Canadians with red maple leaves on their backpacks, Finns in anoraks and tartan golf caps, Indian women in saris, Australian sheep farmers with air-dried wives, Japanese elders who grimace at him with a pain he has never learned the source of: Mundy knows them all by heart, from the colours of their tour buses to the first names of their rapacious minders who wish only to lure them to the gift shops for the greater good of their commissions. All that is missing from this evening's mix is platoons of Midwestern teenagers with barbed wire round their teeth, but America is celebrating its Victory over Evil at home, to the dismay of the German tourist industry.

Removing his bowler and brandishing it above his head, Mundy places himself at the front of his flock and leads the march to the main entrance. In his other hand he clutches a home-built soapbox of marine plywood that he has knocked together in the boiler room beneath the apartment block.

Other guides employ the staircase as a speaker's platform. Not Ted Mundy, our Hyde Park Corner orator. Plonking the box at his feet, he steps smartly onto it, to reappear taller than his audience by eighteen inches, the bowler once more aloft.

'English speakers to *me* then, please, *thank you*. English *listeners*, I should be saying. Though by this time in the day I wish you *were* the speakers. Hah! Not true, really' – the voice kept deliberately low at this stage so that they have to quieten down to hear him – 'not running out of steam yet, I promise you. Cameras welcome, ladies and gents, but no videos, please – that's you too, please, sir, thank you – don't ask me why, but my masters assure me that the merest *whiff* of a video camera will land us in the intellectual-property courts. The normal penalty is a public hanging.' No laughter but he doesn't expect it yet from an audience that has spent the last four hours wedged into a bus, and another hour queuing in the heat of the sun. 'Gather round me, *please*, ladies and gentlemen, a little closer, if you *will*. Plenty of room here in front of me, ladies' – to a bunch of earnest schoolmistresses from Sweden – 'can you hear me over there, young sirs?' – to a clutch of bony teenagers from across the invisible border to Saxony who have wandered into the wrong pen by mistake, but have decided to stay and get a free English lesson – 'You can. Good. And can you *see* me, sir?' – to a diminutive Chinese gentleman – 'You can. One *personal* request, if you don't mind, ladies and gents. *Handies* as we call them here in Germany, known otherwise as your mobile telephones. Kindly make sure they're switched off. All done? Then perhaps the last one in will close those doors behind you, sir, and I'll begin. Thank you.'

The sunlight is cut off, an artificial dusk is lit by myriad candle-bulbs reflected in gilt mirrors. Mundy's finest moment – one of eight in every working day – is about to begin.

'*As* the most observant among you will see, we are standing in the relatively modest entrance hall of the *Linderhof*. Not Linderhof *Palace*, please, because *hof* here means *farm*, and the palace where we are standing was built on the land where the Linder farm once stood. But why *Linder?* we ask ourselves. Do we have a philologist among us? A professor of words? An expert on the old meanings?'

We do not, which is as well, because Mundy is about to embark on one of his illicit improvisations. For reasons that escape him, he never seems quite to have got his head round the plot. Or perhaps it's a blind spot he has. Sometimes he takes himself by surprise, which is part of the therapy when he is fighting other, more persistent thoughts, such as Iraq, or a threatening letter from his Heidelberg bank which this morning coincided with a demand note from the insurance company.

'Well now, we do have the German word *Linde* meaning a lime tree. But does that explain the R? I ask myself.' He's flying now. 'Mind you, the farm may just have belonged to Mr Linder, and that's the end of it. But I prefer a different explanation, which is the verb *lindern*, to relieve, to alleviate, to assuage, to soothe. And I like to think it's the interpretation that appealed most to our poor King Ludwig, if only subliminally. The Linderhof was his *soothing place*. Well, we all need a bit of soothing, don't we, especially these days? Ludwig had had a rough deal, remember. He was nineteen when he took the throne, he was tyrannised by his father, persecuted by his tutors, bullied by Bismarck, cheated by his courtiers, victimised by corrupt politicians, robbed of his dignity as a king, and he hardly knew his mother.'

Has Mundy been similarly mistreated? By the throb in his voice, you would believe so.

'So what does he *do*, this handsome, over-tall, sensitive, abused, *proud* young man who believes he was appointed by God to rule?' he asks, with all the pained authority of one over-tall man empathising with another. 'What does he *do* when he is systematically stripped bit by bit of the power he was born to? Answer: he builds himself a string of fantasy castles. And who wouldn't?' – warming to his subject – 'Palaces with attitude. Illusions of power. The less power he's got, the bigger the illusions he builds – rather like my gallant Prime Minister, Mr Blair, if you want my opinion, but don't quote me' – bemused silence – 'And that's why personally I try not to call Ludwig *mad*. The King of Dreamers is what I prefer to call him. The King of Escape Artists, if you like. A lonely visionary in a lousy world. He lived at night, as you probably know. Didn't like people on the whole and certainly not the ladies. Oh *dear* me, no!'

The laughter this time comes from a group of Russians who are passing a bottle between them, but Mundy prefers not to hear them. Raised on his home-made soapbox, his bowler hat tilted slightly forward, Guards-style, over his unmanageable mop of hair, he has entered a sphere as rarefied as King Ludwig's. Only seldom does he bestow a glance on the upturned heads below him, or pause to let a child bawl or a bunch of Italians resolve a private disagreement.

'When Ludwig was inside his own head, he was ruler of the universe. Nobody, but *nobody*, gave him orders. Here at the Linderhof he was the reincarnation of the Sun King, that bronze gentleman you see riding his horse on the table: Louis in French is Ludwig in German. And at Herrenchiemsee a few miles from here, he built his very own Versailles.

15

At Neuschwanstein up the road he was Siegfried, the great German mediaeval king-warrior, immortalised in opera by Ludwig's idol Richard Wagner. And high up in the mountains, if you're feeling athletic, he built the palace of Schachen, where he duly crowned himself King of Morocco. He'd have been Michael Jackson if he could, but fortunately he hadn't heard of him.'

Laughter from round the room by now, but once again Mundy ignores it.

'And His Majesty had his *little ways*. He had his food put on a gold table and sent up to him through a hole in the floor – which in a minute I'm going to show you – so that nobody could watch him eat. He kept the servants up all night and if they annoyed him he'd order them to be flayed alive. If he had one of his antisocial moods on him, he'd talk to you from behind a screen. And kindly bear in mind, please, that all this is happening in the nineteenth century, not the Dark Ages. Out there in the real world they're building railways and iron ships and steam engines and machine-guns and cameras. So don't let's fool ourselves that this is long-long-ago and once-upon-a-time. Except for Ludwig, of course. Ludwig had put his life into reverse. He was going back into history just as fast as his money would carry him. Which was the problem, because it was also Bavaria's money.'

A downward peek at his wristwatch. Three and a half minutes gone. By now he should be walking up the staircase, his audience trailing after him. He is. Through adjoining walls he can hear the voices of his colleagues, raised like his own: boisterous Frau Doktor Blankenheim, retired teacher, recent Buddhist convert and doyenne of the reading circle; pallid Herr Stettler, cyclist and erotomane; Michel Delarge from Alsace, unfrocked priest. And behind him, coming up the stairs, wave after wave of invincible Japanese infantry led by a tight-stepping Nipponese beauty queen brandishing a puce umbrella that is a far cry from Neville Chamberlain's.

And, somewhere close to him, and not for the first time in his life, the ghost of Sasha.

Is it here on the staircase that Mundy first feels the familiar prickle on his back? In the throne room? In the royal bedchamber? In the Hall of Mirrors? Where does the awareness, like an old premonition, steal over him? A hall of mirrors is a deliberate bastion against reality. Multiplied images of reality lose their impact as they recede into infinity. A figure who face to face might instil stark fear or perfect pleasure becomes, in his numberless reflections, a mere premise, a putative form.

Besides which, Mundy is by necessity and training a most watchful man. Here in the Linderhof he does not undertake the simplest manoeuvre without checking his back and front and all the other approaches to him, either for unwelcome traces of previous lives or for errant members of his present one, such as art thieves, vandals, pickpockets, creditors, writ-servers from Heidelberg, senile tourists struck down by heart attacks, children vomiting on priceless carpets, ladies with small dogs concealed in their handbags, and latterly – on the urgent insistence of the management – suicidally disposed terrorists. Nor must we exclude from this roll of honour the welcome relief, even to a man so happily paired, of a shapely girl whose attributes are best appreciated indirectly.

To assist him in this vigil, Mundy has covertly appointed certain vantage points or static posts: here a dark painting, conveniently glazed, that looks backward down the stairs; there a bronze urn that supplies a wide-angle image of whoever is to either side of him; and now the Hall of Mirrors itself, where a multitude of replicated Sashas hovers in miles and miles of golden corridor.

Or not.

Is he but a Sasha of the mind, a Friday-night mirage? Mundy has seen his share of almost-Sashas in the years since they took leave of one another, as he is quick to remind himself: Sashas down to their last euro who spot him from across the street and, spidery with hunger and enthusiasm, come hobbling through traffic to embrace him; prosperous, sleek Sashas with fur on their coat collars, who wait artfully in doorways to spring out at him or clatter down public stairways yelling, *Teddy, Teddy, it's your old friend, Sasha!* Yet no sooner does Mundy stop and turn, his smile faithfully aloft, than the apparition has vanished or, transmuting itself into an entirely different person, slunk off to join the common crowd.

It is in his quest for solid verification therefore that Mundy now casually changes his vantage point, first by flinging out a rhetorical arm, then by spinning round on his box to point out to his audience the view, the splendid, the magnificent view, afforded from the royal bedstead – just follow my arm, ladies and gents – of the Italian waterfall descending the northern slopes of the Hennenkopf.

'Imagine you're lying there!' he urges his audience with a rush of exuberance to match the spectacular torrent – 'With somebody who loves you! Well, probably *not* in Ludwig's case' – gusts of hysterical laughter from the Russians – 'but lying there anyway, surrounded by all that royal Bavarian gold and blue! And you wake up one sunny morning, and you open your eyes, and you look out of the window at – *bang*.'

And on the word *bang* nails him: *Sasha — good God, man, where the hell have you been?* — except that Mundy says none of this, neither does he indicate it by so much as a slip of the eye, because Sasha in the Wagnerian spirit of the place is wearing his invisibility hat, his *Tarnkappe* as they used to call it, the black Basque beret worn severely across the brow that warns against the slightest indiscretion, particularly in time of war.

In addition to which — lest Mundy has by any chance forgotten his clandestine manners — Sasha has placed a curled and pensive forefinger to his lips, not in warning but rather in the dreamy pose of a man relishing the vicarious experience of waking up one sunny morning and looking out of the window at the waterfall coming down the Hennenkopf. The gesture is superfluous. Not the keenest watcher, not the smartest surveillance camera in the world would have caught a hint of their reunion.

But Sasha all the same: Sasha the midget-sentry, vital even when he is motionless, poised that little bit apart from the person nearest him in order to escape the comparison of height, elbows lifted from his sides as if he's about to take off, his fiery brown eyes aimed just above your eyeline — never mind that, like Mundy, you're taller than he is by a head and a half — bonding, accusing, searching, challenging, eyes to inflame you, question and unsettle you. Sasha, as I live and breathe.

The tour is ending. House rules forbid guides to solicit but allow them to hover at the doorway, nodding their departing audience into the sunlight and wishing them a safe and simply *marvellous* holiday. The take has always varied, but war has reduced it to a trickle. Sometimes Mundy stands empty-handed till the end, his bowler roosting on a convenient bust

19

lest it be mistaken for anything as vulgar as a begging bowl. Sometimes a devoted middle-aged couple or a schoolteacher with unruly charges will dart shyly forward and press a banknote on him, then dart back into the throng. This evening it's a genial building contractor from Melbourne and his wife Darlene who need to explain to Mundy that their daughter Tracey did this *very same tour* way back in the winter, with the *self-same travel company*, would you believe it? And had just *loved* every minute of it – maybe Mundy remembered her, because she sure as hell remembered the big tall Pom in the Bowler Hat! Blonde girl, freckles and a ponytail, boyfriend a medical student from Perth, plays rugby for his university? And it is while Mundy is putting on a show of hunting for Tracey in his memory – the boyfriend's name was Keith, the building contractor confides, in case it's any help – that he feels a hard small hand encircle his wrist, turn it palm upward, insert a folded note and close his fingers over it. In the same moment, out of the corner of his eye, he glimpses Sasha's beret disappearing into the crowd.

'Next time you're in Melbourne, right?' the Australian building contractor yells, tucking a card into the pocket behind Mundy's Union Jack.

'It's a date!' Mundy agrees with a cheery laugh, and deftly palms the note into a side pocket of his jacket.

It is wise to sit down before you start a journey, preferably on your luggage. The superstition is Russian but the axiom originates with Nick Amory, who is Mundy's long-time advisor in matters of self-preservation: if something big is in the air, Edward, and you're part of it, then for pity's sake curb your natural impetuosity and give yourself a break before you jump.

The Linderhof's day is over, staff and tourists are hurrying towards the car park. Like a benign host, Mundy hovers on the steps bestowing multilingual benedictions on his departing colleagues. *Auf Wiedersehen, Frau Meierhof! Still haven't found them then!* He is referring to Iraq's elusive weapons of mass destruction. *Fritz, Tschüss! Love to your dear lady! Marvellous speech she made the other night at the Poltergeist!* – our local culture and debating club where Mundy occasionally goes to let off political steam. And to his French and Spanish colleagues, a married male couple – *Pablo, Marcel, we'll commiserate together next week. Buenas noches, bonsoir the both of you!* The last stragglers disappear into the twilight as he withdraws into the shadows of the western prospect of the palace, immersing himself in the blackness of a stairwell.

He stumbled on the place by luck soon after he took up the job.

Exploring the castle's precincts one evening – a moonlight concert is to be held in the grounds and, Mustafa allowing, he has a mind to stick around and hear it – he discovers a humble basement staircase that leads nowhere. Descending it, he meets a rusted iron door, and in the door a key. He knocks and, hearing nothing, turns the key and steps inside. To anyone but Mundy, the space he enters is no more than a grubby plant room, a dumping ground for watering cans, old hosepipes and ailing plants. No window, just a grille high in the stone wall. Air heavy with the stink of putrid hyacinth and the rumblings of a boiler next door. But to Mundy it is everything Mad Ludwig was looking for when he built the Linderhof in the first place: a sanctuary, a place of escape from his other places of escape. He steps back outside, relocks the door, puts the key in his pocket and for seven working days bides his time while he mounts a systematic reconnaissance of his target. By 10 a.m. when the castle gates open, all healthy plants in the public rooms have been watered and unhealthy plants removed. The plant contractor's van, a flower-painted minibus, leaves the grounds at 10.30 a.m. latest, by which time ailing plants have been consigned to the plant room, or to the van for hospitalisation. The disappearance of the key has raised no eyebrows. The lock has not been changed. It follows that from eleven every morning the plant room is his private property.

It is his tonight.

Standing his full height beneath the frugal ceiling lamp, Mundy extracts a pen-torch from his pocket, unfolds the note until it becomes a rectangle of plain white paper, and sees what he expects to see: Sasha's handwriting, as it always was and ever shall be: the same spiky Germanic Es and Rs, the same adamant downstrokes that declare the man. The expression on Mundy's face as he reads its message is hard to parse. Resignation, anxiety and pleasure all play a part. A rueful excitement dominates. Thirty-four bloody years, he thinks. We're men of three decades. We meet, we fight a war, we separate for a decade. We meet again, and for a decade we're indispensable to each other while we fight another. We part for ever, and a decade later you come back.

Fishing in his jacket pockets he takes out a scuffed book of matches from Zara's kebab café. He plucks a match, strikes it and holds the note in the flame by one corner then another until it's a twisted flake of ash. He lets it fall to the flagstones and grinds it to black dust with his heel, a necessary observance. He looks at his watch and does the arithmetic. One hour and twenty minutes to kill. No point in ringing her yet. She'll just have started work. Her boss goes crazy when the staff take personal calls in peak hours. Mustafa will be at Dina's house with Kamal. Mustafa and Kamal are bosom pals, leading lights of the Westend's all-Turkish national cricket league, President, Mr Edward Mundy. Dina is Zara's cousin and good friend. Scrolling through a mildewed cellphone, he locates her number and dials it.

'Dina. Greetings. The bloody management have called a meeting of tour guides for tonight. I totally forgot. Can Mustafa sleep over at your place in case I'm late?'

'Ted?' Mustafa's croaking voice.

'*Good evening to you, Mustafa! How are you doing?*' Mundy asks, slowly and emphatically. They are speaking the English that Mundy is teaching him.

'I – am – doing – *very – very – well*, Ted!'

'Who is Don Bradman?'

'Don – Bradman – is – greatest – batsman – ever – the – world – was – seen, Ted!'

'Tonight you stay at Dina's house. Yes?'

'Ted?'

'Did you understand me? I have a meeting tonight. I will be late.'

'And – I – sleep – at – Dina.'

'Correct. Well done. You sleep at Dina's house.'

'Ted?'

'What?'

Mustafa is laughing so much he can hardly speak. 'You – very – bad – bad – man, Ted!'

'Why am I a bad man?'

'You – love – other – woman! I – tell – Zara!'

'How did you guess my dark secret?' He has to repeat this.

'I – know – this! I – have – big – big – eyes!'

'Would you like a description of the other woman I love? To tell to Zara?'

'Please?'

'This other woman I've got. Shall I tell you what she looks like?'

'Yes, yes! You – tell – me! You – bad – man!' More hoots of laughter.

'She's got very beautiful legs –'

'Yes, yes!'

'She's got *four* beautiful legs, actually – very *furry* legs – and a long golden tail – and her name is – ?'

'Mo! You love Mo! I tell Zara you love Mo more!'

Mo the stray Labrador, thus named by Mustafa in honour of himself. She took up residence with them at Christmas, to the initial horror of Zara, who has been brought up to believe that touching a dog makes her too dirty to pray. But under the concerted pressure of her two men, Zara's heart melted, and now Mo can do no wrong.

He rings the apartment and hears his own voice on the answerphone. Zara loves Mundy's voice. Sometimes, when she's missing him in the daytime, she says, she plays the tape for company. I may be late, darling, he warns her in their common German over the machine. There's a meeting of staff tonight and I forgot all about it. Lies like this, told protectively and from the heart, have their own integrity, he tells himself, wondering whether the enlightened young imam would agree. And I love you quite as much as I loved you this morning, he adds severely: so don't go thinking otherwise.

He glances at his watch – one hour and ten minutes to go. He advances on a worm-eaten gilded chair and puts it in front of a dilapidated Biedermeier wardrobe. Balancing on the chair, he gropes behind the wardrobe's pediment and extracts an ancient khaki kitbag thick with dust. He pats the dust off, sits down on the chair, sets the kitbag on his lap, yanks the webbing straps free of their tarnished buckles, lifts the flap and peers dubiously inside as if uncertain what to expect.

Gingerly he unpacks the contents onto a bamboo table: one ancient group photograph of an Anglo-Indian family with its many native servants posed on the steps of a grand Colonial house; one buff folder marked FILE in aggressive hand-inked capitals; one bundle of ill-written letters of a similar period; one twist of woman's hair, dark brown, bound round a sprig of dried heather.

But these objects attract only a curt acknowledgement from him. What he is looking for, and has perhaps deliberately left till last, is a plastic folder in which float as many as twenty unopened letters addressed to Mr Teddy Mundy care of his bank in Heidelberg in the same black ink and spiky hand as the note he has this minute burned. No sender's name is supplied, but none is needed.

Floppy blue air-letters.

Coarse-grained Third World envelopes reinforced with sticky tape and blazoned with stamps as radiant as tropical birds from places as far apart as Damascus, Djakarta and Havana.

First he sorts them into chronological order according to their postmarks. Then he slits them open, one by one, with an old tin penknife, also from the kitbag. He starts reading. For what? *When you are reading something, Mr Mundy, first ask yourself why you are reading it.* He is hearing the accented voice of his old German teacher, Dr Mandelbaum, forty years ago. *Are you reading something for* information? *That is one reason. Or are you reading it for* knowledge? *Information is only the path, Mr Mundy. The goal is* knowledge.

I'll settle for knowledge, he's thinking. And I promise I won't fall for dangerous ideology, he adds, with a mental doff of the cap to the imam. I'll settle for knowing what I didn't want to know, and I'm still not sure I want to. How did you find me, Sasha? Why must I not recognise you? Who are you avoiding this time, and why?

Folded among the letters are press cuttings torn impatiently from newspapers and bearing Sasha's byline. The salient passages are highlighted, or indicated by exclamation marks.

He reads for an hour, returns the letters and press cuttings to the kitbag and the kitbag to its hiding place. The mixture as expected, he silently tells himself. No quarter given. One man's war continues as planned. Age is not an excuse. It never was and never will be.

He puts the gilded chair where he found it, sits down again and remembers he's wearing his bowler hat. He takes it off, turns it upside down and peers into it, a thing he does in pensive moments. The maker Steinmatzky's first name is Joseph. He owns to sons, no daughters. His firm's address in Vienna is *No. 19 Dürerstrasse above the Baker's.* Or it was, because old man Joseph Steinmatzky liked to date his handiwork and this example boasts a vintage year: 1938.

Staring into the hat, he watches the scene unfold. The cobbled alley, the little shop above the baker's. The smashed glass, the blood between the cobblestones as Joseph Steinmatzky, his wife and many sons are dragged away to the vociferous approval of Vienna's proverbially innocent bystanders.

He rises, squares his shoulders, lowers them and wriggles

his hands around to loosen himself up. He steps into the stairwell, relocks the door, mounts the stone steps. Strips of dew hover over the palace lawns. The fresh air smells of mown grass and damp cricket field. Sasha, you mad bastard, what do you want now?

Urging his Volkswagen Beetle over the hump between Mad Ludwig's golden gates, Mundy turns onto the road to Murnau. Like its owner, the car is no longer in its first youth. Its engine wheezes, tired wipers have etched half-moons on its windscreen. A home-made sticker on the back, written by Mundy in German, reads *The Driver of This Car Has No Further Territorial Claims in Arabia*. He crosses two small intersections without mishap and as promised encounters a blue Audi with a Munich registration pulling out of the lay-by ahead of him with a silhouetted Sasha in his beret crouched at the wheel.

For fifteen kilometres by the unreliable gauge of the Volkswagen Mundy clings to the Audi's tail. The road sinks, enters forest and divides. Without signalling, Sasha takes a left fork and Mundy in his Volkswagen scrambles after him. Avenues of black trees lead downward to a lake. Which lake? According to Sasha, the only thing Mundy has in common with Leon Trotsky is what the great man called topographical cretinism. At a parking sign the Audi descends a ramp and skids to a halt. Mundy does the same, glancing in his mirror to see what, if anything, comes after him, or what went by slowly without stopping: nothing. Sasha with a carrier bag in his hand is scurrying unevenly down a flight of paved steps.

Sasha believes that before he was born he lacked oxygen in the womb.

A jingle-jangle of fairground music is coming up the path. Fairy lights are twinkling through the trees. A village festival is in progress and Sasha is heading towards it. Scared of losing him, Mundy closes the gap. With Sasha fifteen yards in front they plunge into an inferno of roistering humanity. A merry-go-round belches honky-tonk, a matador on a hay cart undulates before a cardboard bull while crooning in broad Silesian about *amor*. Beer-sodden revellers, oblivious to the war, blow feathered snakes at each other. Nobody is out of place here, not Sasha, not me. Everyone's a citizen for a day and Sasha hasn't forgotten his skills either.

Over a loudspeaker, the *Grossadmiral* of a flag-bedecked steamer is ordering stragglers to forget their troubles and report *immediately* for the romantic cruise. A rocket bursts above the lake. Coloured stars cascade onto the water. Incoming or outgoing? Ask Bush and Blair, our two great war leaders, neither of whom has seen a shot fired in anger.

Sasha has vanished. Mundy looks up and to his relief sees him hauling himself and his carrier bag Heavenwards by way of a spiral iron staircase attached to an Edwardian villa painted in horizontal stripes. His strides are frantic. They always were. It's the way he ducks his head each time he lunges with the right leg. Is the bag heavy? No, but Sasha is careful to nurse it as he negotiates the curves. A bomb perhaps? Not Sasha, never.

After another casual look round for whoever else may be coming to the party, Mundy climbs after him. MINIMUM LET ONE WEEK, a painted sign warns him. A *week*? Who needs a week? These games finished fourteen years ago. He glances down. Nobody is coming up after him. The front door of each apartment as he works his way up is painted mauve and lit by fluorescent strip. At a half-landing a hollow-faced woman in a Sherpa coat and gloves is fumbling in her handbag. He gives her a breathless *grüss Gott*. She ignores him or she's deaf. Take your gloves off, woman, and maybe you'll find it. Still climbing, he glances wistfully back at her as if she were dry land. She's lost her door key! She's locked her grandchild in her flat. Go back downstairs, help her. Do your Sir Galahad act, then go home to Zara and Mustafa and Mo.

He keeps climbing. The staircase turns another corner. On mountain tops around him eternal snow-pastures bask under a half-moon. Below him the lake, the fair, the din – and still no followers that he's aware of. And before him a last mauve door, ajar. He pushes it. It opens a foot but he sees only pitch darkness. He starts to call out *Sasha!* but the memory of the beret restrains him.

He listens and hears nothing except the noise of the fair. He steps inside and pulls the door shut behind him. In the half-darkness, he sees Sasha standing crookedly to attention with the carrier bag at his feet. His arms are as straight to his sides as he can get them and his thumbs pressed forward in the best tradition of a Communist Party functionary on parade. But the Schiller face, the fiery eyes, the eager, forward-leaning stance, even in the flickering dusk, have never appeared so vivid or alert.

'You talk a lot of bullshit these days, I would say, Teddy,' he remarks.

The same smothered Saxon accent, Mundy records. The same pedantic, razor-edged voice, three sizes too big for him. The same instant power of reproach.

'Your philological excursions are bullshit, your portrait of Mad Ludwig is bullshit. Ludwig was a fascist bastard. So was

Bismarck. And so are you, or you would have answered my letters.'

But by then they are hastening towards each other for the long-delayed embrace.

2

The swirling river that winds from Mundy's birth to Sasha's reincarnation at the Linderhof has its source not in the shires of England but in the accursed mountain ranges and ravines of the Hindu Kush that under three centuries of British Colonial administration became the North-West Frontier Province.

'This young sahib of mine you see here,' the retired major of infantry who was Mundy's father would announce in the private bar of the Golden Swan in Weybridge to anybody unfortunate enough not to have heard the story before, or who had heard it a dozen times but was too courteous to say, 'is by way of being a bit of an historical *rarity*, aren't you, boy, aren't you?'

And, slipping an affectionate arm round the adolescent Mundy's shoulder, would muss his hair before turning him to the light for ease of scrutiny. The Major is small, fiery and impassioned. His gestures, even in love, are never less than pugilistic. His son is a beanstalk, already taller than his father by a head.

'And I'll tell you for *why* young Edward here is a rarity, if you'll permit me, sir,' he would continue, gathering steam as he addresses all the sirs within range, and the ladies too, for they still have an eye for him, and he for them. 'On the morning my bearer reported to me that the memsahib was about to do me the honour of presenting me with a child – this very child here, sir – a perfectly *normal* Indian sun was rising over the regimental infirmary.'

A stage pause, of the sort Mundy too will one day learn to make, as the Major's glass also mystically rises and his head dips to greet it.

'*However*, sir,' he would resume. 'However. By the time this same young man deigned to appear on parade' – swinging accusingly round to Mundy now, but the fierce blue gaze as doting as ever – 'without your topee, sir, fourteen days confined to barracks, as we used to say! – that sun up there wasn't Indian any more. It belonged to the self-governing Dominion of Pakistan. Didn't it, boy? Didn't it?'

At which the boy will most likely blush, and stammer out something like, 'Well, so you *tell* me, Father,' which would be enough to earn him a kindly laugh, and for the Major just possibly another drink on someone else's tab, and an opportunity to point the moral of his tale.

'Madame History a very fickle lady, sir' – in the telegramese later inherited by his son – 'you can march for her day and night. Sweat your guts out for her. Shit, shine, shave, shampoo for her. Doesn't make a blind bit o' difference. The day she doesn't want you – *out*. Dismiss. Scrapheap. Enough said.' A fresh glass is by now making its ascent. 'Your good health, sir. Generous man. To the Queen-Emperor. God bless her. Coupled with the name of the Punjabi fighting man. Finest soldier ever lived, bar none. Provided he is led, sir. There's the rub.'

And a ginger beer for the young sahib if he's lucky, while the Major in a fit of emotion whisks a khaki handkerchief from the sleeve of his frayed military sports jacket and, having first hammered his fussy little moustache with it, dabs his cheeks before returning it to base.

The Major had cause for his tears. The day of Pakistan's birth, as the Golden Swan's customers know all too well, robbed him not only of his career, but also of his wife who, having taken one exhausted look at her overdue and over-long son had, like the Empire, expired.

'That woman, sir –' It is the evening watering hour, and the Major is waxing sentimental. 'Only one word to describe her: *quality*. First time I saw her, she was in her riding clothes, out for a dawn canter with a couple of bearers. Done five Hot Weathers in the plains and looked as though she'd come straight from eating strawberries and cream at Cheltenham Ladies' College. Knew her fauna and flora better than her bearers did. And she'd be with us here to this day, God bless her, if that arsehole of a regimental doctor had been halfway sober. To her memory, sir. The late Mrs Mundy. Forward march.' His tearful eye settles on his son, whose presence he appears momentarily to have forgotten. 'Young Edward,' he explains. 'Opens the bowling for his school. How old are you, boy?'

And the boy, waiting to take his father home, admits to sixteen.

The Major, however, as he will assure you, did not buckle under the tragedy of his double loss. He stayed on, sir. He endured. Widowed, a baby son to look after, Raj collapsing round his ears, you might think he'd do what the other buggers did: lower the Union Jack, sound the Last Post and sail home to obscurity. Not the Major, sir. No, thank you. He would rather slop out his Punjabis' shithouses than kiss the arse of some limp-wristed war-profiteer in Civvy Street, thank you.

'I summoned my *derzi*. I said to my *derzi*, "*Derzi*, on the day the Dominion of Pakistan declares itself to be the Republic of Pakistan, and not one day later, you will unstitch the major's crowns on my khaki drills, and you will replace them with the crescent moon of Pakistan – *juldi*." And I pledged my services – for as long as they were appreciated – to the finest body of fighting men in the world bar none, *provided*' – his index finger stabs the air in dramatic warning – 'provided, sir, that they are *led*. There's the rub.'

And there also, mercifully, the bell will ring for last orders, and the boy will slip a trained hand beneath his father's arm and march him home to Number Two, The Vale to finish up last night's curry.

But Mundy's provenance is not as easily defined as these bar-room reminiscences suggest. The Major, so lavish with the larger brushstrokes, is reticent when it comes to detail, with the result that Mundy's memories of his infancy are a succession of camps, barracks, depôts and hill stations that accelerates as the Major's fortunes dwindle. One day the proud son of Empire rules supreme over a whitewashed cantonment complete with red-ochred club, polo, swimming pool, children's games and Christmas plays, including an historic production of *Snow White and the Seven Dwarfs* in which he stars as Dopey. The next, he is running barefoot down the mud streets of a half-empty settlement miles from any town, with bullock carts instead of motor cars, a corrugated-iron cinema for a club, and Christmas pudding served in a regimental institute green with mould.

Few possessions survive so many moves. The Major's tiger skins, his military chests and treasured ivory carvings are all posted missing. Even his late wife's memory has been stolen, her diaries, letters and a box of precious family jewellery: that thieving bastard of a stationmaster at Lahore, the Major will have him flogged, and every one of his rascally *chaprassis* with him! He makes the vow one night in his cups after Mundy has driven him over the edge with his persistent damn-fool questioning. 'Her *grave*, boy? I'll tell you where her bloody grave is! Gone! Smashed to bits by rampaging tribesmen! Not a stone left standing! All we've got of her is *here*!' And he drives his tiny fist against his breast, and pours himself another *chota peg*. 'That woman had class you wouldn't believe, boy. I can see her every time I look at you. Anglo-Irish nobility. Vast estates, razed to the ground in the Troubles. First the Irish, now the bloody Dervishes. Entire clan dead or scattered to the winds.'

They come to rest in the garrison hill town of Murree. While the Major vegetates in a mud-brick barrack hut smoking Craven A for his throat's sake and growling over pay imprests, sick-lists and leave rosters, the boy Mundy is consigned to the care of a very fat Madrassi ayah who came north with Independence, and has no name but Ayah, and recites rhymes with him in English and Punjabi, and surreptitiously teaches him Holy Sayings from the Koran, and tells him of a god called Allah who loves justice and all the peoples of the world and their prophets, even Christians and Hindus, but most of all, she says, he loves children. It is only most unwillingly, after much pressing on Mundy's part, that she admits to possessing no husband, children, parents, sisters or brothers left alive. 'They are all dead now, Edward. They are with Allah, every one. It is all you need to know. Go to sleep.'

Murdered in the great massacres that came of the Partition, she admits under interrogation. Murdered by Hindus. Murdered at railway stations, in mosques and market places.

'How did you stay alive, Ayah?'

'It was the will of God. You are my blessing. Go to sleep now.'

Come evening, to a chorus of goats, jackals, bugles and the insistent twanging of Punjabi drums, the Major will also contemplate mortality, under a neem tree at the river's edge, puffing at cheroots that he calls Burmas and cuts into lengths with a tin penknife. Intermittently he refreshes himself from a pewter hip flask while his overgrown son splashes with his native peers and, acting out the never-ending tales of adult slaughter all around them, plays Hindus versus Muslims and takes turns at being dead. Forty years on, Mundy has only to close his eyes to feel the magic cooling of the air that comes with sundown, and smell the scents that leap out of the sudden dusk, or watch the dawn rise over foothills glistening green from the monsoon, or hear the cat-calls of his playmates give way to the muezzin and the nocturnal bellows of his father berating that damned boy of mine who killed his mother – *Well, didn't you, boy, didn't you? Come here* juldi *when I order you, boy!* But the boy declines, *juldi* or otherwise, preferring to let Ayah clutch him to her flank until the drink has done its work.

Now and then, the boy must endure a birthday, and from the moment it appears on his horizon he succumbs to a variety of illnesses: stomach cramps, feverish headaches, Delhi belly, the onset of malaria, or fears that he has been bitten by a poisonous bat. But the day still comes round, the kitchen wallahs prepare a fearsome curry and make a great cake with *Many Happy Returns to Edward* on it, but no other children are invited, the shutters are closed, the dining table is laid for three, candles are lit and the servants stand silently round the wall while the Major in full mess kit and decorations plays the same Irish ballads on the gramophone again and again, and Mundy wonders how much of his curry he can get away with not eating. Solemnly he blows out his candles, cuts three slices of his birthday cake and lays one on his mother's plate. If the Major is half sober, father and son will do silent combat with a red-and-white ivory chess set brought out for feast-days. The games have no conclusion. They are put aside for tomorrow, and tomorrow never comes.

But there are the other, rarest nights – they never needed to be many – when the Major with a more than usually frightful scowl will stalk to a desk in a corner of the room, unlock it with a key from his chain, and ceremoniously extract from it an elderly red-bound volume called *Selected Readings from the Works of Rudyard Kipling*. Pulling a pair of reading spectacles from their battered metal case and setting his whisky glass in a hole in the arm of his rattan chair, he will bark toneless phrases about Mowgli the jungle boy, and another boy called Kim who became a spy in the service of his Queen and Emperor, though what happened to him when he had become one, and whether he won or was caught, were matters not divulged by the extract. For hours on end the Major will sip and read and sip as solemnly as if he is conducting a one-handed service of Communion, until at length he falls asleep, and Ayah emerges silently from the shadows where she has been crouching all this while and, taking Mundy by the hand, leads him to bed. The Kipling anthology, the Major tells him, is the sole survivor of a vast eclectic library that was once his mother's.

'That woman had more books in her than I've had hot dinners,' he marvels in his soldier's way. Nevertheless, with time it becomes something of a puzzle to Mundy, and a frustration, that such an illustrious reader as his mother should have left him such a ragbag of half-told tales. He prefers Ayah's bedtime stories of the heroic doings of the Prophet Mohammed.

For the remainder of his education the boy attends the dying remnants of a Colonial school for the orphans and children of impecunious British officers, performs in pantomimes and pays weekly visits to a smooth-faced Anglican missionary who instructs him in Divinity and piano, and likes best to guide boys' fingers with his own. But these random spurts of Christianity are only tiresome interruptions in the sunlit passage of each pagan day. His best hours are spent playing ferocious cricket with Ahmed, Omar and Ali on the dust-patch behind the mosque, or gazing in glassy rock pools that flash mother-of-pearl, while he whispers child-love to Rani, a nine-year-old barefoot beauty of the village whom he intends to marry for ever just as soon as arrangements can be made; or bawls patriotic hymns in Punjabi as the shiny new flag of the Islamic Republic of Pakistan is hoisted over the regimental cricket pitch.

And Mundy would have passed the rest of his youth in this undemanding manner, and the rest of his life also, had not a night come when the servants and even Ayah are fled and the bungalow's shutters are once more bolted fast, while father and son in silent haste load their last few life possessions into leather suitcases with brass corners. By first light they are bumping out of camp in the back of an ancient military police truck with two grim Punjabi soldiers riding shotgun. Hunched at Mundy's side the unfrocked major of Pakistani infantry wears a civilian trilby hat and his old school tie, a regimental tie being no longer pukkah for an outcast found guilty of raising his hand to a brother officer. What he did with his hand when he'd raised it was not defined, but if Mundy's experience was anything to go by, he didn't just slip it back in his pocket unfired. At the garrison gates, the dewan who until now welcomed Mundy with a beaming salute is granite-faced, and Ayah stands as white as all the ghosts she fears in her grief, anger and disgust. Ahmed, Omar and Ali howl and wave and scamper after the truck, but Rani is not among them. Dressed in her Brownie tunic, her black hair freshly plaited down her back, she bends double at the roadside, bare feet pressed together as she chokes over her folded arms.

The boat leaves Karachi in darkness and stays dark all the way to England because the Major has become ashamed of his face after seeing it printed in the vernacular press. To hide it from view he takes his whisky in his cabin, and food only when the boy presses it on him. The boy becomes his father's minder, keeping watch for him, making sorties, vetting the ship's daily newspaper in advance for toxic matter, sneaking him on deck for furtive walks before daylight, and in the evenings while the ship changes for dinner. Lying on his back on the other bunk, secondary-smoking his father's Burmas, counting the brass screw-heads in the teak ribs that arch across the bulkhead and listening now to his father's ramblings, now to the chug of the ship's engines, or puzzling his unfulfilled way through Rudyard Kipling, he dreams of Rani, and swimming home to what his father still calls India.

And the Major in his anguish has much to say on the subject of his adored, abandoned India, some of it to the young Mundy's ear surprising. With nothing more to be gained by pretending otherwise, the Major declares himself mortally disgusted by his country's connivance in the disastrous Partition. He heaps curses on the rogues and idiots in Westminster. Everything is their fault, right down to what they did to Ayah's family. It is as if the Major must unload his own guilt onto their shoulders. The blood baths and forced migrations, the collapse of law, order and a central administration are a consequence not of native intransigence but of British Colonial disrespect, manipulation, greed, corruption, cowardice. Lord Mountbatten, the last Viceroy, against whom the Major until now will hear no evil, becomes in the fume-soaked atmosphere of their tiny cabin the Jackass. 'If the Jackass had moved slower on Partition and faster to stop the massacres, he'd have saved a million lives. Two million.' Attlee and Sir Stafford Cripps fare no better. They called themselves socialists, but they were class snobs like the rest of 'em.

'As for that Winston Churchill, if *he'd* been allowed to have his way, he'd have been worse than all the other buggers put together. Know why, boy? Know *why*?'

'No, sir.'

'He thought the Indians were a pack of fuzzy-wuzzies, that's why. Flog 'em, hang 'em and teach 'em the Bible. Don't you ever let me hear you say a good word for that man, d'you understand me, boy?'

'Yes, sir.'

'Give me a whisky.'

The Major's burst of heresy may have its intellectual limitations, but its effect on the impressionable Mundy at this crucial moment in his life is of lightning. In a single flash he sees Ayah standing with her hands clasped in horror, with all her murdered family lying at her feet. He remembers every filtered, unclear rumour of mass murder followed by mass revenge. So it was the British then – it wasn't just the Hindus – who were the villains! He relives the jibes that as an English Christian boy he was obliged to suffer at the hands of Ahmed, Omar and Ali. Too late, he thanks them for their moderation. He sees Rani and marvels that she sufficiently overcame her disgust to love him. Ejected from the country he loves, caught in the twilight of puberty, dragged night and day towards a guilty country he has not seen but must now call home, Mundy undergoes his first exposure to the radical reappraisal of Colonial history.

The England that awaits the young Mundy is a rain-swept cemetery for the living dead powered by a forty-watt bulb. A grey-stone mediaeval boarding school reeks of disinfectant and is ruled by boy quislings and adult despots. Number Two, The Vale weeps and rots as his father cooks inedible curries and pursues his purposeful slide into degradation. There being no native red-light quarter in Weybridge, he retains the services of a flighty Scottish housekeeper named Mrs McKechnie who, aged eternally twenty-nine, disdainfully shares his bed and polishes the last of his collection of Indian silver boxes until one by one they mysteriously disappear. But flighty Mrs McKechnie never strokes Mundy's cheek the way Ayah did, or tells him heroic stories of Mohammed or chafes his hand between both her own until he falls asleep, or replaces his lost talisman of tiger skin to ward off the terrors of the night.

41

Sent off to boarding school on the strength of a legacy from a distant aunt and a bursary for the sons of army officers, Mundy is bewildered, then horrified. The Major's parting words, though well intended, have not prepared him for the impact of his new life. 'Always remember your mother's watching you, boy, and if a chap combs his hair in public, run like hell,' his father urges him huskily as they embrace. On the school train, trying desperately to remember that his mother is watching him, Mundy looks in vain for child beggars clinging to the windows, or station platforms packed with rows of shrouded but unmurdered bodies with their heads covered and their feet poking out, or chaps who comb their hair in public. In place of dung-brown landscapes and blue mountain ranges, he sees only sodden fields and mysterious hoardings telling him he is Welcome to the Strong Country.

On arrival at the place of his incarceration, the former white godling and *baba-log* is summarily reduced to the rank of Untouchable. By the end of his first term he is voted a Colonial freak, and thereafter affects a *chee-chee* accent in order to capitalise on the distinction. To the rage of his fellows he keeps a wary eye for snakes. When he hears the rumbling of the school's ancient plumbing he dives under his desk, yelling, 'Earthquake!' On bath days he equips himself with an old tennis racquet for fending off any bats that should fall out of the ceiling, and when the bell tolls for chapel he muses aloud about whether the muezzin is calling him. Dispatched on early-morning runs to quell his libido, he is given to enquiring whether the Dorset crows circling overhead are kites.

The punishments he attracts do not deter him. During evening prep he burbles half-remembered passages of

Koranic scripture taught to him by Ayah, and when the bell for lights-out sounds he can be discovered in his dressing gown bowed before a cracked mirror in the dormitory washroom, pulling his face about as he hunts for signs of darkening skin and shading round the eyes that will confirm him in his secret conviction that he is *twelve annas in the rupee* rather than the inheritor of his aristocratic mother's dignity. No such luck: he is a Despised One, sentenced to life imprisonment as a snow-white guilty British gentleman of tomorrow's ruling class.

His one spiritual ally is an outcast like himself: a dignified, ageless, diffident, white-haired refugee in rimless spectacles and a shabby suit who teaches German Extra Studies and cello and lives alone in a red-brick bedsitter on the Bristol Road roundabout. His name is Mr Mallory. Mundy discovers him reading in a teashop in the High Street. A grand meeting of masters is currently in progress, so why is Mr Mallory not attending it?

'Because I'm not completely a *master*, Mr Mundy,' he explains, closing his book and sitting bolt upright. 'Maybe one day, when I grow up, I become one. But until now, I am a *temporary* master. Permanently temporary. You wish a piece of cake? I invite you, Mr Mundy.'

Within the week, Mundy has enrolled for twice-weekly cello lessons, German Extra Studies and German Oral. 'I have taken this path because music is all I care about and German is a sort of literary version of music,' he writes recklessly to the Major, in a letter seeking his permission to add fifteen pounds to the annual tuition charges.

The Major's reply is equally impulsive. It comes by telegram or, as the Major would say, signal. 'Your application whole-heartedly approved. Your mother musical genius.

If he's related to the Mallory who took part in assault on Everest he's prime human material. Ask him and report back. Mundy.'

Mr Mallory is not, alas, prime human material, or not of the sort the Major has in mind. His real name, he regrets, is Dr Hugo Mandelbaum, he comes from Leipzig and has no taste for heights. 'But don't tell this to the boys, please, Mr Mundy. With such a name as Mandelbaum, they have too much fun.' And he laughs and nods his white head with the resignation of one who has been the object of quite a bit of fun already.

The cello is not a success. At first, Dr Mandelbaum is concerned only with bow action. Unlike the Anglican missionary in Murree he treats Mundy's fingers as if they were live electric wires, gingerly attaching them to their points before leaping back to safety at the other side of the room. But by the end of their fifth session, his expression has changed from one of technical concern to simple grief for a fellow human being. Perched on his piano stool, he clasps his hands together and leans over them.

'Mr Mundy, music is not your refuge,' he pronounces at last, with great solemnity. 'Maybe later, when you have experienced the emotions that music describes, it will become a refuge for you. But we cannot be sure. So maybe better for now you take refuge in *language*. To possess another language, Charlemagne tells us, is to possess another soul. German is such a language. Once you have it in your head, you can go there any time, you can close the door, you have a refuge. You allow me to read you a little poem by Goethe? Sometimes Goethe is very pure. When he was young like you, he was pure. When he was old like me, he became pure again. So I tell you once in German a most beautiful little poem, then I tell you what it means. And next time we meet, you will learn this little poem. So.'

So Dr Mandelbaum recites the loveliest and shortest poem in the German language, then provides his translation: *Over all the mountains is peace . . . but wait, soon you too will be at rest*. And the cello goes back into Dr Mandelbaum's cupboard where he keeps his shabby suit. And Mundy, who has learned to hate the cello and is not used to tears, weeps and weeps at the shame of seeing it go, while Dr Mandelbaum sits on the far side of the room at the lace-curtained window, staring into a book of spiky Gothic lettering.

Nonetheless the miracle happens. By the end of a couple of terms Dr Mandelbaum has acquired a star pupil and Mundy has found his refuge. Goethe, Heine, Schiller, Eichendorff and Mörike are his secret familiars. He reads them furtively in scripture prep, and takes them to bed to read again by torchlight under the sheets.

'So, Mr Mundy,' Dr Mandelbaum declares proudly over a chocolate cake he has bought to celebrate Mundy's success in a public examination. 'Today we are both refugees. For as long as mankind is in chains, maybe all good people in the world are also refugees.' It is only when he speaks German, as now, that he allows himself to lament the enslavement of the world's downtrodden classes. 'We cannot live in a bubble, Mr Mundy. Comfortable ignorance is not a solution. In German student societies that I was not permitted to join, they made a toast: "Better to be a salamander, and live in the fire."'

After which he will read him a passage from Lessing's *Nathan der Weise* while Mundy listens respectfully, nodding to the cadence of the beautiful voice as if it were the dream-music that he will one day understand.

'Now tell me once about *India*,' Dr Mandelbaum will say, and in turn closes his eyes to Ayah's plain tales from the hills.

Periodically, seized with a desire to exercise his parental duty, the Major will descend unannounced on the school and, supported by a cherrywood walking stick, inspect the lines and roar. If Mundy is playing rugby, he will roar at him to break the blighters' legs; if cricket, to swipe the buggers over the pavilion. His visits end abruptly when, angered by defeat, he accuses the sports master of being a bloody pansy and, not for the first time in his life, is escorted from the field. Outside the school's walls the Swinging Sixties are in full cry, but inside them the band of Empire plays on. Twice-daily chapel services praise the school's war dead to the detriment of its living, value the white man above lesser breeds, and preach chastity to boys who can find sexual stimulation in a *Times* leader.

Yet while the oppression Mundy suffers at the hands of his jailers entrenches his loathing of them, he cannot dodge the curse of their acceptance. His real enemy is his own good-heartedness and his inextinguishable need to belong. Perhaps only those who have had no mother can understand the emptiness he has to fill. The change in the official attitude is subtle and insidious. One by one, his gestures of insubordination pass unnoticed. He smokes cigarettes in the most perilous places but nobody catches him at it or notices his breath. He reads the lesson in chapel while drunk on a pint of beer gulped down at the back door of a nearby pub, yet instead of the mandatory flogging he has the rank of prefect thrust on him with the assurance that the post of head boy is within his grasp. There is worse to come. Despite his ungainliness he is capped for rugby, promoted to the first eleven cricket team as a fast bowler, and appointed the unlikely hero of the hour. Overnight his heathen practices and subversive tendencies are forgotten. In a dreary production of *Everyman* he is given the title rôle. He leaves school covered in unwanted glory and, thanks to Dr Mandelbaum, with an Exhibition in Modern Languages to Oxford.

'Dear boy.'

'Father.'

Mundy allows time for the Major to muster his thoughts. They are seated in the conservatory of the Surrey villa and as usual it is raining. Rain shades the blue pines in the neglected garden, seeps down the rusted frames of the french windows and pings onto the cracked tile floor. Flighty Mrs McKechnie is on home leave in Aberdeen. It is mid-afternoon and the Major is enjoying an interval of lucidity between the last of the lunch hour and the first of the evening. A scrofulous retriever farts and mutters in a basket at his feet. Panes of glass are missing from the conservatory, but this is all to the good since the Major has developed a horror of enclosure. In accordance with new regimental orders, no doors or windows to the house may be locked. If the bastards want him, he likes to insist to his diminished audience at the Golden Swan, they know where they can find him; and he indicates the cherrywood walking stick which is now his constant companion.

'You're set on it, are you, boy? This German thing you're up to?' – drawing shrewdly on his Burma.

'I think so, thank you, sir.'

Major and retriever reflect on this. It's the Major who speaks first.

'Still some decent regiments out there, you know. Not everything's gone to the devil.'

'All the same, sir.'

Another prolonged delay.

'Reckon the Hun will come at us again, do you? Twenty years since the last show. Twenty years since the show before that. They're about due for another, I grant you.'

A further period of rumination follows, until the Major suddenly brightens.

'Well, there we are then, boy. Blame your mother.'

Not for the first time in recent months, Mundy fears for his father's sanity. My dead mother responsible for the next war with the Germans? How can this be, sir?

'That woman could pick up languages the way you and I pick up this glass. Hindi, Punjabi, Urdu, Telegu, Tamil, German.'

Mundy is astonished. 'German?'

'And French. Wrote it, spoke it, sang it. Mynah bird ear. All the Stanhopes had it.'

Mundy is gratified to hear this. Thanks to Dr Mandelbaum, he has for some while been privy to the classified information that the German language has beauty, poetry, music, logic and unlikely humour, as well as a romantic soul incomprehensible to anyone who can't decode it. Short of a KEEP OUT sign on its door, it possesses everything a nineteen-year-old Steppenwolf in search of a cultural safe haven could decently ask. But now it has genealogy as well. Any further doubts he may have are quickly dispelled by Fate. Without Dr Mandelbaum he would never have plumped for German. Without German he would never have signed up for weekly tutorials on Bishop Wulfila's translation of the Bible into Gothic. And if he hadn't signed up for Wulfila, he would never have found himself, on the third day of his first term at university, sitting buttock-to-buttock on a chintz sofa in North Oxford with a diminutive polyglot Hungarian spitfire called Ilse who takes upon herself the task of leading a motherless six-foot-four virgin to the sexual light. Ilse's interest in Wulfila, like Mundy's, is an accident of life. After an academic safari through Europe, she has descended on Oxford to expand her understanding of the roots of contemporary anarchism. Wulfila wormed his way into her syllabus.

Summoned at darkest night to the Surrey villa, a bereft Mundy cradles his father's sweated head and watches him spew out the remaining fragments of his wretched life while Mrs McKechnie treats herself to a ciggy on the landing. Other mourners at the funeral include a fellow alcoholic who is also a solicitor, an unpaid bookmaker, the landlord of the Golden Swan and a handful of its regulars. Mrs McKechnie, still firmly twenty-nine, stands to attention at the open graveside, every inch the courageous Scottish widow. It is summer and she is wearing a black chiffon dress. A languid breeze presses it against her, revealing a pair of fine breasts and a frank outline of her remaining assets. Masking her mouth with her Order of Service, she murmurs to Mundy from so close that he can feel her lips fluttering the little hairs inside his ear.

'Look at what you might have had if you'd asked nicely,' she says in her mocking Aberdonian brogue, and to his outrage brushes her hand across his crotch.

Safely back in his college rooms, a trembling Mundy takes stock of his humble patrimony: one red-and-white carved ivory chess set, much damaged; one army-issue khaki kitbag containing six handmade shirts by Ranken & Company Limited, Est. Calcutta 1770, By Appointment to HM King George V, with branches in Delhi, Madras, Lahore and Murree; one pewter hip flask, much dented, for sitting under neem trees at sundown; one tin penknife, Burmas for the use of; one truncated ceremonial Gurkha kukri engraved *To a Gallant Friend*; one multi-generational tweed jacket with no maker's attribution; one copy of *Selected Readings from the Works of Rudyard Kipling*, foxed and much thumbed; and one heavy leather suitcase with brass corners, found hidden or forgotten beneath a sea of empty bottles in the Major's bedroom wardrobe.

Padlocked.

No key.

For several days he keeps the suitcase under his bed. He is the sole possessor of its destiny, the only person in the entire world who knows of its existence. Will he be mountainously rich? Has he inherited British American Tobacco? Is he the sole owner of the secrets of the vanished Stanhopes? With a hacksaw borrowed from the college butler he spends an evening trying to cut his way through the padlock. In desperation he lays the suitcase on his bed, draws the ceremonial kukri from its scabbard and, in thrall to its power, makes a perfect circular incision in the lid. Drawing back the flap, he smells Murree at sunset and the sweat on Rani's neck as she crouches at his side peering into the rock pool.

Official army files, British, Indian, Pakistani.

Faded parchments appointing Arthur Henry George Mundy to the rank and condition of second lieutenant, lieutenant, captain in this regiment, then a lesser regiment, then the one below it.

One yellowed, hand-printed playbill of the Peshawar Players' production of *Snow White*, featuring E.A. Mundy in the rôle of Dopey.

Letters from unhappy bank managers concerning 'mess

bills and sundry other debts that can no longer be covered by this account'.

Official protocol of a court martial convened in Camberley, Surrey, in September 1956. Exquisitely hand-written witness statements sworn and signed in Murree, Pakistan, together with summary of evidence. The prisoner confesses his crime, no defence offered. Statement by Prisoner's Friend: *Major Mundy was drunk. He went berserk. He is sincerely sorry for his actions and throws himself on the mercy of the court.*

Not so fast. Sorry is not enough. What actions? Mercy for what?

Summary of evidence, submitted in writing to the court but not read out. It is alleged by the prosecution and agreed by the accused that Major Mundy while refreshing himself in the officers' mess took exception to certain words spoken in flippant jest by one Captain Gray, an honourable British technical officer on temporary attachment from Lahore. Seizing said respected captain by the collars of his uniform in a manner totally contrary to good order and military discipline, he three times head-butted him with great accuracy causing extensive facial bleeding, kneed him purposefully in the groin and, resisting the efforts of his perturbed comrades to restrain him, dragged the captain onto the verandah and administered such an horrendous rain of blows with his fists and feet as might have gravely endangered the captain's very life and being, let alone jeopardised his marital prospects and distinguished military career.

Of the words spoken by the captain in flippant jest, there is so far no clue. Since the prisoner does not offer them in mitigation, the court sees no purpose in repeating them. *He was drunk. He is sincerely sorry for his actions.* End of defence, end of career. End of everything. Except the mystery.

One fat buff folder with pockets, the word FILE inked in the Major's hand. Why? Would you write BOOK on a book? Yes, you probably would. Mundy spills the contents of the folder onto his frayed eiderdown. One sepia photograph, quarto size, on presentation cardboard mount with gilt surround. An Anglo-Indian family and its many servants cluster in a rigid group on the steps of a multi-turreted Colonial mansion set in the foothills of upper India amid formal lawns and shrubberies. Union Jacks fly from every pinnacle. At the centre of the group stands an arrogant white man in stiff collars, next to him his arrogant unsmiling white wife in twinset and pleated skirt. Their two small white boys stand either side of them, wearing Eton suits. Either side of the boys stand white children and adults of varying ages. They can be aunts, uncles and cousins. On the step below them stand the uniformed servants of the household, colour-coded for precedence, the whitest at the centre, darkest at the edges. The printed caption reads: *The Stanhope Family at Home, Victory in Europe Day, 1945. GOD SAVE THE KING.*

Conscious that he is in the presence of the Maternal Spirit, Mundy takes the photograph to his bedside light, tipping it this way and that while he scans the ranks of the female members of the family for the tall polyglot Anglo-Irish aristocrat who will turn out to be his mother. He is looking particularly for marks of dignity and erudition. He sees fierce-eyed matrons. He sees dowager ladies long past child-bearing age. He sees scowling adolescents with puppy fat and plaits. But he sees no potential mother. About to set the photograph aside he turns it over to discover a single scrawl of brown handwriting, not the Major's. It is the hand of a semi-literate girl – perhaps one of the scowling adolescents

– blobbed and reckless in its excitement. *Here's me with me eyes shut, tippical!!*

No signature, but the exuberance is infectious. Returning to the photograph, Mundy examines the group for a pair of shut eyes, English or Indian. But too many are shut on account of the sun. He lays the photograph face-up on the eiderdown and rummages among the other offerings in the folder and selects, at random but not quite, a wad of handwritten letters bound in string. He turns the photograph face-down again and makes the match. The writer of the letters is also the writer of the illiterate inscription on the back of the photograph. Dealing the letters onto the eiderdown, Mundy counts off six. The longest is eight unnumbered sides. All are scrawls, all are painfully, atrociously spelled. Marks of dignity and erudition are conspicuously absent. The earliest start *My dearest* or *Oh Arthur*, but the tone quickly deteriorates:

Arthur, bloody hell, for the love of God listen to me!
The bastad that done this to me is the same barstad that your Nell gave herself willing and week to, your Gods judgmint on me, Arthur, don't bloody deny it. If I go home ruined my dad will kill me. I'll be a scarlit whore with an illigitment to feed they'll give me to the nuns and take me baby I've heard what they make you do for repintince. If I stay in India its me with the halfcarst prostutes in the market God help me I'd rather drown meself in the Ganges. Confessions not safe here, nothing is, that dirty bogger Father M'Graw would as soon tell Lady Stanhope as put his hand up your skirt and that Housekeeper stayring at me belly like I've stolen the lunch off her. Are you pregnant by any chance, Nurse Nellie? God help me

Mrs Ormrod whatever makes you think such a thing, it's
all the good food you're feeding us in the servants hall.
But how long will she believe that pray Arthur when I'm
six months gone and still swelling? And me playing the
Holy Virgin Mary in the staffside Christmas tablo for
Christs sakes, Arthur! But it wasn't the Holy Spirit
done it to me, was it? It was you! THEYRE FOCKIN TWINS
ARTHUR I CAN FEEL THEIR BLOODY HARTS GOING HEAR
ME!

Mundy needs a magnifying glass. He borrows it from a
first-year student on his staircase who collects postage
stamps.

'Sorry, Sammy, something I need to look at a bit closer.'

'At fucking midnight?'

'At any fucking time,' says Mundy.

He has focused his attention on the lower step and is
searching for a tall girl in nurse's uniform with her eyes
closed, and she isn't hard to spot. She's a sunny, overgrown
child with a head of black curls and her Irish eyes clamped
shut exactly the way she says they are, and if Mundy ever
wore a nursemaid's drag and a black wig and squeezed up
his eyes against the Indian sun, this is what he'd look like,
because she's the same age as I am now, and the same height,
he thinks. And she's got the same damn-fool all-weather grin
I'm wearing while I gawp at her through the magnifying
glass, which is the closest I will ever be to her.

Or hang on, he thinks.

Maybe you're smiling out of shyness because you're
too tall.

And there's something of the wild spirit about you too,
now I come to look at you more closely.

Something spontaneous and trusting and joyful, like a tall, white Rani full-grown.

Something that is actually a great deal more to my taste than the stuck-up, tight-arsed aristocrat of dignity and erudition that I've had shoved down my throat from the day I was old enough to be lied to.

<u>Personal and Confidential to Yourself</u>
Dear Captain Mundy,

I am directed by Lady Stanhope to draw your attention to your obligations to the person of Miss Nellie O'Connor, a nursemaid in Her Ladyship's employ. Her Ladyship asks me to advise you that if Miss O'Connor's position is not promptly regulated in a manner befitting an officer and gentleman, she will have no alternative but to apprise your Regimental Colonel Commanding.

Yours faithfully,
Private Secretary to Lady Stanhope

One marriage certificate, signed by the Anglican Vicar of Delhi in what looks like rather a rush.

One death certificate, signed three months later.

One birth certificate, signed the same day: Edward Arthur Mundy is hereby welcome to the world. He was born, to his surprise, not in Murree but in Lahore, where both his mother and his baby sister were certified dead.

Mundy deftly completes the equation. The nature of Captain Gray's words spoken in flippant jest is no longer in question. *Mundy? Mundy? Aren't you the fellow who put the Stanhope nursemaid in the family way?* By providing no cause to have them repeated in court, the Major secured an embargo on them. But only in court. The secretary's letter may have been personal and confidential to the Major – but so it was to the entire strength of the Stanhope household and its outstations. His head still buzzing with images of the berserk Major raining blows on luckless Captain Gray, Mundy searches his heart for the appropriate rage, anger and recrimination that he tells himself he should be mustering, but all he can feel is a helpless pity for two inarticulate souls trapped in the conventional cages of their time.

Why did he lie to me for all those years?

Because he knew he wasn't enough.

Because he thought she wasn't.

Because he was sorry and guilty.

Because he wanted me to have the dignity.

It's called love.

The brass-cornered suitcase has one more trick up its sleeve: an ancient leather-bound box embossed with a gold crest containing a Pakistani War Office citation dated six months after the birth of the infant Mundy. By directing the operations of his platoon with reckless disregard for his own safety and firing his Bren gun from the hip, Major Arthur Henry George Mundy emptied twenty saddles and is hereby appointed an honorary bearer of the Pakistani Something-or-Other of Honour. The medal, if it was ever struck, is missing presumed sold for drink.

Dawn has broken. With tears streaming down his cheeks at last, Mundy pins the citation to the wall above his bed and next to it the group photograph of the victorious Stanhopes and their minions, and hammers them both home with his shoe.

Ilse's radical principles like her eager little body are un-appeasable, and Mundy in the flush of his initiation can be forgiven for not spotting the difference. Why should he care that he knows even less about Mikhail Bakunin than he does about the parts of the female anatomy? Ilse is giving him the crash course in both, and it would be downright impolite to accept the one without the other. If she rails against the State as an instrument of tyranny, Mundy passionately agrees with her, though the State is about the last thing on his mind. If she lisps of *individualisation*, extols the *rehabilitation of the I* and *the supremacy of the individual*, and promises to cut Mundy free of his submissive self, he implores her to do exactly that. That she talks in the same breath of radical collectivism disturbs him not at all. He will make the bridge. If she reads aloud from Laing and Cooper, while he dozes temporarily sated on her naked belly, a nod of appreciation can scarcely be accounted hardship. And if making love appeals to her more than making war – for in her spare moments away from anarchism and individualism Ilse is also an evangelising pacifist – he will hang up his musket for her any day, just as long as her impatient little heels keep hammering his rump on the coconut matting of her anchorite's horsebox in St Hugh's – gentlemen callers tolerated between the hours of 4 and 6 p.m. for Earl Grey tea and Marmite sandwiches with the door open. And what more soothing, in the afterglow of lust temporarily assuaged, than the shared vision of a social paradise ordered by the free agreement of all component groups?

Yet none of this should imply that Ted Mundy is not by predisposition committed to the New Jerusalem that Ilse has revealed to him. In her starry radicalism he has found not only echoes of the venerable Dr Mandelbaum, but evidence of his own vague stirrings of revolt against most of the things that England means to him. Her just causes are his by adoption. He's a hybrid, a nomad, a man without territory, parents, property or example. He's a frozen child who is beginning to thaw out. Occasionally, trotting off to a lecture or library, he will brush up against a former schoolmate in sports jacket, cavalry twill trousers and polished brown toecaps. Awkward exchanges pass before each hurries on his way. *Christ, that fellow Mundy*, he imagines them thinking, *gone completely off the rails*. And they're right. Pretty much, he has. He belongs neither to the Gridiron nor the Bullingdon, the Canning nor the Union. At raucous if dismally attended political meetings he relishes his tussles with the hated right- ists. His height notwithstanding, his favoured position away from Ilse's arms is perching cross-legged with his knees up by his ears in the cramped rooms of left-leaning dons while he listens to the gospel according to Thoreau, Hegel, Marx and Lukacs.

That he is not persuaded by intellectual argument, that he hears it as music he can't play rather than the iron logic it professes to be, is neither here nor there. He is undaunted by belonging to a tiny band of gallant comrades. When Ilse marches, Mundy the great joiner puts his whole good self where her loyalties are, boarding the coach with her at Gloucester Green at daybreak equipped with the Mars bars she likes, and the carefully wrapped egg-and-cress sand- wiches from the market, and a thermos of tinned tomato soup, all stowed for her in the Major's army-issue kitbag. Shoulder to shoulder and often hand in hand, they march to protest against Harold Wilson's support of the Vietnam war, and – since they are robbed of the chance to dissent through the parliamentary process – proclaim themselves members of the Extra-Parliamentary Opposition. They march to

Trafalgar Square to protest against apartheid and issue passionate declarations of support for American students burning their draft cards. They cluster in Hyde Park, are politely dispersed by the police, and feel vindicated if a little hangdog. Yet hundreds of Vietnamese are dying every day, bombed, burned and thrown out of helicopters in the name of democracy, and Mundy's heart is with them, and so is Ilse's.

To protest the seizure of power in Athens by the CIA-backed Greek Colonels and the torture and killing of unnumbered Greek leftists, they linger vainly outside London's Claridge's Hotel where the Colonels are believed to be residing during a furtive visit to Britain. None emerges to receive their jeers. Undaunted, they repair to the Greek Embassy in London under banners reading *Save Greece Now*. Their most satisfying moment comes when an attaché leans out of a hotel window and shouts, 'In Greece, we would shoot you!' Safely back in Oxford, they still feel the wind of that imaginary bullet.

In the winter term, it's true, Mundy takes time out to stage a German-language production of Büchner's *Woyzeck*, but its radical sentiments are impeccable. And in the summer, if a little sheepishly, he opens the bowling for his college and would have a high time drinking with the boys if he didn't remind himself of his allegiances.

Ilse's parents live in Hendon, in a semi-detached villa with a green roof and plaster dwarfs fishing in the garden pond. Her father is a Marxist surgeon with a wide Slav brow and fuzzy hair, her mother a pacifist psychotherapist and disciple of Rudolf Steiner. Never in his life has Mundy met such an intelligent, broad-minded couple. Inspired by their example, he wakes up in his rooms one morning seized with a determination to propose marriage to their daughter. The case for doing so strikes him as overwhelming. Bored out of her wits by what she perceives as half-baked British protest, Ilse has for some while been hankering for a campus where students go the whole hog, such as Paris, Berkeley or Milan. Her choice, after much soul-searching, has fallen on the Free University of Berlin, crucible of the new world order, and Mundy has pledged himself to accompany her there for his year out.

And what more natural, he argues, than to go as man and wife?

The timing of his proposal is not perhaps as propitious as he imagines, but Mundy in the grip of a great plan is blind to tactic. He has turned in his weekly essay on the symbolic use of colour by the early Minnesänger, and feels master of the moment. Ilse on the other hand is worn out by two days of ineffectual marching in Glasgow in the company of a Scottish working-class history student named Fergus, who she claims is irredeemably homosexual. Her response to Mundy's declaration is muted, if not downright contemptuous. *Marriage?* This was not one of the options they considered when they were debating Laing and Cooper. *Marriage?* Like a real bourgeois marriage, he means? A *civil ceremony* conducted by the *State?* Or has Mundy so far regressed in his radical education that he covets the blessing of a religious institution? She stares at him, if not angrily, with profound gloom. She shrugs, and not with grace. She requires time to reflect on whether such an outlandish step can be reconciled with her principles.

A day later, Mundy has his answer. A squat Hungarian angel wearing nothing but her socks stands feet splayed in the only corner of her anchorite's horsebox where she can't be spotted from across the quad. Her pacifist-anarchist-humanist-radical philanthropy has run out. Her fists are clenched, tears are streaming down her flushed cheeks.

'You have completely bourgeois heart, Teddy!' she bawls in her charmingly accented English. And as an afterthought: 'You wish stupid marriage and you are complete infant for sex!'

3

The aspiring student of the German soul who steps off the interzonal train into the vibrant Berlin air possesses six of his late father's shirts that are too short for him in the sleeve but mysteriously not in the tail, one hundred pounds sterling, and fifty-six Deutschmarks that a weeping Ilse has discovered in a drawer. The grant that kept him just below water at Oxford, he has been advised too late, is not available for study overseas.

'Sasha *who*, Sasha *where*, for God's sake?' he yells at her on the platform of Waterloo station while Ilse, racked by Magyar remorse, decides for the umpteenth time to change her mind and jump aboard with him except she hasn't brought her passport.

'Tell him I sent you,' she implores him as the train mercifully pulls out. 'Give him my letter. He is a graduate but democratic. Everyone in Berlin knows Sasha,' which to Mundy sounds about as convincing as everybody in Bombay knows Gupta.

It is 1969, Beatlemania is no longer at its zenith, but nobody has told Mundy. In addition to a monkish mop of brown hair that flops over his ears and bothers his eyes, he sports his father's webbing kitbag to denote the rootless wanderer he intends to become now that life has lost its meaning for him. Behind him lies the wreckage of a great love, ahead of him the model of Christopher Isherwood, illusionless diarist of Berlin at the crossroads. Like Isherwood, he will expect nothing of life but life itself. He will be a camera with a broken heart. And if by some remote chance it should turn out that he can love again – but Ilse has obviously put paid to that – well, just maybe, in some sleazy café where beautiful women in cloche hats drink absinthe and sing huskily of disenchantment, he will find his Sally Bowles. Is he an anarchist? It will depend. To be an anarchist one must have a glimmer of hope. For our recently anointed misanthrope, nihilism is closer to the mark. So why then, he might wonder, this spring in my stride as I venture forth in search of Sasha, the Great Militant? Why this sense of arriving in a fresher, jollier world, when all is so demonstrably lost?

'Go to Kreuzberg,' Ilse is howling after him, as he waves his last tragic farewells from the carriage window. 'Ask for him there! *And look after him, Teddy,*' she commands as a peremptory afterthought which he has no time to explore before the train conveys him on the next stage of his life.

Kreuzberg is not Oxford, Mundy observes with relief.

No kind lady in blue curls from the University Delegacy of Lodgings is on hand with cyclostyled lists of addresses where he must behave himself. Priced out of the better parts of town, West Berlin's unruly students have set themselves up in bombed-out factories, abandoned railway stations and tenement blocks too close to the Wall for the sensibilities of property developers. The Turkish shanty towns of asbestos and corrugated iron, so reminiscent of Mundy's childhood, sell neither academic books nor squash racquets, but figs, copper saucepans, halva, leather sandals and strings of plastic yellow ducks. The scents of jeera, charcoal and roasting lamb are a welcome-home to Pakistan's lost son. The fly-bills and graffiti on the walls and windows of the communes do not proclaim college productions of the plays of minor Elizabethan dramatists, but pour invective on the Shah, the Pentagon, Henry Kissinger, President Lyndon Johnson and the Napalm Culture of US Imperialist Aggression in Vietnam.

Yet Ilse's advice is not misplaced. Bit by bit, in cafés, impromptu clubs, at street corners where students lounge, smoke and rebel, the name Sasha raises the odd smile, rings a distant bell. Sasha? You mean Sasha the Great Rouser – *that* Sasha? Well now, we have a problem here, you see. We don't give just anybody our addresses these days. The *Schweinesystem* has long ears. Best leave your name with Students for Democratic Socialism and see if he wants to get in touch with you.

Schweinesystem, Mundy the new boy repeats to himself. Remember that phrase. The Pig System. Does he feel a momentary wave of resentment against Ilse for launching him into the eye of the radical storm with no charts or instruments? Perhaps. But evening is drawing in, his path is set and despite his state of mourning he has a great appetite to begin his new life.

'Try Anita, Commune Six,' a somnolent revolutionary advises him, in a clamorous cellar dense with pot smoke and Vietcong flags.

'Maybe Brigitte can tell you where he is,' another suggests, over the strains of a girl guitarist in a Palestinian keffiyeh giving her rendering of Joan Baez. A child sits at her feet, a big man in a sombrero at her side.

In a bullet-pocked former factory as high as Paddington railway station hang likenesses of Castro, Mao and Ho Chi Minh. A portrait of the late Che Guevara is draped in black bunting. Hand-daubed slogans on bed sheets warn Mundy that *It is Forbidden to Forbid*, urge him to *Be Realistic, Demand the Impossible, Accept No Gods or Masters*. Strewn across the floor like survivors from a shipwreck, students doze, smoke, breastfeed babies, play rock music, fondle and harangue each other. Anita? Left, oh, hours ago, says one advisor. Brigitte? Try Commune Two and fuck America, says another. When he asks to use a lavatory, a tender Swede escorts him to a line of six, each with its door smashed in.

'Personal privacy, comrade, that's a bourgeois barrier to communal integration,' the Swede explains in earnest English. 'Better that men and women piss together than bomb Vietnamese kids. *Sasha?*' he repeats, after Mundy has courteously declined his advances. 'Maybe you find him at the Troglodyte Club, except they call it the Shaven Cat these days.' He detaches a cigarette paper from its packet and, using Mundy's back to press on, draws a map.

The map leads Mundy to a canal. With the kitbag slapping his hip, he sets off along the towpath. Sentry towers, then a patrol boat bristling with guns, glide past him. Ours or theirs? It is immaterial. They are nobody's. They are part of the great impasse he is here to unblock. He turns into a cobbled side street and stops dead. A twenty-foot-high breeze-block wall with a crown of barbed-wire thorns and a sickly halo of floodlights bars his way. At first he refuses

65

to recognise it. You're a fantasy, a film set, a construction site. Two West Berlin policemen call him over.

'Draft dodger?'

'English,' he replies, showing his passport.

They take him to the light, examine his passport, then his face.

'Ever seen the Berlin Wall before?'

'No.'

'Well look at it now, then go to bed, Englishman. And stay out of trouble.'

He retraces his steps and finds a side road. On a rusted iron door, amid Picasso peace doves and Ban the Bomb signs, a hairless cat on two legs brandishes its penis. Inside, music and argument combine in a single feral roar.

'Try the Peace Centre, comrade, top floor,' a beautiful girl advises him, cupping her hands.

'Where's the Peace Centre?'

'Upstairs, arsehole.'

He climbs, his feet clanging on the tile steps. It's close on midnight. At each floor a fresh tableau of liberation is revealed to him. On the first, students and babies lounge in a Sunday-school ring while a stern woman harangues them on the crippling effect of parents. On the second, a post-coital quiet reigns over bundles of intertwined bodies. *Support the Neutron Bomb!* a handmade poster urges them. *Kills your mother-in-law! Doesn't harm your TV set!* On the third, Mundy is thrilled to see some sort of theatre workshop is in progress. On the fourth, shaggy Septembrists pummel typewriters, confer, feed paper into hand-presses and bark orders into radio telephones.

He has reached the top floor. A ladder rises to an open trapdoor in the ceiling. He emerges in an attic lit by a builder's inspection light. A passage like the entrance to a mineshaft leads from it. At its end, two men and two women are bowed over a candlelit table strewn with maps and beer bottles. One girl is black-haired and grim-faced, the other fair and large-boned. The nearer man is as tall as Mundy: a Viking with a golden beard and mop of yellow hair bound in a pirate's headscarf. The other man is short, vivid and dark-eyed, with uneven, spindly shoulders that are too narrow for his head. He wears a black Basque beret drawn dead level across his pale brow, and he is Sasha. How does Mundy know this? Because all along, he realises, he has known intuitively that Ilse was talking about someone as small as herself.

Too diffident to intrude, he hovers at the opening to the mine-shaft, clutching her letter in his hand. He hears fragments of war talk, all Sasha's. The voice is stronger than the body and carries naturally. It is accompanied by imperious gestures of the hands and forearms. . . . *don't let the pigs cram us into side streets, hear me? . . . Stand up to them in the open, where the cameras can see what they do to us* . . . Mundy is already deciding to tiptoe back down the ladder and make his entrance another time when the party breaks up. The black-haired girl folds up the maps. The Viking rises and stretches. The blonde girl hugs him to her by his buttocks. Sasha stands too, but is no taller than when he was sitting. As Mundy steps forward to present himself, the others move instinctively to shield the little emperor at their centre.

'Good evening. I'm Ted Mundy. I've got a letter for you from Ilse,' he says in his best head prefect's voice. And when he receives no answering light of recognition from the wide, dark eyes: 'Ilse the Hungarian student of political philosophy. She was here last summer and had the pleasure of meeting you.'

Perhaps it is Mundy's politeness that catches them off balance, for there is a moment of shared suspicion among them. Who is he, this courtly English arsehole with the Beatle haircut? The tall Viking is first to respond. Placing himself between Mundy and the rest of them, he accepts the envelope on Sasha's behalf and subjects it to a quick examination. Ilse has stuck down the flap with sticky tape. Her peremptory scrawl of *Private, Strictly Personal!* twice underlined, is a clear claim to intimacy. The Viking hands the envelope to Sasha who rips it open and extracts two blotchy pages of Ilse's densely packed handwriting, with afterthoughts charging up the margins. He reads the first few lines, turns to the back page to find the signature. Then he smiles, first to himself, and then at Mundy. And this time it's Mundy who is taken off balance, because the wide dark eyes are so brilliant and the smile is so young.

'Well, well. *Ilse!*' he muses. 'That's quite a girl, yes?' – slipping her letter into the side pocket of his threadbare lumber jacket.

'One can really say that,' Mundy agrees in his best High German.

'Hungarian' – as if to remind himself. 'And you are *Teddy.*'

'Well, Ted actually.'

'From Oxford.'

'Yes.'

'Her lover?' It's a straight question. 'We are all lovers here,' he adds, to laughter.

'I was until a few weeks ago.'

'A few weeks! That's a lifetime in Berlin! You are English?'

'Yes. Well, not completely. Foreign born, but English bred. Oh, and she sends you a bottle of Scotch. She remembers you liked it.'

'Scotch! What a memory, my God! A woman's memory will hang us all. What are you doing in Berlin, Teddy? Are you a revolutionary tourist?'

Mundy is pondering his reply when the black-haired girl with the grim face cuts in ahead of him. 'He means, do you sincerely wish to take part in our Movement, or are you here for the purposes of human zoology?' she demands, in a foreign accent he can't place.

'I took part in Oxford. Why not here?'

'Because here is not Oxford,' she snaps. 'Here we have an Auschwitz generation. In Oxford you do not. In Berlin we can lean out of the window and shout "Nazi swine", and if the arsehole on the pavement is more than forty years old we shall be right.'

'What are you proposing to study here in Berlin, Teddy?' Sasha enquires, in a softer tone.

'Germanistic.'

The dark-haired girl takes immediate exception to this. 'Then you will have to be lucky, comrade. The professors who teach that archaic shit are so scared they won't come out of their bunkers. And the twenty-year-old stooges they send us are so scared they sign up with us.'

Now it's the turn of the blonde girl beside her. 'Have you any money, comrade?'

'Not very much, I'm afraid.'

'You are without *money*? Then you are a worthless human being! How will you eat cutlet every day? How will you buy a new hat?'

'Work, I suppose,' says Mundy, trying his best as a good fellow to share their unfamiliar brand of humour.

'For the Pig System?'

The girl with dark hair is back. She wears it pushed behind

her ears. She has a strong, slightly crooked jaw. 'What is the purpose of our revolution, comrade?'

Mundy has not expected a viva-voce, but six months of Ilse and her friends have not left him unprepared. 'To oppose the Vietnam war by all means . . . To arrest the spread of military imperialism . . . To reject the consumer state . . . To challenge the nostrums of the bourgeoisie . . . To awaken it, and educate it. To create a new and fair society . . . and to oppose all irrational authority.'

'*Irrational?* What is *rational* authority? All authority is *irrational*, arsehole. Do you have parents?'

'No.'

'Do you share the opinion of Marcuse that logical positivism is a load of shit?'

'I'm not really a philosopher, I'm afraid.'

'In a state of unfreedom, nobody has a liberated consciousness. Do you accept this?'

'It seems to make pretty good sense.'

'It is the only sense, arsehole. In Berlin the student masses are in permanent movement against the forces of counter-revolution. The city of the Spartacists and the capital of the Third Reich has rediscovered its revolutionary destiny. Have you read Horkheimer? If you have not read Horkheimer's *Twilight*, you are ridiculous.'

'Ask him whether he is *eingebläut*,' the blonde girl suggests, using a word Mundy has never heard before – at which everyone laughs except Sasha who, having observed this exchange in quick-eyed silence, decides to come to Mundy's rescue.

'Okay, comrades. He's a nice fellow. Let's leave him alone. Maybe we all meet later at the Republican Club.'

Watched by Sasha, one after the other of his aides descends

the ladder. Finally he lowers the trapdoor on them, locks it, and to Mundy's surprise reaches up and claps a hand on his shoulder.

'You have that whisky with you, Teddy?'

'In my bag.'

'Don't mind Christina. Greek women have too much mouth. The day she has an orgasm, she won't speak another word.' He is opening a small door low in the wainscoting. 'And everyone's an arsehole here. It's a term of affection, like comrade. The revolution doesn't like circumlocutions.'

Is Sasha smiling as he says this? Mundy can't tell. 'What does *eingebläut* mean?'

'She was asking whether you have had your first beating from the pigs. She wants you to have nice blue bruises from their truncheons.'

Stooping double, Mundy follows Sasha into a long, cavernous chamber that at first sight resembles the belly of a ship. Two skylights appear high above him, and slowly fill with stars. Sasha removes his beret and reveals a revolutionist's mop of untamed hair. He strikes a match and lights a lantern. As its flame rises, Mundy makes out a *bombé* desk with brass inlay, and on it heaps of pamphlets and a typewriter. An iron double bedstead strewn with worn-out cushions of satin and brocade stands along one wall. And on the floor, like stepping stones, stacks of books.

'Stolen for the revolution,' Sasha explains, waving a hand at them. 'Nobody reads them, nobody knows the titles. All they know is, intellectual property belongs to the masses, not to bloodsucking publishers and booksellers. Last week we held a competition. Whoever brings the most books has struck the biggest blow against petit bourgeois morality. Have you eaten anything today?'

'Not much.'

'*Not much* being English for nothing? Then eat.'

Sasha pushes Mundy towards an ancient leather armchair and sets down two empty tooth-mugs, a chunk of sausage and a loaf of bread. His bony left shoulder rides higher than its companion. His right foot trails as he darts around. Mundy unfastens the buckles of his kitbag, extricates Ilse's bottle of St Hugh's Buttery Scotch whisky from the Major's shirts and pours two shots. Sasha perches opposite him on a wooden stool, pulls on a pair of spectacles with thick black frames and settles to a purposeful examination of Ilse's letter while Mundy cuts himself a slice of bread and sausage.

'*Teddy will never let you down*,' he announces, reading aloud. 'That's a quite subjective judgment, I would say. What's it supposed to mean? That I'm going to invest my confidence in you? Why should she make that assumption?'

No answer springs to Mundy's mind but Sasha doesn't seem to need one. His German has a regional accent of some kind, but Mundy is not yet equipped to place it.

'What did she tell you about me?'

'Not much. You were a graduate but democratic. Everybody knows you.'

Sasha doesn't appear to hear this. '*A good companion, loyal in all circumstances, a stranger to deceit − belongs to no group* − am I supposed to admire you for that? − *in his head a bourgeois, but has a socialist heart*. Maybe with a capitalist soul and a Communist prick you'll be complete. Why does she write to me like this?' A thought occurs to him. 'Did she walk out on you, by any chance?'

'Pretty much,' Mundy concedes.

'Now we're getting to the bottom of it. She walked out

on you so she feels guilty – and what's this? I don't believe it – *He wanted me to marry him.* Are you crazy?'

'Why not?' Mundy says sheepishly.

'The question is *why*, not *why not*. Is it your English practice to marry every girl you sleep with a few times? We had that here in Germany once. It was a disaster.'

No longer sure how he is expected to reply, Mundy takes another mouthful of sausage and washes it down with a swig of whisky while Sasha returns to the letter.

'*Teddy loves peace as much as we do, but he's a good soldier.* Jesus Christ. What does she mean by *that*? That Teddy obeys orders without questioning them? You shoot whoever you're told to shoot? That's not a virtue, that's grounds for criminal proceedings. Ilse should pick her compliments more carefully.'

Mundy grunts, partly in agreement, partly in embarrassment.

'So why does she say you're a good soldier?' Sasha insists. 'Good soldier like I'm a good democrat? Or does she mean you're a great hero in bed?'

'I don't think so,' says the complete infant for sex.

But Sasha won't leave the point alone. 'Did you fight somebody for her? Why are you a good soldier?'

'It's a phrase. We went on demos together. I took care of her. I play sport a bit. What the hell?' He is standing, his bag slung over his shoulder. 'Thanks for the whisky.'

'We haven't finished it.'

'She sent it to you, not me.'

'But you brought it. You didn't keep it, you didn't drink it. You were a good soldier. Where do you propose to sleep tonight?'

'I'll find somewhere.'

'Wait. Stop. Put your stupid bag down.'

Compelled by the insistence in Sasha's voice, Mundy pauses, but doesn't quite put down the bag. Sasha tosses the letter aside and stares at him for a while.

'Tell me something truthful, no bullshit, okay? We get a little paranoid here. Who sent you?'

'Ilse.'

'Nobody else? No pigs, spies, newspapers, clever people? This town is full of clever people.'

'I'm not one of them.'

'You're who she says you are. Is that what you're telling me? A political tyro, reading Germanistic, a good soldier with a socialist heart, or whatever the hell? That's the whole story?'

'Yes.'

'And you always tell the truth.'

'Mostly.'

'But you're queer.'

'No. I'm not.'

'Me neither. So what do we do?'

Looking down on Sasha, puzzling how to reply, Mundy is again struck by his host's fragility. It's as if every bone in his body has been broken and stuck back the wrong way.

Sasha takes a pull of whisky and, without looking at Mundy, hands him the glass to drink from. 'Okay,' he says reluctantly.

Okay what? Mundy wonders.

'Put that fucking bag down.'

Mundy does.

'There's a girl I like, okay? Sometimes she visits me up here. She may come tonight. She's young. Bourgeois. Shy, like you. If she shows up, you sleep on the roof. If it's raining,

I'll lend you a tarpaulin. That's how shy she is. Okay? If necessary I do the same for you.'

'What are you talking about?'

'Maybe I need a good soldier. Maybe you do. What the fuck?' He takes back the glass, drains it, and refills it from the bottle, which seems too big for his wrist. 'And if she doesn't show up, you sleep down here. I've got a spare bed. A field bed. I don't tell that to everyone. We can put it the other end of the room. And tomorrow I get you a desk for your Germanistic, we put it over there under the window. That way you get daylight. If you fart too much, if I don't like you after all, I ask you nicely to fuck off. Okay?' He goes straight on, not bothering with Mundy's answer. 'And in the morning I put you up for selection to the commune. We have a discussion, then a formal vote, it's all bullshit. Maybe you get a couple of questions from Christina about your bourgeois origins. She's the biggest bourgeois of us all. Her father's a Greek shipowner who loves the Colonels and pays for half the food here.' He takes another pull of whisky, and again hands the glass to Mundy. 'Some squats are legal. This one isn't. We don't like Nazi landlords. When you register with the university, you don't give this address, we provide you with a nice letter from a guy in Charlottenburg. He says you live with him, which isn't true, you're a good Lutheran boy, which isn't true, you're in bed alone every night at ten o'clock, you marry everyone you fuck.'

Which is how Mundy learns that he is to become Sasha's room-mate.

A golden age has unexpectedly dawned in Ted Mundy's life. He has a home, he has a friend, both new concepts to him. He is part of a brave new family determined to rebuild the world.

An occasional night of exile under the stars is no hardship to a soldier's son serving at the front line of the revolution. He is not offended when a red ribbon round the attic door handle advises him that his general is not receiving. While Sasha's dealings with women are swift and purposeful, Mundy remains true to his vow of abstinence. Occasionally he is obliged to exchange a platonic word or two with one of the squat's indecently high proportion of beautiful girls, but that is only because within hours of his admission he is gallantly providing free conversation lessons in English three times a week to any fellow communard so inclined.

And the salamander is living in the flames. Dr Mandelbaum would be proud of him. The awareness of being in a combat zone, the knowledge that any moment he may be summoned to join his fellow partisans at the barricade, the night-long debates on how the world's rotten wood can be swept away and the new growth planted act on him like a constant stimulant. If Mundy arrived in Berlin a greenhorn, under the guidance of Sasha and the comrades he becomes an eager inheritor of the Movement's noble history. The names of its heroes and villains are soon as familiar to him as those of great cricketers.

It was the Iranian exile Bahman Nirumand, on the eve of the Shah of Iran's visit to West Berlin, who informed a packed student audience in the Free University's Auditorium Maximum of the true awfulness of the Shah's American-backed régime.

It was Benno Ohnesorg who demonstrated against the Shah's visit to the city and was, on the very next day, shot through the head by a plainclothes police inspector outside the West Berlin Opera House.

It was Benno's funeral, and the denial of all wrongdoing

by the police and the Mayor, that drove the students to greater militancy and sped the rise of Rudi Dutschke, founder of the students' Extra-Parliamentary Opposition.

It was the fascistic rhetoric of the press baron Axel Springer and his odious *Bild Zeitung* that incited a deranged workman with far-right fantasies to shoot down Rudi Dutschke in Berlin's Kurfürstendamm. Dutschke survived for a time. Martin Luther King, shot the same month, did not.

He knows the dates and places of the great sit-ins and bloody confrontations of the recent past. He knows that the student revolt is raging across the world on a thousand battle-fields, and that the students of America have been as brave as any, and as savagely put down.

He knows that the finest publication in the world is *Konkret*, founded by the Movement's high priestess, the immaculate Ulrike Meinhof. Germany's two great revolutionary writers of the moment are called Langhans and Teufel.

So many brothers and sisters everywhere! So many comrades who share the dream! Even if the dream itself is not yet entirely clear to him, but he's getting there, wherever *there* is.

So a life begins. First thing in the morning the chaste English boarding-school boy and as yet unbruised recruit to the cause of world liberation springs from his field bed while Sasha sleeps off the night's great arguments. After a communal shower enlivened by girls he studiously ignores, he takes his turn in the squat's cookhouse chopping stolen sausages and vegetables for the day's soup then hurries out to pound West Berlin's precious parks and open spaces, trawl the libraries and attend whatever lectures have survived the student body's edict against fascistic indoctrination. Later in the day, he will offer himself as an apprentice at the print-shop to help run off salient passages from the works of the fashionable revolutionaries and, packing them into the Major's kitbag, stand bravely at street corners foisting them on the passing bourgeoisie on their way home to unawakened lives.

And this isn't just a matter of handing out free newspapers. This is risky work. Not only does the Berlin bourgeoisie refuse to awaken, but it has had enough of students to last it several generations. Less than twenty-five years after Hitler, the good citizens are not pleased to see their streets seething with riot police with truncheons, and mobs of foul-mouthed radicals hurling rocks at them. State-funded Berlin students exempted from conscription should pay their fees, obey, study and shut up. They should not smash glass, advocate copulation in public, cause traffic jams and insult our American saviours. More than one good citizen's fist is raised at him. More than one old lady of the Auschwitz generation screams into his face to take his stupid pamphlets *nach drüben* where they can be used as toilet paper – she means, over the Wall to East Germany – or makes a grab for his long hair, but he's too tall for her. More than one taxi driver from the forces of reaction bumps his cab over the kerb, sending Mundy scampering for cover and his wares flying over the street. But the good soldier is not fazed. Or not for long. Come evening of the same day, as soon as he has finished his conversation lessons, he can as likely be found relaxing over a beer at the Shaven Cat or the Republican Club, or enjoying Turkish coffee and an arak in one of Kreuzberg's many ramshackle cafés, where the aspiring novelist likes to spread his notebook and indulge his Isherwood persona.

But there are times when, for all his determined good

spirits, Mundy is infected by the unreality of the divided city, its gallows humour and doomed atmosphere of unassured survival. Surrounded by angers that are new and often alien to him, he does wonder in his lowest moments whether his comrades are in fact searchers and puzzlers like himself, drawing their strength from the presumed convictions of their neighbours rather than from their own hearts, and whether, in his quest for the larger truths of life, he has after all ended up living in what Dr Mandelbaum called a bubble. Clutching his end of a banner at a street demonstration, protesting the latest act of despotism by the terrified university authorities, or waiting manfully at the barricades for a police charge that fails to materialise, the expatriate son of a British army major does occasionally ask himself which war he is fighting: the last one or the next.

Yet his search for connection continues. There is an evening when, inspired by the benign weather and an arak, he improvises a game of cricket for the many Turkish children hanging around the shanties. A dust-patch serves as a pitch, a stack of empty beer cans makes a wicket. Mundy grabs a handsaw and a plank from Faisal, the proprietor of his favourite café, and hacks out a bat. No Rani steps out of the evening sunlight to greet him, but the shouts of encouragement and despair, the skimming faces and olive limbs lift his heart. The Kreuzberg cricket club is born.

On restless safaris in the shadow of the Wall, he seeks out foreign sightseers and regales them with inspiring tales of escape. Should a factual episode elude him, then he will invent one, and feel rewarded by their gratitude. And if these remedies are not enough to rescue his occasionally flagging spirits, there is Sasha to come home to.

* * *

79

At first they are wary of each other. Like a couple who have rushed to the altar without benefit of courtship, each is inclined to fall back until he sees what he's got. Is Mundy really the good soldier Sasha took him for? Is Sasha really the limping, charismatic firebrand who needs Mundy's protection? Though they share the same territory, they live their lives in parallel, only overlapping at mutually agreeable moments. Of Sasha's personal background, Mundy knows next to nothing, and the word around the squat is that the subject is taboo. He is of Saxon Lutheran origin, an East German refugee, an avowed enemy of all religion and like Mundy an orphan – though he has this last from hearsay only. That is all that need be known. It is not till Christmas Eve, or as the Germans have it, Holy Evening, that they experience one of those moments of mutual self-revelation from which there can be no retreat.

Already by the twenty-third of December the squat is three-quarters empty as communards abandon principle and slink home to celebrate in the bosom of their reactionary families. Those who have nowhere to go remain behind like uncollected children in a boarding school. Heavy snow is falling, and Kreuzberg is a sentimental dream of Yule. Waking early the next day, Mundy is exhilarated to see the attic skylights above him whited over, but when he calls this to Sasha's attention he receives only a groan and the injunction to fuck off. Undaunted, he flings on all the clothes he possesses and wades down to the Turkish settlement to build a snowman and cook kebabs with Faisal and the kids from the cricket club. Returning to the attic at dusk, he finds the radio playing carols and Sasha looking like Charlie Chaplin in *Modern Times*, wearing his beret and an apron, and stooped over a mixing bowl.

The desk is set as a dinner table for two. An Advent candle burns at its centre beside a bottle of Christina's father's Greek wine. More candles are balanced on the piles of stolen books. An unpromising chunk of red meat sits on a wooden board.

'Where the fuck have you been?' Sasha demands, without lifting his eyes from his work.

'Walking. Why? What's wrong?'

'It's Christmas, isn't it? The fucking family feast. You're supposed to be at home.'

'We haven't *got* families. We've got dead parents and no brothers and sisters. I tried to wake you up, but you told me to fuck off.'

Sasha has still not raised his head. The bowl contains red berries. He is preparing some kind of sauce.

'What's the meat?'

'Venison. Do you wish me to take it back to the shop and change it for your eternal fucking Wienerschnitzel?'

'Venison's fine. Bambi for Christmas. Is that whisky you're drinking, by any chance?'

'Probably.'

Mundy chatters but Sasha will not be humoured. Over dinner, trying to jolly him along, Mundy rashly relates the tale of his aristocratic mother who turned out to be an Irish nursemaid. He selects a merry tone, designed to assure his listener that he has long ago come to terms with an amusing byway of family history. Sasha hears him out with ill-concealed impatience.

'Why do you tell me this bullshit? Do you wish me to shed tears for you because you are not a lord?'

'Of course not. I thought you might laugh.'

'I am interested only in your personal liberation. There comes a moment for all of us when our childhood ceases to be an excuse. In your case, I would say that, as with many English, the moment is somewhat delayed.'

'All right. What about *your* dead parents? What did *you* have to overcome in order to arrive at the perfect state in which we find you?'

Is the taboo of Sasha's family history to be broken? Apparently so, for the Schiller head is giving a succession of tight nods as if overcoming its reservations one by one. And Mundy notices how the deep-set eyes have aged somehow, and appear to absorb the candlelight rather than reflect it.

'Very well. You are my friend and I trust you. Despite your ridiculous preoccupations with duchesses and housemaids.'

'Thank you.'

'My late father is not quite as late or as dead as I would wish him to be. If we are to judge him by normal medical criteria, he is in fact offensively alive.'

Either Mundy has the wit to stay silent, or he is too bemused to speak.

'He did not assault a brother officer. He has not succumbed to drink, though periodically he tries. He is a religious and political *Wendehals* – a turncoat whose existence is so intolerable to me that even today, when I am forced to think of him, I can only bring myself to refer to him as the Herr Pastor, never *Father*. You look bored.'

'I'm anything but bored! Everyone told me your private life was holy ground. How could I imagine it was *this* holy?'

'From his earliest childhood the Herr Pastor believed unquestioningly in God. His parents were religious but he was super-religious, a puritanical Lutheran fanatic of the most incorrigible sort, born 1910. When Our Dear Führer came to power' – his invariable term for Hitler – 'the Herr

Pastor was already an enthusiastic member of the Nazi Party, twenty-three years old and recently ordained. His faith in Our Dear Führer was even greater than his faith in God. Hitler would work magic. He would give Germany back its dignity, burn the Versailles Treaty, get rid of our Communists and Jews and build an Aryan heaven on earth. You are really not bored?'

'How can you ask? I'm riveted!'

'But not so riveted that you will rush out and tell your ten best friends that after all I have a father, I hope. The Herr Pastor and his fellow Nazi Lutherans called themselves *Deutsche Christen*. How he survived the last years of the war is unclear to me, since to this day he refuses to discuss such matters. At some desperate moment he was sent to the Russian front and captured. That the Russians didn't shoot him is a dereliction of good sense that I have long held against them. Instead they sent him to prison in Siberia, and by the time he was released and returned to East Germany, Herr Pastor the Christian Nazi had become Herr Pastor the Christian Bolshevik. As a consequence of this conversion the East German Lutheran Church gave him a job curing Communist souls in Leipzig. I will confess to you that I greatly resented his return from captivity. He had no right to take my mother from me. He was a stranger, a violator. Other children had no father: why should I have one? This broken little coward of a man, sniffing a lot, preaching himself up to twice his size, with the words of Jesus and Lenin, was repulsive to me. To please my poor mother I was obliged to declare myself a convert. It is true that there were times when I was confused by the bond between the two deities, but since they both had beards it was possible to assume a symbiosis. In 1960, however, God was good enough to appear to the Herr Pastor in a dream and order him to take his family and everything he owned to the West while there was time. So we put our Bibles in our pockets and fled over the sector border, leaving Lenin behind.'

'Did you have brothers and sisters? This is *really* appalling, Sasha.'

'An elder brother whom my parents greatly preferred to me. He died.'

'At what age?'

'Sixteen.'

'What of?'

'Pneumonia, complicated by respiratory problems. A long, slow dying. I envied Rolf because he was our mother's favourite, and loved him because he was a good brother to me. For seven months I visited him every day in hospital and was present at his end. It was not a vigil I remember with pleasure.'

'I'm sure not.' He risks it. 'So what happened to your body?'

'It appears that I was conceived while the Herr Pastor was on home leave, and subsequently born in a ditch while my mother was attempting to escape from the Russian advance. Her later information, probably inaccurate, was that I was deprived of oxygen in the womb. What my mother was deprived of, I can only imagine. It was not a salubrious ditch.' He resumes. 'The Herr Pastor made the spiritual transition from East to West with his customary agility. Having caught the eye of a Missouri missionary organisation of dubious connections, he was flown to St Louis for a course of religious instruction. He graduated summa cum laude and returned to West Germany an ardent Christian conservative of the seventeenth century and a devotee of free-market

Christian capitalism. Appropriately, a curacy was found for him in the old Nazi stamping-ground of Schleswig-Holstein, where every Sunday, to the enchantment of his congregation, he may be heard singing the praises of Martin Luther and Wall Street from the pulpit.'

'Sasha, this is truly terrible. Terrible and fantastic. Can we go up to Schleswig-Holstein and listen to him?'

'Never. I have disowned him totally. As far as my comrades are concerned he is totally dead. It is the one point on which the Herr Pastor and I have found common ground. He does not wish to acknowledge an atheist radical militant for a son, and I do not wish to acknowledge an aggressive hypocritical religious turncoat for a father. That is why, with the Herr Pastor's collusion, I have expunged him from my past. All I ask is that he will not die before I have a chance to tell him once more how much I hate him.'

'And your mother?'

'Lives but does not live. Unlike your Irish nursemaid, she did not have the good fortune to die in childbirth. She walks the fens of Schleswig-Holstein in a mist of grief and confusion for her children, and speaks constantly of taking her life. As a young mother she was of course repeatedly raped by our victorious Russian liberators.'

His empty glass before him, Sasha is seated at his desk as stiffly as a condemned man. Watching him, listening to his self-ironies, Mundy experiences one of those surges of spiritual generosity that make all things clear to him. And so it is the undemonstrative English pragmatist rather than the anguished German seeker after life's verities who fills their glasses and proposes a humble Christmas toast.

'Well, here's to us, anyway,' he mumbles, with appropriate reserve. '*Prosit*. Happy Christmas and so on.'

Still frowning, Sasha lifts his glass and they drink to each other in the German way: raise your glass, look into the other fellow's eyes, drink, raise it again, look again, allow a moment's silence to put down your glass and dwell reverently upon the moment.

Relationships must deepen or die. In Mundy's later remembering, that Christmas was the night when their relationship deepened, and found an unforced ease. Henceforth, Sasha pays no visit to the Republican Club or the Shaven Cat without tersely enquiring whether Mundy is coming along too. In student bars, on slow, unequal walks along frozen canal towpaths and river banks, Mundy plays Boswell to Sasha's Johnson and Sancho Panza to his Quixote. When their commune becomes richer by a herd of stolen bourgeois bicycles, Sasha insists the two friends extend their horizons by exploring the outer limits of the half-city. The ever-willing Mundy prepares a picnic – chicken, bread, a bottle of red burgundy, all honestly bought from his earnings as a Berlin Wall tour guide. They set out, but Sasha insists they first push their bicycles a distance because he has something to discuss and it is best discussed on foot. They are safely out of sight of the squat before he says what it is.

'Come to think of it, actually, Teddy, I don't believe I have ever ridden one of these fucking things,' he confesses with monumental casualness.

Fearing Sasha's legs may not be equal to the job, and cursing himself for not having thought of this earlier, Mundy walks him to the Tiergarten and seeks out a gentle grass slope with no children looking on. He holds Sasha's saddle, but Sasha smartly orders him to let go. Sasha falls, swears foully, struggles back up the slope, tries again, falls again, swears more foully still. But by the third descent he has learned to trim his uneven body so that he remains aloft, and a couple of hours later, flushed with pride, he is squatting in his greatcoat on a bench, eating chicken and with frosted breath dilating on the sayings of the great Marcuse.

But Christmas, as is usual in warfare, is only a temporary suspension of hostilities. No sooner has the snow melted than the tensions between the students and the city return to breaking-point. It is incidental that every university in West Germany is crawling with unrest; that from Hamburg, Bremen, Göttingen, Frankfurt, Tübingen, Saarbrücken, Bochum and Bonn come stories of strikes, mass resignations of ruling professors and the triumphant advance of radical bodies. Berlin has larger, older and more vicious scores to settle than the whole lot of them put together. In the shadow of the approaching storm, Sasha makes a dash to Cologne, where rumour reports that a brilliant new theoretician is pushing out the borders of radical thought. By the time he returns, Mundy is braced for action, and in facetious mood.

'And did the Oracle pronounce on how men of peace should bear themselves in the forthcoming confrontation?' he enquires, expecting at the very least one of Sasha's tirades against the repressive tolerance of pseudo-liberalism, or the cancer of military-industrial colonialism. 'Tomatoes, stink-bombs, thunder-flashes – Uzi machine-guns, perhaps?'

'We intend to *reveal the social genesis of human knowledge*,' Sasha replies, stuffing bread and sausage into his mouth before he hurries off to a meeting.

'What's that when it's at home?' Mundy asks, slipping into his familiar rôle of test audience.

'Man's preternatural state, his *Ur*state. Day One is already too late. We must begin on Day Zero. That is the entire point.'

'You're going to have to spell this one out for me,' Mundy warns, brows appropriately puckered. And the notion is indeed surprising to Mundy, since Sasha has until now insisted that they must deal with harsh political realities rather than fancy visions of Utopia.

'As a first stage, we shall wipe the human slate clean. We shall detoxify the brain, cleanse it of its prejudices, inhibitions and inherited appetites. We shall purge it of everything old and rotten' – another chunk of sausage – 'Americanism, greed, class, envy, racism, bourgeois sentimentality, hatred, aggression, superstition and the craving for property and power.'

'And enter *what* exactly?'

'I fail to understand your question.'

'It's simple enough. You've wiped my slate clean. I'm pure, I'm not American, racist, bourgeois or materialistic. I've got no bad thoughts left, no bad inherited instincts. What do I get in return, apart from a policeman's boot in the balls?'

Standing impatiently at the door, Sasha has ceased to take kindly to this inquisition. 'You get what is needful to a harmonious society and nothing more. Brotherly love, natural sharing, mutual respect. Napoleon was right. You English are totally materialistic.'

All the same, it is a theory of which Mundy hears no more.

4

'Those girls are total dykes,' insists the Viking, now better known to Mundy by his kennel name of Peter the Great. Peter is a pacifist from Stuttgart. He came to Berlin to escape military service. His rich parents are whispered to be *Sympis*, members of the guilt-ridden higher bourgeoisie who secretly give succour to those bent on their destruction.

'A lost cause,' Sasha, taken up with larger matters of revolutionary strategy, distractedly agrees. 'Don't waste your stupid time on them, Teddy. Freaks, the pair of them.'

They are speaking of Legal Judith and Legal Karen, so named because they are studying jurisprudence. The fact that they happen to be the two most desirable females in the squat only adds to their offence. Sexual choice for women, in the opinion of the two great liberators, does not include refusing to go to bed with important male activists. Take a look at the sackcloth skirts they wear, for God's sake, Peter urges. And those mannish shoes like army boots, where do they think they're marching to? And the way they put their hair up in messy buns and slop around the squat like a couple of lovesick Burghers of Calais! Peter claims they take out one law book from the library at a time so that they have something to read together in bed. Karen moves her finger along the line, he says, Judith does the words.

The only person they consort with apart from one another is Mundy's erstwhile inquisitor, the Greek Christina, who is suspected of sharing their sexual predilections. Mundy has never previously encountered the phenomenon of lesbianism, but has to concede that all known evidence supports the rumour. The two women refuse to shower communally. From the day they arrived in the squat they insisted on having their own room, and fitted a padlock to the door with a sign saying FUCK OFF. It's still there. Mundy has been to see it. Any further proof he should require, let him try his luck and see what he gets apart from a broken jaw, says Peter.

Yet for all these doom-laden prognostications, Legal Judith is imposing grave strains on Mundy's vows of Isherwood detachment. Her efforts to disguise her beauty are futile. Where Karen hunches her shoulders and acts grumpy, Judith is wispy and ethereal. At protest meetings Karen snarls like a bulldog, but Judith in anger merely shakes her golden head. Yet as soon as the meeting's over, there they are again: Legal Judith and Legal Karen, nicely-brought-up North German girls, received in Berlin's best radical drawing rooms, strolling hand in hand along the shores of Lesbos.

So forget her, Mundy orders himself each time he catches his hopes rising. Those straight looks she gives you during English conversation lessons are because you're weird and tall and Oxford. Our verbal flirtations — of Judith's contrivance, admittedly – are opportunities for her to try out her English on you, nothing more.

'Did I speak that sentence accurately, Teddy?' she will ask, with a smile to melt glaciers.

'Marvellous, Judith! Not a syllable out of joint.'

'*Joint?*'

'Out of place. Slip of the tongue. You're immaculate. Official.'

'But do I suffer from an American accent, Teddy? If I do, you will please *immediately* correct me.'

'Not a *hint* of one, scout's honour! English to the core. Fact,' Mundy blurts in the agony of his frustration.

And the blue metallic eyes not believing him, but staying on him like a child's till he says it all to her again the way children need you to. 'Thank you, Teddy. Then I wish you a pleasant day. Not a *nice* day, for that would be American. Yes?'

'Absolutely right. You too, Judith. And you, Karen.'

Because she's never alone, naturally. Legal Karen is sitting right there at her side, tessellating with her, learning about glottal stops with her, breathing out with her as they try to say *go away* without the fricative bump in the middle. Or so things stand until a day comes when without warning it is tacitly acknowledged that Legal Karen has left the squat, whereabouts unknown. At first she is reported sick, then she is visiting her dying mother until someone remembers that both her parents were killed on the last day of the war. But after a raid by police on a nearby cooperative, a different rumour starts the rounds. Legal Karen has become illegal, meaning she has followed the sainted Ulrike Meinhof on her journey underground. Ulrike our moral angel, our leading leftist, high priestess of the Alternative Life, the Movement's

Joan of Arc in all matters of courage and integrity, who has recently announced to the radical world that shooting may begin. It is also rumoured that Christina has accompanied her, in one stroke depriving Judith of her life's companion and the squat of half its income. But for Mundy it is the sight of Judith drifting like Ophelia down the corridors of the commune that is too much to bear. All the more surprising, therefore, when one evening she lays a frail hand on his upper arm and enquires whether he would care to accompany her on a *sleepwalk*.

'*Sleep*walk, Judith? My God! Walk *any*where with you!' He is going to add sleep anywhere with you too, but changes his mind in time. 'Sure that's what you mean? What's the German, if you don't mind my asking?'

She gives it. *Nachtwandlung*. 'It is an action of political importance, also completely secret. It is to force Berliners to confront their fascist past. You are willing?'

'Will Sasha be there?'

'Unfortunately he will be in Cologne consulting certain professors. Also he is not appropriate on a bicycle.'

Loyal Mundy hastens to protest. 'Sasha's fine on a bicycle. You should see him. Goes like a hare.'

Judith does not relent.

It is by now early spring, but the weather doesn't know this. Flurries of wet snow pursue him through the darkness as he makes his way to a derelict schoolhouse close to the canal. Peter the Great and his girlfriend Magda are there ahead of him. So is a Swede called Torkil and a Bavarian Amazon called Hilde. On Judith's orders, each conspirator has supplied himself with one hand torch, one can of crimson spray paint and one can of waterglass, a mysterious solution that allegedly etches itself so deeply into glass that to remove it you must remove the whole window. Peter the Great, as the appointed quartermaster, has furnished a stolen bicycle for each combatant. Mundy wears three of his father's shirts, a scarf and an old anorak. His torch and waterglass and paint are in his kitbag. Torkil and Peter the Great have brought balaclava helmets. Hilde sports a Chairman Mao face-mask. Placing herself before a city plan, Judith briefs her troops in crisp North German accents. She has thrown aside her sackcloth in favour of a fisherman's sweater and extremely long white woollen tights. If she is wearing a skirt, it is not in evidence.

Our targets for tonight are the former houses, ministries and headquarters of the Third Reich, presently masquerading as innocuous buildings, she announces. The aim of our operation is educational. It is to redress the amnesia of the city's bourgeoisie by indicating the function of each building during the Nazi period. Past experience has proved that the West Berlin pigs are incensed by such markings, and mount special actions to replace windows and eradicate the graffiti. We shall therefore be scoring a double victory: against the bourgeois love of property, and the efforts of the Pig System to deny its Nazi past. Prime objectives – she indicates them on the map – will include Tiergartenstrasse 4, home of the Euthanasia Programme, and afterwards Adolf Eichmann's offices in the Kurfürstenstrasse, now all but removed to make way for a spanking new hotel; also Heinrich Himmler's headquarters on the corner of the Wilhelmstrasse and the Prinz Albrechtstrasse, now unfortunately a victim of the Berlin Wall, but we'll do whatever we can in the circumstances. Subject to operational considerations, we shall also attack the marshalling points where Berlin's Jews were assembled for transportation to the death camps, including Grunewald railway station which still has the very ramps built for the job, and the old military courthouse with its entrance in the Witzlebenstrasse where the gallant few who plotted against Hitler are proudly commemorated, in contrast to the millions who supported him to the hilt and are conveniently forgotten. Our inscription at the Schlosspark will address this injustice.

The possibility of riding out to Wannsee where Hitler's Final Solution for the Jews was agreed upon has also been discussed, but prevailing weather conditions are against it. Wannsee will therefore be the target of a separate action. Tonight's secondary objectives will however include the city's much-admired lamp-posts originally designed by Hitler's personal architect, Albert Speer. Peter will have the responsibility of pasting them with leaflets exhorting all good Nazis to rally to the American genocide in Vietnam.

Judith will ride point, Teddy and Torkil will make up the second echelon, Peter and Hilde will keep up the rear. Magda will hang back, watch out for pigs and engage them in diversionary tactics if they attempt to foil the operation. Laughter. Magda is pretty and shameless. To earn money without compromising her revolutionary principles, she is proud to hire herself out as an occasional prostitute. She is also considering bearing the child of an infertile petit bourgeois couple as a means of furthering her studies.

The team sets off, Mundy shooting ahead by mistake on account of his long legs, then braking to let Judith overtake him, which she does at full tilt. Head down, white backside lifted to the sky, she races past him whistling the 'Internationale'. He gives chase, discipline is abandoned, hoots of merriment follow him through the freezing air, the

'Internationale' becomes their battle-cry. Fair hair flowing free as she jives to the rhythm of her singing, Judith embellishes one shop window, and Mundy her comrade-in-arms another. A message is passed breathlessly down the line: pigs approaching at forty degrees. The rearguard peels away but Judith goes on writing, first in German and afterwards, for the benefit of our British and American readers, in English. Mundy, her self-appointed bodyguard, watches over her while she calmly pursues her work. After hot pursuit through cobbled back alleys the team regroups, heads are counted and Peter the Great produces a welcome thermos of bourgeois mulled wine before they advance on their next target. Orange streaks of dawn are appearing through the swirling snow-clouds as the victorious troops return exhausted to their squat. Alight with cold and the exultation of the hunt, Mundy escorts Judith to her door.

'Wondered whether you'd like a spot more English conversation, if you're not too tired,' he proposes airily, only to watch the door, with its injunction to fuck off, close softly in his face.

For an age he lies wakefully on his bed. Sasha was right, damn him: even when she's left high and dry, Judith is a lost cause. In his frustration he is visited first by Ilse, then by Mrs McKechnie in her see-through black chiffon. He brushes them wearily away. Next comes Legal Judith herself, with her fountain of fair hair tumbling over her shoulders and otherwise stark naked. 'Teddy, Teddy, I require you to wake up, please,' she is saying, as she rocks his shoulder with increasing impatience. I'll bet you do, he thinks sourly. He tries opening his eyes and closing them again, but the mirage is still there despite the unpleasing morning light. Irritably he throws out an arm and meets not, as he is expecting, empty air, but Legal Judith's extremely naked bum. His first thought, idiotically, is that, like Christina and Legal Karen, she is on the run and needs a place to hide.

'What's happened? Have the police come?' he asks, in English since it is their lingua franca.

'Why? Would you prefer to make love to the police?'

'No. Of course not.'

'Do you have an engagement today? Perhaps with another girl?'

'No. I haven't. Nothing at all. I haven't got another girl.'

'We shall take time, please. You are my first man. Are you discouraged by this information? You are too English perhaps? Too respectable?'

'Of course I'm not. I mean, I'm *not* discouraged by this information. I'm not respectable at all.'

'Then we are fortunate. It was necessary to wait till everyone was asleep before I came to you. This is for security. Afterwards you will please not tell anybody that we have made love, otherwise all the men in the commune will demand to make love to me, which would not be convenient. You agree to this condition?'

'I agree. I agree to everything. You're not here. I'm asleep. Nothing's happening. I'll keep everything under my hat.'

'Your hat?'

Thus does Ted Mundy, the complete infant for sex, become the triumphant lover of Legal Judith, total dyke.

The intensity of their lovemaking unites them as a single rebel force. Their first passions slaked, they transfer themselves to Judith's lair. The FUCK OFF sign remains, but by evening of the same day the bedroom has become their love nest. Her insistence on security, and speaking only

English even in their extreme moments, ensures that they inhabit a sphere apart from other terrestrials. He knows nothing of her, nor she of him. To ask the banal questions would be to commit the mortal sin of conformity. Only now and then does an answer slip unbidden through the lines.

She is not yet *eingebläut* but is confident that once the spring marches begin she will be.

She expects, like Trotsky and Bakunin, to spend the rest of her life as a professional revolutionary, probably half of it in prison or Siberia.

She sees frozen exile, hard labour and privation as necessary stages on her path to radical perfection.

She is studying law because law is the enemy of natural justice and she wishes to know her enemy. A lawyer is always an arsehole, she proclaims contentedly, quoting a favoured guru. Mundy finds nothing inconsistent in her selecting a profession populated by arseholes.

She is impatient to sweep away all repressive social structures and believes that only by ceaseless struggle will the Movement succeed in forcing the Pig System to abandon its mask of liberal democracy and reveal its true face.

The exact form of the forthcoming struggle was, however, the stumbling block between herself and Karen. Like Karen, Judith accepts the thesis of Regis Debray and Che Guevara that if the proletariat is not ready or mature, then the revolutionary vanguard must put itself in the place of the masses. She also agrees that in such a situation, the avant-garde acquires the right to act on behalf of the deficient proletariat. What is at issue between them is method. Or, as Judith puts it, method and morality.

'If I am putting sand into a pig's petrol tank, do you

consider this action to be morally acceptable, or not morally acceptable?' she demands to know.

'Acceptable. Absolutely. Just what pigs deserve,' Mundy assures her gallantly.

The debate is taking place as usual in Judith's bed. Spring has announced itself. Sunshine is streaming through the window and the lovers are entwined in its rays. Mundy has spread her long gold hair over his face like a veil. Her voice comes to him through a dreamy haze.

'But if it is a hand-grenade I am putting into a pig's petrol tank, is this still morally acceptable, or is it morally unacceptable?'

Mundy doesn't recoil, but even in his state of permanent ecstasy he misses a beat and sits up before replying. 'Well, *no*, actually,' he says, taken aback that the English for hand-grenade should trip so lightly from his loved one's lips. 'Emphatically *un*. No go. Not in the petrol tank, not anywhere. Motion *not* carried. Ask Sasha. He agrees.'

'To Karen such a hand-grenade is not only morally acceptable, it is desirable. Against tyranny and lies, all methods are for Karen legitimate. To kill an oppressor is to perform a human service. It is to protect the oppressed. This is logical. A terrorist for Karen is someone who has a bomb but no aeroplane. We should not have bourgeois *Hemmungen*.'

'Inhibitions,' Mundy translates obligingly, doing his best to ignore the didactic edge that has entered her voice.

'Karen subscribes completely to the words of Frantz Fanon that violence exercised by the oppressed is invariably legitimate,' she adds as a defiant afterthought.

'Well, I don't,' Mundy retorts, flopping back onto the bed. 'And neither does Sasha,' he adds, as if that clinches the matter.

A long silence follows.

'You wish to know something, Teddy?'

'What, my love?'

'You are a totally insular, imperialistic English arsehole.'

See it as just another fixture, Mundy urges himself as he once again dons his father's shirts, this time by way of body armour. Demos are mock battles, never the real thing. Everybody knows where they're going to happen, and when and why. Nobody gets seriously hurt. Well, not unless they ask for it. Not even on a field day.

And I mean, for Heaven's sake, how many times have I stood shoulder to shoulder with Ilse, except that her shoulder came up to my elbow, and jostled along in jam-packed crowds all the way down Whitehall, with policemen marching close on either side of us in order not to have to use their truncheons? And what happened? A few knocks here and there, the odd kick in the ribs, but nothing half as bad as being an overgrown, underpowered rugby forward versus Downside away. It is true that, by an act of divine malice or mercy, he's never sure which, he was not among those present at the great Grosvenor Square march. But he's demo'd here in Berlin, he's occupied university buildings, participated in sit-ins, manned barricades and, thanks to his prowess as a fast bowler, earned his colours as a prodigious thrower of stink-bombs and rocks, usually at armoured police vans, thereby delaying the advance of fascism by at least a hundredth of a second.

And all right, Berlin isn't Hyde Park, it isn't Whitehall. It's less sporty, a rougher deal. And all right, the odds aren't exactly evenly distributed, what with one team all geared up with guns, truncheons, handcuffs, shields, helmets, gas masks,

99

tear gas, water-cannon and busloads of reinforcements round the corner; and the other side with – well, come to think of it – not very much at all, beyond boxes of rotting tomatoes and bad eggs, a few heaps of rocks, a lot of pretty girls and a shining message for mankind.

But I mean, we're all civilised – well, aren't we? Even on Sasha's special day: Sasha our charismatic orator, our coming man for the leader's throne, our Quasimodo of the social genesis of knowledge, who according to the prevailing pot-talk could fill the Aula with the girls he's screwed. For this same Sasha – quoting information covertly obtained by the ubiquitous Magda while in bed with a policeman – has today been singled out for particular attention, which is why Mundy, Judith, Peter the Great and other members of his supporters' club are rallied to him on the university steps. It is also why the pigs themselves have turned out in such spectacular numbers to acquaint themselves in greater detail with the doctrines of the Frankfurt School before politely inviting Sasha to step into a *grüne Minna*, which is what Germans call a Black Maria, and ride with them to the nearest police station where he will be requested with due respect for his constitutional rights under the Basic Law to make a voluntary statement listing names and addresses of his comrades and their plans to cause mayhem and rapine in the highly inflammable half-city of West Berlin, and gener-ally return the world to where it was before it succumbed to the multiple diseases of fascism, capitalism, militarism, consumerism, Nazism, Coca-Colonisation, imperialism and pseudo-democracy.

Exactly these topics are Sasha's text for today's sermon on the hallowed lawn of the Free University, and the sight of the police cordon as it closes round him inspires him to develop his themes to their extremity. He has poured scorn and hatred on America for the carpet-bombing of Vietnam's cities, the poisoning of her crops and napalming of her jungles. He has called for the Nuremberg Tribunal to be reconvened, and the fascist-imperialist American leadership arraigned before it on charges of genocide and crimes against humanity. He has accused the morally degenerate American lackeys of the so-called government in Bonn of sanitising Germany's Nazi past with consumerism, and turning the Auschwitz generation into a flock of fat sheep with nothing in their heads but new refrigerators, TV sets and Mercedes cars. He has railed against the Shah and his CIA-backed secret police, the Savak, and spread himself on the subject of the American-sponsored Greek Colonels and the 'American puppet state of Israel'. He has listed America's wars of aggression, from Hiroshima through Korea by way of Central America, South America and Africa to Vietnam. He has sent fraternal greetings to our fellow activists in Paris, Rome and Madrid and saluted America's courageous students of Berkeley and Washington DC, 'who blazed the trail we are all now marching'. He has lashed out at a mob of infuriated rightists who are yelling at him to shut his big mouth and get on with his studies.

'Shut our mouths?' he yells at them. 'You who were silent under the Nazi tyranny are telling us we should be silent under *yours*? We are good children! We have learned our lessons too well! From *you*, arseholes! From our silent Nazi parents! And we can promise you this. The children of the Auschwitz generation will never, NEVER be silent!'

He is raised on a soapbox of Mundy's manufacture in order to say this. Mundy has run it up on Faisal's workbench at the back of the café. Judith stands at Mundy's side wearing a fireman's helmet and a keffiyeh bound across her lower face. Her Chairman Mao jacket is bulked out with Mundy's cricket pullover. But her best-kept secret is the peerless body that she keeps hidden under all the shapeless tat, and it is a secret that Mundy shares with her. He knows it better than his own, every fold and contour of it. Each cry of indignant pleasure that he draws from her is a cry from his own heart. In politics as in lovemaking she is never content until they have crossed together into the wild borderlands of anarchy.

Suddenly, absolutely nothing is happening. Or nothing Mundy is aware of. It is as if film and soundtrack have stopped simultaneously, then started up again. Sasha is still speechifying from his soapbox, but the extras are screaming. Rings of armed police are tightening round the protesters, the beating of truncheons on shields has become thunderous, the first tear-gas canisters have gone off, which doesn't bother the police, because very sensibly they've put on their masks. Amid the mist of smoke and water-cannon, students are escaping in all directions, howling and whining from the gas. Mundy's ears, nose and throat are dissolving with the heat, tears are blinding him but he knows better than to wipe them away. Jets of water are crashing into his face, he sees flying truncheons and hears horses' hooves clattering on the cobble and the childlike whimpering of the wounded. In the scrum of yelling, punching bodies round him, there is only one player showing any class, and that's Legal Judith. To his amazement, she has produced a family-sized baseball bat from inside her Mao jacket and, ignoring Sasha's exhortations to passive resistance, whacks a young policeman so hard on the side of his new helmet that it falls into his hands like a gift from Heaven as he sinks smiling stupidly to his knees. 'Teddy, *du gibst bitte Acht auf Sasha!*' she advises Mundy politely, speaking for once the delicious language of Thomas Mann rather than the English of their passion. Then she vanishes under a snake-heap of brown and blue uniforms and there is no way on earth he can reach her. The last he sees of her she has swapped her fireman's hat for a cap of blood, but her exhortation is burning in his ears: *Teddy, you will kindly take care of Sasha,* and he remembers that Ilse made the same request of him, and that he has made the same request of himself.

The water-cannon are being wheeled up but the two armies are now so intermingled that the pigs are reluctant to drench their own, and Sasha is still yelling out his message from his soapbox. The pigs are within truncheon range of him, a very fat sergeant screams, 'Get me this shit-faced poison dwarf!' and Mundy is doing what he never dreamed of doing, and if he had planned it he would never have done it. The son of Major Arthur Mundy, holder of the Pakistani Something-or-Other of Honour, emptier of twenty saddles, is charging the enemy. But it is Sasha, not a Bren gun, he is holding in his arms. Blindly obedient to Legal Judith's command as well as his own good impulses, he has whisked Sasha from his soapbox and slung him across his shoulders. He has Sasha's thrashing feet in one arm and flailing hands in another and he is wading through the enemy tear gas and the mass of howling, bleeding bodies, not feeling the truncheons that rain on him and not hearing anything except Sasha's bitching and complaining – let me down, you arsehole, run, get out of here, the pigs will kill you – until the sun comes out and Mundy is lighter by an entire millstone because by now he has carried out Judith's orders to the best of his ability, and Sasha has slipped from his shoulders and hightailed it across the open square, and it is Mundy, not Sasha, who sits in the police van with his hands cuffed to a bar above his head while two policemen take turns to beat the living daylights out of him: Ted Mundy is being *eingebläut*, and he doesn't need Sasha's translation to tell him what it means.

It was never afterwards easy for Mundy to document what followed. There was the van, there was the police station. There was the cell that smelled of the things cells are supposed to smell of: excreta, salt tears, vomit and, from time to time, warm blood. For a while he shared it with a bald-headed Pole who proclaimed himself a multiple murderer, rolled his eyes a lot and giggled. In the interrogation room there was no Pole. It was the private domain of Mundy and the same two policemen who had given him his first beating in the van, and were now giving him another under the mistaken impression that he was Peter the Great with his beard shaved off, pretending to be a British subject. He possessed a perfectly good student's card they could have looked at, even if it had the wrong address on it, not to mention a British passport, but unfortunately he had left them back in the attic for fear of losing them in the fray. He offered to go and fetch them, but obviously he couldn't tell his inquisitors where to find them for themselves because to do so would have been to point them straight at Sasha and the illegal squat. His stubbornness on this point drove them to new heights of fury. They stopped listening to him and whaled into him for the hell of it: groin, kidneys, soles of the feet, groin again, but for cosmetic purposes leaving the face relatively intact, though ultimately not as intact as any of them might have wished. Periodically he dropped off. Periodically they carted him back to his cell while they had a rest. How many times this happened was always a blur to him, just as the sudden end of it all, and the ambulance ride to the British military hospital, were blurs. He had an impression of blue lights that flashed inside his head instead of in the street where they belonged, and of clean bed sheets that smelled of Dettol. And of a glistening ward presided over by a children's nursemaid with a silver-plated stopwatch pinned to her white linen bosom.

'Mundy? Mundy? Not related to a little shit called Major Arthur Mundy, are we, ex-Indian Army? Can't be,' the Chief Medical Officer asks suspiciously, peering down at the bandaged length of him.

'I'm afraid not, sir.'

'Don't be afraid, old boy. Count yourself bloody lucky is all I can say. How many fingers am I holding up? Well done. Jolly good.'

He is lying in the ship's cabin, but without the comfort of the Major's Burmas. He is crouched beside Rani at the rock pool, but can't stand up. He has his head in a handbasin and is clutching the taps in the school washroom while the prefects take it in turns to beat him for his lack of Christian reverence. He is out of bounds, a plague case. The sight of him could be infectious. He's an untouchable, and there's a stencilled notice hanging just the other side of his door to prove it:

AUTHORISED MILITARY PERSONNEL ONLY

– or as Judith would say, fuck off. In earnest of this, there is also a red-capped military police sergeant to watch over his well-being. The sergeant makes his feelings clear on the first occasion Mundy is strong enough to shuffle down the corridor to pee.

'We'd have put the manners on you if *we'd* had you, son,' he assures him. 'You'd be bloody dead, *and* grateful for it.'

A British official comes to visit. He is Mr Amory, and brings a printed card to say so: Mr Nicholas Amory, Vice-Consul, the British High Commission, Berlin. He is only a few years older than Mundy and, for an unredeemed bourgeois Englishman of the oppressive classes, disconcertingly agreeable. He wears a good tweed suit but is shaggy in a reassuring way. His suède shoes are particularly disgraceful. The Major's kitbag dangles from his nicely tailored shoulder.

'Whoever sent you these grapes, Edward?' he enquires, fingering them and grinning.

'The Berlin police.'

'Did they by Jove? And the chrysanths?'

'The Berlin police.'

'Well, I think that's mighty handsome of them, don't you, given the strain the poor chaps are under these days?' – laying the kitbag at the foot of Mundy's bed – 'This *is* the front line, you know. Nobody can be blamed for losing their rag now and then. Specially when they're provoked by a bunch of State-funded students who don't know their radical arses from their elbows – any more than you do, I suspect.' He has pulled up a chair and is studying Mundy's face critically in close-up. 'Who's your nice friend, Edward?'

'Which one?'

'The little twerp who came storming into our office like the bloody SS,' he replies, helping himself to a grape. 'Jumped the queue, slammed your passport on the reception desk and barked at our German clerk to secure your immediate release from the West Berlin police, or else. Then barged out again before anyone could take his name and address. The poor clerk was scared out of his wits. A submerged Saxon accent, he said. Audible but not ridiculous. Only a Saxon would be such an oaf. Do you have a lot of chums like that, Edward? Angry East Germans who won't leave their names?'

'No.'

'How long have you been in Berlin?'

'Nine months.'

'Living where?'

'My grant ran out.'

'Living where?'

'In Charlottenburg.'

'Someone told me Kreuzberg.'

No answer.

'You should have come and signed the book. Distressed British students are what we do best.'

'I wasn't distressed.'

'Well, you are now. You bowled for the public schools, didn't you?'

'A couple of times.'

'We've got quite a decent side here. Too late now. Pity. What's his name, as a matter of interest?'

'Whose?'

'Your short-arsed Saxon knight with a hobble. His ugly face struck our clerk as familiar. Thought he might have seen it in the papers.'

'I don't know.'

Amory seems quietly amused by this. He consults the disgraceful suède shoes. 'Well, well. Question is, Edward, what are we going to do with you?'

Mundy has no suggestions. He is wondering whether Amory is one of the prefects who beat him in the washroom.

'You could raise a stink, I suppose. Call in six lawyers. We can give you a list. The coppers would press charges of their own, of course. Causing a breach of the peace, for openers. Abusing your status as a foreign guest, which the judges won't like. Registering yourself under a false address. We'd do our best for you, naturally. Feed you French bread through the bars. Did you say something?'

Mundy hasn't said a word, Amory can beat him as much as he likes.

'As far as the police are concerned, you're simply a case of mistaken identity. If you'd been the right person, they'd have been highly commended. They say some mad Polish murderer did it to you. Is that possible?'

'No.'

'However, they *are* prepared to cut a deal, if we are. *They* won't throw the book at you, and *you* won't press charges for any little mishap that may or may not have occurred while you were in the nick. And *we* will save our British blushes at this delicate time of international crisis by smuggling you out of Berlin disguised as a Nubian slave. Done?'

The night nurse is as big as Ayah, but she tells no stories about the Prophet Mohammed.

He arrives as a doctor, the way clever heroes do in movies: at crack of dawn while the sergeant's man is dozing in the sentry's chair, and Mundy is lying on his back sending messages to Judith. The white medical coat has three pips on each shoulder and is several sizes too big for him. A stethoscope dangles haplessly round his neck, and a pair of enormous surgical galoshes cover his fraying sneakers. The whole of West Berlin must have been looking out for a shit-faced poison dwarf, but that hasn't stopped him, he's resourceful. He's wriggled or talked his way past the sentries at the gate, and once inside the hospital he's made a beeline for the MO room and forced a locker. There is a yellowy sickness round his eyes. His forelock is too young for him, his revolutionist's scowl replaced by deep uncertainty. The rest of him is smaller and more crumpled than ever.

'Teddy, I am without words. What you did for me – saving my life, no less – this was the gesture of a friend I do not deserve. How can I repay you? Nobody has ever performed such an absurd act of sacrifice on my behalf. You are English, and for you, all life is a silly accident. But I am German, and for me, if it has no logic it is meaningless.'

Lakes have formed in the brown eyes. His oversized voice is husky inside the little chest. His words sound carefully prepared.

'How's Judith?' Mundy asks.

'Judith? Legal Judith?' He seems to have difficulty remembering the name. 'Judith, ah well, she is in good form, thank you, Teddy, yes. Affected, as we all are, by this outrage but, as you would expect of her, not bowed. She suffered a small head wound, she breathed too much gas. She is *eingebläut* like you, but she is recovered. And she asks to be remembered to you' – as if that settles the matter – 'warmly remembered to you, Teddy. She admires you for what you did.'

'Where is she?'

'In the squat. A small bandage for the first few days. Then nothing.'

The *nothing*, and the silence that follows it, prompt Mundy to pull a humourless grin. '*To the girl who has got nozzings on,*' he intones idiotically in English, quoting a line of doggerel the Major was fond of reciting in his cups. 'She knows they're throwing me out, does she?' he asks.

'Judith? Of course. A totally unconstitutional act. The lawyer in her is outraged. Her immediate instinct was to go to the courts. I had to use all my persuasive powers to convince her that your legal position here is not as strong as she would wish.'

'But you managed.'

'Only with great difficulty. Like many women, Judith does not take kindly to arguments of expediency. However, you would be proud of her, Teddy. Thanks to you, she is completely liberated.'

After that, as good friends may, Sasha sits at Mundy's bedside, holding his friend's wrist rather than his smashed-up hand but somehow contriving not to look Mundy in the eye. Mundy lies staring at him, Sasha sits staring at the wall, until Mundy out of politeness finally pretends to be asleep. Sasha leaves and the door seems to close twice: once on Sasha and once on the completely liberated Judith.

5

Flat years, frustrating years, years of directionless wandering are about to blight the progress of Ted Mundy, life's eternal apprentice. He later thinks of them as his Empty Quarter, though in number they amount to less than a decade.

Not for the first time in his brief existence, he is hustled out of town at first light. He has no disgraced father to care for, the road is flat and metalled. No weeping Rani hunches as if crippled at the compound gates and, though he searches everywhere for her, no Judith. Murree's ancient army truck has been replaced by a polished Jeep with white spats, and it's the military police sergeant, not a Punjabi warrior, who offers a last piece of friendly advice.

'Come back any time you like, son. We'll remember you, and we'll be bloody waiting for you.'

The sergeant need not worry. After three weeks of studying the ceiling of his hospital ward, Mundy has no plans to return, and no destination in mind. Should he return to

Oxford? As who? In what disguise? The prospect of resuming a degree course among a bunch of over-educated children who have never seen an ideal fired in anger is repugnant to him. Landing at Heathrow he heads on an impulse for Weybridge, where the inebriated lawyer who attended his father's funeral receives him in a dark mock-Tudor house called The Pines. It's raining, but then it always was.

'One had *rather* hoped you'd have the decency to reply to one's letter,' the lawyer complains.

'One did,' Mundy says, and helps find the missing document among a heap of chewed files.

'Yes, well, there we are then. Something in the kitty after all. Your late father Arthur signed a banker's order on his savings fund, stupid bugger. He'd have stopped it years ago if he'd known. Don't mind if I knock off the first five hundred for fees?'

A lawyer is always an arsehole, Mundy reminds himself as he slams the garden gate behind him. Striding down the road, he meets the fairy-lit outline of the Golden Swan. The night's last revellers are departing in the rain. Mundy spots himself and his father among them.

'Good crowd tonight, boy,' the Major is remarking, dragging on his arm like a drowning man. 'High level of conversation. You don't get that in a Mess. All shop.'

'It was really interesting, sir.'

'If you want to feel the heartbeat of England, they're the ones to listen to. I don't say much, but I listen. Specially Percy. Fund of knowledge. Can't understand where the fellow went wrong.'

Number Two, The Vale has been razed to the ground. All that remains, so far as Mundy can make out by the street lamp, is a builder's board offering family homes with three bedrooms and a ninety per cent mortgage. At the railway station, the last train to anywhere has left. An old man with an Alsatian dog offers bed and breakfast for five pounds cash in advance. By midday Mundy is a new boy again, riding westward on the school train, looking out for chaps who comb their hair in public.

The Abbey with its flag of St George looms like a risen crypt over the dismal town. At its foot lies The Close, and up the hill the ancient school. But Mundy doesn't climb the hill. Somehow there was never quite the space up there for impecunious refugees from Hitler's Germany to teach cello or the language of Goethe. They were deemed more comfortable living above a red-brick shoe-shop on the roundabout. The side door is in an alley. The same faded handwritten notice in Mandelbaum's pedantic German hand is fastened to it with rusted drawing pins. *For out of hours, press only LOWER. For Mallory, press only TOP and afterwards please WAIT.* Mundy presses *only TOP* and is pleased to wait. He hears footsteps and starts to smile until he realises they are not the footsteps he wants. They are swift and flurried and whoever owns them is yelling back up the stairs as she descends: *Hang on, Billy, Mummy will be back in a minute!*

The door opens six inches and stops dead. The same voice says, *Shit.* The door slams shut, he hears the chain come off. The door flies open.

'Yes?'

Young mothers never have time. This one has a pink, flustered face and long hair she has to sweep away to let him see her.

'I was hoping for Mr Mallory,' Mundy says. He indicates the faded notice. 'He's a teacher at the school. Top floor.'

'Is he the one that's dead? Ask in the shop. They'll know. *Coming*, Billy!'

He needs a bank. Somewhere they cash cheques from lawyers in Weybridge for young men in search of Godot.

Airborne once more, Mundy drifts between dream and reality. Rome, Athens, Cairo, Bahrain and Karachi receive him without comment and pass him on. Landing in Lahore, he declines the airport's many imaginative offers of a night's accommodation and delivers himself into the hands of a driver called Mahmoud who speaks English and Punjabi. Mahmoud has military moustaches and a 1949 Wolseley car with a mahogany dashboard and wax carnations in a vase fixed in the rear window. And Mahmoud knows his way to the *very precise location, sahib, no ifs and buts, the perfectly exact position* where an Irish Roman Catholic nursemaid and her dead daughter would have been *most reverently laid to rest*. Mahmoud knows this because by coincidence he is a lifelong friend and also first cousin of an ancient white-turbaned Christian sacristan who says his name is Paul after the saint, and is the owner of a leather-bound register which, when encouraged by a small donation, indicates where the most gracious sahibs and memsahibs are buried.

The cemetery is an enclosed oval of descending terraces beside a derelict gasworks. It is strewn with decapitated angels, bits of ancient car and smashed concrete crosses with their intestines open to the sky. The grave lies at the foot of a tree whose spreading branches make such a pool of black-ness under the glaring sun that Mundy in his half-dazed state fancies it is open. The headstone is sandy-soft, the carved inscription so faded that he has to guess the words with his finger. *In memory of Nellie O'Connor of County Kerry Ireland*

and her baby daughter Rose. Beloved of her husband Arthur and son Edward. Rest in God.

I'm Edward.

A score of children have attached themselves, tendering flowers from other graves. Unheeding of Mahmoud's protests, Mundy presses money into every small hand. The hillside becomes a hive of begging children, and the tall, stooping Englishman longs to be one of them.

Crammed into the passenger seat with his knees knocking against the mahogany dashboard of the ancient Wolseley, the Returning Son watches himself enter the dusty haze that in India you must always pass through on your way to somewhere. And when you arrive, the haze is waiting for you. On lush hillsides he recognises the deserted stone breweries built by the Raj to wash down the Major's curry. It's the road we drove down when they sent us back to England, he thinks. These are the bullock carts we hooted at. These are the children who stared at us but I didn't stare back.

The bends have acquired a rhythm. Like a willing drayhorse the Wolseley responds to it. Brown mountains with their peaks sawn off by haze lift ahead of them. To their left lie the foothills of the Hindu Kush, presided over by the mother-peak of Nanga Parbat.

'Your very town, sahib!' cries Mahmoud, and there it is: a glimpse of brown houses perched on a ridge, gone again with the next turn. Now the relics of the departed British take on a military note: a collapsed sentry post, a dying barrack hut, an overgrown saluting base. A final push by the Wolseley, a few more turns. They are in the town. From tour guide and chauffeur Mahmoud promotes himself to estate agent, conversant with every fine property in Murree and the bargain price that will secure it. This main street, sahib, is today one of the most fashionable in all of Pakistan: note the fine restaurants, food stalls and clothes shops. In these secluded side streets you may observe the elegant summer villas of the richest and most discerning citizens of Islamabad.

'Kindly reflect upon the most superb views, sahib! Admire the distant plains of Kashmir! As to the climate, it is most jolly. And the pine forests are full of animals at all times of year! Smell also the sweet Himalayan air! Oh gladness!'

Please drive on uphill, says the Returning Son.

Yes, this way. Past the Pakistani Air Force base and keep going.

Thank you, Mahmoud.

The Air Force base is made of smart tarmac instead of grass. A second floor has been added to the officers' quarters. *Those bloody pansies in blue, they hog the budget every time*, Mundy hears the Major fume. The road is pitted now, and overgrown. Dusty poverty replaces the affluence of the town. After a couple of miles they reach a brown slope strewn with abandoned military cantonments and poor villages.

Stop here, please, Mahmoud. Thank you. Here is fine.

Goats, pi-dogs and the eternal poor drift across the overgrown parade ground. The dust-patch next to the mosque where the great cricketers of tomorrow honed their skills is today a hostel for the dying. The same hand that erased Number Two, The Vale has turned the Major's bungalow into a half-dried skull, ripping off its tin roof, doors and balcony but leaving the eyeless sockets of the windows to stare at the destruction.

Do the asking, please, Mahmoud. I have forgotten my Punjabi.

Ayah? Everyone's an ayah, sahib! What's her name?

She had no name but Ayah. She was very big. Mundy wants to add that she had a huge bottom and perched on a tiny stool in the corridor outside his bedroom, but he doesn't want the children to laugh. She worked for an English major who lived here, he says. The Major left suddenly. He drank too much whisky. He liked to sit under that neem tree over there and smoke cheroots called Burmas. He mourned his wife, loved his son and regretted the Partition.

Does Mahmoud translate this? Probably not. He too has his delicacy. They find the oldest man in the street. *Oh, I remember Ayah most well, sahib! A Madrassi, as I recall. All her family had perished wretchedly in the many massacres, except for the good lady herself. Well, sir, yes, there we are, as we say. After the English left, nobody wanted her any more. First she begged, then she died. By the end, she was most diminutive. The sahib would not have recognised her as the large lady he is describing. Rani?* he speculates, warming to his work. *Now which Rani would that be, sahib?*

The Rani whose father ran a spice farm, Mundy replies, by a feat of memory that bewilders him until he recalls how she used to bring him gifts of spices wrapped in leaves.

Suddenly the oldest man in the street remembers Rani exactly! *Miss Rani, she is married most suitably, I assure you, sahib. You will rejoice to hear of her good fortune, thank you, sir. When she was but fourteen years of age her father gave her to a rich factory owner resident in Lahore, what we call in this region a most suitable match. To date they have been blessed with three fine sons and one daughter already, which I say is not bad going, thank you, sahib. You are most gracious, like all the British.*

They are walking back to the Wolseley but the oldest man is still with them, clutching Mundy's arm and peering into his eyes with unearthly benevolence.

And now I beseech you to go home, sir, please, he advises, with the utmost good humour. *Don't bring us your commerce, I implore you. Don't send us any more soldiers, we have quite enough, thank you. You British have taken what you need from us. You have enough now. It's time you gave us a bit of a rest, I say!*

Wait here, Mundy tells Mahmoud. Look after the car.

He treads softly down the forest path, thinking he is barefoot. In a minute, Ayah will call to me, telling me I mustn't go too far. The two great tree trunks are as vast as they ever were. The zigzag footpath between them leads down to the stream's edge. The rock pool still flashes with mother-of-pearl. But the only face he sees in it is his own.

Very dear Judith, Mundy writes the same night in stern school English, from his hotel room in a poor part of Lahore. *You owe me at the very least some sign of yourself. I need to know that our time together meant as much to you as it did to me. I have to believe in you. It's one thing to keep searching in life. It's another to have no firm ground under one's feet. I believe you would love this place. It is populated by what you would call the true proletariat. I know about Sasha and I don't mind. I love you. Ted.*

Which doesn't sound like me at all, he decides. But what does? The postbox in the hotel bears Queen Victoria's insignia. Let's hope Her Majesty knows where to find the Kreuzberg squat.

He is in England again. Sooner or later you have to turn yourself in. Perhaps his visa ran out. Perhaps he grew tired of his own bad company. Availing himself of time-honoured tradition, the former head prefect and cricket hero signs up with a rural preparatory school that accepts unqualified teachers at a discount. Embracing its discipline like an old friend, he throws himself with his habitual zeal on the Germanic mysteries of verb-comma-verb, gender and plurality. In the hours left him after correcting schoolwork, he masterminds the school's production of *Ambrose Applejohn's Adventure* and makes furtive love to a Judith substitute, who happens to be the science master's wife, in the scorers' shed beside the first eleven cricket field. In the school holidays he persuades himself that he is the coming Evelyn Waugh, a view not shared by publishers. Between times he dashes off ever more desperate letters to the squat. Some propose marriage, some profess a broken heart, but all are mysteriously dogged by the prosaic tone of his letter from Lahore. Knowing only that her family name is Kaiser and she is from Hamburg, he ploughs through telephone directories in the local library, besieges Overseas Enquiries, and pesters Kaisers across the North German seaboard in case they have a Judith. None points him in the direction of his former language pupil.

Towards Sasha he adopts a reserved approach. There are too many bits of his erstwhile room-mate that in retrospect he finds difficult to enjoy. He resents the spell Sasha cast over him when they were face to face. He regrets his undue reverence for Sasha's zany philosophical abstractions. He is irked, despite his protestations to the contrary, that Sasha went before him as Ilse's lover, and after him as Judith's. One day I'll write to him. Meanwhile, I'll write my novel.

All the more disconcerting, therefore, that a full three years after being thrown out of Berlin, he should receive a battered bunch of readdressed envelopes sent care of his Oxford college and forwarded to his bank after long months of convalescence in the porters' lodge.

There is a round dozen of them. Some are as long as twenty sides of single-spaced typescript from Sasha's Olivetti portable, with addenda and postscripts in his spiky Germanic hand. Mundy's first dishonourable thought is to consign the whole lot to his dustbin. His second is to hide them somewhere he won't find them: behind the chest of drawers, or in the rafters of the scorers' shed. But after days of shifting them from place to place he pours himself a stiff drink and, laying out the letters in their chronological order, works his way through them.

He is at first moved, then ashamed.

All his self-indulgent obsessions disappear.

This is Sasha in despair.

This is a cry of real pain from a fragile friend who has not left the battle front.

Fled the snappish tone, the dogmatic statements from the throne. In place of them, a desperate appeal for a glimmer of hope in a world that has collapsed around his ears.

He asks nothing material. His daily wants are few and easily taken care of. He can cook his own food – Mundy shudders – he does not lack for women – when did he ever? He is owed money by magazines; one or other will pay before it goes under. Faisal at the café makes an illicit arak that can blind a horse. No, the tragedy of Sasha's life is of a grander, nobler order altogether. It is that West Germany's radical left is a spent force and Sasha is a prophet without a country.

'Passive resistance has become no resistance, civil disobedience has become armed violence. Maoist groups are fighting each other for the entertainment of the CIA, the extremists have taken over from the radicals, and those who do not conform with the Bonn reactionaries are banished from what is to be called society. Perhaps you did not know that we now have a law which officially bars from public life all who do not pledge allegiance to the *basic principles of liberal democracy*? One fifth of West German employees, from train drivers to professors to myself, are to be considered non-persons by the fascists! Think, Teddy! I am not allowed to drive a train unless I agree to drink Coca-Cola, bomb the Red River dam and napalm Vietnamese children! Soon I shall be forced to wear a yellow S declaring me a socialist!'

Mundy is by now searching hungrily for word of Judith. He finds it submerged in a footnote devoted to matters not associated with the letter's central theme, which as usual is Sasha.

'People leave Berlin in the night, often we cannot tell where they go. Peter the Great, one hears, has gone to Cuba. He will fight for Fidel Castro. If I had two good legs and Peter's shoulders I would perhaps offer myself to the same great cause. Of Christina, we have depressing rumours that through her father's influence she has been permitted to return to Athens. By kind consent of her country's American-backed fascistic military dictatorship she will join her family's shipping company. Judith, ignoring my advice, has joined Karen in Beirut. I fear for her, Teddy. The path she has taken is heroic but misguided. Even among revolutionaries, there are too many cultural differences to be resolved. According to a friend who recently returned from those regions, not even the most radical Arabs take kindly to our sexual revolution, dismissing it as decadent Westernism. Such prejudice does not bode well for Judith's libertarian appetites. Unfortunately by the time of her departure I exerted little influence over her actions. She is a wilful woman, led by her senses and not easily persuaded by arguments of moderation.'

Such an unjust portrait of Mundy's true love rekindles his romantic longings: *Go to her! Fly to Beirut! Comb the Palestinian training camps! Join the struggle, separate her from Karen, bring her back alive!* Discovering that he is still sitting in his chair, however, he reads on.

'I am so sick of *theory*, Teddy. I am so sick of bourgeois posturers whose idea of revolution is smoking pot instead of tobacco in front of their children! The hated Lutheran in me will not sleep, I admit it, I admit it. Writing to you at this moment I am ready to give up half of what I believe in exchange for one clarifying vision. To see one great rational truth glowing on the horizon, to go to it regardless of cost, regardless of what must be left behind, is what I dream of beyond all things. Will tomorrow change me? Nothing changes me. It is only the world that changes. And here in West Germany there is no tomorrow. There is only yesterday, or banishment, or enslavement to the forces of imperialism.'

Mundy begins to feel the old fuzziness descend on him. If he were listening, he would by now have switched off. Somehow he continues reading.

'Any acts of protest currently performed by the left only legitimise the rightist conspiracy that we are forced to call democracy. Our very existence as radicals underpins the authority of our enemies. Bonn's military-industrial junta has strapped West Germany so tight to the American warwagon that we shall never be able to raise a finger against its atrocities.'

He thunders on. Mundy is by now reading him diagonally.

'Our officially tolerated voices are all we have left to fight the corporate tyranny . . . True socialist ideals have become the court eunuchs of the Bonn Pantheon . . .'

Did the Pantheon keep eunuchs? Mundy the pedantic schoolmaster doubts it. He licks a finger and skims a couple more pages, then a couple more. Great news. Sasha is still a cyclist. *I have taken no more falls since that day you taught me in the Tiergarten.* The news of his former mentor in Cologne is less good: *The bastard has retracted half his writings and done a bunk to New Zealand!*

Mundy pushes the letter aside and takes up the last of all. It opens with an ominous announcement: *Here beginneth the second bottle of arak.* The writing is freer and, for all its high-flown style, more intimate.

'I do not begrudge you your silence, Teddy. I grudge you nothing. You saved my life, I stole your woman. If you are still angry with me, please remain angry. Without anger we are nothing, nothing, nothing.' Good to hear it. *Now* what? 'If you are guarding your literary muse with silence, guard her well, write well, tend your talent. I shall never again take you for granted. When I talk to you I talk to that good ear that has listened to so much of my bullshit that I blush.' Well, now you know. 'Does it listen still? I believe so. You are not ideologically encumbered. You are my bourgeois confessor as I pursue my odyssey of logical metamorphosis. To you alone I am able to think aloud. Therefore I will whisper to you through the grille that I am like the Persian poet who, having heard all the world's great arguments, evermore comes out of the same door he went in through. I see the dark door before me now. It is open, waiting for me to enter.' *Dark door?* What the hell's he bleating about – suicide? For

Christ's sake, Sasha, get a grip on yourself! thinks Mundy, but he is seriously alarmed.

Unfinished page. Turn to the next one. The writing is now hectic, a message in a bottle from a marooned man contemplating the jump off the rocks.

'Therefore, Teddy, you see your friend standing at the crossroads of his life' – a crossroads, or a dark Persian door? Get on with it, arsehole! 'What names do I read on the signpost? The fog is so thick I can barely decipher them! For answer me this, dear friend. Or better, answer my new seducers – If our class enemy is capitalist imperialism – and who can doubt that it is? – who ultimately is our class friend? Do I hear you warn me that Sasha is venturing into a quicksand?' – ah, got it, your dark door opens onto a beach, naturally – 'You are right, Teddy! You are right as always! Yet how many times have you not heard me declare that it is the duty of every true revolutionary to throw his weight where it will be most effective to the Cause?' Mundy recalls no such times, but then probably he wasn't listening. 'Well, Teddy, now you may see for yourself how neatly I am impaled on the imperfect logic of my own convictions! Go well, dear Teddy. You are my absolute friend! If I decide as I fear I have already decided, I shall carry your loyal heart with me!'

Groaning theatrically, Mundy pushes the letter away from him, but he has one more page to go.

'Write to me care of Faisal at the Istanbul Café. I shall arrange for your letters to reach me in whatever improbable circumstance I find myself. Have the pigs left you with a limp? Oh, what bastards those fellows are! Can you still found a dynasty? I hope so, for the more Teddys there are in the world, the better place it will be. What about the headaches?

All this I need to know. Yours in Christ, in agape, in friendship, in despair, Sasha.'

Seized with guilt and concern, as well as some kind of habitual unease whenever Sasha's shadow falls across his path, Mundy grabs pen and paper and applies himself to the task of explaining his silence and vowing eternal loyalty. He has not forgotten how precarious was Sasha's hold on life; or the feeling, whenever he hauled his little body out of the room, that he might never come back. He remembers the uneven shoulders, the dramatic head, the daffy, uncoordinated hobble, on or off a bicycle. He remembers Sasha by Christmas candlelight, soliloquising about the Herr Pastor. He remembers the brown, over-studious eyes, fervently searching for a better world, incapable of compromise or diversion. He determinedly forgives him Judith. He forgives Judith too. He has been forgiving her for longer than he cares to think, and failing every time.

The writing starts well but dries.

Do it in the morning when I'm fresh, he tells himself.

But morning is no better than the night before.

He tries a moment of post-coital lassitude after a particularly satisfying encounter in the scorers' shed, but the fond, lightly humorous letter that he plans remains stubbornly unwritten.

He makes the usual feeble excuses to himself. It's three bloody years, for God's sake. Four probably. Faisal will have closed down the Istanbul, he was saving up to buy a taxi.

Anyway, whatever mad step Sasha was contemplating, he'll have taken it. And besides, I've got this pile of fifth-form German compositions staring at me.

Mundy is still prevaricating in this way when the science

master's wife, yielding to an implausible fit of remorse, makes a clean breast of her misdemeanours to her husband. The trio is summoned to the headmaster's study where a solution is crisply arrived at. By adding their signatures to a document the headmaster has obligingly prepared for them in advance, all parties contract to put their passions on hold until exams are over.

'You wouldn't care to take her on for the holidays, would you, old boy?' the science master murmurs in Mundy's ear in the village pub while his wife pretends not to listen. 'I've been offered this rather good part-time job at Heathrow airport.'

Mundy regrets that he has already made his holiday arrangements. And it is while he is debating what these arrangements might be – and not just for the holidays – that he is freed from his writer's block. In a few warm-hearted sentences, he echoes Sasha's pledge of undying loyalty, urges him to cheer up and not be so serious – Dr Mandelbaum's term *foolishly earnest* springs happily to his pen. He recommends the middle way. *Don't be so hard on yourself, man, give yourself a break! Life's a botch and you can't solve it single-handed, nobody can, least of all your new seducers, whoever the hell they are!* And for amusement's sake, but also as a way of saying he has put male jealousy behind him, he provides a Rabelaisian and not wholly accurate account of his recent affair with the science teacher's wife.

And I *have* put it behind me, he reasons. Judith and Sasha had a bit of free love and I paid for it. And as Sasha so rightly says, without anger we are nothing.

Launching himself upon a career in journalism as a stepping stone to literary immortality, Mundy submits to a correspondence course and enrols as a cub reporter with a dying provincial newspaper in the East Midlands. At first, all bodes well. His coverage of the decline of the local herring fleet is admired; his descriptions, sensitively embroidered, of the goings-on in the mayoral parlour are found amusing, and no colleague's wife offers herself as a Judith substitute. But when, during the absence on holiday of his editor, he files an exposé of underpaid Asian labour in a local canning factory, the idyll ends abruptly. The owner of the factory is the proprietor of the newspaper.

Transferring his talents to a pirate radio station, he interviews local celebrities and plays songs of yesteryear to Mum and Dad on their golden day until a Friday evening when the producer suggests they pop down the road together for a jar.

'It's the class bit, Ted,' the producer explains. 'The punters say you sound like some over-fed geezer from the House of Lords.'

Bad months follow. The BBC turns down his radio play. A children's story about a pavement artist who produces a chalk masterpiece and recruits a gang of street kids to help him remove the flagstone finds no favour with publishers, one of whom responds with unwelcome frankness: *We find the actions of your German police violent and their language offensive. We fail to see why you have set your story in Berlin, a city of unpleasant connotations for many of our British readers.*

But from the depths of gloom Mundy as ever sees a chink of light. In a quarterly periodical devoted to readers with literary ambitions, an American foundation offers travelling scholarships to writers under thirty who seek the inspiration of the New World. Undaunted by the prospect of venturing into the giant's castle, Mundy beams his charm at three kindly matrons from North Carolina over tea and muffins in an elderly hotel in London's Russell Square. Six weeks later he finds himself once more aboard ship, this time bound for the Land of Opportunity. Standing on the afterdeck, watching the imperial outlines of Liverpool fade into the drizzle, he has the unaccountable feeling that it is Sasha and not England that he is leaving behind.

The years of directionless wandering have yet to run their course. In Taos, a real writer at last, Mundy rents an adobe hut with a fine view of desert sagebrush, telegraph poles and a pack of shiftless pi-dogs wandered in from Murree. Seated at his window, he drinks tequila and rhapsodises about the long mauve dying of each day. There are many such days and many tequilas. But so there were for Malcolm Lowry and D.H. Lawrence. The natives are not merely friendly, they are sun-soaked, benign and frequently stoned. He has no sense of the ravening world-colonisers he deplored in Berlin. His efforts to raise a local drama group are balked not by unbridled aggression but differences of ethereal perception.

Achieving fifty pages of a novel about civil strife in a fictional European country, he packs them off to a publisher with the suggestion that he should advise him how to complete it. The publisher is not inclined to do so. Next comes a slender volume of poems to Judith, privately printed on handmade paper and entitled *Radical Love*. Undiscovered talents like himself are unanimous in their admiration, but the cost is twice the estimate.

Time loses its impact. Ambling down the dusty streets on his evening pilgrimage to the Spanish Inn and Motel, Mundy wears a perpetual and slightly shameful grin. News of causes that were once dear to him reaches him like the Major's incomplete readings of Kipling. The Vietnam war is a continuing tragedy. All Taos says so. Several of its young have burned their draft cards and disappeared to Canada. The Palestinians have launched a campaign of terror, he reads in an old copy of *Time*, and Ulrike Meinhof's Red Army Fraktion is giving them a helping hand. Is Judith the face behind the mask behind the gun? Is Karen? The notion appals him but what can he do? *Karen subscribes completely to the words of Frantz Fanon that violence exercised by the oppressed is invariably legitimate*. Well, I don't. And nor does Sasha. But you do, presumably. And your sexual liberation is not compatible with the moral standards of Rejectionist Arabia.

If Mundy feels the occasional pang of conscience because he isn't marching and being beaten up, a couple of tequilas can suppress it any time. In a paradise where everyone around you lives for art alone, it's only civilised to do the same. But paradise has other snags that no number of tequilas can quite overcome. Shut out your past at the front door, and it creeps in at the back. Sit on the verandah of your adobe hut with a yellow pad on your lap watching the same damned sun disappear yet again behind the same damned mountain top – prowl round your typewriter night after night glowering at the blank paper or the blank window and cranking up your genius with tequila – and what do you *hear*, if not Sasha with his mouth full of garlic sausage lecturing you on the genesis of human knowledge? On your way to the Spanish Inn and Motel, when the desert loneliness hits you with the sunset and you start to count old friends – who if not Sasha hobbles along beside you over the Berlin cobble as the pair of you make your way to the Shaven Cat for Sasha to put the world to rights? And when you are in the arms of one of the many female painters, writers, transcendental meditators and truth-seekers whose road to enlightenment includes a detour in your bed, whose peerless body, plus or minus its long white woollen tights, presides over your dutiful endeavours?

And then – as Hemingway might say – there is poor little Bernie Luger, the bearded, rich, undersized action-painter with his Cuban model Nita, who never poses for him, because how can she? – Bernie's not painting fucking female flesh any more, he's way beyond that shit, man! His eight-foot-tall masterpieces are black and crimson infernos of the Last Day, his work-in-progress is a triptych of the Napalming of Minnesota, so tall he needs a ladder. Do all small painters paint large canvases? Mundy suspects they do.

Bernie – if you believe him and you'd better – is the greatest libertarian and freedom fighter since Thoreau, whose work he reads aloud at his all-night parties, while he peers over the brown precipice of a Spanish pulpit that he claims was given him by Che Guevara in gratitude for services he may not name. Bernie has done civil disobedience in Memphis. He's been clubbed insensible by National Guardsmen more times than he remembers – see this scar? He's led marches on Washington and stewed in jail for insurrection. The Black Panthers call him Brother and the FBI taps his phone and reads his mail – or that's if you believe him, which few do.

So how on earth can Mundy put up with him, this loud-mouthed rich boy with his oily-thick spectacles, his awful paintings, grey pony-tail and ludicrous pretensions? Perhaps it's because Mundy understands the state of constant terror Bernie lives in – one puff could knock him down. Nita understands it too. Fierce-eyed, rude and fearless, she sleeps with all male Taos in the name of human liberty, but protects her baby Bernie like a lioness.

'That shit you did in Berlin,' Bernie declares late one night, raising himself on one elbow to bark at Mundy across the recumbent Nita stretched between them.

The scene is Bernie's dude *hacienda*, an old Spanish farmhouse at the meeting of two stony rivers. A dozen guests are sprawled round them, relishing the hallucinogenic wisdom of *peyote*.

'What about it?' says Mundy, already regretting that a few days back, in a moment of weakness or nostalgia, he confessed his radical past.

'You were a Communist, right?'

'Only with a small "c".'

'What the fuck does "small c" mean, Limey?'

'Communist philosophically maybe. But not institutionally. A plague on both your houses, basically.'

'So you were the *Middle Way*,' Luger sneers, starting to heat up despite the soothing tones of Simon & Garfunkel in the background. 'A fucking *safe Liberal* with a big L and a small dick.'

Mundy knows from experience that it is best to offer no opposition at these moments.

'Well *I* was that person once,' Luger goes on, leaning right across Nita now but lowering his voice. 'I did Middle Way, the path of peace and fucking concord. And I'll tell you something, man. There *is* no Middle fucking Way. It's a cop-out. When the chips are down, there's one way only. Do we jump aboard the fucking train of history, or do we stand at the track-side scratching our British candy-asses while we watch the fucking train go by?' Mundy remembers how Sasha posed much the same question in his letters, but keeps the thought to himself. 'And *Jesus*, man, am I on that train! I'm on that train in ways you could never dream of, ways you would never *dare* to dream of – hear me, comrade? Hear me?'

'Loud and clear, old boy. Just don't know what you're telling me exactly.'

'Then count yourself fucking lucky, man, because you could *die* from knowing.' In his passion he has seized Mundy's forearm with a trembling hand. Now he relaxes his grip and pulls a beggar's smile. 'Just joking, okay? I love you, Limey. You love us. I never said it, you never heard it. Not if they pull out our fucking fingernails. Swear to me, man. Swear!'

'Bernie, I've forgotten already,' Mundy insists and, wandering home, reflects uneasily that there are no lengths a deceived lover will not go to in order to disguise his frailty.

One day a letter reaches him, but it is not from Sasha. The envelope is of high quality, and this is fortunate since, having begun its journey in Canada, it has twice crossed the Atlantic and, while on dry land, passed through many hands. The sender's name is printed in waxy capitals in the top left corner: Epstein, Benjamin & Longford, suite something-or-other, assume grand offices in Toronto. Mundy duly assumes them, and assumes further that he is about to be sued by an outraged husband. Leaving the envelope to mature for a week or two, therefore, he waits until the right number of tequilas has brought him to the right level of insouciance, and rips it open. The letter inside is three and a half pages long. The home address and telephone number, also in Toronto, are unfamiliar. The signature, which he has not seen before, is an executive scrawl, one name, illegible.

Dear Teddy,

Well, I guess you will be surprised to hear from me after all these years, but what goes around comes around. I am not about to weary the shit out of you with an account of my travels (travails!) after we all split from Berlin – Jesus, who *were* we in those days? – except to say that I have discovered that in life, if you take enough wrong turnings, at a certain age you end up right where you started, and I guess in a way, if I'm totally rational, which in my job I have to be, that's where I am now. From Berlin, I thought I couldn't go any further downhill but I was wrong, but maybe if I hadn't hit bottom I would never have realised just how crazy my life had become, and I would never have gone to the embassy in Beirut or called my parents and told them to get me the hell out before I killed someone, or got blown to fuckareens like Karen, making some fucking awful bomb in a Nairobi back street.

So what am I now? (A) I am a respected member of the Ontario Bar, a successful Toronto lawyer and (B) the mother of a cute little girl called Jasmine who is going to look *just* like me, if you remember how *that* was!! and (C) married to the sweetest, dearest man, a *great* father, who adores his little girl and her mother, naturally, and is the creepiest, the most fucking boring and the most deceitful little shit in the world. And rich, which by Canadian middle-class standards we both are, except don't run away with the idea that Canadian lawyers get paid US rates, which is a subject I could dwell on at considerable length! (Larry is kind of placid about LCD – Lawyers' Comparability Drive – but you know me: I'm right up there with the ringleaders!)

I left (D) to the end and I guess that's why I'm writing this, Teddy. Maybe it's a long shot, but I have a hunch it may not be. You know something? Jesus, Teddy, I love you too. All that hot talk you put into your letters – well, it *really* chimed my bells, and not just my bells, but a few other parts of me that you know pretty well! One day, I thought, I'm going to write and tell Teddy just how hot I am for him! But well, fuck, I guess I'm just the world's second lousiest correspondent with no first prize yet awarded. So let's just say I *would* have told you if I'd gotten around to it. Okay, you were my first straight fuck, you had my cherry if that means anything these days, but, dammit, Teddy, there's *more to it than that*. Why did I go first for Teddy when I could have gone for Peter the Greatest Stud on Earth, or Sasha our charismatic Socrates (who later admitted me to his harem, I may add, to absolutely *no* great effect) or for any of the pretty boys hanging around the Republican? Why did I go *wet* every time I saw you strolling through the squat with everybody screwing and jawing and doping around you, and you not even fucking *looking* at them, you were so cool! It's because you were something special, Teddy, and you for me still are. If I bitched at you from time to time, well, I guess that's just because you opened my mind and my something else to normality, which thank Jesus is where I am at these days . . .

But by now Mundy is doing what he did when he was reading Sasha's letters: hurrying through the rest to see what she wants. He doesn't have to search for long: she wants

134

Teddy instead of Larry. She's checked Larry out, and she's confirmed what she long suspected: he's cheating on her. She doesn't handle divorces herself, but a partner in the firm who does has told her strictly off the record that he reckons that, with the evidence she has, a settlement could come in at around two to two-five. And she's talking millions, not peanuts.

So Teddy, here's what I propose. Like I said, it's a long shot. We have a cabin on Lake Joseph. Winterised. It's all mine. I made Larry buy it that way. He doesn't even get to own a key. I want you to take me there, and I want it to be our second Berlin. You remember how you called it our fuckathon? Well, let's have another, and take life from there. I have an excellent maid for Jasmine.

Judith

In short, further proof, thinks Mundy, if proof were ever needed, that a lawyer is always an arsehole.

The same night, in a secret ceremony, Mundy burns his remaining copies of *Radical Love*. His bed companion of the moment is an expatriate painter named Gail who in a former life worked for something called the British Council which, according to Gail, does for British art what the Foreign Office does for British politics but better. Prompted by Mundy she appeals urgently to her former employer, a married man who is the cause of her exile. By return of post an application form arrives, accompanied by a two-line unsigned letter advising Mundy to complete the enclosed and never tell anyone where he got it from. In offering the British Council his services, Mundy neglects to mention that he does not, strictly speaking, possess a university degree. Propped on the railings of his slow boat back to England, he watches Liverpool's same muddy shoreline reach out to reclaim its own. Sooner or later, he thinks for the second time, I had to turn myself in.

Everybody in the British Council likes him from the start, and Mundy likes everything about the British Council and everybody in it: breezy, unfettered people, keen on art and spreading the good word, and above all, no politics.

He likes getting up in the morning in his bedsit in Hampstead and catching the bus to Trafalgar Square. He likes his monthly pay cheque and pottering down the corridor for a coffee and a natter in the canteen. He even likes the suit he has to wear. And he likes Crispin, whose job in Greeting Section he'll be taking over as a way of cutting his milk teeth, just as soon as Crispin hits sixty – though actually, old boy, don't tell Personnel, it's seventy, they got it wrong – as he confides to Mundy over lunch in the little Italian around the corner. In honour of the occasion, Crispin has donned the Greeter's full monty: the black Homburg and the red carnation in the velvet collar of his coat.

'Best job in the world, ducky. The hardest part is avoiding being promoted out of it. All one does is ride up and down to Heathrow in one's slow-but-steady government limo – ask for Henry the driver, he's a brick – *flash* one's pass to the nice boy at the barrier, and make the *hugest* fuss of one's distinguished foreign guest in the name of Her Maj's government before dumping him in his cut-rate hostelry in King's Cross. *Pray* the plane will be delayed so that you can have a little glass of something helpful in the VIP room while you wait. *Pray* his room won't be ready when you arrive at the hotel so you'll have to give him another in the bar. *Hurry* back to base to fill in your expenses with *just* the right amount of panache, and Bob's your uncle. I say, are you paying *all* the bill? Oh, you'll go a *long* way.'

And Mundy will. In no time at all, he's the best Greeter in the business.

'Well, *what* an honour, sir – or *señor, monsieur, madame*, or *Herr Doktor*,' he cries, sometimes twice in one day, stepping forward from behind the Immigration Officer's desk and flinging up an arm. 'No, no, for *us*, not for *you*! – never *dreamed* you'd accept our invitation – Minister absolutely *beside* himself with pleasure – and may I just say what an *enormous* fan I personally am of your [fill in as appropriate] – here, let *me* take that – my name's Mundy, by the way, and I'm the Minister's humble emissary – no, no, just plain *Mr*, I'm afraid – I'm in charge of your comfort while you're here and anything at all we can do to make your stay more enjoyable, here's my card. The phone rings right on my desk. And here I am at home if ever there's an emergency –' Or the same in German, or passable French. And a buttonhole like Crispin's for that extra touch.

But life in the British Council is not all Greeting. Unlike Crispin, Mundy has his eye on higher things. For the right man, plum jobs abound, as the kindly lady in Personnel, who seems to have taken a liking to him, makes clear at their first interview. There are British ballet and theatre groups to be escorted to faraway places, not to mention painters, writers, musicians, dancers and academics of every stripe. Under her motherly encouragement, Mundy begins to form a vision of himself as a kind of cultural roving ambassador, nurturing the talents of established artists while discreetly cultivating his own. If a post is advertised that in Personnel's estimation might serve him as a springboard, he applies for it – which is how within months he advances from mere Greeting to the richer pastures of Twinning, with the delicate task of forging cultural links between reluctant British communities and their more eager counterparts in the land of their former enemy.

With the new job comes an office of his own and a map of Britain indicating the most stubborn pockets of anti-German resistance. In whistle-stop tours around the shires, he blandishes village elders, mayors and masters of the hunt. He acquires an opposite number in a reserved but amiable Frau Doktor of the Goethe Institute. British schools also feature large in his ambit. And thus it happens that without fanfares he meets Kate, a pretty, bespectacled North London deputy headmistress who teaches mathematics and gives up her spare evenings to licking envelopes for the St Pancras Labour Party.

Kate is fair-haired and practical. She is tall and topples slightly as she walks, a thing that touches Mundy in ways he can't explain until he recalls the string-bean Irish nursemaid in the group photograph of the victorious Stanhope Family at Home. Her complexion is creamy and always slightly out of focus. Her hazy smile seems to stay on him after she has switched it off. A low sun beats through the nineteenth-century windows of her study at the edge of Hampstead Heath as Mundy makes his pitch. The Frau Doktor nods gravely at his side. The trick is in the *matching*, he insists: no good marrying a lame duck with a high-flyer. And *this* marvellous school, Miss Andrews, if you don't mind my saying so, is a high-flyer if ever I saw one.

'I say, we haven't kept you from *class*, have we?' he cries in alarm, after administering twice his usual dose of charm. 'Well, look here – *anything* you're worried about – the *smallest* thing, call me at this number. And here's me at *home* if ' – he does a double-take – 'well, *probably* quicker just to pop up the road, turn left at the lights, it's Number Seven, and ring the top bell!'

'And here is *my* card, Miss Andrews,' the Frau Doktor murmurs, in case they have forgotten her.

A courtship gets quickly under way. On Friday evenings Mundy will collect Kate from school, arriving early for the pleasure of watching her cope with swarms of multi-ethnic children. At the Hampstead Everyman cinema Kate pays for her own ticket. Over Dutch dinners at the Bacchus Greek taverna they laugh over Mundy's tales of Council intrigues and Kate's raging feuds inside the St Pancras Labour Party. Mundy admires her for being a mathematician and says he can't add for toffee. Kate respects his interest in things German, though she has to confess that, purely practically speaking, she regards languages as a poor investment, given that the whole world will soon be speaking English. Mundy confides to Kate his dream of promotion to Overseas Drama & Arts. Kate thinks he's absolutely cut out for it. At week-ends they walk on Hampstead Heath. When Kate's school puts on an exhibition of artwork, Mundy is first on the doorstep. Her solid socialist values – in her family home they were the only ones to have – mesh comfortably with what-ever remains of Mundy's, and before long he too is giving up a couple of hours a week to lick envelopes for Labour. His posh voice and manners are at first a butt for the wit of his new comrades, but soon he has them laughing with him rather than at him. Away from headquarters, Kate deplores the infiltration of the party she loves by Trotskyists and other militants. Mundy judges that the moment is not yet ripe for him to confess that he once played room-mate and batman to a red-toothed anarchist who stole his girl.

A couple more months must pass before the pair manage to go to bed together. It is Kate who takes the initiative. Mundy feels oddly shy. She selects his flat, not hers, and a Saturday afternoon when downstairs are watching an international soccer match on television. It's a day when Hampstead is bathed in the browns and golds of autumn. Their walk on the Heath has been a journey through sloping shafts of sunlight scented with wood smoke. Closing Mundy's front door behind her and putting the chain across, she takes off her coat, then continues to take off her clothes until she has none left. Then she buries her face in Mundy's shoulder while she helps him off with his. It is afterwards a secret joke between them that they won their first match three-love. And yes, of course she will marry him. She's been hoping he will ask. They agree that the Frau Doktor must come to the wedding.

The great decision taken, everything else, as so often in life, slots neatly into place. Kate's father Des provides the down-payment on an unconverted Victorian house in Estelle Road. Des is a bruised-up former boxer turned builder, and a man of solid opinions, all rebellious. The house is an honest red-brick worker's cottage, nothing fancy, one of a row in a street where dads of all colours kick footballs at their kids between inexpensive cars. But as Des remarks when they have their first look round together, it's got all the trimmings and then some: the Heath and the lido just across the footbridge, a soccer pitch, swings and roundabouts and even an adventure playground!

The walk to Kate's school takes her ten minutes and they've got the railway from Gospel Oak if they're feeling like a day in Kew. And if we're talking money, Ted, that house is a snip, believe me. Only last week, Number Sixteen over the way went for twenty grand more than what yours ever did, and it's got one bedroom less which is stupid, half the sun, and a lounge you couldn't swing a cat in, well, could you?

Was there ever a time when Mundy's life looked so good to him? He refuses to believe there was. He loves it all, his job, her family, the house and the sense of belonging. And when Kate comes home from the doctor grinning like the baby she's just heard she's going to have, he knows that his cup of happiness is full. At the wedding, he wasn't able to whistle up a single relative to call his own. Well, just you wait till the christening!

And to cap it all, only days later, Mundy's good fairy in Personnel comes up with her own little piece of good news. In recognition of his fine performance in the Twinning Department, Mr E.A. Mundy is promoted to Deputy Field Assistant, Overseas Drama & Arts, with immediate effect. He will be away from home more, which they'll both hate, particularly now Kate is pregnant. But if he keeps proper expense accounts for once, and lives small, he can help pay off the mortgage.

And as if all *that* weren't enough, to their shared delight his particular responsibility will be Youth. Mundy's days of directionless wandering are over at last.

6

Bloody angels, says Mundy. No honestly, darling, I mean it.

Well, maybe not angels exactly, but the sort of kids you'd give your last rupee for, he enthuses to Kate in a hasty call from Harwich docks before he embarks. He's speaking of the Sweet Dole Company, a bunch of volatile working-class kids from across the North of England, an ethnic free-for-all of black, white and caroline, Geordies, Mancunians and a couple of them from Doncaster where Kate grew up. They are his first twenty-five-and-under theatre group, and from the day their psychedelic double-decker British Leyland bus lumbers onto the ferry bound for Holland they call him Pop.

The oldest is a freckled gamine called Spike and she's their producer, reckoned over the hill at twenty-two. The youngest is a soulful black Hamlet called Lexham who's pushing sixteen, and costumes are the work of Sally the Needle, who is minute and Portuguese. Their stock-in-trade is potted Shakespeare on the hoof, and in their short existence together as an acting troupe they've played doss-houses, picket lines, soup queues, factory gates and works canteens in the lunch hour, and they are Mundy's gypsy family for the next forty days and nights of gigs, welcome and farewell parties, love-tangles and bush-fire punch-ups that flare and go out so fast he often doesn't know they've happened till one fellow is wiping blood off his face with the other fellow's handkerchief.

Officially he's their travelling representative and tour supervisor. Unofficially, he's their co-driver, wardrobe keeper, sparks, interpreter, prompter, understudy, stills man, agony aunt, and – when Spike the producer is sent home in tears with glandular fever on day nine – willy-nilly her stand-in. Hooked up to the double-decker is a two-wheel farmer's trailer for the props they can't squeeze onto the top deck, and there's a rack that runs the full length of the roof of the bus where they can lash the rolled-up backdrop.

Their tour of Holland, West Germany and Austria is a sleepless march of heroes. Amsterdam and The Hague adore them, they enchant Cologne, win first prize at a youth *Dramafest* in Frankfurt and are cheered to the echo in Munich and Vienna before stiffening their backs and buttoning their tongues – thus Mundy's exhortation on their last evening in the West – to cross the Iron Curtain for their swing through Eastern Europe.

The troupe by now is beginning to fray, and the puritan-ical constraints of socialist society do not improve their manners. In Budapest Mundy must sweet-talk a drunken Polonius out of jail; in Prague march Falstaff to a poxdoctor. In Cracow he must interpose himself in a fist-fight between Malvolio and a pair of plainclothes policemen, and in Warsaw receive the tearful confession of Ophelia that she is preg-nant, probably by Shylock.

Yet not even the sum of these misfortunes accounts, to Mundy's watchful eye, for the mood of sullen resentment that has descended over the troupe by the time the bus pulls up before the cluster of flags, huts, sentry towers, border policemen and customs officials that marks the crossing point from Poland to East Germany, and they are once more ordered to dismount and line up along the roadside while their passports, possessions and the bus itself are subjected to the usual tedious examination.

So what the hell's got into them? Mundy wonders wearily. They stand about like prisoners, they visit the vile lavatories singly, come back and scowl at the ground. They barely speak to one another, let alone to Pop. What are they scared of? He suspects the worst. They've scored drugs in Warsaw. They're waiting for the yell of discovery that will land them in jail.

More extraordinary still, they scarcely notice the changing of the guard. Their beloved Polish interpreter and travel escort – nicknamed Spartacus on account of his spindly frame – is shuffling tearfully down the line, making his emotional goodbyes. Until now, they have treated Spartacus like a prince. They've flirted with him, adopted him, taught him all the worst English swear-words, showered him with cigarettes and invitations to Huddersfield. Now all they can muster is a few listless hugs and 'Cheers, Sparts', and the odd pat on his bird-like shoulders. His East German replacement is a heavyweight blonde matron in a shiny black suit, yet not a single wisecrack or *sotto voce* wolf-whistle escapes them. She has small quick eyes in big white cheeks, and hair plaited in a ring loaf. She delivers her English in a series of rapid-fire statements for the record.

'Good morning, Mr Mundy' – nearly breaking Mundy's

hand – 'My name is Erna. I am from Leipzig. I am your official escort during your goodwill visit. Welcome to the
German Democratic Republic.' After which, like an
inspecting general, she requires to be presented to each
member of the troupe in turn while Spartacus watches
mournfully from the touchlines. And they submit. Nobody
is cheeky. Nobody protests or comes up with a funny name
for her. There is no impromptu performance of a piece of
Shakespearean slapstick.

And while they submit, East German frontier guards in
fatigues storm their bus, ransack their trailer, scale the roof
and bounce up and down on the rolled-up backcloth that is
lashed along the length of it. And after that, like so many
vultures, they savage their way through the troupe's suitcases and rucksacks, even shaking pregnant Ophelia's stuffed
rabbit in case it rattles. But nobody protests, not even Lexham
when they give him that extra bit of attention because he's
black. Everybody complies. Passively. Shiftily. And when
they are finally herded back into the bus, the boom lifts and
they enter the territory of their new hosts, not a single cheer
goes up, which in Mundy's recollection is a first. By now he
is seriously concerned. Weimar is their last stand, their
grandest gig, their prize number. In Weimar, cultural jewel
of East Germany, it will be Shakespeare Week, and the Sweet
Dole Company is the only British theatre company invited.
They will play to students, schools and Weimar's hallowed
National Theatre itself before setting course for West Berlin
and home.

So why not cheer up? Why no song from Sally the Needle
and her accordion? Why aren't they trying to winkle a smile
out of Erna's frozen features as she towers massively at
Mundy's side on the box seat next to the driver, and glowers

ahead of her at the pitted autobahn? On any other day, Lexham would by now have come up with a nickname for her: Moby Dick, Tinkerbell, the Sugar Plum Fairy. But not today.

It is not until late the same night, when they have been settled into a grim youth hostel in Weimar's Humboldtstrasse and, over meat and dumpling in the canteen, treated to an exquisitely boring address by a male representative of the Weimar Shakespeare Society on Socialist Harmony and the Healing Powers of a Shared Literary Heritage, that Mundy out of the corner of his eye catches sight of Viola secreting a chunk of meat, two pieces of bread and an apple in her Tibetan bag.

For what? Who's she feeding? Viola is famous for eating nothing.

Is she providing extra rations for Ophelia who, like Kate, is feeding two?

Or has Viola, who is mad about animals, befriended a dog? She can't have done. She hasn't had time.

Hostel rules require that boys and girls are segregated. Mundy's bed is in a cubicle in the corridor between the two dormitories. At midnight he wakes from a half-sleep to the rustle of bare feet on wooden stairs.

Viola.

He allows her a moment, then follows her down the stairs into a rear courtyard where the psychedelic bus is parked. Big stars, a warm moon, a scent of blossom. He is in time to see Viola, wearing only a short nightdress and her Tibetan bag, enter the bus and mount the spiral staircase to the upper deck. He waits. She doesn't emerge. He climbs softly after her and discovers her, bottom up, on a pile of stage costumes.

Closer inspection reveals that the costumes conceal a young, beautiful and naked Polish actor named Jan who attached himself to the troupe in Warsaw and insisted on following it around night and day wherever it went.

In a tearful whisper Viola admits all. She is hopelessly, desperately, eternally in love with Jan, and he with her. But Jan has no passport. He is brave, and therefore hated by the Polish police. Sooner than be parted from him for ever, she hid him in the costume chest and with the connivance of the rest of the troupe smuggled him across the border from Poland into East Germany. She regrets nothing. Jan is hers, her stowaway, her great love. She will take him to Berlin, to England, to wherever she needs to take him. She will never give him up. Ever, ever, Pop, and I don't care what you do to me, I swear.

Jan has about five words of German and none of English. He is small and vivid, and obviously packs up beautifully. Mundy disliked him in Warsaw, but dislikes him a great deal more now.

Mundy must wait till morning rehearsal. In the afternoon they will give an open-air performance to conscripted school-children. Their stage will be this patch of meadow in front of the ruined Tower of the Temple Lords in the historic park that stretches either side of the River Ilm. A jolly sun smiles on them, the park is alight with flowers. Erna who has no nickname roosts implacably on a long iron bench, knees apart, watching over her charges. For reinforcements she has the same official who last night bored the company to death with his speech, but also two sallow boys in leather jackets who have renounced facial expression. Their bench stands twenty yards from the improvised stage. Mundy rallies the

147

cast around him inside the ruined tower, he hopes out of earshot and out of sight.

As things stand at the moment, he informs his audience, he calculates that they're in for about twenty years' hard labour per head: ten for smuggling Jan out of Poland, ten more for smuggling him into East Germany. So if anyone has any bright suggestions about where to go from here, Mundy would be grateful to hear them.

He is expecting contrition, but he has forgotten about actors. In a dread, theatrical silence, all heads turn to Viola, who does not fail them. Hands clenched below her chin, she gazes bravely upward at Goethe's blue Heaven. She will kill herself if she is parted from Jan. Jan has assured her he will do the same. Of her friends, she expects nothing. If they have lost faith, then go, go, and she and Jan will throw themselves on the mercy of the East German authorities. God knows, someone somewhere in this country must have a human heart.

Mundy doubts it. Moreover, it won't just be yourselves you'll be throwing at the mercy of the East Germans, he tells Viola. It will be the whole bloody lot of us. So does anyone else have a suggestion?

For a moment no one has. Viola has played her big scene to the hilt, and it would take a brave actor to follow her. Mainly, Mundy suspects, the kids are scared stiff by what they've done, but see no way back. It falls to their self-appointed lawyer, an eighteen-year-old redhead called Len, to put the motion to the vote. His tone is necessarily muted, his courage perhaps also.

'All right, gang. Which is it? Do we desert a fellow thesp in his hour of need? Forget the love angle a minute. He's getting shit from the authorities in his own country, right?

So what are we supposed to do? Help get him out of it, or send him back to it? How many're for helping him out?'

Carried unanimously, if uncertainly – the only abstention being Mundy himself. He is now in a serious quandary. He'd like to talk it through with Kate, but without the East German secret police listening. He doesn't need reminding that the chances of smuggling a Polish actor or anybody else across the Berlin Wall are wafer-thin. The chances of setting back Anglo-East German cultural relations by ten years, on the other hand, are excellent.

'From now on, we act happy and bright,' he orders the troupe. 'We're proud of ourselves, we're stars, we've won a prize and we're on the home run. All the rest to follow. Got it?'

Got it, Pop.

The matinée for schools is a riot. Shorn kids crammed in rows on the grass forsake their gravity and dissolve in hysterics at the posturings of Lexham as Malvolio in love. Even Erna has a bit of a chuckle. The Walter Ulbricht Youth Club the same evening is a rave, and next morning under the all-seeing eye of Erna and her two sallow boys, the whole troupe including Mundy is marched through Goethe's town house and thence to admire the Red Army heroes' memorial with its blood-red hammer and sickle on the gate.

And nobody misbehaves, everybody's good as gold. They pose for photographs in front of Shakespeare's statue. They swap acting notes with Russians, Vietnamese, Palestinians and Cubans. They play chess, and drink to the fellowship of all mankind in a students' bar in a tower in the city's ramparts.

In quick tense visits, while the troupe covers for her, Viola takes Jan food and comfort, but Mundy times her visits to

the bus, and keeps them short. The day of their last performance dawns. Tonight they play the National Theatre,
tomorrow they drive to Berlin and home. There will be no
more rehearsal. The troupe will pass the morning in super-
vised group discussion with fellow actors of other nations,
but Mundy is intent on having the day he has long planned.
Weimar is his holy city, the shrine of his beloved German
muse. He will treat himself to a tour of its treasures, even
if Erna insists he do so in the company of a professor of
arts from Leipzig who just happens, by the most delightful
of coincidences, to be in Weimar.

The Professor turns out to be an elegant, silvery fellow
in his sixties who is determined to show off his unnaturally
good English. His manner is so proprietorial that Mundy
keeps racking his brain to fathom where they might have
met along the road – say in Prague, or Bucharest, or one of
the score of cities that have flitted past him in the last five
weeks. And with the Professor comes the shapely Comrade
Inge, who claims to represent the Goethe Institute.

'And you are *Ted*, are you not?' the Professor enquires,
with that amused smile he has.

'Ted. Yes.'

'And I of course am Wolfgang. *Comrade* is really too bourgeois, don't you think?'

Why of course? Mundy wonders, as the Professor's eyes
continue to signal their mysterious familiarity.

With Comrade Inge one side of him and the Professor
the other, Mundy inhales the tomb-like air of Goethe's tiny
summer house and touches the very desk at which the poet
wrote. He hovers dutifully in the rooms where Liszt made
music, eats sausage in the cellar bar of the Hotel Elephant
and clinks glasses with a group of drunken Chinese publishers

while he struggles to evoke the ghost of Thomas Mann. But that damned Polish boy gets in his way each time.

In the afternoon they travel by unsprung limousine to Ilmenau to worship at the hilltop shrine of the loveliest and shortest poem in the German language. The Professor sits in the front beside his driver, Comrade Inge jogs carelessly against Mundy in the back. The road is pitted and often flooded. Crumbling farmhouses vie with slab apartment blocks jammed into green fields. They pass a horde of cyclists and another of Soviet soldiers in grey singlets taking their afternoon run. The air is wet with smuts, black smoke billows from the chimneys of sprawling roadside factories, the trees beside the road are sickly yellow, gigantic signs remind him that he is in the Land of Peace and Progress. The sky opens and they are on the edge of the Thuringian forest. Flowing wooded hills surround them. They climb a snake road and pull into a lay-by. Their driver, a gangling boy in fancy Texan-style boots, springs to open the doors. Leaving him to watch over the car, they set off up a rocky track between pine trees, the Professor leading.

'You are happy, Ted?' asks Comrade Inge tenderly.

'Blissfully, thank you.'

'Maybe you are missing your wife.'

No, actually, Inge. I'm worrying about how to smuggle a Polish actor across the Berlin Wall. They have reached the summit. Before them, range after range of forested mountains fades into the distance. The famous hut is locked. An ancient iron plaque in Gothic script provides the only testimony to an old poet's thoughts as he gazes upon eternity. For a fleeting moment, it is true, Mundy hears the lost, melodious voice of Dr Mandelbaum intoning the sacred lines: *Over all the mountains is peace . . . soon you too will be at rest.*

'You are moved, Ted?' Comrade Inge enquires, laying the flat of her hand along his upper arm.

'Enormously,' says Mundy grimly.

They descend the hill, the Professor once more leading. Comrade Inge wants to know whether socialism will ever be possible in Britain without a revolution. Mundy says he hopes so. The unsprung limousine is waiting. The gangling driver hovers beside it, finishing a cigarette. As he opens the doors for them, a mud-spattered Trabant lurches inexpertly out of the shadow of the trees and coasts past them before gathering speed and setting off down the hill. One driver, probably but not certainly male, Mundy registers. Woollen cap pulled low over the forehead.

'I imagine that will be the curator of our museum,' the Professor remarks in his perfumed English, noticing Mundy's interest. 'Poor Herr Studmann is a great worrier. He is aware we have a distinguished guest today, so he is wishing to ascertain that everything is in order for you.'

'Then why didn't he stop and introduce himself?'

'Poor Herr Studmann is shy. A bookish fellow. Social contact is anathema to him. Also a little eccentric, which you English appreciate.'

Mundy feels a fool. It was nothing, nobody. Cool down. Somehow the day is passing, which is all that matters. On the journey back, the Professor treats them to a dissertation on Goethe's relationship with Nature.

'If you are in Weimar again, will you *please* call me at my office,' Comrade Inge insists, handing Mundy a card.

The Professor confesses airily that he has no card. He seems to be implying that he is too well known to bother with one. They agree to remain lifelong friends.

* * *

Backstage in Weimar's National Theatre, just a stone's-throw from their youth hostel and the psychedelic bus, the Sweet Dole Company is gearing itself up for the last performance of its tour and Mundy has decided to distract himself by packing up props and costumes in the theatre's basement in preparation for an early getaway tomorrow. Every sane bone in his body is urging him to dump the Polish boy overboard but the Major's son can't do that. Neither can the father of his unborn child or the husband of Kate.

The basement doubles as a conference room. A honey-coloured table occupies the centre. Leather-backed thrones are arranged either side. The floorboards are of finest rain-forest teak, iron delivery doors give onto a rear courtyard. Picking up Hamlet's crown, Mundy hears directly above him the booming voice of Lexham our Jamaican Macbeth over claps of witches' thunder. Wrapping the crown in strips of rag, he stuffs it in a packing case. But as he starts to do the same with Polonius's chain of office, he spots Banquo staring at him from one of the brick arches to his left, and Banquo tonight is being played by Sasha in modern dress.

No smoke, no strobe lights. Just a very thin, very small Sasha with his hair cropped short and his hollowed eyes larger than ever, sporting an undertaker's black suit and a boy scout's brown tie, and holding a Party-issue imitation-leather brief-case in his left hand and keeping his right hand to his side as he stands crookedly at attention in the archway. So obviously the producer has told him: this is what you do with your right hand while your left hand is carrying the brief-case and you are giving your friend Teddy the hairy eyeball.

The packing case is on the floor and Mundy is hunkered beside it with Polonius's chain lying across his hands exactly as if he's about to make a presentation of it. It is in this position that, for a while, he simply denies the evidence of his senses. You're not Banquo and you're not Sasha, you're not anyone. How can you be Sasha in that ridiculous suit?

Then reluctantly he must admit that the figure who is so patently not Sasha is speaking to him. And nobody, Mundy included, can do Sasha's voice except Sasha.

'God's blessings on you, Teddy. We must be quick and quiet. You are well?'

'Flourishing. You too?'

In a dream, instead of saying what's in your head you say something totally absurd.

'And married, I hear. And about to found a dynasty, despite the efforts of the West Berlin police. I congratulate you.'

'Thanks.'

For a moment the two men share the duellists' stillness. Sasha does not venture forward from his archway. Mundy remains on his haunches in front of the packing case with Polonius's chain draped across his palms. From where he crouches the distance to Sasha is as long as the Kreuzberg cricket pitch, or longer.

'Teddy, I require you to pay close attention to me and keep your comments to a minimum. It will come hard to you, but try. In West Berlin we were partisans, but in this petit bourgeois kindergarten we are criminals.'

Mundy lays the chain in the packing case and stands up. He turns to find Sasha at his side peering up at him, a web of fine lines round each dark, dependent eye, but otherwise the basic model with no extras.

'Are you listening to me, Teddy?'

He is.

'The first act of your bizarre production will end in fifteen

154

minutes. I must return to my seat in the audience in time for the ecstatic applause. At the official reception afterwards you and I will spontaneously recognise each other for the first time, express due astonishment and disbelief, and embrace as old friends. You follow me?'

He does.

'A certain embarrassment will colour our public reunion. You are knocked a little off balance, you are not expecting to be reminded so graphically of your radical past, least of all here in the German Democratic paradise. I also shall be overjoyed but restrained, and a little evasive. This is normal in a society where every word has several meanings and many listeners. What do you propose to do with your besotted Polish actor?'

'Smuggle him into West Berlin.' Does he say this? Does Sasha hear him? Sometimes in a dream, everyone hears you except yourself.

'How?' Sasha demands.

'On the roof of the bus. Roll him up in the backdrop.'

'Do exactly as you plan. The frontier guards are under orders not to find him. Your Comrade Erna is an old hand and will make sure they are not overzealous by mistake. The boy is a plant: the product of a joint operation by ourselves and the Poles to penetrate the corrupt bastions of the West. When you arrive in West Berlin, go immediately to the British Political Advisor's office. Demand to speak to Mr Arnold, which is the workname of the head of your secret service station. If they try to persuade you he is in London or Bonn, reply that you know he arrived at Tempelhof from London this evening at five o'clock. While you're about it, you will hand over your Pole to him. Are you already working for British Intelligence?'

'No.'

'You will be. You will also inform Mr Arnold that the Polish boy is a plant, but he should not act on this information or he will compromise an excellent potential source. He will understand the logic of this instruction. Have you noticed how this country stinks?'

'I suppose so.'

'Every filthy corner of it. Of cheap cigarettes, cheap sweat, cheap deodorant, and briquettes of compacted brown coal that gas you without heating you. We are stuck in the glue of State bureaucracy. Society begins at the rank of captain, every waiter and taxi driver is a despot. Have you slept with any women here?'

'Not as far as I remember.'

'Without first acclimatising oneself, the experience is not to be recommended. And avoid the wine at all costs. The Hungarians poison us with something they call Bull's Blood. It is considered a great delicacy, but I suspect it is a vengeance for suppressing their counter-revolutionary uprising in 1956. We have entered the Second Cold War. In the East we have Comrade Brezhnev and Afghanistan, in the West we have Pershing and Cruise missiles. Kindly tell your Mr Arnold to direct them at East Germany before anywhere else.'

While Sasha talks this way, he unpacks his briefcase in quick order onto the conference table. In the last weeks Mundy has been given the same junk six times over and he's being given it again now: one blurred picture book of the Bolshoi Ballet, one chrome statuette of a virile worker in baggy cap and plus-fours, one blue-and-white imitation Meissen pottery box with ill-fitting lid bound to the base with transparent tape. And one departure from the usual script: a sealed pack of unexposed thirty-five-millimetre

Kodak Tri-X film, the type Mundy uses for the camera that takes all the pictures he's going to show Kate when he gets home.

'These precious gifts are all for you, Teddy, with the heartfelt affection of your old friend. However, when you reach West Berlin they will be for Mr Arnold. They contain among other things the terms and conditions of my recruitment by his organisation. In the pottery box you will find walnuts. On no account attempt to eat these walnuts during your journey, not even if you are in the last stages of starvation. Pack the films with the rest of your camera gear. They are not for you to use, but to give to Mr Arnold also. A Summer Festival of Dance is to be held in Prague starting on the first of June. Does the British Council propose to send you?'

'Not as far as I know.' The first of June, he remembers from another life, is six weeks away.

'It will. Mr Arnold must arrange for you to escort some British dancers. I shall be there also. Like you, I will have discovered a belated passion for cultural diplomacy. I shall work only with you, Teddy. I am what we call in the spy business a one-man dog, and you are my man for as long as I bark. I have informed Mr Arnold that I trust nobody else. I am embarrassed to impose this condition on you, but you are a chauvinist at heart and you will enjoy serving your ridiculous country.'

'What happens if they find this stuff when we're searched? It'll lead straight back to you.'

'The search of your acting company's bus and effects will be intrusive but unrevealing. For this we may thank the heroic Jan.'

Mundy has found his voice at last, or one like it. 'Sasha, what are you doing? This is bloody crazy!'

157

'After our dramatic encounter at tonight's reception, the nature of our former relationship will become official knowledge to my masters. You enjoyed your day with Professor Wolfgang?'

'I had too much on my mind.'

'At Ilmenau, through my car window, you gave every impression of getting along swimmingly. The good Professor is very taken by you. He considers you an excellent subject for cultivation. I have warned him that you will not be an easy conquest. A sophisticated courtship will have to be mounted in order to obtain you and he has agreed to entrust it to me as your old friend and ideological mentor. In Prague, if I deem the moment right, I shall make the first pass. You will be reluctant and a little shocked. That is normal. You are Teddy, my student friend, still secretly critical of capitalist values perhaps, but fully integrated into the consumerist society. After a period of reflection, however, you will discover that the old rebellious fires still burn in you, and you will succumb to our blandishments. You are as usual broke?'

'Well – you know – up against it.'

In a dream, one does not have to explain that the combined salaries of a State school teacher and a junior civil servant leave little to spare after hefty monthly payments to a mortgage company. But Sasha understands anyway.

'Then money may play a discreet part in your motivation. My masters will be reassured. Ideology without greed embarrasses them. Do you covet the beautiful companion we provided for you today, or do you intend to remain stubbornly faithful to your wife?'

Mundy must have spoken up for marriage, because Sasha is already withdrawing his offer of the beautiful interpreter.

'It is immaterial. A dalliance would place you more firmly in my masters' grasp, but we can do without it. You will insist on working to me exclusively, however, Teddy. You too will be a one-man dog. It is said by one of your English writers that with double agents one never knows whether one is getting the fat or the lean. I shall supply Mr Arnold with the lean. In return you and he will supply Comrade Sasha with the fat.'

'How on earth did you get here, Sasha? Why do they trust you? I don't understand.' In a dream, one asks the questions too late, with no expectation of a reply.

'Did you have an opportunity to visit Buchenwald concentration camp during your stay in Weimar?'

'It was offered but there wasn't time.'

'And just eight kilometres up the road. What a pity. In addition to Goethe's celebrated beech tree, the camp's crematorium is particularly noteworthy. You didn't even have to be dead to be burned in it. Did you know the Russians kept the camp running after they liberated it from fascism?'

'I don't think I did.'

'Oh yes. And provided us with a fine example of socialist realism while they were about it. We call it Buchenwald Two. They brought in their own prisoners and treated them much as their predecessors had done before them. Their victims weren't all Nazis by any means. Most were social democrats and other anti-Party elements who wished to revive capitalism and restore the rule of the bourgeoisie. Tyranny is like the electric wiring in an old house. A tyrant dies, the new tyrant takes possession, and all he has to do is drop the switch. Do you not agree?'

Mundy supposes he does.

'The British Council is a hive of anti-socialist propaganda,

I hear, a factory for counter-revolutionary lies. I am shocked that you should be associated with it.'

In a dream, protests are futile, but we make them all the same. 'That's nonsense! How can capsule Shakespeare be counterrevolutionary?'

'Never underrate our paranoia, Teddy. You will soon be a vital tool in the people's constant struggle against ideological subversion. A little imagination on the part of Mr Arnold, and you will realise that your poor Council exists only to provide cover for the perpetrators of anti-proletarian sabotage. I hear poor Macbeth crying his last. I shall see you at the reception. Will you remember to be astonished?'

An elderly London bus barging its way through peaceful Communist countryside, belching out offensive Western rock music and diesel fumes and flaunting crazy-daisies and coloured balloons, is asking to be arrested, whether or not a fourteen-stone Valkyrie with her hair in a twisted loaf is sitting beside you on the box seat. Every village they pass through, old people scowl and press their hands to their ears and kids leap around and wave as if the circus has come to town. The exhaust pipe must be stoved or else it's the silencer, because the engine's din has gone up several decibels – which perhaps explains why a police car with its lights on has been following the bus for the last half-hour and a police motorcycle is dawdling out ahead of it. Any moment now, thinks Mundy, we're going to be pulled over and charged with about fifteen offences under the Workers' Paradise Transport Act, including possession of a lovesick Polish actor rolled up in the backdrop on the roof, a pottery box full of unopenable walnuts, and a pack of unexposed Kodak film to be handed to the head of British Intelligence immediately on arrival in West Berlin.

They are driving across drab yellow fields. The only visual relief is the occasional cluster of broken-down farmhouses, decaying churches, or a brutalist Soviet-style pylon positioned to cause maximum offence to the eye. Steve their toothless driver is at the helm, Mundy sits in his usual place on the box beside him with the passports and visas and permits and insurance papers in an attaché case wedged between his knees. Erna sits next to him. From the back of the bus come bursts of jolly singing that die without explanation until Sally the Needle strikes up on her squeeze box to get everybody going again. In the mirror above him he can watch the blue fishtail of the backdrop flapping in the rear window, and the trailer bobbing along behind it. And a hundred yards behind the trailer he can watch the police car keeping the same distance all the time, slowing down when we slow down and putting on the speed if we get a straight stretch. When the bus goes into a corner he hears the backdrop creaking on its moorings. When he clambers up to the top deck to check you're all okay up here, he tries not to look too hard at the sugar-paper bundles in the luggage racks and the muscled silver arm of the socialist worker's statuette sticking out of its wrapping.

'Does everyone around here get a police escort?' he asks Erna, resuming his place beside her.

'Only if they are very distinguished, Ted.'

Mundy has taken refuge in his own thoughts. The staged reunion of two old friends at the official farewell reception passed off exactly as Sasha forecast. They catch sight of each other at the same moment, their eyes widen simultaneously. Sasha is the first to find the words to express his astonishment: 'Good God – *Teddy!* – my dear friend – the fellow who saved my life – whatever are you doing here in Weimar?' And Mundy, looking suitably confused, which in the circumstances is not a problem to him, comes back with: 'Sasha – my old cell-mate – of all the people – this is plain daft – explain!' After the embraces and the backslapping, the pained separation is just as smooth, with its ostentatious exchange of addresses and telephone numbers and imprecise talk of a get-together in the near future. Then back to the hostel with the troupe, to toss on his iron school bed and listen to the whisperings of his wards through the paper-thin walls and hope to goodness nobody else is listening because how many times has he told them already that careless talk costs lives?

All night he lies awake turning the unanswerable questions round and round in his head. When he tries to sleep he dreams of Jan the Pole slipping a hand-grenade into the bus's petrol tank. When he stays awake, his nightmares are worse. If Sasha is to be believed, their Polish stowaway and the packages will get through and that will be the end of it. But *is* he to be believed? And assuming he *is* to be believed, is the game he is playing going to work? At six o'clock while it's still dark Mundy sits bolt upright and bangs on the partition walls to either side of him and yells, ' *All right, gang, wakey-wakey! To hell with breakfast and let's get this show on the road!*' in the sort of gung-ho military voice he would never normally use. But what he means is clear to all of them: we smuggle the little bastard out exactly the way we planned it, and we do it now and get it over. For his operational team he has selected Lexham, Viola and Sally the Needle.

'The rest of you act natural, arse around and try to look relaxed,' he has told them, none too kindly.

Whatever you say, Pop.

At crack of dawn, with Viola leading, Mundy, Sally and

Lexham cross the courtyard, climb to the top deck and shake Jan from his slumbers. They strip him naked and smear him from head to toe with axle grease. The aim is to confuse the sniffer dogs. Viola, you do the close work for us. Next they wind him in mothball-scented stage curtains and pack layers of kapok over his heart and pulse points. Crossing into East Germany, Mundy remembers seeing frontier guards armed with earphones and oversized stethoscopes for listening to suspicious objects. When they've finished wrapping him, Mundy presses his ear against the place where Jan's heart should be and hears nothing. Probably hasn't got one, he tells Sally under his breath. By now their stowaway looks like an Egyptian mummy. They have given him an airhole but in case it closes by mistake Mundy shoves a piece of metal tubing in his mouth before rolling him up in a dusty carpet.

They are still on the top deck of the bus and Jan is no longer Jan but a carpet standing on its end. Half toppling and half carrying him, they feed him down the staircase to the courtyard, where the blue-painted canvas backdrop is spread out on the ground awaiting them. It has veins of red puddle water running over it, and its trawler-like stink of size and fish-glue hits them before they reach it. Erna has yet to arrive. They told her seven-thirty, and it's only quarter past. While Viola looks on, Mundy and Lexham dump the carpet with the boy inside it along one edge of the backdrop, and roll. And keep on rolling until Jan and the carpet are inside a thirty-foot blue sausage which, to sailor-like cries of 'There she blows' and 'Heave, lads, heave', Mundy and a bunch of willing helpers manhandle onto the roof of the bus, then strap lengthways down the rack with its tail drooping over the end.

* * *

To the shriek of worn brakes and bald tyres, black smoke fills the window on Mundy's left. Ten yards short of a red-and-white boom the psychedelic bus staggers to a halt. They have reached their first checkpoint. Not your five-star number, but the country version: half a dozen armed Vopos, a sniffer dog, a *grüne Minna*, the police motorcyclist who till now was riding out ahead of them, and the police car with its lights on that's been following them since Weimar. Mundy bounds from the bus, briefcase in hand. Erna, serene on the box seat, remains aloof to all of it.

'Gentlemen — Colonel — comrades — a very good day to you all!' he cries facetiously. But he keeps his distance because the colonel who is actually a captain is, like Sasha, short of stature, and Mundy doesn't want to fan his insecurity by towering over him.

The guards board the bus, offer gruff salutations to Erna and scowl at the festively dressed girls in their funny hats before ordering everyone out while they rip the tarpaulins off the trailer, rummage through suitcases, and leave everything for the hated Westerners to clear up. The captain broods over the passports, hunting for irregularities while he fires questions at Mundy in a thick Silesian accent. How long have you been in Weimar, comrade? When did you arrive in the GDR, comrade? How long did you spend in Czecho, Hungary, Romania, Poland? He compares Mundy's answers with the stamps in the passports, eyes the psychedelic bus and, more severely, the vamped-up girls. He glowers up at the blue sausage on the roof with its balloons and streamers, and at the lump that has developed in the middle, which to Mundy's eye resembles a swallowed mouse halfway down the body of a boa constrictor. At last he makes the gesture Mundy has learned to recognise: a sullen and contemptuous tip of the head, a grimace, part hatred, part warning and part envy. *Go, damn you.* Mundy and the troupe pile back into the bus, Sally's squeezebox strikes up 'It's a long, long way to Tipperary' and – damn them – they go.

Erna appears to have seen nothing. Her small round eyes are peering out of the window. 'There was a problem?' she asks Mundy.

'Everything in order. Nice chaps,' Mundy assures her.

With variations of landscape, the scene is enacted three more times. With each search the tension is cranked up a notch, and by the third, nobody is singing any more, nobody is bothering to speak. Do whatever the hell you want with us, we can't take any more, we surrender. Erna suddenly stands up, gives them all a jovial wave, dismounts from the bus and keeps on waving till she is out of sight. Did anybody wave back? Mundy doubts it. They pass through a chicane, he looks glumly down. American soldiers are grinning at them through the windows, bystanders gawp at the crazy-painted giant horse that has emerged from the darkness of *over there*, a couple of cameras flash and all the lights of Las Vegas are winking at them from the wet cobbles. They are safe in West Berlin but nobody inside the bus has anything to say. Except Lexham possibly, who is doing some heavy cursing – all the worst words as usual, but without the energy we expect. And Viola who is quietly sobbing her heart out and saying, 'Thank you, everyone, thank you, oh Christ.'

Up on the top deck, one of the boys is having hysterics, and that will be Polonius.

The over-tall British arts diplomat with a thirty-six-hour beard who strides into the British Political Advisor's office close to Our Dear Führer's old Olympic stadium armed with two bulky carrier bags and a briefcase looks as if he has just come off the sea and the deck is still rolling under him, which is how he feels. The receptionist is a middle-aged Englishwoman with greying hair and nice, stern manners. She could be a schoolmistress like Kate.

'I need to speak to Mr Arnold,' Mundy blurts, slapping his passport on the counter, together with his British Council visiting card. 'I've got a double-decker bus parked in your courtyard with twenty very tired young actors on board and your sentries are telling the driver to get lost.'

'Now which Mr Arnold would *that* be, sir?' the receptionist enquires as she leafs her way through Mundy's passport.

'The one who arrived at Tempelhof yesterday evening.'

'Ah. That one. Thank you. The sergeant will show you to the waiting room, and we'll see what we can do about your poor actors. Are those useful bags for Mr Arnold or would you be wanting to leave them with me?' She has pressed a bell and is speaking into an internal telephone. 'For Mr Arnold, please, Jack. As soon as he can manage would be best. And there's a bus-full of impatient actors in the courtyard to be cared for. Always the same on a Monday morning, isn't it?'

The sergeant is a benign version of the sergeant who guarded Mundy in the military hospital ten years ago. He wears a sports jacket, grey flannels and highly polished toecaps. The waiting room is Mundy's private ward without the bed: white walls, frosted windows, the same photograph of our dear young Queen. And the same chrysanthemums, courtesy of the West Berlin police. It is therefore not at all surprising to Mundy when the same Vice-Consul ambles

166

in – shaggy-elegant Nick Amory, wearing the same suède shoes and tweed suit that he wears for his hospital visits, and the same clever, self-deprecating smile. He is a decade older, but in a bad light he could, like Sasha, play the age he has remained in Mundy's memory. A deeper tan, perhaps, a wider brow where the hair has started to recede. A touch of frost on the ginger sideburns. A new, intangible authority. It takes Mundy a moment to realise that Amory is conducting a similar inspection of his visitor.

'Well, you look a damn sight better than when last seen, I must say,' says Amory carelessly. 'What's the story?'

'We've got a Polish defector on the roof of our bus.'

'Who put him there?'

'We all did.'

'*All* being your acting troupe?'

'Yes.'

'When?'

'This morning. In Weimar. We had a gig there.'

Amory goes to the window and cautiously parts the net curtain. 'He's lying very still for a liberated stowaway. You sure he's alive?'

'I've told him to shut up and lie still till we say it's safe to come out.'

'*You* told him.'

'Yes.'

'You run a pretty tight ship then.'

'Somebody had to.'

And for a while nothing but Amory's shaggy grin and the sounds of shunting traffic in the courtyard outside.

'You don't seem very pleased about it,' he remarks at last. 'Why are we all just sitting here? Why aren't we dancing in the streets and whistling up the champagne?'

'The boy says his family will suffer if he's identified. We've all agreed to keep mum.'

'Who told you to ask for Arnold?'

'Sasha.'

The smile is not a smile, Mundy realises. If it were, it would have gone by now. The smile is what he wears while he watches you and thinks.

'Sasha,' Amory repeats, after an age. 'The chap you roomed with while you were playing at being a pinko. *That* Sasha. The one who came here that day and made a stink.'

'He's in the East now. He's some kind of spy.'

'Yes, I think we heard that, actually. Do you know *what* kind?'

'No.'

'Did he also tell you I flew into Tempelhof yesterday evening?'

'Yes. Why?'

'It's a sort of silly code we have, when one side wants to tell the other side something frightfully important. What's in the bags?'

'Secrets, according to him. And he says the Pole's a plant but it wouldn't be sensible to do anything about him.'

'For risk of compromising Comrade Sasha?'

'He said the police searches of the bus would be a sham to let the boy get through. The stuff in the bags would be safer that way.'

'Well, that makes a fair amount of sense, doesn't it? Is this all he's giving us, or are we looking at trade samples with a view to placing a serious order?'

'He says he's got more.'

'With you in the loop?'

'He says he's written to you. It's in the stuff.'

'Is he asking for money?'

'He didn't say so. Not to me, anyway. It would be a first if he is.'

'Are you?'

'No, I bloody well am not.'

'What's your next move? Now? This minute?'

'Home to England.'

'This afternoon as ever is?'

'Yes.'

'With your actors?'

'Yes.'

'Mind if I unpack my stocking? I'm going to call you Edward, if you don't mind. I think I did that before, didn't I? I've got an Uncle Ted I simply can't abide.'

Still smiling, Amory empties the carrier bags onto the white plastic coffee table: the virile socialist worker, the book on the Bolshoi, the pack of Kodak film and the blue pottery box. He examines the socialist worker's glued edges, sniffs the book, turns the pack of film over with his fingertips, studies the use-by date, the customs duty stamps, holds the blue pottery box to his ear and gently rattles it, but doesn't pick at the sticky tape that binds the lid to the base.

'And these are walnuts inside?'

'So he says.'

'Well, well. It's been done before, of course. But then most things have, haven't they?' Setting the box on the table beside the rest, he lays a hand flat on the top of his head while he admires the collection. 'You must have been shitting bricks.'

'We all were.'

'But only about the Pole. You didn't tell your troupe about *this* lot?' – eyes drifting lazily back to the table – 'They don't know about our – crock of gold?'

169

'No. They only know about the boy. They must be raising hell by now.'

'Don't worry. Laura is feeding them buns and fizz. Did the Vopos search seriously for him, d'you think? Or was it a sham, the way Sasha said it would be?'

'I don't know. I tried not to look.'

'No doggies?'

'Yes, but they didn't find him. We'd covered him with axle grease to put them off the scent.'

'Edward's idea?'

'I suppose so.'

'Didn't they provide you with a travel escort?'

'Yes. But she was part of the scam.'

'To plant the boy on us?'

'According to Sasha, yes. Called herself Erna. Blonde. Fights at about sixteen stone.'

Amory's smile widens in fond recognition. 'And are we still a pinko, or have we put away childish things?' Waiting for an answer that doesn't come, Amory replaces the box of film on the table and smiles at it until it's nicely in line with the rest of his crock of gold. 'Where do we live?'

'Hampstead.'

'And we work full time with the Brit. Coun.?'

'Yes.'

'Twenty-four bus to Trafalgar Square?'

'Yes.'

'Got anyone? Wife, friend, whatnot?'

'Wife. Pregnant.'

'First name?'

'Kate. Short for Catherine.'

'With a C?'

'Yes.'

'Maiden name?'

'Andrews.'

'British subject?'

'Yes. Schoolteacher.'

'Born where?'

'Doncaster.'

'Know how long ago?'

'Two years before me. April the fifteenth.'

Why do I submit to this? Why don't I tell Amory to mind his bloody business?

'Well, bravo,' Amory remarks, still reviewing his find. '*Very* bravo, in case I forget to say it later. To the manner born, in fact. I'll just stick this lot in the fridge if you don't mind, then you can take me to your charges. I'm a Foreign Office flunkey as far as they're concerned, so don't peach on me or I'll be mortified.'

The West Berlin police station, for all Mundy knows, is the very one where he was beaten up, but in his state of dazed anticlimax he hardly cares. Amory has phoned ahead to arrange things, Amory and his sergeant have perched themselves in Mundy's place on the box next to Steve the driver and put Mundy in the seat behind them, and it is Amory, not Mundy, who orders the troupe to dismount in the windowless hangar where the bus has magically arrived. It is Amory again who with his sergeant's help gathers the troupe in a circle round him while he addresses them with just the right mix of irreverence and warning.

They've done a wonderful thing, he tells them. They've got every right to congratulate themselves.

'But we have a secret. We have actually two secrets. One of them is on the top of the bus, because we don't want his mum and dad and brothers and sisters back in Poland getting hurt. And the other one is Edward here, because if the British Council gets to hear what he's stage-managed it will pop its bureaucratic garters and Edward will be out on his ear. Smuggling refugees is not supposed to be what the Council is about. So what we're asking you to do is the hardest thing we can ask *any* actor to do, and that's to keep your big mouths shut. Not just for tonight but for ever and ever, amen.'

And after the sergeant has read aloud an official declaration under the Official Secrets Act, and each one of them has separately signed an impressive form, Amory calls a jaunty *Also los, bitte, meine Herren!* across the hangar to a squad of policemen in dungarees who promptly lay their ladders against the British Leyland bus and swarm onto the roof, barking orders at each other until, with infinite circumspection, the backdrop is laid like a precious archaeological find on the concrete floor, and unrolled. An explosion of clapping breaks out as a naked tar-baby rises like Adonis from the shreds of rag and kapok and, wild-eyed in his euphoria, rushes to his deliverers and embraces every one of them, Viola last and longest. After that, everything is suddenly very quick and matter of fact. The police put a blanket round him and whisk him away. Viola bustles after him. One wave from the door is all she is allowed. Standing on the platform of the bus, Amory has a final word for them.

'Now the *really* bad news is – we've got to keep Edward here in Berlin for a day or two. So I'm afraid you're going to have to say your goodbyes to him now, and leave him here to do the dirty work.'

To hugs, howls and stage tears that turn to real tears, the

psychedelic double-decker wheezes out of the hangar, leaving Pop to do the dirty work.

Returning to Estelle Road four days later than either he or Kate had bargained for, Mundy slips easily into his rôle of indignant employee. It makes no difference that he's already telephoned her on each one of those days with the same outraged message. He was incensed in Berlin, and he's incensed now.

'I mean why didn't they think of it earlier?' he insists, not for the first time – *they* being as usual his luckless employers. 'The sheer *incompetence* is what gets me down. Why does everything have to be so bloody *hand to mouth*?' he demands, and somewhat disloyally gives a scathing imitation of his good fairy in Personnel. '"Oh *goody*! Darling Ted Mundy's in *Berlin*. How *nice* for him. Let's give him a few days in our office there so he can meet all the boys and girls." Three bloody months, she's known I was headed for Berlin. Then suddenly, bingo, it's news to her.'

Kate has put serious forethought into making his home-coming a success after five weeks of separation. She is waiting for him with the car when he arrives at London airport and she listens with a patient smile to his rant during the drive. But once in Estelle Road she puts her fingers over his lips and marches him straight upstairs to bed, pausing only to light a scented candle she has bought for the occasion. An hour later, they agree it's time to eat and he shepherds her to the kitchen and insists on lifting the Burgundy beef out of the oven for her and generally getting in the way in his efforts to spare her needless exertion. His gestures, like his conversation, might strike her as a little theatrical but after so much exposure to theatre people, what else should she expect?

Over supper, with similar conscientiousness, he earnestly debriefs her about her pregnancy, her family, and the ructions inside the St Pancras Labour Party. But as she obligingly chatters for him, he finds his eyes wandering furtively round the kitchen, treasuring each sacred detail as if he's just come back from hospital: the tongue-and-groove pine dresser that, with a bit of help from her dad, he ran up to her specifications, because as Des likes to say, there's a real carpenter in our Ted if he'd only put his mind to it; the non-stick saucepans that her brother Reg and his wife Jenny gave them as a wedding present; and the top-flight German washing machine and dryer that Kate bought out of her savings because she's one of the old-fashioned ones, she says, and doesn't mind admitting it: their baby's going to have real nappies, not those blotting-paper jobs with the plastic rompers.

And after leading her through every hour of the past five weeks, he goes round to her side of the table and kisses and caresses her until there's nothing to be done but go upstairs again and make more love until, bit by bit, he ventures upon a censored version of his adventures with the kids, interrupting his narrative with gusts of hearty laughter to give himself the extra thinking time, and mimicking the voices of the main players till she swears she'll be able to recognise Lexham anywhere.

'And, thank God, I don't have to go through it all again until June,' he ends with a careless sigh of relief.

'Why? What's in June?'

'Oh, they want to give me *Prague*' – as if Prague is a bit of a downer.

'Whatever for?' – her wry humour at it again – 'Prague's lovely.'

'International dance festival. Minding the British entrants. Full subsistence, plus responsibility allowance.'

'How long?'

'Ten days, I'm afraid. Twelve if we count travel.'

She goes quiet a moment, then gives her stomach a friendly pat. 'Well, that's all right, isn't it? As long as he doesn't decide to put in an early appearance.'

'If she does, I'll be here before her,' Mundy vows.

Which is a game they play. She says it's a boy, he says it's a girl. Sometimes, to vary the joke, they change rôles.

7

The psychedelic bus has lumbered out of view, the troupe's last tragic howls of farewell have merged into the din of traffic. Mundy and Amory are seated opposite one another in a soundproofed airing cupboard across the corridor from Amory's bare office, a tape recorder turns on the cork table between them. Even as we speak, says Amory, the crock of gold is winging its way to London. The analysts can't wait to get their thieving hands on it. Meanwhile here's what they want from us by yesterday, says Amory: a self-portrait warts and all of Edward; a blow-by-blow account of the Sasha–Mundy love affair from first blush to Weimar; and a description of the man who calls himself Professor Wolfgang, omitting no detail however slight.

Dog-tired and over-stimulated at once, Mundy answers Amory's questions brilliantly for an hour, then raggedly for another, before he starts to doze off for want of oxygen in the womb. Back in the reception room where he waits for

Amory to dispose of the tape, he falls fast asleep, barely wakes for the short car journey to wherever Amory is taking him, and comes round to discover that he is shaved and showered and holding a whisky-and-soda in his hand, and standing at the lace-curtained window of a pleasant flat overlooking the Kleistpark, with sturdy representatives of Berlin's petit bourgeoisie, including many unawakened mothers with prams, strolling in the pleasant evening sunlight fifty feet below him. If he is an object of curiosity to Amory, he is a mystery to himself. The stress, the realisation of what he has unleashed, and a bunch of accumulated anxieties that he has put aside till now, have left him drained and bewildered.

'So maybe it's time you called your Kate while I powder my nose,' Amory suggests, with the smile that never leaves his face.

To which Mundy says, oh, well, yes, that's what's bothering him actually: Kate, and the problem of what exactly to tell her.

'Not a problem at all,' Amory corrects him cheerfully. 'Your conversation will be monitored by at least six intelligence services, so all you can do is play it down the middle.'

'What middle?'

'You're being kept here by the British Council, reasons to follow. "Held up, darling – trouble at mill – my lords and masters are begging me to stay on till it's sorted. *Tschüss*, Edward." She's a professional girl. She'll understand.'

'Where am I staying?'

'Here. Tell her it's a bachelor officers' hostel, that'll put her mind at rest. Same number as on the phone. Don't gild the lily too much and she'll believe you.'

And she does. While Amory powders his nose, Kate believes Mundy with a conviction that accuses him almost beyond bearing. Yet minutes later he's back in Amory's car swapping jokes with Cliff the sergeant at the wheel, and the next thing he knows he's sitting in this new fish place in the Grunewald that a lot of people don't know about yet, thank God, because Berlin's so bloody incestuous these days. And over dinner, which they enjoy head to head in a timbered cubicle darkened for lovers and conveniently bombarded with live music and hubbub, Mundy again magically recovers his spirits – so much so that, when Amory playfully asks him whether, as a confirmed lefty, he regrets forsaking the sanctuary of Communist Europe for the decadence of the capitalist West, Mundy startles not just Amory but himself with a full-throated condemnation of Soviet Communism and all its works.

And perhaps he really feels all this, or perhaps he's having a last shudder as he looks back with horror on his foolhardiness. Either way, Amory is not about to let the moment pass.

'If you want it straight, Edward, you're a born One of Us,' he says. 'Onward and upward is the cry. So thanks and welcome aboard. Cheers.'

And it is from there – Mundy is never afterwards sure why, but it seems at the time perfectly natural – that the conversation shifts to the strictly academic question of what a chap should or shouldn't reasonably tell his wife in *a situation like this*, without anybody precisely identifying what situation they are referring to. And Amory's point, which he offers tentatively but on the strength of a certain amount of experience, Edward, is that burdening people one loves with information they don't need and can't do anything about is as hurtful – and self-indulgent – as not telling them anything at all, and arguably more so. But that's just Amory's personal view, and Edward may feel differently.

For example, if the person one is proposing to confide in is pregnant, Amory goes on lightly.

Or if they're naturally warm-hearted and trusting, and haven't got the checks and balances to keep something as big as this bottled up inside them.

Or if they're someone of high principle, say, who might have problems reconciling their political beliefs with – well, certain activities directed against a certain enemy or ideology which they don't see in the same light as we do.

In short if they're Kate and have enough to worry about already, what with a school department to run, and a house to run, and a husband to take care of, and a first baby on the near-horizon, and a bunch of Trotskyists to flush out of the St Pancras Labour Party – because somewhere along the line, Mundy must have told Amory about them too.

The Kleistpark flat is not Amory's. And it's not a bachelor officers' hostel either. It's a place he keeps for what he calls the odd chum who's floating through town and doesn't necessarily want to announce his presence. And anyway Amory needs to get back to the office for an hour in case anything new has come in from London.

But Cliff here will be in the bedroom next to you if you need anything.

And Cliff always knows how to find me.

And if you're thinking of an early walk, which you tell me you're a devil for, I'm game. Meanwhile, get some sleep. And well done again.

I'll try.

Mundy lies wide awake – as awake as last night in Weimar – counting off the quarters and halves of West Berlin's over-synchronised clocks.

Cut and run, he tells himself. You don't need this stuff. You've got Kate, the baby, the job, the house. You're not a Taos layabout any more, you've cleared the pit. You're Ted Mundy, cultural diplomat and father-to-be. Grab your bag, sneak downstairs without waking Cliff and hightail it to the airport.

But while he gives himself this advice he remembers, and elsewhere in his head was remembering all along, that Nick Amory has his passport – only a formality, Edward, you'll get it back in the morning.

And he also knows that, in handing over the passport, he was entirely alive to the significance of what he was doing, and so was Amory.

He was joining. A Born One of Us was signing up to His Own.

He wasn't submitting, he wasn't being press-ganged. He was saying, 'I'm in,' just as he was saying it over dinner when he was winging off about the awfulness of Communist life. He was offering himself as a playing member of Amory's team because that was how he saw himself in the flush of his success, and how Amory saw him too.

So just remind me, please, how I got into this mess in the first place. It wasn't Amory who recruited me, it was Sasha. Amory didn't dump a sackful of secrets in my lap and say, 'Here, take this lot and give it to the British Secret Service.'

Sasha did.

So am I doing this for Mother England, or for a self-flagellating anti-Lutheran on the run from God?

Answer: I'm not bloody well doing it at all. I'm jumping ship.

All right, Sasha's my friend. Not a friend I necessarily like, but a friend, a loyal one, and an old one, a friend who needs my protection. And, God knows, has had it. A friend who also happens to be a chaos addict, waging a fanatical one-man war against all forms of established order.

And now he's found himself another temple to pull down, so good luck to him. But he's not pulling me down with it.

Or Kate.

Or the baby.

Or the house. Or the job.

And that's what I'm going to be telling Amory in a couple of hours' time when I take him up on that early walk he was talking about. 'Nick,' I'll be saying. 'You're a fine professional, I respect London, and yes, I totally agree, Soviet-style Communism is a legitimate enemy and I wish you every success in your efforts to frustrate it. So if you'd kindly let me have my passport back and maybe rustle me up a car to the airport, you can make your own arrangements with Sasha and we'll shake hands and call it a day.'

But there is no early walk. There is Nick Amory hovering over him in the grey light of dawn, telling him to get dressed *now*.

'Why? Where are we going?'

'Home. The shortest route.'

'Why?'

'The analysts have given you an alpha double plus.'

'What the hell's that?'

'Best there is. Vital to national security. Your chum must have been hamstering the stuff for years. They're asking whether you'd prefer a VC or a peerage.'

To be conveyed.

To take no decisions.

To sit back and be a spectator to your own life. That's spying too, apparently.

Tempelhof airport, yet again, by early-morning Jeep, a different sergeant.

Goodbye, Cliff.

And goodbye to you, Ted, and good luck.

The RAF plane waiting, propellers turning, Amory the only other passenger. Hold tight, we're already taking off. The pilots don't look at us. Trained not to. Land at Northolt airport, step out of the plane straight into a green van with extended wing mirrors and two blackened windows in the rear doors.

She'll be walking to school by now. She'll be about halfway up the concrete path between the Hampstead lido and the mansion flats. The big kids are chatting her up, the little ones are swinging on her fingers, and she thinks I'm talking Morris dancing with the British Council in Berlin.

Through the van's rear windows Mundy begins to recognise the road to Oxford. He's got an alpha double plus so they're giving him a degree. Ilse is in her anchorite's horsebox telling him he's a complete infant for sex. They enter rolling hills and pass between brick gateposts capped by sandstone griffins. The daylight switches on and off as beech trees close over them. The van stops, but only for the driver to be waved forward. No beech trees now, but paddocks with white fences, a cricket pavilion and a round pond. The van stops again, the rear doors fly open, a tight-lipped steward in a white jacket and plimsolls commandeers Mundy's kitbag and ushers him past a cluster of parked cars, along a flagstoned passage, up a back staircase to a servants' corridor.

'My guest gets the bridal suite, Staff,' Amory tells the steward.

'Very good, sir. I'll send the bride up directly.'

The bridal suite has a single narrow bed, a washbasin and jug, and a very small window looking onto an ivy-covered wall. In his last year as a school prefect, Mundy had a room just like it. More cars are arriving. He hears muted voices and footsteps on gravel. The greatest change in his life is about to begin. Behind closed doors, over four days of unrecorded time, the Born One of Us meets the family.

They are not the family he expected but that's nothing new to him.

No grim-faced men with secretive glances measure him for the drop. No super-graduettes in twinsets and pearls tie him in knots with courtroom-style questions. They're excited to meet him, proud, impressed by him, they want to shake his hand, and do. Decent, ordinary, jolly folk, at first reading – no names, no side, but good faces, sensible shoes and scuffed brown briefcases that look anything but official, the womenfolk ranging from the slightly scatty – now where on *earth* did I put my purse? – to the quiet motherly type with dreamy wet eyes who listens to him dotingly for hours on end before drifting in with a question about something he's totally forgotten until she puts her finger on it.

As to the male of the species – well, they too come in all shapes and sizes, but they're a genus nonetheless. Mid-life academics, you might say. Archaeologists working happily together on the same site. Medics, with that benign but purposeful detachment that says we go for the disease and not the man. Bony young men with bad suits and faraway eyes – Mundy imagines them as descendants of the classic school of Arabian explorer, crossing the Empty Quarter by camel with nothing but the stars, a bottle of lemonade and a bar of fruit-and-nut.

So what is it, he wonders, that paints them with a single brush, other than their flattering obsession with the person of Ted Mundy? It's the unexpected belly laughs, the bounce, the shared enthusiasms, the slightly faster tongue and eye. It's the nearly hidden spark of larceny. It's the belonging together.

Backwards over his past they go, first with Amory's debriefing in Berlin to guide them, then striking off in their own directions. All his personal history stretched out before him like a cadaver and, in the most tactful British way, dissected. But Mundy doesn't mind this. He's part of it, an alpha double plus player capped for England.

Connections about his life he's never made before, dug out of the entrails of his memory and held up for him to inspect and comment on: *Gosh, well, I suppose that's true*, or *Come to think of it yes, bang on, in fact*. And Amory always at his side, ready to catch him if he falls, and iron out any little misunderstandings in case our Edward here gets stroppy, which he sometimes does, because not everything that has to be asked makes comfortable fare. They never pretended it would, quite the contrary. That's how families are.

'Nobody who's done something as important as you have can survive this sort of mauling without a blush or two, Ted,' a motherly one warns him kindly.

'Agreed. Absolutely. Fire away, ma'am.'

Is she a shrink? How would he know? He wants to call her Flora or Betty or whatever her name would be if he knew it, but all he can think of in his good-spirited way is ma'am like the Queen, which raises a ripple of friendly laughter round the mahogany table.

So that's the first day, and by the time it's over except for a few last stragglers in the bar, they have celebrated the version of Ted Mundy that he afterwards thinks of as Mundy

One: hero of Weimar, the Major's loyal only son, former captain of cricket at his public school, doughty second-row rugby forward who went a bit pink in his undergraduate days – and what good man doesn't? – but now the bugle's sounded he's rallied to the family regiment with the best of 'em.

But unfortunately that is only Mundy One. In spying, there is always a second version.

Can schizophrenia be induced?

Certainly it can, provided the patient is complicit.

In Weimar, Sasha gave Mundy a foretaste of what to expect. Here in Oxford, thanks to certain microfilmed instructions conveyed to Mr Arnold in various concealment devices, they are serving up the whole unpleasant feast. If yesterday's Mundy One represented the best of everything Mundy might aspire to, today's Mundy Two is a caricature of everything that until a couple of years ago he feared he was becoming.

A Bolshie ex-schoolboy and ex-Oxford leftist-turned-anarchist drop-out and Berlin rowdy who, after a well-merited beating, was run out of town at crack of dawn; an unqualified prep-school master expelled for venery who fell foul of a provincial newspaper before setting up as a failed writer in New Mexico, only to creep back to England and lose himself in the no-hope basements of the arts bureaucracy, a has-been to his grubby fingertips.

The image of himself in this insufficiently distorted mirror is at first so familiar that he can hardly contemplate it without screwing up his face in ridiculous expressions, pulling at his hair, blushing, groaning and shooting his arms around. How much of the portrait comes from his confessions to Amory, and how much from London's researches over the last forty-eight hours, he has no means of knowing. It makes no odds: Mundy Two is too close to the bone, whether lovingly sketched by the dreamy-eyed ladies, or raunchily by a mid-life academic in full flow.

A parsonical man in a Bible-black Homburg has arrived by helicopter. Through the bay window of the conference room, Mundy watches him scurry across the lawn clutching his hat to his head and holding out his briefcase as a counterweight. The men stand up and a hush greets him as he enters. He takes his place at the centre of the table. A respectful silence collects while he whisks a file from his briefcase and pores over it before bestowing a twinkly smile, first upon the gathering at large, and then upon Mundy.

'Ted,' he says. It is afternoon by now, and Mundy is washed up: both elbows on the conference table and long hands wedged into his tousled hair. 'A question of you, dear boy.'

'Any number,' Mundy replies.

'Did Kate ever mention to you that your father-in-law Des was a paid-up member of the British Communist Party till fifty-six?' – much as he might ask, does Kate like gardening?

'No, she absolutely didn't.'

'Did Des?'

'No.'

'Not even over your Saturday-night game of bar billiards?' – the twinkle very bright – 'I'm shocked.'

'Not over our game of bar billiards or anywhere else.' And I'm shocked too, but Mundy is too loyal to Des to say so.

'The Soviet invasion of Hungary scuppered him, of course, as it scuppered a lot of them,' the Parson laments, consulting his file once more. 'Still one never *completely* leaves the Party, does one? It's always *there*, in the blood, in its way,' he adds, cheering up.

'I suppose it is,' Mundy agrees.

But the file is full of good things, the Parson's smile suggests as he goes back to it. Des is only the beginning.

'And Ilse. What do you know of *her* politics – in formal terms, as it were?'

'She was a bit of everything. Anarchist, Trot, pacifist – I never really worked it out.'

'But she did. In 1972, under the influence of your successor, she became a fully paid-up member of the Leith branch of the Scottish Communist Party.'

'Well done her.'

'You're being too modest. It was all your doing, I swear it was. You began the good work, your successor completed it. I see you as primarily responsible for leading her to the light.'

Mundy only shakes his head but the Parson is undaunted.

'Regarding your Dr Mandelbaum, first name Hugo, your fellow refugee and inspiration at boarding school,' the Parson goes on, making a Norman arch out of his fingertips. 'What did he teach you *exactly*?'

'German.'

'Yes, but what *type* of German?'

'Literature and language.'

'Nothing else?'

'What else should there be?'

'How about a little philosophy? Hegel, Herder, Marx, Engels?'

'God no!'

'Why God?' – the Parson's hooped eyebrows are cordially lifted.

'I wasn't up to philosophy, that's why. Not at that age. Not at any age. And least of all in German – I wouldn't have made head nor tail of it. Not much better now. Ask Sasha.' And he puts the back of his hand to his mouth and lets out an uncertain bark.

'Then let me put it *this* way, Ted. I'm being contrary, but bear with me. Would I be right in saying Dr Mandelbaum *could* have taught you philosophy? Had he wanted to. Had you been precocious.'

'Well – my hat! – on *that* basis, he *could* have taught me any bloody thing! The fact is, he didn't. You asked me, I said no. Now you're putting the same question hypothetically and I'm supposed to say yes.'

The Parson finds this huge fun. 'So what we're saying is, surely, that Dr Mandelbaum *could* have brainwashed you with Marx, Engels or whoever he wished, and as long as you didn't bubble to your peer group or the rest of the staff, nobody would have been a penny the wiser.'

'And *I'm* telling you it never happened. All he did – in the most indirect way – legitimately and professionally – nothing more to it than that – was breathe a kind of vague revolutionary vapour over me –' He dries, and goes back to massaging his scalp.

'Ted. Dear chap.'

'What?'

'This profession – yours by adoption – does not live in the real world. It visits it. However, in this case reality is on our side. The entire Mandelbaum clan were hoof-and-horn lefties, and all honour to them. Three of them fought with the Thälmann brigade in the Spanish Civil War. Hugo's elder brother was in the Comintern. Stalin hanged him for his pains. Your very own Hugo joined the Communist Party in

Leipzig in 1934 and went on paying his dues till he went to his reward in Bath General Hospital forty years later.'

'So?'

'So Sasha's masters aren't idiots. You met one. The good Professor. He may have his little ways but he's nobody's fool. He'll want to know he's catching a real fish. Or Sasha is. And the first thing he'll do is turn you inside out. And what he'll find – and his numberless mates will find – is a thick red line of radical involvement starting with Dr Hugo Mandelbaum and continuing without a break through Ilse, Oxford and Sasha to the present day. Of course you didn't join the Party! Why should you? – you didn't want to imperil your career. But your tutor was a Red, your first girlfriend is a Red, you're a member of the St Pancras Labour Party, which is good and left, you're married to a woman of left-wing lineage whose father was a full-blown comrade till he lapsed in fifty-six. You're a miracle, dear boy! If we'd had to invent you, you wouldn't be *half* as convincing. You'll be God's gift to them. As, I have to say, you are to all of us.'

Seconded by all present, to jolly laughter from everyone except Mundy. Slowly he sits straight, pushes his hands over his hair to tidy it, and lays them softly on the table. He is smiling, a happy lad. He is gradually getting the hang of the family game. The failed writer is not failed after all. He is a creator like themselves. He is visiting reality, as they are, and plundering it for art's sake.

'You've forgotten Ayah,' he says reproachfully.

They glance at each other uncertainly. Ire? Eire? Where's the file on Eyer?

'There was this substitute mother I had in India,' Mundy goes on. Then amends the text: 'Pakistan.'

Ah, *that* sort of *ayah*, their faces say in relief. Yes, yes of course. You mean a *maid*.

'What about her, Ted?' asks the Parson encouragingly.

'Her entire family was slaughtered in the massacres at Partition time. My father blamed Partition on British Colonial misrule. She ended her days begging in the streets of Murree.'

Now it is the turn of the Parson and his crew to see the light. *Marvellous*, Ted, they agree. A sob story like that is *just* what they love! Ayah gets star billing. And soon they are all toiling together on Ayah under the working title of Early Influences, firing each other up with their ideas as they bash out the storyline: how the infant Mundy was a social lie, born of a working-class mother and passed off as the son of an aristocrat; how he was adopted by this native peasant woman – fat, Ted? Terrific, let's blow her up like a balloon! – who gave nothing for his purported origins; and how this enormously fat peasant woman called Ayah – a nursemaid *just like your mother, for Christ's sake!* – was herself the victim of Colonial oppression. But without Ted, they all agree afterwards in the bar, they would never have got there: those extra touches made all the difference between something *felt* and just another run-of-the-mill bit of cover.

'We're Carmelites,' Amory announces without embarrassment, as he and Mundy make an after-dinner tour of the grounds. 'We can't talk about what we do, we get no visible promotion, normal life goes for a burton. Our wives have to pretend they've married failures and some believe it. But when the captains and the bullshit artists depart, we'll be the boys and girls who made the difference. And by the looks of it, you'll be another.'

But who is Mundy Three, when Mundys One and Two have gone to bed? Who is this third person who is neither of the other two, who lies awake while they sleep, and listens for the chimes of country bells he doesn't hear? He is the silent spectator. He is the one member of the audience who doesn't applaud the performances of his two familiars. He is made up of all the odd bits of his life that are left over after he has given the rest away.

Have there ever been so many busy hours in a young husband's day?

Whether Mundy is slaving in the British Council's head-quarters in Trafalgar Square writing up his report on the Sweet Dole Company's triumphant tour or preparing the ground for the Prague Festival of Dance, now less than four weeks away, or hurrying home for a Dads-2-Bee session at the South End Green Maternity Clinic or lending a hand with the school production of *The Pirates of Penzance*, he vows he was never in his life so stretched and – dare he say it? – useful.

And if there's a spare moment, it's nip into the woodshed with Des to do a bit of work on the baby's cradle that Des and Ted together are running up for Kate as a surprise, and Kate's mum Bess is crocheting the blanket for. Des has found this lovely batch of old applewood, you wouldn't believe the grain or the colour. The cradle has become a mystical object in Mundy's order of things, a mixture of talisman and life-goal: for Kate, for the baby, and for keeping everything on course. As always, Des likes to talk high politics.

'What would you do – you, Ted – supposing you had your hands on her – apart from the obvious – with that Margaret Thatcher?' he will muse as they labour.

But Mundy knows he must provide no answer because that's Des's job.

'Know what *I'd* do?' Des asks.

'Tell me.'

'I'd ship her off to a desert island with Arthur Scargill and leave them to get on with it.' And the notion of Margaret Thatcher enduring a forced marriage with the hated miners' leader has him laughing so much that the cradle's progress is delayed by several minutes.

Mundy has always liked Des, but since his recent visit to Oxford there is new spice to their relationship. How on earth would the old ex-Communist react, he wonders, if he found out that his son-in-law was spying on Mother Russia's most obedient vassal? If Mundy knows anything, Des would ceremoniously take off his cap and shake him silently by the hand.

And the baby isn't the only excitement on the horizon either. Only a few days ago, the Labour Party took a trouncing in the General Election and Kate lays the blame for this squarely on the militants and extremists who have infiltrated its ranks. To save the Party she loves, she intends to put herself forward as the officially backed moderate candidate in the forthcoming Council elections in direct competition with the Trots, Communists and closet anarchists who are the plague of St Pancras. It takes her three days to break this news to Ted. She's so worried *he'll* worry. But she underrates his good heart. Within a week Mundy is sitting in the front stalls at St Pancras Town Hall, willing her forward as she modestly declares her candidature in terse, cogent sentences that remind him of Sasha.

Mundy's fairy godmother in the British Council's Personnel Department would like to see him when he has a moment. She suggests around closing time when people are going home. She has her hands pressed flat on her desk like somebody who has promised to keep her temper. She enunciates her lines with care. She has obviously rehearsed them.

'How's the writing going?'

'Well. You know. Coming along.'

'You had a novel in the pipeline.'

'Yes. Well, I'm afraid it still is.'

Small talk over. She takes a breath.

'When I was informed by higher authority that your presence was required in Berlin to clear up certain security matters relating to your tour, I was not unduly perturbed' – breath – 'similar things have happened before. Experience has taught us to be incurious and wait for them to pass. However.'

Unprepared for this discussion, Mundy waits for the *however*.

'When I was informed by the same authority that you were to be given Prague, I came to the conclusion, wrongly as I now know, that you were pulling strings. So I refused to play' – breath – 'only to be instructed by a still *higher* authority, not only to do as I was told, but to obey virtually without question any further instruction relating to your future, unless that instruction is so blatantly at odds with our personnel policy as to be *ostentatious to an outside eye*.' Long pause. 'Short of resigning, which seems excessive in view of the fact that what you are doing is apparently vital to the public interest, I have no alternative but to buckle under what I regard as – *un*pardonable *in*tolerable meddling in the Council's affairs.' There. She's said it. 'May I ask you one question?'

'Absolutely,' says Mundy, with none of his usual verve. 'Fire away.' *Play it dumb*, Amory has strenuously advised him. *She's as leaky as a basket. She's not allowed to know a bloody thing.*

'Clearly you don't have to reply. Equally clearly I shouldn't be asking it. Are you a Trojan Horse?'

'A *what*?'

'At the time when you joined our organisation, were you already – I don't even know what the word is – and I'm sure if I did know, I wouldn't be allowed to say it – I believe the expression is, *doing a little of this and that* for them?'

'No. I wasn't. Not for anybody.'

'And what has happened since – whatever it is, which obviously I can't know and don't want to – has that happened by accident, or by design, would you say?'

'Total accident,' Mundy blurts, keeping his head down in order to examine his hands. 'Fluke of life. One in a million chance. Frightfully sorry about it.'

'And do you wish – *please* don't answer this if it's too painful – do you secretly rather wish it hadn't happened at all?'

'Now and then, I suppose.'

'Then I'm sorry too, Ted. I thought I was helping you by overlooking the fact that you've no degree. Now it seems I've only landed you in trouble. Still, I suppose we're all working for the same queen. Though in your case she can't know, can she?'

'I suppose not.'

'I feel so badly, just giving you a roof. It just seems such a *waste* somehow. Will you – and I'm *sure* you can't tell me – will you get promotion from somewhere else?'

Returning home by the slowest possible route, Mundy ponders the high cost of living a double life for his country. He likes Personnel, and has come to count on her goodwill. Now it seems he must get along without it. He's beginning to understand what Amory meant when he said that normal life went for a burton. But by the time he gets home he has cheered up.

Who wants a normal life, anyway?

British Council memo from Head of Personnel Department to E.A. Mundy marked 'Private and Confidential':

> We are informed that your presence is requested at an out-of-town Arts Festival Organisers' Convention at the McCullough Hall, Edinburgh from 9 to 16 May, in preparation for your attendance at the Prague Festival of Dance. We understand that travel, accommodation and subsistence will be borne by the organisers. Salary and leave entitlements will be subject to review.

'We call it the School of Deportment,' Amory explains as they ride round Hyde Park munching smoked salmon sandwiches in a black cab driven by Cliff, his sergeant. 'They'll tell you the ten best things to do in Prague when it rains, and a few things about how to cross the road on your own.'

'Will you be there?'

'Darling. Would I leave you at a time like this?'

Kate is less enthusiastic. 'A whole *week* talking about festivals?' she marvels, taking a break from composing A Personal Promise to My Supporters. 'You arts bureaucrats are worse than the United Nations!'

It's a midweek afternoon, a fine spring day, and the eve of Mundy's departure for Scotland. Kate's official nomination arrived in the post this morning. She rings Mundy at the Council. She's perfectly calm but she needs him at once. He leaves his meeting and rushes home to find her standing white-faced but composed on the path to the front door. He takes her arm and coaxes her as far as the porch where she stops dead, like a horse refusing the fence. She has the teething knuckle of her right forefinger jammed in her mouth.

'I disturbed them. They weren't expecting me. I was supposed to have classes all day,' she says without expression. 'One of my girls won a top scholarship to Leeds so the Head announced a half-holiday for the Sixth.'

Mundy puts an arm round her to hold her more tightly.

'I walked home. I opened the front gate. I saw shadows in the window. In the lounge.'

'Through the net curtains?'

'They had the door to the kitchen open. They were moving back and forth across the doorway.'

'So more than one.'

'Two. Maybe three. They were light.'

'Light *shadows*?'

'Light on their feet. She saw me. The woman did. Girl. She was wearing a sort of catsuit. I saw her head turn, then she must have dived for the floor and crawled into the kitchen. The door to the back garden was open.' Kate could be giving evidence in court, she's so precise. 'I ran round the back in case I could see them. A van was driving away but I was too late to get its number.'

'What sort of van?'

'Green. Black windows in the back doors.'

'Mirrors?'

'I didn't look. What do mirrors matter? It was just a glimpse, for God's sake. For all I know the van had nothing to do with it.'

'Old van or new one?'

'Ted, stop interrogating me, will you? If it was conspicuously old or new, I would have said so. It was neither.'

'What did the police say?'

'They put me through to the CID and the sergeant asked if anything was stolen. I said no. He said they'd come when they could.'

They go into the lounge. The desk is an antique kneehole job they bought for a song from a crook in Camden Town. Des says it's so hot he's surprised it hasn't caught fire. It has a flat top with imitation leather and a pillar of drawers on either side. The left pillar is Mundy's, the right pillar is Kate's. He pulls open his three drawers, one after the other, snap, snap.

Old typescripts, some with their rejection slips still attached.

Jottings for a new play he has in mind.

The file marked FILE that contains his mother's letters to the Major and the minutes of the Major's court martial and the group photograph of the victorious Stanhopes.

Displaced, all of them.

Displaced, but not disordered. Or almost not.

Shoved back, *almost* in their right sequence, by somebody who wanted to make them look as though they hadn't been disturbed in the first place.

Kate is watching him, waiting for him to speak.

'Mind?' he asks.

She shakes her head. He pulls open the top drawer on her side. She is breathing heavily. He fears she may faint. He should know her better: she's angry.

'The bastards put them back upside down,' she says.

Her Sixth Form exercise books go in the bottom drawer because it's the deepest, she explains in clipped sentences.

Work to be corrected by Wednesday goes on top of work to be corrected by Friday. That's why I dish out colour-coded exercise books to my students. Yellow, you're a Wednesday student. Red, you're a Friday. The bloody burglars turned them upside down.

'But why would a bunch of Trots be interested in your students' essays?' Mundy reasons.

'They wouldn't. They were going for Labour Party stuff.'

When the police arrive at ten o'clock the same night, they are not much help.

'Know what my wife does, sir, when she's in the family way?' the sergeant asks over the cup of tea Mundy makes, while Kate puts her feet up in the bedroom.

'I'm afraid I don't.'

'Eats the toilet soap. I have to hide it or she'd be blowing bubbles all night. Still, I suppose we could arrest everyone with a green van with black windows. That would be a start.'

Watching the police drive away, Mundy privately debates whether to make use of the emergency number Amory has given him, but what does he hope to gain? The sergeant, though odious, was right. Thousands of people own green vans.

Kate's right. It was the Trots.

It was a couple of thieving kids, and she disturbed them before they could take anything.

It was a normal incident in a normal life, and the only thing that isn't normal is me.

8

'You are tired, Teddy?' asks the ponderous, ginger-headed Lothar, ordering up another round of Pilsners.

'Oh, just a bit stretched, Lothar, nothing terminal,' Mundy confesses. 'We did a lot of dancing today,' he adds, to over-appreciative laughter.

'Tired but happy,' Frau Doktor Bahr suggests primly from the head of the table, and her young neighbour, the intellectual Horst, seconds this.

Sasha says nothing. He sits, chin in hand, frowning into the middle distance. He has pulled his beret low over his brow, perhaps for irony. It's their second evening together, so Mundy is familiar with the pecking order. Lothar is Sasha's minder. Horst, the blond intellectual, is Lothar's minder. The stern Frau Doktor Bahr from the East German Embassy here in Prague is minding all three of them. And all four of them are minding Ted Mundy.

The third day of the Prague Festival of Dance has just

ended. They are sitting in the cellar bar of a conference hotel at the edge of town, a Soviet-style monster of glass and steel, but the cellar is supposed to recreate Habsburg times, with fat stone pillars and frescoes of knights and maidens. A few late drinkers sit at other tables, a few girls drink cola out of straws, still hoping to catch a foreigner. In a far corner a middle-aged couple are drinking tea, and they have been drinking the same tea in the same tender way for half an hour.

You'll be followed and that's par for the course, Edward. It will be professional surveillance, so the important thing for you is not to be aware of it. They'll shake out your room, so don't be too tidy or they'll think you're playing games with them. If they make eye contact with you by mistake, best to smile vaguely and tell yourself you bumped into them at a party somewhere. Your most convincing weapon is your innocence. With me?

With you, Nick.

In the last seventy-two hours Mundy has sat through bone-wearying displays of sword-dancing, folk dancing, tribal dancing, country dancing and Morris dancing. He has clapped his hands off for Cossacks, Georgians, Palestinians doing the *dabke*, and numberless enactments of scenes from *Swan Lake*, *Coppélia* and *Nutcracker* in a packed baroque theatre with no ventilation. He has drunk warm white wine in half a dozen national tents, and in the British tent he has bantered with the usual good chaps and dutiful wives, including a chubby first secretary with circular spectacles who says he once opened the batting for Harrow and Mundy bowled him out first ball, which is the agreed recognition signal. He has been plagued by loudspeaker systems that don't work, scenery going to the wrong theatre and stars refusing to perform because there is no hot water in their hotel. And between-whiles he has grudgingly allowed himself to be wooed by Sasha and his outriders. Last night they wanted him to go with them to a private party in town and when Mundy declined, saying he must tend his flock, Lothar suggested a nightclub. Mundy declined that too.

Make the buggers sweat for you, Edward. The only reason they've come to Prague is to get inside your knickers. But you don't know that. You don't know anything except Sasha's your old buddy. You're mixed up, unhappy, drinking a bit, a loner. You're all over them one minute and cagey the next. That's the way Sasha's sold you to them, and that's who he wants you to be.

Thus Nick Amory, Ted Mundy's drama coach, at the Edinburgh School of Deportment, relaying the stage directions of Sasha our Producer.

Lothar is trying to draw Mundy out, assisted by Frau Doktor Bahr. They tried to draw him out last night, at this same table and at this same hour, and in the same contrived atmosphere of weary geniality. In the low moments of his drinking curve, Mundy has been monosyllabic. In high moments he has regaled them with embroidered tales of his anti-Colonial past and, to the huge amusement of his audience and his own secret shame, Ayah's enormous bottom. He has described the horrors of a bourgeois English education and let slip the magic name of Dr Hugo Mandelbaum, the man who first got him thinking, but nobody has taken him up on it. They won't, of course. They're spies.

'So what do you think about England's great lurch to the right, Teddy? Does Mrs Thatcher's brand of belligerent capitalism alarm you a little, or are you a natural friend of the free-market economy?'

The question is so cumbersome, and Lothar's archness so insinuating, that Mundy disdains a reasoned reply.

'Not a *lurch*, old boy. Not even a twitch, actually. They've changed the name on the shop front, and that's about all that's happened.'

Frau Doktor Bahr manages her banalities better. 'But if America is going to the right, and Britain also, and the right is gaining ground all over Western Europe, don't you shudder a little for the future of world peace?'

Horst, who fancies himself an expert on all things British, needs to parade his knowledge.

'Could the pit closures lead to actual *revolution*, Teddy? – somewhat on the lines of the hunger marches of the thirties maybe, then spinning totally out of control? Can you give us a few tips about how the British man in the street is reacting at the moment?'

They are getting nowhere, and must be aware of it. Mundy is yawning and Lothar is about to order up another round of drinks when Sasha emerges like a jack-in-the-box from his stupor.

'Teddy.'

'What?'

'This is total bullshit, actually.'

'What is?'

'Have you brought your bicycle?'

'Of course I haven't.'

Suddenly Sasha is standing, hands wide, appealing to all of them. 'He's a cyclist, didn't you know? He's crazy. You know what this crazy man did in West Berlin? We rode bicycles round the streets. We spray-painted the old Nazi houses, then rode like hell to get away from the pigs. And I had to go with him – me, with my legs, on a bloody bicycle! – to look after him. Teddy organised it all. He was a genius. Weren't you, Teddy? Are you trying to pretend you have forgotten?'

Mundy's hand is rising to hide a rueful smile. 'Of course I haven't. Don't be bloody silly. Best fun we ever had,' he asserts, determinedly sharing the wilful distortion of history.

Sasha's toughest job will be getting you on your own, Amory is saying. *He'll work on it but you're going to have to help him. You're a restless sod, remember? Always wanting to go for a walk, run round the park, jump on a bike.*

'Teddy. We have a date tomorrow,' Sasha is announcing excitedly. 'Three o'clock outside the hotel. In Berlin we did night-time. Here we do daytime.'

'Sasha. Honestly. For God's sake. I've got a hundred and six neurotic British artists to worry about. I can't make three o'clock or any other o'clock. You know that.'

'Artists survive. We don't. We get out of town, the two of us. I steal the bicycles, you bring the whisky. We talk about God and the world, like the old days. Fuck it.'

'Sasha – listen to me.'

'What?'

Mundy is pleading now. He's the one person at the table who isn't smiling. 'I've got modern ballet all afternoon. And I've got the British Embassy reception in the evening and mad dancers round the clock. I can't just –'

'You are being a total arsehole as usual. Modern ballet is pretentious shit. Skip the ballet, I'll get you back to town in time for the Queen. Don't argue.'

Sasha has carried the company. Frau Doktor Bahr is beaming her blessing, Lothar is chuckling, Horst is saying he will come too, but Lothar is wagging his finger in an avuncular way and saying these boys deserve a bit of time on their own.

And the great thing about bicycles, Edward, is they're hell on wheels to follow.

Hotel rooms are not sanctuaries, Edward. They're glass boxes. They're where they watch you and search you and listen to you and smell you.

And marriage is not a sanctuary either, or not for the British Council has-been, closet radical and resentful failed writer who haunts the basements of the arts bureaucracy. His phone calls to Kate must reflect this. First thing this morning he filled in a laborious application form at hotel reception: foreign number to be called, foreign party to be spoken to, purpose of foreign call, proposed duration of foreign call, practically the content of the foreign call in advance – which strikes him as pretty bloody silly, seeing that they'll all be listening in, and ready to cut him off if the talk gets dirty. Crouched on the bed, with the silent phone beside him, he discovers he is shivering. When the phone finally rings it screams so loud he imagines it's about to commit suicide by hurling itself off the bed. Speaking into the mouthpiece, he notices that his voice is higher and slower. Kate notices it too, and wonders whether he is ill.

'No fine, really. Just a bit danced out. Miranda's being an absolute bitch, as usual.'

Miranda his boss, the regional supervisor. He asks after the baby. It's kicking, she says. Jolly hard too: maybe one day he'll play football for Doncaster. Maybe one day she will, he agrees in a lacklustre voice, but the joke, like Mundy, sounds flat. And how are all the drama kings and queens of St Pancras? he asks. They're all fine, thank you, she replies, irritated by his low spirits. And has Ted met anyone nice, she asks pointedly, or done anything *amusing*?

Well. Not really.

You don't mention Sasha to her EVER, Amory is saying. *Sasha belongs to your secret heart. Maybe you've got a crush on him, maybe you want to keep him to yourself. Maybe you're already thinking exactly what they hope you're thinking: that you want to jump over the Wall and sign up with them.*

Mundy rings off and sits at the table, head in hands. He is acting 'Christ, life is awful' – but it is. He loves Kate. He loves his family-in-the-making.

I'm doing this so that our unborn child and other people's unborn children will be able to sleep at night, he tells himself with one voice.

He goes to bed and doesn't sleep. He doesn't expect to.

Five o'clock. Cheer up. There's hope just around the corner. In a couple of hours our first ballerina of the day will be throwing her tutu out of her cot because her hairdryer doesn't work.

For Mundy, Sasha has obtained a giant-sized English policeman's black bicycle complete with a basket in front of the upright handlebars. For himself, a child's version of the same thing. Side by side they ride between tramlines to a suburban railway station at the edge of town. Sasha wears his beret, Mundy an anorak over his one good suit, and his trousers tucked into his socks. The day is beautiful, the city brave and careworn, its Habsburg glory crumbling in the sun. There are few cars. The people walk warily, not looking at each other. At the station the two friends board a three-coach local train. Sasha insists they sit in the guard's van with their bicycles. The straw reeks of cow manure. Sasha is still wearing his beret. He unbuttons his jacket to show Mundy a tape recorder in the inside pocket. Mundy nods, to say I understand. Sasha makes small talk. Mundy does the same: Berlin, girls, old times, old friends. The train stops at every lamp-post. They are entering deep countryside. The recorder is voice-activated. Its pin light goes out when things are quiet.

At a village with an unpronounceable name they unload their bicycles onto the platform. With Mundy practically free-wheeling and Sasha pedalling for all he is worth they bump down an unmade road past horse-drawn carts and flat fields dotted with red barns. Only the occasional motor-tricycle or truck overtakes them. They draw up at the roadside for Sasha to consult a map. A straight yellow track makes an avenue between tall fir trees. They advance in single file, Sasha in his beret leading. They enter a clearing pocked with mining grottoes overgrown with moss, sawn logs and bits of ancient brickwork. Large bearded irises nod in the breeze. Dismounting, Sasha wheels his bicycle up and down the mounds until he finds one that he likes, lays the bicycle in the grass and waits for Mundy to do the same. Reaching inside his jacket, Sasha extracts the tape recorder and holds it in his palm. His small talk acquires a sneering and impatient edge.

'So you are content with your lot, Teddy,' he says, watching the pin light flicker. 'That is good news, I would say. You have a mortgage, a wife and a petit bourgeois in the pipeline, and you are leaving the revolution for the rest of us to fight. There was a time when we despised such people. Now you are one of them.'

Mundy the ham actor is quick to spot his cue: 'That's not a fair description of who I am, Sasha, and you know it!' he protests angrily.

'Then what are you?' Sasha demands, unyielding. 'Tell me what you are, for once, not what you are not!'

'I am who I always was,' Mundy retorts hotly, as the tape turns in its window. 'No more and no less. What you see isn't always what you get. Not with you, not with me. Not even with your bloody Communist Party.'

It's a radio play. Mundy's lines sound to him like bad improvisation, but Sasha seems content with them. The pin light is out, the tape has stopped turning, but as a precaution Sasha ejects it, drops it into one pocket and the recorder into another. Only then does he tear off his beret, let out a great cathartic cry of '*Teddy!*' and fling up his arms for the unequal embrace.

The ethics of the Edinburgh School of Deportment now require Mundy to ask a number of routine questions of his field agent before they settle down to the business of the day, and Mundy the natural has them waiting in his head:

What is the cover for this meeting?
What is the fallback if we are interrupted?
Do you have any immediate anxieties?
When shall we next meet?
Are you sitting comfortably or do you see people you recognise, and did they follow you here?

But the School of Deportment can go hang. Sasha's uncensored monologue is sweeping such mundane considerations aside. He is glaring across the lumpy clearing into the distant blue pines, seeing nothing. Confession and revelation pour from him in a stream of outrage and despair.

'In the months and years after you were removed from West Berlin I entered a total darkness. What use were a few burning cars and broken windows? Our Movement was inspired not by the will of the oppressed classes but by the liberal guilt of the affluent. In my personal turmoil I considered the miserable alternatives available to me. According to our anarchist writers, world conflict should lead to creative chaos. If such chaos is intelligently exploited, a free society will emerge. But when I looked about me, I was forced to accept that the preconditions of creative chaos did not exist, neither did the intelligent exploiters. Chaos presupposes a vacuum of power, yet bourgeois power was gaining everywhere, and so was the military might of America, for whom West Germany was by now the arsenal and craven ally in the world war that appeared inevitable. As to the intelligent exploiters, they were too busy making profits and driving Mercedes cars to avail themselves of the opportunities we had created for them. In the same period the Herr Pastor also rose to rank and influence among the fascistic élite of Schleswig-Holstein. From the politics of the pulpit, he had moved to the politics of the pseudo-liberal ballot box. He joined secret right-wing societies and was admitted to certain very select Masonic committees. There was talk of putting him into Parliament in Bonn. His success inflamed my hatred of fascism. His American-inspired adoration of the God of Wealth goaded me to the point of dementia. My future, if I was to remain in American-owned West Germany, was a desert of compromise and frustration.

'If we are to build a better world than this, I asked myself, where do we turn, whose actions do we support, how do we frustrate the endless march of capitalist-imperialist aggression? You know I have the Lutheran curse. Conviction without action has no meaning for me. Yet what is conviction? How do we identify it? How can we know that we should be guided by it? Is it to be found in the heart, or in the intellect? And what if it is only to be found in the one and not the other? I spent much time considering the example of my good friend Teddy. You became my virtue. Imagine. Like you, I had no conscious faith, but if I acted, then the faith would surely follow. After that, I would believe because I had acted. Perhaps that is how faith is born, I thought: by action and not by contemplation. It was worth a try. Anything was better than stasis. You had sacrificed yourself for me without thought of reward. My seducers – you have met one – were wise enough to appeal to me in the same terms. No inducement would have persuaded me. But offer me a long stony path with a single light shining at the end of it, and throw in the opportunity to reverse the hypocrisies of the Herr Pastor, and perhaps I shall listen to you.'

He has left the mound and is hobbling impatiently round it with his strange, uneven stride, stepping over the push-bikes, gesturing with open hands while he talks, clamping his elbows to his sides as if there is no room to raise them. He is describing covert meetings in apartments in West Berlin, furtive border crossings to safe houses in the East, and solitary lost weekends in the Kreuzberg attic while he struggles to reach his great decision, and his erstwhile comrades slip away to permanent confinement in the open prisons of materialism.

'By the end of many days and nights of deliberation and with the aid of my tireless and by no means stupid seducers, not to mention a good few bottles of vodka, I had reduced my dilemma to two simplistic questions. I described them to you in my letters. Question one: who is the ultimate class enemy? Answer, unhesitatingly, American military and corporate imperialism. Question two: how do we realistic-ally oppose this enemy? Is it by relying on the enemy to destroy himself, but only after he has destroyed the world? Or is it by swallowing our objections to certain negative tendencies on the part of international Communism and allying ourselves with the one great socialist movement that, for all its blemishes, is capable of bringing the victory?' A long silence, which Mundy does not feel inclined to interrupt. Theory, as Sasha has observed, was never his thing. 'Do you know why my name is Sasha?'

'No.'

'Because it is the Russian abbreviation of Alexander. When the Herr Pastor brought me to the West, he wished for reasons of respectability to rechristen me Alexander. I refused. By keeping my name Sasha, I was able to demonstrate to myself that I had left my heart in the East. One night, after many hours of discussion with my seducers, I agreed to make the same demonstration with my feet.'

'The Professor?'

'Was one of them,' Sasha confirms.

'Professor what of?'

'Corruption,' Sasha snaps.

'Why did they want you so badly?' This is not Amory asking, this is Mundy wanting to know how they both got here. 'Why did you matter to them so much? Why go to all this trouble, just for Sasha?'

'You think I didn't ask them?' His mood is black again. 'You think I am so vain that I believe I take the whole world with me when I cross one shitty frontier? At first they flattered me. To win over such a great intellect as mine would signify a notable moral victory for the forces of progress. I told them that was bullshit. I was a left-wing minor West German academic with no chance of acceptance by a major university. I was no sort of victory for anybody. Then they admitted me to what they blushingly described as their little secret. My defection would frustrate the counter-revolutionary activities of the increasingly influential Herr Pastor and his fascistic fellow conspirators in Schleswig-Holstein. Millions of American dollars were being siphoned through Church channels into the coffers of anti-Communist agitators in North Germany. Local newspapers, radio and television were being infiltrated by capitalistic subversives and spies. For the Herr Pastor's only son to return freely and publicly to his democratic homeland would strike a blow against the imperialist saboteurs and undermine the Herr Pastor's standing. It might even cause the CIA to withdraw some of its covert funding of West German counter-revolutionary elements. I will not conceal from you that this argument compelled me more than any other.' He draws to an abrupt halt and fixes Mundy with an imploring stare. 'You understand that there is nobody on God's earth with whom I can share this story apart from you? – that all the rest of them are enemy, to a man, to a woman – liars, frauds, informants, living in permanent duplicity, as I am?'

'Yes. I believe I do.'

'I was not so foolish as to expect a warm welcome from the GDR. Our family had committed the crime of fleeing the Republic. My seducers knew I was not a Communist by conviction and I anticipated – they had prepared me for it – a humbling period of re-education. What future I had after that could only be resolved by time. At best, an honourable place in the great anticapitalist struggle. At the least, a quiet Rousseau life, perhaps on a collective farm. Why are you laughing?'

Mundy isn't, but he has allowed himself a small smile, forgetting for a moment that jokes about Sasha are in bad taste. 'I don't see you milking cows, that's all. Not even on a collective farm.'

'It is immaterial. All that matters is, in a fit of culpable lunacy that I shall regret for the remainder of my life, I boarded the S-bahn to the Friedrichstrasse station and, on the advice of my seducers, surrendered myself to the East German frontier guards.'

He stops speaking. It is prayer time. His fine hands have found each other and are clasped beneath his chin. His devout gaze is directed away from the clearing and sightlessly upward.

'Whores,' he whispers.

'Frontier guards?'

'Defectors. All of us. While we are fresh, we are handed round and used. When our tricks are known and we are past our prime, we are tossed onto the rubbish heap. For the first weeks after my arrival I was accommodated in a pleasant apartment on the outskirts of Potsdam, and subjected to searching but benign questions about my life, my memories of my childhood in East Germany and the Herr Pastor's return from imprisonment in the Soviet Union.'

'By the Professor?'

'And by his underlings. At their request, I composed an impassioned statement designed to cause the maximum consternation among the fascists and conspirators of the Herr Pastor's inner circle. I took great satisfaction in this task. I proclaimed the futility of anarchism in the face of modern realities, and my unbounded joy at returning to the bosom of the GDR. "Anarchism destroys but Communism builds," I wrote. It was my hope, if not yet my conviction. But I had acted. Faith would follow. I also voiced my contempt for those members of the West German Lutheran movement who, while posing as messengers of Christ, accepted Judas-money from their spy-masters in America. My statement, I was assured, had found wide circulation in the Western media. Professor Wolfgang himself went so far as to declare it a world sensation, though I was shown no evidence to prove this.

'I had been led to believe, before crossing over, that immediately upon my arrival in East Berlin I would be the occasion of an international press conference. Also at the request of my hosts, I posed for a photographer and did my best to appear as happy and reconciled as was possible in the circumstances. Photographs of me were taken on the steps of the apartment house in Leipzig where I had grown up, in order to provide pictorial evidence that the erring son had returned to his socialist roots. But I waited in vain for my press conference, and when I questioned the Professor during one of his rare visits to the apartment, he was evasive. Press conferences were a matter of timing, he said. Perhaps the moment was past and my statement, together with the photographs, had done the job. I asked again: where has my statement appeared, please? In *Spiegel? Stern? Welt? Tagesspiegel? Berliner Morgenpost?* He replied curtly that he was not a student of reactionary disinformation and advised me to be more modest. I told him, which was the truth, that I listened daily to West German and West Berlin radio news broadcasts and had heard not a word anywhere of my defection. He replied that if I chose to immerse myself in fascist propaganda, it was unlikely that I would attain a positive understanding of Marxism–Leninism.

'A week later, I was transferred to a secure encampment in remote countryside close to the Polish border. It was a limbo, part refuge for political vagrants, part penitentiary, part interrogation centre. Above all it was a place where you are sent in order to be forgotten. We called it the White

Hotel. I would not award it many stars for excellence. You have heard of an East German prison called the U-boat, Teddy?'

'Afraid not.' He has long ceased to be surprised by Sasha's switches of mood.

'The U-boat is a revered feature of our East German gulag. Three of my fellow guests at the White Hotel spoke enthusiastically of its facilities. Its official title is Hohenschönhausen prison in East Berlin. It was built by the considerate Soviet secret police in 1945. To keep the inmates alert, the architecture provides that they should stand, not lie. To keep them clean the cells are flooded with icy water up to the inmates' chests and for their entertainment penetrating sounds are played at varying volume through loudspeakers. You have heard of the Red Ox?'

No, Mundy has not heard of the Red Ox either.

'The Red Ox is situated in the ancient town of Halle. It is the U-boat's sister establishment. Its mission is to provide constructive therapy for political malcontents, and to rebuild their Party awareness. Our White Hotel in East Prussia boasted several of its graduates. One, I remember, was a musician. His awareness had been so thoroughly rebuilt that he was unable to pick up his spoon to feed himself. You may say that after a few months of the White Hotel, the last of my misplaced illusions about the nature of the German Democratic paradise had been forcibly expunged. I was learning to detest its monstrous bureaucracy and thinly disguised fascism with an ardent but secret passion. One day, without explanation, I was ordered to pack my possessions together and present myself at the guardhouse. I will admit that I had not always been a model guest. My unexplained isolation, my horizonless existence, and the horror stories told by other detainees, had not improved my manners. Neither had the wearisome interrogations about my opinions on every stray subject – political, philosophical and sexual. When I asked our distinguished hotel manager where I was being taken, he told me, "Somewhere that will teach you to keep your fucking mouth shut." The five-hour drive inside a wire cage fitted into the back of a builder's van did not prepare me for what lay ahead.'

He stares straight ahead of him, then, like a puppet whose strings are let go, flops to Mundy's side on the grassy mound.

'Teddy, you bastard,' he whispers. 'Let us for God's sake have some of your whisky!'

Mundy has forgotten all about the whisky. Unearthing his father's pewter flask from the recesses of his anorak, he hands it first to Sasha, then takes a pull himself. Sasha resumes his story. His expression is fearful. He seems afraid he will lose a friend's respect.

'Professor Wolfgang has a nice garden,' he announces. He has drawn up his spindly knees and is resting his forearms on them. 'And Potsdam is a beautiful town. You have seen those old Prussian houses where the Hohenzollerns used to put their officials?'

Mundy may have done, but only on the bus drive from Weimar, when his interest in nineteenth-century architecture was limited.

'So many roses. We sat in his garden. He gave me tea and cake then a glass of the finest Obstler. He was apologetic for having abandoned me, and complimentary about my behaviour in stressful circumstances. I had acquitted myself excellently before my interrogators, he said. They had formed a high opinion of my sincerity. Since I had more than once advised my interrogators to go fuck themselves, you may imagine that I wondered where this was leading. He asked me if I wished to take a bath after my long drive. I replied that since I had been treated like a dog, it might be more appropriate if I jumped into the river. He said I had my father's sense of humour. I answered that this was scarcely a compliment, since the Herr Pastor was an arsehole and I had never in my life seen him laugh.

'"Oh, you have him wrong, Sasha. I believe your father has a famous sense of humour," he replied. "He merely keeps it to himself. The best jokes in life are surely those that we can laugh at when we are alone. Don't you think so?"

'I did not. I didn't know what he was talking about, and told him. He then asked me whether I ever considered making up my quarrel with my father, if only for my mother's sake? I replied that at no time in my life had such a thought occurred to me. It was my conviction that the Herr Pastor did not qualify as an object of filial affection. To the contrary, I said, he represented everything that was opportunistic, reactionary and politically amoral in society. I should add that, by this stage, the Professor had ceased to impress me intellectually. When I demanded to know at what point according to his Marxist beliefs he expected the East German State to wither away and a State of true socialism to begin, he replied with Moscow's stock answer that, for as long as the socialist revolution was menaced by the forces of reaction, such a possibility was remote.' Sasha passes a hand through his cropped black hair as if to assure himself that the beret is not in place. 'It was, however, no longer the subject of our discussion that was interesting me. It was his manner. It was the insinuation – manifested by the favours he was lavishing on me, the Obstler, the garden, and the civilised nature of our conversation – that, in ways I could sense but not define, I belonged to him by right. There was a bond between us, known to him but not to me. It was like a bond of family. In my confusion, I went so far as to speculate whether my host was homosexual, and intended to force his attentions on me. It was in the same light that I interpreted his mysterious tolerance towards the Herr Pastor. By intruding upon my filial feelings, I reasoned, he was by implication offering himself as a father substitute, and ultimately as my protector and lover. My suspicions were misplaced. The explanation for the Professor's intimacy was far more terrible.'

He stops. Has he run out of breath – or courage? Mundy ventures not a word, but there must be comfort in his silence, for gradually Sasha rallies.

'It was soon clear to me that the Herr Pastor was to be the only material topic of our conversation in the garden. In the White Hotel I had touched no alcohol, except for one experience of Château Moonshine, which nearly killed me. Now the Professor was plying me with fine Obstler, and simultaneously with insinuating questions about the Herr Pastor. I would go so far as to say respectful. He referred to my father's *little ways*. Did my father drink? How should I know? – I replied – I hadn't seen him for almost twenty years. Did I remember my father talking politics in the home? Here in the GDR before he fled the Republic, for example? Or afterwards in West Germany when he came back from his indoctrination course in America? Did my father ever quarrel with my poor mother? Did he have other women, sleep with colleagues' wives? Did my father take drugs, visit brothels, gamble on racehorses? Why was the Professor interrogating me like this about a father I didn't know?'

Not the Herr Pastor any more, Mundy records. My father.

Sasha has no defences left. He must face his father as a man, no longer as a concept.

'Dusk fell and we went indoors. The furnishings were not exactly proletarian: imperial-style furniture, fine paintings, everything of the best. "Any fool can be uncomfortable," he said. "There is nothing in the Communist Manifesto that forbids a little luxury to those who have deserved it. Why should the devil wear all the best suits?" In a dining room with an ornate ceiling we were served roast chicken and Western wines by docile orderlies. When the orderlies retired, the Professor took me to the drawing room and beckoned me to sit beside him on the sofa, thus immediately reviving my fears regarding his sexuality. He explained that what he had to say to me was extremely secret, and that while his house was regularly swept for microphones, no word of our conversation must be overheard by the staff. He told me also that I should listen to him in complete silence, and reserve whatever comment I might have until he had finished. I can give you his exact words, since they are branded on my memory.'

Sasha closes his eyes for a moment, as if preparing himself for a leap into the blue. Then begins again, speaking as the Professor.

'"As you may have gathered for yourself, my colleagues in State Security are divided as to how we should regard you, which explains the regrettable inconsistencies in your treatment. You have been the football between two opposing teams and for this I offer you my personal apologies. But be assured that from now on, you are in safe hands. I shall now put to you a certain question but it is a rhetorical one. Which would you prefer to have for a father? A *Wendehals*, a false priest, a corrupt hypocrite who consorts with counter-revolutionary agitators, or a man so dedicated to an ideal, so committed to the great cause of the revolution and the highest principles of Leninism, that he is prepared to endure the contempt of his only son? The answer, Sasha, is obvious, so you need not provide it. Now I shall put a second question to you. If such a man, from the day of his providential incarceration in the Soviet Union, had been selected by the Party organs for a life of supreme self-sacrifice – and were now lying on his deathbed far behind the enemy's lines – would you wish, as his only beloved son, to give him comfort in his last hours, or would you leave him to the mercy of those whose conspiratorial actions he has devoted his life to frustrating?" It was as well that he had forbidden me to speak, because I was struck mute. I sat. I stared at him. I listened in a trance when he told me that he had known and loved my father for forty years, that it was always my father's greatest wish that I should return to the GDR and take up his sword when it fell from his hand.'

He breaks off. His eyes widen in entreaty. '*Forty years,*' he repeats incredulously. 'You know what that means, Teddy? *They knew each other when they were both good Nazis together.*' His voice recovers its strength. 'I did not point out to the Professor that I had come to the GDR in the expectation of destroying my father, and that it was therefore a surprise to be asked to adulate him. Perhaps, after my intransigence in the White Hotel, I was learning to conceal my emotions. Nor did I say anything when the Professor explained to me that, though my father had long dreamed of dying in the Democratic Republic, the imperatives of his mission required him to remain in exile till the bitter end.' He assumes the Professor's voice again. '"The greatest joy of your beloved father's life was your statement renouncing anarchism and embracing the Party of Social Renewal and Justice."' Sasha seems to go to sleep for a moment, then starts awake, and becomes once more the Professor. '"His delight at the photograph of his beloved son standing on the doorstep of his old apartment is not to be described. When it was shown to him by our trusted intermediary, your father was deeply moved. It was your father's wish and also mine that there would be an occasion when we might smuggle you to his bedside so that you could clasp his hand, but this has been reluctantly overruled by the highest authority on security grounds. As a compromise it has been agreed that you will be informed of the truth concerning his life before it ends, and write him an appropriate letter from the heart. You will adopt a conciliatory and humble tone, begging his forgiveness and assuring him of your respect and admiration for his ideological integrity. Nothing less will lighten his passing."

'I do not remember how I walked the short distance from the drawing room to the desk in his study where he provided me with the necessary writing paper and pen. My head was swimming with repulsive and simultaneous revelations. *From the day of his incarceration in the Soviet Union*: do you know what those words meant to me? That on his arrival in Russian prison camp my father at once became a stool pigeon and gained the protection of the Politkommissars, who recruited him as their spy and trained him for the future use of East German State Security. That when he returned to the GDR and set up as a good priest in Leipzig, any member of his flock who had oppositional tendencies was tempted to confide them to him, not knowing he was a professional Judas. Until this moment I believed I had plumbed the depths of my father's baseness. Now I realised I had been living in a fool's paradise. If there was any single moment when I came face to face with the idiocy of my decision to throw in my lot with the Communist cause, it was this. If a desire for retribution has a moment of conception, this was when it occurred. I do not remember what words of sycophantic adoration I wrote through my secret tears of rage and hatred. I remember the Professor's consoling hand on my shoulder as he informed me that I was henceforth the bearer of a considerable State secret. The Party, he said, was therefore faced with the choice of returning me to the White Hotel for an indefinite period, or permitting me to enter the portals of State Security in a lowly capacity so that my movements could at all times be observed. In the short term, it was accepted that I would have some transient value as an authority on aspects of West Berlin's disintegrating anarchist and Maoist groups. In the longer view, he hoped I would aspire to become a dedicated Chekist, exhibiting my father's aptitude for conspiracy, and following in his footsteps. Such was the Professor's ambition for me. Such was the course of action that, as my father's most loyal friend and controller, he had personally urged upon his illustrious comrades. "Now it is up to you, Sasha," he told me, "to show them I was right." He assured me that my future path in the Stasi would be hard and long, and that much would depend on the extent to which I submitted my temperamental personality to the Party's will. His final words were his most vile. "Always remember, Sasha, that henceforth you are the Comrade Professor's favourite child."'

Does the story end here? For the time being it seems so, for Sasha, volatile as ever, has looked at his watch and, with an exclamation, sprung to his feet.

'Teddy. We must be quick. They will waste no time.'

221

'To do what?' – for now it is Mundy's turn to lose his way.

'I must seduce you. Secure you for the Cause of Peace and Progress. Not all at once, but from me a compelling overture, and from you a less than convincing rejection of my advances. And tonight you will be morose – it is arranged, yes?'

Yes, tonight it is arranged that I will be morose.

'And a little drunk?'

Also a little drunk, though not as drunk as I may appear.

Sasha takes the tape recorder from his pocket, then a fresh cassette, which he brandishes in Mundy's face in warning. He slips the cassette into its housing, presses the start button, replaces the recorder in an inside pocket of his jacket, puts on his beret and with it the impassive scowl of the apparatchik who has submitted his temperamental personality to the Party's will. His voice hardens and acquires a hectoring edge.

'Teddy, I will ask you this frankly. Are you telling me you have turned your back on everything we fought for together in Berlin? That you are leaving the revolution to take care of itself? – *undermining* it even? That you are in love with your bank account, and your sweet little house, and you have put your social awareness to *sleep*? Okay: we didn't change the world that time! We were kids, playing soldiers of the revolution. But what about joining the *real* revolution? Your country's fallen under the spell of a fascistic warmonger: *but you don't give a fuck!* You are the paid lackey of an anti-democratic propaganda machine: *and you don't give a fuck!* Is this what you will be telling your petit bourgeois when it grows up? *I didn't give a fuck?* We need you, Teddy! It makes me sick to watch you, for two nights already, how you flirt with us, show us one tit then put it back in your shirt, then show us the other one! Smirking while you sit there with the fence halfway up your arse!' His voice drops. 'You know something else, Teddy? Shall I tell you something in very great confidence, just you and me and the rabbits? We're not proud. We understand human nature. When it's necessary we even pay people to listen to the voice of their political conscience.'

Everyone is charmed by the sight of a lanky Englishman on a bobby's pushbike arriving at the British Embassy gates dressed in a dark suit and tie and cycle-clips. And Mundy, as always when he is called upon to do so, plays the part for all it's worth. He sounds the silver bell on his handlebars as he weaves precariously between parking and departing cars, he yells, 'Pardon me, madam,' to a diplomatic couple whom he narrowly misses scything down, he flings up an arm to assist the braking process, and gives a drayman's 'Whoa, there, girl!' as he brings his steed to a halt and takes up his place at the back of the ragged queue of fellow guests – Czech officials, British cultural representatives, dance masters and mistresses, organisers and performers. Shuffling his bike towards the sentry box, he chatters merrily with whomever he happens to be alongside, and when it's his turn to show his passport and invitation card, he takes exaggerated umbrage at the suggestion that he might leave his bicycle in the street rather than inside the embassy compound.

'Wouldn't dream of it, old boy! Your gallant citizens would pinch it in five minutes cold. Got a bike shed? Bike stand? Anywhere you say except on the roof. How about over there in the corner?'

He's in luck. His protests have been heard by a member

of the embassy staff who happens to be hovering at the opening of the tented walkway that leads to the front door.

'Problem?' he enquires blandly, taking a casual look at Mundy's passport. He is the chubby man with circular spectacles who complained that Mundy had bowled him out first ball.

'Well, not really, officer,' says Mundy facetiously. 'I just need somewhere to park my bike.'

'Here. Hand it over. I'll shove it round the back. You'll be going home on it, I take it?'

'Absolutely, if I'm sober. Got to get my deposit back.'

'Well, give me a yell when you decide it's time to go. If I'm AWOL, ask for Giles. No troubles on the road?'

'None.'

He walks. This is how tarts feel. Who are you, what do you want and how much will you pay for me? He is in Prague on a perfect moonlit night, striding down cobbled alleys. He is drunk, but drunk to order. He could drink twice as much and not be drunk. His head is swirling, but from Sasha's story, not from alcohol. He feels the weightlessness that he felt in Berlin on Christmas Eve when Sasha told him for the first time about the Herr Pastor. He feels the shame that comes on him when he encounters pains he can only imagine, never share. He is walking Sasha-style, one leg leading as he pounds unsteadily along. His head is everywhere, now with Kate at home, now with Sasha in his White Hotel. The streets are lit by wrought-iron lanterns. Dark shrouds of washing drift across them. The ornate houses are slatternly, their doorways barred, windows shuttered. The eloquent silence of the city accuses him, the atmosphere of quelled revolt is palpable. While we gallant students of Berlin were hoisting

224

our red flags over the rooftops, you poor bastards were pulling yours down and getting crushed by Soviet tanks for your trouble.

Am I being followed? *First assume it, then confirm it, then relax.* Am I sufficiently morose, distraught? Am I wrestling with a great decision, angry with Sasha for putting me on the spot? He no longer knows which parts of him are pretending. Perhaps all of him is. Perhaps he has never been anything but pretended man. A natural. A naturally pretended man.

At the embassy reception he was also a natural, the soul of wit. The British Council should be proud of him, but he knows it isn't. *Then I'm sorry too*, says Personnel, the fairy godmother he never had.

From the embassy, he has ridden the policeman's bicycle triumphantly back to his hotel and left it in the forecourt for Sasha to reclaim. Did it feel different after Giles had removed its contents? – lighter? No, but I did. He has again telephoned Kate from his hotel room and this time he made a better job of it, even if in retrospect his end of the conversation sounds more like a letter home from school.

This city is more beautiful than you can imagine, darling . . . I just so wish you were here, darling . . . I never knew I liked watching dance so much, darling . . . Tell you what, I've had a brilliant idea! – it comes to him as he speaks. He hadn't thought of it till now – *When I get home, let's take out a couple of those season tickets to the Royal Ballet. The Council might even come up with the cost. After all, it's their fault I've become a dance junkie. Oh and to confirm: the Czechs are really super. It's always the way, isn't it, with people who have to make do on next to nothing? . . . And you too, darling. Deeply, truly . . . And our baby. Sleep well. Tschüss.*

He *is* being followed. He has assumed it, he has confirmed it, but he has not relaxed. Across the road from him, he has recognised the staid couple who were sitting in the corner of the bar last night. Behind him two dumpy men in baggy hats and raincoats are playing Grandmother's Footsteps with him at thirty yards' distance. Abandoning the tenets of the Edinburgh School of Deportment, he stops, squares himself, swings round, cups his hands to his mouth and screams blue murder at his pursuers.

'Get off my fucking back! Get out of my hair, all of you!' His voice ricochets up and down the street. Windows are slapping open, curtains are being cautiously parted. 'Fuck off, you ridiculous little people. *Now!*' Then he plonks himself on a convenient Habsburg bench and demonstratively folds his arms. 'I've told you what to do, so now let's see you do it!'

The footsteps behind him have stopped. The staid couple across the road have disappeared up a side street. In about half a minute they'll be popping up pretending to be someone else. Great. Let's all pretend to be someone else, and then perhaps we'll find out who we are. A large car crawls into the square but he refuses to be interested in it. It rolls past him, stops, reverses. Let it. His arms are still folded. He has his chin on his chest and his eyes down. He is thinking of his new baby, his new novel, tomorrow's dance contest. He is thinking of everything except what he is thinking about.

The car has drawn up. He hears a door open. And stay open. He hears footsteps climbing towards him. The square is on a slope, and he is at the upper end of it, which is why there has to be a short climb, then a levelling-out as the footsteps cross the cobbled platform and come to a halt a yard away. But Mundy is too fed up, too confused and put upon, to lift his head.

Fancy German shoes. Mushroom-coloured leather with brogue toecaps. Brown trousers with turn-ups. A hand descends on his shoulder and gently shakes it. A voice that he refuses to recognise speaks perfumed German English to him.

'Ted? Is it you? Ted?'

After a very long pause, Mundy agrees to look up and sees a parked black saloon at the kerbside with Lothar at the wheel and Sasha in his beret peering at him from the rear seat. He looks higher and sees the elegant features of the silken-haired Professor as he gazes down on him with fatherly concern.

'Ted. My dear fellow. You remember me. Wolfgang. Thank God we found you. You look all in. I understand you had a jolly interesting conversation with Sasha this after-noon. This is not the behaviour we expect from a disciple of the late, great Dr Mandelbaum. Why don't we go somewhere quiet and talk about God and the world?'

Mundy stares at him for a while in mystification. Gradually he lets the penny drop. 'And why don't you move your fucking shadow,' he suggests, and remains seated, his face buried in his hands, until the Professor, with Sasha's assistance, carefully raises him to his feet and guides him to the car.

Traitors are opera stars, Edward. They have nervous break-downs, crises of conscience and outrageous needs. The Wolfgangs of this world know that. If you don't make it hard for them they'll never believe you were worth buying.

A classic Cold War double-agent operation is taking its first cautious steps towards consummation. If the seduction is agonisingly slow, that is because Ted Mundy in his many parts turns out to be a master of prevarication.

At an international convention of Egyptologists in Bucharest he flourishes a tantalising sample of the sort of material he thinks he might be able to provide: a top-secret plan to disrupt a forthcoming World Federation of Trade Unions in Warsaw – but can he bear to deceive his colleagues? His tempters hasten to reassure him. In the service of the true democracy, they tell him, such scruples are misplaced.

At a book fair in Budapest he provides an enticing, if retrospective, overview of how anti-Communist disinformation is fed to the Third World press. But the risk he took still scares him. He'll have to think about it. His tempters wonder aloud whether fifty thousand capitalist dollars will assist his thought processes.

At the Leningrad Festival of Peace and Song, exactly at the point where the Professor and his people dare to believe they have landed their fish, Mundy throws a convincing five-star tantrum about the proposed terms of his remuneration. What proof can they give him, when he shows up at the Bank Julius Bär in Geneva five years from now and utters the magic password, that the cashier will hand over the cash and not ring for the police? It takes a five-day seminar of international oncologists in Sofia to iron out the final details. A discreet but lavish dinner in the upper room of a grand hotel overlooking Lake Iskur marks the breakthrough.

Faking illness to Kate and his notional employers at the British Council, Mundy allows himself to be spirited from Sofia to East Berlin. In the Professor's villa in Potsdam where Sasha was first told that his father the Herr Pastor was a Stasi spy, glasses are raised to the brilliant new agent at the heart of Britain's subversive propaganda machine, and his recruiter, Sasha. Seated shoulder to shoulder at the centre of the candlelit table, the two friends proudly listen as the

Professor reads aloud a telegram of congratulation from his masters in Moscow.

Triumph on one side is matched by triumph on the other. In London a safe house in Bedford Square is acquired and a team assembled to perform the double duty of processing Sasha's alpha double plus material and confecting disinformation ingenious and plausible – and alarming enough – to satisfy the paranoid appetites of Mundy's masters for the next hundred years at least, since everybody on both sides knows that's how long the Cold War's going to last.

Insiders including Mundy learn to refer to the house as the Wool Factory, wool being the commodity that it proposes to pull over the Stasi's eyes.

The effect of the twin victory upon Mundy himself is mixed. At the age of thirty-two, the pseudo-artist, pseudo-radical, pseudo-failure and pseudo everything else he accuses himself of being has finally discovered his natural art form. On the other hand, there are snags. The strains of running two successful careers within a single marriage are well known; the strains of running three, less so – particularly when one of them is a top-secret mission vital to the security of your nation, rated alpha double plus and not discussable with your partner.

9

Kate is getting along splendidly.

So is young Jake, now aged eight.

Jake is a boisterous, rough-cut fellow who, according to family lore, bears no resemblance to either of his parents but is the dead spit of his granddad Des: stocky, outspoken, large-hearted, but quick to anger, and no friend of fine distinctions. Unlike Mundy or Sasha, Jake entered the world without mishap. After a squally infancy, he passed his first year at primary with flying colours, to the relief of his parents who were beginning to fear he might need specialised attention. The present anxiety is how he will handle the move to Kate's home town of Doncaster where, if she is to stand any chance of reversing the pro-Tory swing in her marginal constituency, she must reclaim her roots.

In the years between, Kate's political ambitions have made impressive strides. She is billed as one of the Labour Party's rising modernisers. Her blistering denunciation of the wreckers of St Pancras – FEARLESS SCHOOL-MARM BLASTS 'ENEMIES WITHIN', *Hampstead & Highgate Express* – did not escape the eye of Labour Party headquarters. Her fighting nomination speech as parliamentary candidate for her native constituency of Doncaster Trent, praised for its unsparing realism, earned her loud applause from the new centrists. And while she is heartbroken to be saying goodbye to her pupils and colleagues in Hampstead – not to mention uprooting Jake just when he's settling down at last – well, the best-rated secondary in South Yorkshire is bidding for her services, there's a house that comes with the job, and a primary for Jake right round the corner and a kids' sports centre where he can let off steam.

But it's Ted, as the whole family agrees, who's come through this looking like the trooper Des always said he was. Without Ted's support, Kate would never have made it out of the trap, says Des, who loves a greyhound. He goes one further, inspiring a family joke that never quite goes to rest, much as Mundy might wish it to:

'I'll tell you this, and in a minute I'm going to drink to it,' he warns, while Mundy carves the Sunday beef and Jake tries to get everyone to join him in 'One Man Went to Mow'. 'When our Kate takes up residence at Number Ten, which she will, I'm not joking – *Jake, shut up a minute, will you?* – when she does, *Ted* here is going to do a bloody sight better job than what Denis Thatcher is doing today, or should I say *not* doing? Ted here will *not* be playing golf all day, and he will *not* be auntie-cissed by four o'clock in the afternoon or somewhat sooner – *in a minute, all right, Jake darling?* – Ted here, unlike Denis the Menace, will be where he belongs, at my darling daughter's side, giving her moral support from every angle in exactly the way – *belt up, Jake!* – in the same way that Prince Albert did for Queen Victoria – don't laugh, Kate, please, I am totally serious. He'll be your *consort* is what he'll be. And he'll be the best bloody consort there ever was, bar none. So here's to you, Ted old son, and God bless you. All right, Jake, let's have a sing then.'

The move to Doncaster raises complications for the whole family, but Kate and Ted, as two rational people, are not about to be thrown by them. With Jake they hope asleep upstairs, Kate sets out the invariables of the situation. Ted has passed the big four-O, so it would be daylight madness for him to give up his pension rights and promotion prospects unless something equally good and preferably better comes along. And that's putting the best face on it, says Kate. Because frankly, Ted, at your age, in your position – she tactfully leaves the sentence unfinished, just as she has left unfinished an earlier speech on the subject of Our Marriage and its Shortcomings, principal among which are Mundy's frequent absences, and his peculiar other-worldliness before and after them, which might well lead any other wife to conclude he had *another interest*, but since he swears he hasn't, she'll let that go.

Returning to Ted's career prospects, or lack of them, Kate takes it to be common ground that he has hit a plateau at the Council. This special job they gave him as Travelling Representative Eastern Europe all those years ago has not turned out to be quite the path to glory Ted was led to expect. Put bluntly, it's become a backwater, not to say dead end, she goes on. And why they now insist on calling him an *auxiliary* travelling representative strikes her as most extraordinary. She can only imagine Ted blotted his copybook in some way that he won't tell her about. Or perhaps, after all, they have found out about his not having a degree. She just wishes she could confront those wretched people in his personnel department, who according to Ted look straight through him these days.

'And you, my darling, as we all know, are the very *last* person to speak up for yourself. It's your public-school hang-up about not being pushy. Well, these days we *all* have to be pushy because that's what Thatcherism's brought us to.'

Kate next applies her analytical head to the feasibility of Mundy living in Doncaster and commuting to London. Unfortunately, that too is a non-starter. Quite apart from the astronomic cost of a Doncaster–King's Cross season ticket, neither of them can see Ted sitting on a train for four hours a day, *plus* the Underground – particularly if Thatcher does what she's threatening to do with the railways. Also, Kate's going to need some paid help with looking after Jake while she's getting round her constituency. Her political agent, a mother herself, says there's a good supply of Sri Lankans if you tap into the right lot, but they cost.

'Anyway, completely rationally, if you count up weekends, bank holidays *and* your leave entitlement' – which, as it happens, Kate has already done – 'they amount to very nearly half the year. So let's think of it that way, shall we? Bearing in mind that, ever since you took up your present job, you've been averaging nine weeks abroad per year, thanks to the academic conferences and student exchange programmes which for some *extraordinary* reason they've thrown at you in addition to your cultural festivals.'

Not for the first time in recent years, Mundy wonders who Kate is. The woman before him seems to have no relation to the woman he longs for when he is away from her. She has not evolved, she has simply been replaced. If she were

Kate's double, he wouldn't be surprised. On the other hand, it occurs to him that Kate may well be having similar thoughts about himself.

'Next question, obviously: can we afford to maintain two households and, following on from *that*, what do we do with Estelle Road, particularly given that the housing market, after being deliberately inflated by the City banks for their own purposes, is in a state of collapse? Might we, for instance, keep the house, but let off the two spare bedrooms – say to medical students or nurses from the Royal Free Hospital? You could keep the master bedroom, drawing room and kitchen, and they could have the rest.'

Mundy is not attracted by the prospect of adding boarding-house keeper to his many rôles in life, but doesn't say so. They agree to discuss the possibilities with Des. Maybe a loft conversion is the answer. But Mundy also feels obliged to obtain a second opinion from Amory, who together with the Professor owns the controlling interest in Mundy Incorporated.

Amory finds much to commend the idea of two households. If there is a financial shortfall, he adds cautiously, London might make it up to him. And London can afford to, he might have added. As a prized Stasi agent, Mundy receives a fat retainer, bonuses and incentive payments. The conventions of the trade, however, require him to turn these sums over to his true masters, whose remunerations are more modest, since London, unlike the Stasi, takes his loyalty for granted. Obscure lockaway trusts and life policies lodged in City banks have little meaning for him. A monthly brown envelope containing what Amory calls 'play money' is all he is otherwise allowed, since an unnatural improvement in his lifestyle would not only attract the curiosity of British Security, from which Amory's Service likes to keep a healthy distance, but of the family accountant, Kate.

'Perfect way to keep your flavours apart, Edward. Once Jake knows the form, he'll settle down in no time. How's his cricket coming on?'

'Fine. Super.'

'What's the problem?'

'Kate likes to do her door-to-door stuff at weekends when voters are at home.'

'Tell her to do it on weekday evenings when you're not there,' Amory advises, and perhaps he really has a wife to whom he can talk like that.

Suddenly the schism is real. Mundy hires a van, Des and a friend of his called Wilf help load it up with the bits of furniture that Kate has marked in advance with lengths of sticky pink tape. Jake, who is no supporter of the move, barricades himself in his room and lobs its contents out of the window, including his duvet, blankets, toy fire station and, for the finale, the cradle Des and Mundy made for him before he was born.

With Jake firing off abuse from the back of the van they arrive at a very new housing estate on the outskirts of Doncaster. Its dominant feature is a red-brick church with a free-standing bell tower which to Mundy resembles a hanged man swinging from a gibbet. The semi-bungalow which is henceforth the candidate's family home is an orange-roofed box with picture windows and a rectangle of mown lawn front and back like two fresh graves. After two days of boisterous unpacking, punctuated by bursts of kids' cricket on the community playground, and Mundy's entire repertoire of funny voices, not to mention the glad-handing of next-door neighbours and other members of the electorate, he drives the empty van back to London and begins his new life as a weekly boarder.

In his early mornings he pounds the Heath and tries not to remember the mornings when he walked Kate to work, and the evenings when he stood around with the mothers waiting for her to come out of class, and the sandpit where he and Jake fought the Battle of Waterloo, and the corner of the playing field where they threw frisbees, and played England versus Pakistan Test cricket until Jake made it clear that he preferred his disobliging peers to anything Mundy had to offer.

Jake's rages are accusing. He seems to be having them for all the family: for Kate, who in anger merely purses her lips, and for Mundy whose first line of defence is to make silly jokes and bark with laughter till the cloud has passed. But Jake has inherited neither of these tactics. When Jake is shushed, he roars. When he feels frustrated or perplexed or disregarded, he roars. To Mundy in despondent mood, Jake's message is clear: *You're a fraud, Dad. I've observed your clowning, I have listened carefully to your funny voices and your crappy bird noises. I am familiar with the full range of your insincere facial expressions, and I've rumbled you. You're a revolutionary tourist turned capitalist spy and there's not a true bone in your ugly, over-long body. But because my tender years preclude me from articulating these sentiments, I roar. Signed Jake.*

But look on the bright side, Mundy urges himself, with one of those compulsive reaches for the sky which his right arm undertakes by itself these days. All right, I'm not quite the father I hoped I'd be. But I'm not a cashiered ex-Indian Army drunk either, and Jake's got a real, live, upwardly mobile mother instead of a dead aristocrat turned bog-Irish housemaid. It's not my fault that I'm six different people.

At first, Mundy's daily routine proceeds much as before. All morning he sits or paces in his room at the British Council, engaging in what Amory is pleased to call his cover job, making the odd phone call, signing off the odd policy document and being affable in the canteen where he is regarded as some sort of remittance man. It is required of him by Amory that he present, where challenged, a soured, anti-establishment sort of image and despite his affability he contrives this without too much difficulty: the old rebellious fires may not be exactly raging, but thanks to Mrs Thatcher there are plenty of embers around.

Lunch, always a relief, is a variable affair. If he's lucky, his cover work will require him to be entertained by a fellow cultural diplomat from an Iron Curtain embassy, someone who may be reckoned to wear more than one hat. On such occasions Mundy will adopt an even more seditious attitude on the reasonable assumption that his words will get back to the Professor. Sometimes his host will venture an intelligence pass, which Mundy will politely decline. He can hardly explain that he is already fully engaged on both sides of the ideological abyss.

Afternoons are again a mixed feast. Under the terms of whatever murky deal Amory's Service has thrashed out with Personnel, they are ostensibly given over to outside meetings with artists and their representatives. In reality, they are Amory's to dispose of, but nothing in Mundy's life is neat, and he frequently finds himself with a couple of empty hours on his hands. To fill them he has until now patronised the National Gallery, the Tate, the British Museum and other worthy institutions of self-instruction. In the spirit of his greater liberty, he now transfers his custom to the little strip clubs that pop up and disappear like brightly coloured mushrooms in the fertile pastures of Soho.

His motives are not prurient. It is the church-like atmosphere of sanctuary that draws him, the mute devotion of his fellow worshippers, and the disinterested good nature of the performing priestesses. Seated in the smoky half-darkness he is as sovereign and untouchable as the creatures he observes. Of shame, contrition, guilt or whatever is supposed to afflict him, he feels nothing. I deserve this. Mundy Two would be proud of me. And Doncaster isn't cleared for access.

And come four o'clock or thereabouts – he must first ring a certain number from a phone box– he will make his way by one of several routes to Bedford Square, to a terrace of stately pillared houses variously occupied by publishers, benevolent societies or, in the case of Number Twelve, the Foreign Debenture Ownership Company Limited, which to his knowledge owns nothing but the brass plate mounted in its porch.

And having unobtrusively reconnoitred the square for familiar or suspicious faces – repeated visits to the Edinburgh School of Deportment have made such things second nature to him – he admits himself with his own door key and enters his other home – or not quite, for once inside he must wait in front of a second door until a jolly girl called Laura with freckles and a pony-club smile and her father's signet ring on her right hand admits him to the inner bailey, known to its denizens as the Wool Factory.

Here at last, in Bedford Square, the many disparate fragments of Ted Mundy – actor, novelist, befriender, major's son, misfit, dreamer and pretender – come together to make a single hero.

Here in the Wool Factory he is welcomed with the veneration that is absent from his other lives. Gone the contemplative humility of the strip club. This is Mundy *erectus*.

Here his true feelings are understood, his talents appreciated for what they are.

Does anyone in the great outside know, for instance, that Ted Mundy is a master of the subminiature camera, with a failure rate of less than nine per cent in eight years and literally thousands of exposures? Well, here in the Wool Factory they know.

A deception operation is a complex affair and Mundy is the hub of it, the point man, the racing driver who will pay the price for the loose nut or bit of slack in the steering wheel.

First, in some distant catacomb of secret Whitehall, a huddle of mandarins determines what antiquated State secrets may be compromised without loss, or subtly altered to mislead. To these they will add their wish-list of 'desirable untruths' – fabrications which, if successfully planted, believed and acted on, will cause the enemy to point his guns in the wrong direction.

The Bedford Square creation team, alias the wool-spinners, now get down to work. There are ultra-secret files to be faked, loose minutes, interdepartmental memos between committees whose notional existence is already enough to spark the enemy's paranoia. There are indiscreet conversations to be overheard – in the canteen, the men's room, or the pubs around Trafalgar Square where the plotters like to drown their sorrows of a weekday evening.

But who are these non-existent villains, these artful

wreckers and intriguers of Whitehall's secret overworld? Where do they meet to do their dirty work and when, who are their ringleaders? Which social stratum are they drawn from, what skills do they bring to the table? What are their appetites, rivalries, failings? And how did Mundy Two, this vengeful, unpromoted malcontent who stalks their murky corridors, ever get their documents in his sights?

The team functions under Amory's theoretical stewardship, but it is Mundy who is the star, the driving force, roaming the room with his hand thrust into his hair, tossing out ideas, retracting them, trying on stories like clothes. Because when the lights go down everybody in the house knows – from Laura who opens the door to him, to the forgers and scriptwriters who compose the documents for him to steal, to the technicians in the basement who help him photograph his booty with just the right amount of clumsiness, to the dispatchers who rehearse his lines with him right up to the moment when he boards the bus to London airport – all of them know that Ted is on his own, it's Ted's arse on the line if anything goes wrong, and Ted who will spend the next ten years rotting in some hellish Communist prison.

And Mundy knows it too, and is frightened stiff. It takes all the sterling qualities of Mundy One, patriotic public-school prefect and major's son, not to mention a couple of sharp ones at the departure lounge bar, to get him onto the plane at all. If he is escorting a delegation, he is pathetically grateful for their protection; if not, he burns alone.

But once in the air, all that changes. The fears fall away and a sensation comes over him that is like a kind of grateful peace. Soon Mundy Two is replacing Mundy One. The England he is leaving behind becomes his enemy, and by the time he enters the grim chicanes of whichever East European airport is receiving him, he could almost hug the hard-faced frontier guards, so effectively has he persuaded himself that the pretending is over, he can breathe free air, he is among real friends at last.

And he is. As often as not, these days, Sasha himself will be waiting at the airport, for their relationship is by now well attested. And if Mundy is worried that one of his compatriots may raise an eyebrow at such a close friendship with an East German official, then Sasha or the ponderous Lothar or the intellectual Horst will fix a more discreet reunion, in a hotel or a safe flat rented for the occasion. But this is not to undermine the intense companionship that the two one-man dogs continue to enjoy.

Faithful to Sasha's instructions, later ratified by Amory, Mundy has refused from the day of his recruitment by the Professor to be handled by anybody but Sasha personally. He will not, for example, consort with one of the Professor's many fine operatives attached to the East German Embassy in London. He will not at any price hover outside Harrods after dark, waiting for a car with a certain number plate to slow down so that he can shove a package through the window. He will not bury his microfilm in a flower bed beside the Serpentine, or make chalk-marks on iron railings, or exchange shopping bags with a lady in a green hat standing in the Waitrose fish queue. The very most that this temperamental and demanding Stasi agent will do is hand-deliver his material to Sasha each time he meets him — which is when, and only when, the British Council sees fit to send him to an East European country.

Therefore it is Sasha alone who in the first breathless hours of Mundy's return to the Communist fold takes delivery of his crop of hidden microfilm in whatever concealment device the Professor's people provided last time round – a tin of talcum powder, a tube of toothpaste, a transistor radio. It is Sasha again who questions Mundy about exactly how he brought off some recent spectacular coup. And no trip is ever complete until the two friends have enjoyed a jaunt together just like old times – a walk alone in the forest, a bicycle ride, or a meal in some country hostelry without benefit of minders. And Sasha, like any good case officer pleased with his agent, will not forget on these occasions to provide him with a personal token of his gratitude – nothing that could embarrass him, naturally – but perhaps an antiquarian copy of a German literary classic to add to his growing library back in London, or a piece of Dresden porcelain that he might have picked up at a flea market, or a tin of Russian caviar.

Only rarely, and with unfeigned reluctance, does Sasha consent to parade his ewe-lamb for the Professor's inspection. For instance, at yet another interminable dinner held in the Professor's villa in Potsdam. Addressing Mundy – and Sasha incidentally at his side – the Professor eschews the tawdry details of espionage in favour of a grand vision of world affairs.

'The day will come, Teddy – and you two boys will live to see it, I assure you – when the walls of the capitalist citadel will be toppled from within.' Since the Professor is showing off his English, Sasha has no need to conceal his boredom. 'The consumerist society will consume itself. When your manufacturing declines and your service industries abound, we already see the writing on the wall. And I am not referring to a certain Wall not far from here, either!' Risqué joke. 'Do you not feel, Teddy, in your own country, that while the poor starve and the rich choke on their own greed, the wheels of industry are grinding slowly to a standstill?'

What Mundy says in reply to such banalities is immaterial. What matters is how well he scores in the searching viva-voce examination that follows just when he is feeling most relaxed.

'That was a very interesting report you gave us last month concerning the activities of your clandestine Black Propaganda Committee. We were most taken with the proposal to spread rumours of an outbreak of typhus in Romania in order to coincide with the Conference of the World Federation of Trade Unions.'

'Well, I was pretty pleased with it too,' Mundy confesses. 'Mind you, it's only a draft working paper. If the Foreign Office has anything to do with it, it'll never get off the ground.'

'And how did you obtain it, exactly?'

'Photographed it.'

If they start to question your integrity — which they periodically will — clam up, Amory advised him long ago. *Traitors resent being distrusted. You're no exception.*

'I think we know that, Teddy. What we are not quite clear about is the *circumstances* in which you photographed it.'

'It was lying in Mary Outhwaite's in-tray.'

'Mary Outhwaite who is —'

'Officially, she runs the overseas students' desk. Unofficially, she heads up the Special Intervention Group which acts as the umbrella for the Black Propaganda Committee.'

As you bloody well know, he nearly adds.

'And is Mary in the habit of leaving hand-delivered, top-secret, subscriber-only documents lying in her in-tray for stray members of other departments to come along and photograph?'

'No,' Mundy snaps, bridling at *stray members*.

'Then to what happy circumstance may we owe your triumph?'

'Mary's in love.'

'So?'

'There's a picture of him on the desk.'

'Thank you, the left half of his face is in the shot. He appears a pretty fellow from what we could see of him. Perhaps not over-endowed with intellect.'

Pretty fellow? Who the hell taught him his English? Mundy imagines a queer Shakespearean pedagogue locked away in the Stasi language school.

'He's been cheating on her,' he replies. 'I walked into her room and found her sitting at her desk crying her eyes out.'

'Under what pretext did you walk into her room?'

'It wasn't a *pretext*,' Mundy retorts waspishly. 'She'd been asking my opinion on whether a modern historian I'd escorted to Budapest would be a suitable person to sit on one of her advisory committees. When I found her weeping, I started to walk out of the room but she called me back. She needed to talk to someone. She flung her arms round me and sobbed. When she'd calmed down she looked a mess and needed to clean up. She's a senior officer so her office has its own anteroom and lavatory and I insisted on waiting for her till she came back in case she broke down again.'

'How very gallant of you.'

'I was lucky.'

The Professor is already grinning broadly. 'And as Napoleon would say, since you are lucky you are a good officer.'

And to prove his point he produces a little box, and from the box a garish medal appointing Mundy a Hero of the Democratic Struggle Class II, which happens to be roughly the equivalent, in the hero ratings, of a medal conferred on him not six weeks earlier at a private ceremony in Bedford Square conducted by no less a dignitary than Amory's chief, known otherwise to Mundy as the Parson, and – for all Mundy knows – of yet another medal, conferred a generation earlier on a certain gallant British major for emptying twenty saddles.

And this is not the only interrogation Mundy must withstand by any means, either at the hands of the Professor and his minions, or of one Orville J. Rourke – which, if it isn't a made-up name, ought to be.

Rourke is an American, and people don't call him Orville, they call him Jay. He descends on Bedford Square in a cloud of mystery, purportedly on attachment from the Central Intelligence Agency in Langley, Virginia.

'Then he can bloody well go back there,' Mundy flares, when Amory breaks the news to him that Rourke is henceforth added to the team.

'Want to explain why?'

Mundy searches for a reason for his indignation. He is only recently returned from a harrowing tryst in Kiev, and there is a lot of Mundy Two left in him.

'What am I supposed to tell Sasha?' he demands.

'Nothing. There are things we don't tell you, for your own health as well as ours. This is something you don't tell Sasha. He can never have supposed his stuff wasn't being passed to the Americans, but there's no need to shove it in his face.'

'What job's Rourke supposed to be doing?'

'Liaison. Research. Cost-effectiveness. What do I know? Mind your own business.'

And of course Rourke fails to live up to Mundy's sulky expectation of a bullet-faced, short-back-and-sides CIA automaton. He is spare, civilised, travelled and good-looking, a black-haired Celt with a widow's peak. He is patrician, in a lazy sort of way, with a droll brand of curiosity that invites you in: 'Oh my God, you think *that*?' he will murmur in his Boston Irish drawl. 'Well, you're a scream, I will say. Why don't you tell me all about it?' When he discovers that one of the team is half French, he talks good French with her. His German turns out to be equally efficient. His face is wide and decent, his gait a little sloppy, a little tentative, which adds to his generally pleasing manner. He has his suits made in Dublin and wears Harvard shoes with no toecaps and heavy-welted soles. He's quaintly fastidious about where he puts his large feet. To Mundy's horror, he served with the Agency in Vietnam, a crime to which he cheerfully confesses at their first encounter in Amory's office.

'Well, I opposed that war and I still do,' Mundy declares pompously.

'Oh but you're so *right*, Ted,' Rourke assures him, with a disarming smile. 'It was all just so much worse than you peaceniks ever knew about. We killed everybody we could think of, then denied the shit out of it. We did stuff so bad it makes me puke. Where does it *end*, for Christ's sake? Nobody told us. There was no stop-sign, so we went right off the reservation.'

Against such frankness, there is no protection: least of all, for a man who is living a lonely lie in London and has a weekend wife and son in Doncaster.

'Rourke wants me to go to dinner with him,' he informs Amory, half expecting an objection. The invitation is unprecedented. Team protocol and the interests of security dictate that Amory alone has dining rights over his agent.

'Then go.'

'What does that mean?'

'He wants you to go. You want to go. He's read your file. He's probably read all our files. There's nothing he can get out of you that he doesn't know. Bubble your heart out, if that's what you need to do.'

Jealousy? Indifference? Mundy has no idea.

The house is in Eaton Place, a pretty mews mansion on three floors. He has no time to ring the bell before a butler in a black suit opens the door to him. In a long, brand-new, Georgian-style drawing room that is instant home to Colonial America, Rourke is stooped gracefully over a brass drinks trolley. Advancing towards him, Mundy nearly trips over the deep pile of the carpet. In one corner, a rocking chair with an embroidered cushion. On the walls, pictures of the Way West and Andrew Wyeth reproductions. In a glass corner-cupboard, a collection of New England scrimshaw.

'Dry Martini okay for you?' Rourke enquires, without raising his head.

'Martini's fine.'

'Want to take a look at that map over there? Seems we're kind of neighbours.'

A *Times Atlas* lies on a reproduction music stand. It is open at Ireland.

'Go southwest. See the little red arrow there?'

'Got it.'

'That's where your late mother Nellie O'Connor first opened her fair eyes on the mountains of Mullaghareirk. Go south a tad. Cross the River Blackwater. Sixteen miles as the crow flies if Irish crows fly straight, which I beg leave to doubt. The white arrow. Got it?'

Mundy has.

'That's where my own illustrious father was born. Orville Senior. In the shadow of the mountains of Boggeragh, he played his first game of poker at the age of seven. Your good health.' Rourke hands him his Martini and Mundy does his best to fend off the feelings of instant kinship he knows he's being told to have. But he has them all the same. A friendship, if a cautious one, is born.

Rourke, like Mundy, has time. In the afternoon when Mundy is free, so is Rourke. On evenings when Mundy would otherwise take himself to the cinema or hang around the pubs of Hampstead, Rourke, a grass bachelor with a lawyer wife in Washington and a daughter at Yale, is also at a loose end. Rourke, like Mundy, loves to walk. Sitting indoors on a fine day, he swears, is an offence against the soul. Mundy's view entirely. Rourke loves London, even if he has a couple of Irish relations who would happily blow the place to kingdom come. Mundy has some too, though he has never met them, but he assumes their intentions are similar. The butler who opens the door in Eaton Place doubles as a chauffeur. His name is Milton. With Milton to ferry them, they pound the parks and the docks, and the byways of the City. They pay homage to Karl Marx in Highgate Cemetery, and to his dead comrades who had themselves shipped halfway across the globe to lie beside him. Mundy says the Professor would be so proud. So would Dr Mandelbaum – but he doesn't say that.

They talk about pretty well everything under the sun, but

their recurrent theme is Ted Mundy's life and loves from Murree to Bedford Square. It's been a long time since Mundy confessed himself to a stranger, if he ever did. But Amory's advice was clear enough and he needs no second telling. And Rourke is a good listener, never judgmental. His air of looking back on life is catching. They walk side by side. Without eye contact, frankness comes more easily. Even Mundy's marriage is not exempt, though he blames himself at every turn, flails himself for all manner of real and imagined failings. The name Sasha is never mentioned. He is 'our Welsh friend'. Berlin is 'Cardiff'. East Germany, 'East Wales'. A casual eavesdropper would wander away, uninterested. They are both old hands.

When Rourke is physically exerting himself, the pitch of his voice turns squeaky and endearing. His Harvard shoes hit the pavement with jolly slaps. Mundy finds himself keeping step with him. Rourke flings his arms around a lot. So does Mundy. To see the lanky pair striding across Regent's Park gesticulating at each other, you would suppose they were slightly eccentric brothers, resolving the problems of the world.

Their dinners at Eaton Place have a different, but equally infectious sort of intimacy. The routine never varies. My house is swept weekly, Rourke assures Mundy, and I'm not talking about the cleaning lady. After a couple of Martinis — Rourke calls them *belts* — they get down to the nitty-gritty of the Sasha–Mundy operation. Come on, Ted, I need it all. This time there's no messing around with circumlocutions. Rourke will have selected a recent coup, some nugget Sasha has procured. The content hardly matters since Rourke's interest is purely technical. Call it the GDR's relations with China, no big deal, but all grist to the intelligence mill.

'I'm a nuts and bolts man, Ted. Let's just follow the yellow-brick road through the system, if you don't mind. Let's hear Sasha's story about how he got his hands on it.'

He means: let's track this same little piece of film about the GDR's relations with China from Stasi headquarters to Bedford Square. Tell me what concealment device Sasha used and where he got it from. Does he *really* have that kind of access to Stasi operational stores? Can he *really* just march in, sneak a doctored bar of Yardley's soap and finagle a roll of undeveloped microfilm into it without somebody yelling 'Hey!'? And then let's do the moment when he hands that same roll of film to his friend Teddy.

And finally, Ted, let's do the bit when you palm the film to Amory's man on the spot. Or – since there have also been times when a covert handover to the local representative was reckoned more risky than having Ted smuggle the product out of Badland himself – let's have what happened when you hit the frontier.

And Mundy beats his brains to provide Rourke with every last detail. Perhaps it's just vanity, but he has a feeling he may be handing down his knowledge for posterity. This isn't the Professor trying to fault him. This is about young fellows new to the game who will one day turn up the Sasha–Mundy case history, by then released for general reading, and marvel at its brilliance, its simple beauty. And Rourke is not the Professor. Rourke can monitor both flow and contraflow, whereas the Professor – pray God – can only monitor the contraflow.

'Ted.'

It has been one of those dinners. They are at the Calvados stage. Calvados is Rourke's favourite tipple. One of his many fights with the Agency bean-counters over the years was when he put down five hundred bucks for a bottle of eighty-year-old. It was for a joe, for Christ's sake! What was he supposed to give the poor bastard? Perrier water?

'You did the right thing,' Mundy pronounces, from the depths of his balloon glass.

'Ted, when you were in Taos, searching for your soul, do you recall coming across an artist friend of mine called Luger? Bernie Luger? Big canvases, mixed media, visions of the apocalypse, played guitar?'

Luger? Bernie? Of course Mundy bloody does! And not with a lot of pride, if he is honest, given his afternoons in bed with Nita while Bernie is up his ladder, napalming Minnesota. But he recovers himself. He doesn't yell out or blush. He's a spy, Edinburgh-trained, he can dissemble.

'Bernie Luger, coke-head and Yale drop-out,' he muses lightly through his Calvados. 'Forsook dictatorship of the bourgeoisie in favour of half a million a year from the family trust fund. How could I forget?'

'Ever go to one of his parties?'

'You bet I did. *And* lived to tell the tale.'

'Was Bernie political in Taos?'

'When he remembered to be. When he wasn't too high or too low.'

'Way out there, still? Wild? *Communist?*'

'Well, not *real* Communist, not as such. More contrary than Communist, I'd say. If you were for it, Bernie was agin it.' And he puts his hand to his mouth because he has a momentary feeling he may be letting Bernie down.

'You ever meet his girl? Cuban girl?'

'Nita? Sure.' So it's Nita, he thinks.

'She Communist too?'

'I assume so. But only with a small "c",' he adds.

'Love Castro?'

'Probably. She loved most chaps.'

'Did Bernie or Nita ever try to get you to *do* anything for them? Like meet somebody they knew, hand them a letter, talk to someone when you got home to England? Why are you laughing?'

'I wondered for a minute whether you were going to ask me if I'd packed my own suitcase.'

So Rourke laughs too, good rich laughter while he refreshes their glasses.

'So no, right? You did them no favours? No little errands. I'm relieved.'

There is no way out. He has to ask 'Why? What have they done?'

'Oh, they haven't *done* it yet. But they will. Thirty years apiece for spying for the Sovs. No kids, thank God. It's always hardest on the kids.'

Mundy watches Rourke smile into his balloon glass while he cradles it in his palm. But in his mind's eye it is Nita he sees, stretched beside him in the *hacienda*, and bearded little Bernie leaning wild-eyed across her, boasting that he is riding on the revolutionary train.

'But Bernie's a fantasist,' he manages to protest. 'He'd say anything that came into his head, just for effect. What could they possibly know that would be useful to the Russians? You'd have to be a fool to believe anything Bernie told you.'

'Oh, they never got to the Russians, we made sure of that. Bernie called up the Sov consulate in Miami, gave a funny name, said he was pro-Cuban and would like to serve the Cause. Sovs didn't take him up on his offer. We did. Sweetest little sting I ever saw. Ran for six long months before it dawned on Bernie that he was working for Uncle Sam and not the Sovs.'

'Where does Nita come in?'

Rourke shakes his head in happy reminiscence. 'Carried for him. Smarter than he was by a mile. Women usually are.'

He rolls genially on.

'Ted.'

'Jay.'

'Can I ask you this one more question before you tear me limb from limb? A really *bad* one.'

'If you must.'

'You're public school, right?'

'Not my choice actually.'

'A lost boy.'

'In those days. Probably.'

'Parentless.'

'Well, not always.'

'But by the time you got to Berlin.'

'Yes.'

'So we have one Brit, one Kraut, both parentless, even if Sasha wants to be but isn't. Both lost boys, both – I don't know – *mouvementé*, kinetic, thirsting for life. You mentioned Isherwood. I liked that. Can I go on?'

'Can I stop you?' He already wishes he could.

'And you *bond*. You're creating a perfect society together. You share your dreams. You share a radical lifestyle. You share a room. You share a girl – okay, okay, calm down, you share her consecutively, *not* concurrently. There's a difference, I respect that. But Ted, hand on Bible, no taboos, no microphones, man-to-man within these four well-swept walls – are you *really* telling me you and Sasha never shared each *other*?'

'Didn't happen,' Mundy barks, blushing. 'Didn't anywhere *near* happen. Never on the cards. That answer your question?' And puts his hand to his mouth again to cover his embarrassment.

'Good session with Jay last night?' Amory asks next afternoon.

'Fine. Great.'

'Did he call you a scream?'

'Once.'

'Bubbled yourself dry yet?'

'Probably. He wants to take me to Glyndebourne next week. I thought I should clear it with you.'

'Ever been?'

'No.'

'Well, now's your chance then, isn't it?'

But Glyndebourne never comes. A few days later – following a trying weekend in Doncaster devoted to persuading Jake's headmaster to give him another chance while Kate conducts her parliamentary candidate's clinic – Mundy arrives at Bedford Square to find Rourke's desk gone, his room empty and the door wide open as if to air it. A burning joss-stick in a milk bottle stands in the centre of the bare floor.

For a month and more Amory refuses to remark on Rourke's disappearance. In itself this has no significance. Other members of the team have disappeared from time to time with as little explanation. But Rourke's different. Rourke, detached, urbane, easy to talk to and cleared for access, is the closest thing Mundy has had in recent years to a confidant, apart from Amory himself.

'He's done his job and gone home. That's all you need to know.'

'So what *was* his job?' Mundy insists, refusing to back down. 'Why couldn't he at least say goodbye?'

'You've passed,' Amory replies tersely. 'Be thankful and shut up.'

'I've *what*?'

'On the advice of Orville J. Rourke, the CIA has of its goodness decreed that you are a loyal British agent, a double but not a triple, and that Sasha, though German and mad, is another.' Then most unusually his anger gets the better of him. 'And for Christ's sake stop looking as if somebody's stolen your fluffy dog. It was a legitimate concern. He did a good job. You're Persil white.'

Then why the joss? Mundy wonders.

Is there room, among all these Mundys, for another? The answer, unfortunately, is that since the door to his life is wide open, everyone is invited in and no one who has made himself at home there is ever turned away.

Enter then Ted Mundy, hero of the Helmstedt autobahn and the Steel Coffin. He is so scared of what these versions of himself get up to that it's like opening the bowling for the public schools at Lord's every time, multiplied by about a hundred.

The logic is simple enough. Sometimes there just aren't enough East European arts festivals and book fairs and academic seminars to keep up with Sasha's rate of productivity. Sometimes Sasha has an important scoop in his sights, and the Communist culture circuit can't deliver soon enough to satisfy Amory's customers in London. Sometimes the prudent side of Amory decides that the frequency of Mundy's Eastern jaunts is making things a little bit too easy for the Professor, and that it's time for Mundy to go sick, throw a tantrum at having to live out of a suitcase, or be lent to some other, harmless section pending a reshuffle among the Black Propaganda espiocrats.

But Sasha will accept no substitutes. He wants Mundy and nobody but Mundy, if only for as long as it takes to pass a matchbox from hand to hand. Sasha is a one-man dog but, unlike Mundy, a real one. So every few months an altogether different kind of meeting must be achieved between the players. The instructions are Sasha's, conveyed by way of the most recent batch of microfilm, and executed with due professionalism by Amory and his team.

It is thus that Mundy finds himself at dead of night, wearing night-vision glasses and wading over a boggy strip of borderland that for a few hours has been left unguarded for the convenience of some unknown Stasi agent from West Germany who requires a moment with his controller – only for Sasha to get wind of the arrangement, and exploit it for his own purposes.

Or Mundy is a humble soldier for a day, his father's son at last, wrapped in a Tommy's greatcoat and riding in the back of a fifteen-hundredweight truck that is part of a convoy of British troops making its way up the corridor from Helmstedt to the Berlin garrison. The convoy slows down, its tail crawls, a dispatcher slaps Mundy on the shoulder. Masked by trucks behind and in front of him, he tears off his greatcoat and, dressed as an East German labourer, leaps from the moving truck and in the best Edinburgh tradition hits the ground running. A bicycle is flung after him, he rides hell for leather down an unmade track until a pin light winks at him from a cattle shed. The two men embrace, Sasha hands over his package. Leaving the bicycle to look after itself, Mundy returns by hidden paths to wait in a ditch for the truck, car or lorry that, with false papers and a recently vacated seat, will smuggle him to safety.

But worst by far is the Steel Coffin, his Room 101, his ultimate nightmare come true. Like the Major in his final days, Mundy has a living horror of enclosure. Perhaps his fear is commensurate with the length of him that has to be enclosed. To climb into the coffin, lie face down with his mouth over the airholes while Amory's dispatchers screw him in, takes more courage than he thought he possessed. Staring wide-eyed into the pitch darkness as he is clamped underneath the railway truck, he commends his sinner's soul to Heaven, and reminds himself of Dr Mandelbaum's advice not to live in a bubble. And though there's an abort button, and it's only a few sweltering, bone-breaking minutes across the border to the marshalling yard where Sasha will be waiting with a monkey-wrench to receive him, he can't help feeling there are better ways to spend a summer's evening in the prime of his confusing life.

10

A mood of muted festivity informs Mundy's forty-ninth mission behind the Iron Curtain, and all Bedford Square shares it.

'One more trip, Ted, and you'll have notched up the half-ton,' says Paul the head dispatcher, as he makes a last check of Mundy's pockets, suitcase, wallet and diary for the nightmare clue that could spell the end of ten years of alpha double plus material. 'And after that, you won't want to know us, will you?'

At the door, the girls give him a kiss and Amory, as usual, tells him to watch his arse.

It's a beautiful day, six in the morning. Spring is in the air and so is Gorbachev's perestroika. The marionette dictatorships of Eastern Europe are under serious threat at last. A few months earlier in New York, Gorbachev unilaterally volunteered massive tank and troop withdrawals, and repudiated the Brezhnev doctrine of intervention in the affairs of client States. The old oligarchs, he was telling them, are on their own. Though on the surface relations between Washington and the Evil Empire remain as frozen as ever, the stirrings beneath the ice are enough to persuade the wishful that one day, maybe not in our generation but the next, sanity will break through. And Mundy, as he sets course for Victoria station air terminal on his way to the International Convention of Mediaeval Archaeologists in Gdansk, is one of the wishful. Maybe Sasha and I have played a part, he thinks. Maybe we've helped the thaw. Amory says they have, but then he would.

True, Mundy has the usual pre-departure butterflies – when didn't he? Amory and the sages of Edinburgh will never let him forget that the longer an operation runs, the hairier it gets and the more there is to lose. But as soon as he starts to compare his lot with Sasha's – which he does every time he embarks on one of these journeys, and on this day particularly – he sees himself as the spoiled dilettante and Sasha as the real thing.

Who briefs Sasha? he argues. Nobody does. Who grooms him, dispatches him? Nobody. Who dresses the shot for him when he steals his photographs? Nobody. The finger-shadows and the camera-shake and the misfires happen in the heat of battle while he waits for the footfall in the corridor that could lead straight to a bullet in the back of the head.

And look at the sheer distance the man's covered, the miles and miles of impossible achievement! How in Heaven's name did he ever get from there to here? How does a lame East German child-refugee-turned-West-German-anarchist recross the border and emerge as the improbable provider of information vital to the national security – theirs as well as ours – all in the space of a few years?

All right, thanks to the Herr Pastor, the Professor adopted him as his favourite son, and for love of his old chum gave him a head start in the family business. But that doesn't include a free pass to roam the Stasi's archives at will, cherry-picking whatever he reckons will do most damage to his employers.

Mundy's British delegation of mediaevalists is travelling independently to Gdansk. Tomorrow he will field them as they land. Sipping his Bloody Mary in the departure lounge, or seated in the half-empty plane and staring out of the window at a white nothing, he pieces together as much as he knows of the pilgrim Sasha's progress over the last decade. The picture is far from complete. Sasha does not take gracefully to being questioned about how he obtains his information. Perhaps his prickliness conceals a certain shame.

In the beginning was the anger. That much Sasha admits.

And the source of Sasha's anger was the revelation that he had been lured across the border under false pretences and had been hating his father for the wrong reasons.

And after the anger, hatred.

Hatred of the malodorous and heartless bureaucracy that by its size and weight squeezed the very breath out of its citizenry in the name of democracy.

Of the police state that posed as the cradle of liberty. Of its craven subservience to Moscow.

Above all, of its systematic, wholesale betrayal of the sacred socialist dream.

And with the anger and the hatred came the cunning. Sasha was a prisoner in a bourgeois fascist state posing as a workers' paradise. To prevail against his captors he would use their own perfidious weapons. He would dissemble, lie and ingratiate himself. To strike at the very source of their unlawful power, he would steal what they loved most: their secrets.

His plan at the outset was modest.

He would bear witness.

He would steal their secrets and make of them an archive for posterity.

Working entirely alone, he would make sure that the lies, deceptions and hypocrisies that were being perpetrated all round him by the Nazis in red shirts could not be hidden from later generations.

And that was all. The sole beneficiaries of his endeavours would be future German historians. That was the limit of his ambition.

The only question was how to achieve it. For enlightenment he availed himself of the Stasi library and consulted the leading authorities on guerilla warfare. *To float on the enemy's current . . . to conceal yourself among his hordes . . . to use the enemy's weight to bring him down.*

Following his incarceration in the White Hotel, Sasha passed weeks of unlikely recuperation lounging around the Professor's house in Potsdam, walking the Professor's Alsatian dogs in the People's Park, weeding the Professor's flower beds, chauffeuring his wife when she went shopping. For yes, the Professor who was not after all homosexual possessed a wife, a veritable dragon of a wife, whose single merit in Sasha's eyes was that she detested her husband.

But not even she can restrain the Professor from exercising his self-appointed rôle of Sasha's patron, power-broker and protector. If Sasha promised to behave himself like a true comrade — the Professor's words — and guarded his tongue, and was respectful at all times to other highly placed protectors of the State, the Professor would undertake to guide his footsteps to the light. For the Professor — it is a point he is never tired of repeating — loved Sasha's father like a brother, and possessed no son of his own.

And Sasha gritted his teeth and promised. He behaved himself. He took other wives shopping as well as the Professor's. He carried their shopping up to their apartments for them, and sometimes all the way into the bedroom. Sasha never boasted about his conquests. Discretion was his watchword. But like a bartered bride, he put a metaphorical handkerchief in his mouth, and did not cry out in his repugnance. In the People's Paradise, compliant silence was everything.

'Did you get any fun out of it, or was it all strictly business?' Mundy enquires, as the two of them stroll in one of Leningrad's parks.

Sasha rounds on him in fury. 'Go down to the Smolny docks, please, Teddy,' he snaps, flinging an arm towards the bleak grey outlines of ships and cranes. 'Pick up a ten-rouble whore, and ask her whether it's fun or strictly business.'

Under the Professor's auspices, Sasha the favoured son acquired a tiny one-room apartment all his own, and was admitted to the lowest rungs of the Stasi's ladder of beings. By the time of his initiation he had mastered, as best his crabby body allowed, the official Party walk. With it went the official Party expression — a non-look, delivered with the chin raised, to the pavement fifteen yards ahead of him. He wore it as he wheeled the coffee trolley down the disinfected corridors of the Professor's linoleum empire, and set china cups on the desks of State protectors too elevated to acknowledge his existence.

And just occasionally, when Sasha held open the door of a limousine for a great protector, or delivered a package to a comrade's sumptuous villa, a hand would grasp his arm confidingly and a voice would murmur, 'Welcome home, Sasha. Your father was a great man.'

Such words were balm to his ears. They told him he was one of them, and refuelled the fires of his secret anger.

Did Sasha ever *advance* inside the Stasi? Mundy used to wonder. And if he did, to what rank, office, and when?

It is a question that after all these years Sasha still brushes irritably aside. And when London's analysts from time to time dig out their Stasi orders of battle in search of him, his name does not feature among the distinguished section heads, nor even in the lowest categories of archivist or clerk.

'Promotion, Teddy, I would say, is in inverse proportion to knowledge,' he pontificates. 'The butler knows more than the lord of the manor. The lord of the manor knows more than the Queen. I know more than all of them.'

Sasha does not advance, he entrenches, which in a spy is probably a better way to go. Since his aim is not power but knowledge, he devotes himself to the systematic acquisition of menial responsibilities, keys, combination numbers and protectors' wives. Put together, they make a traitor's kingdom. What Mundy Two pretends to do in the virtual world, Sasha does in the real one.

A secure storeroom is to be established for files that are out of action but not yet officially dead? *But of course, Comrade Counsellor, yours to command, Comrade Counsellor, three bags full, Comrade Counsellor!*

An immediate destruction programme is to be implemented for certain sensitive material that should have been got rid of months ago? *No problem, Comrade Counsellor! Sasha will give up his free weekend so that State protectors burdened with heavier responsibilities than his own may take their well-deserved ease.*

The Frau Oberst is expecting an important visitor from Moscow and has nobody to mow her lawn for her? *The Frau Oberst's grass need not wait another minute. Sasha is standing brushed and shiny on her doorstep with a mower and an able-bodied serf!*

Yet how can all this take place, Mundy asks himself repeatedly over the years, in such an immense, all-powerful and vigilant State Security system as the Stasi? Is not the Stasi a model of legendary Prussian efficiency, of the sort that accounts for every ball-bearing, stub of pencil and gold tooth?

Under London's promptings, the long-suffering Mundy has put the question to Sasha in a dozen different ways, and always received the same answer: in a mammoth bureaucracy obsessed with its own secrecy, the fault lines are best observed by those who, instead of peering down from the top, stand at the bottom and look up.

Sasha's entrenchment quickly yielded unexpected prizes. One of the earliest was an old safe, locked and apparently disused, that stood inside the antechamber to the office of the Professor's prodigiously overweight female first assistant, a Sasha conquest. Its only perceptible function was to act as a table for a vase of wax flowers with which she brightened her drab surroundings. She said the safe had long been empty and, when Sasha accidentally on purpose banged his coffee trolley into it, it rang reassuringly hollow. Undertaking a discreet search of the sump of her enormous handbag one night, he came upon an orphan key with a label on it. The safe became his treasure chest, the deniable storehouse for his expanding crock of gold.

In the absence of a fellow underling on holiday, Sasha was given custody of a box room full of obsolete operational equipment awaiting shipment to a Third World ally in the common struggle against the imperialist enemy. By the time the colleague returned, Sasha was the unofficial owner of a subminiature camera, a user's handbook and two family-size cartons of subminiature film cartridges. Henceforth, instead of attempting to smuggle his stolen documents out of the building, Sasha could photograph them and then destroy them or, if needful, return them to their rightful homes. Smuggling out subminiature film cartridges presented no problem unless he was intimately searched. By tacit edict, the Professor's chosen son is not subjected to this indignity.

'Any qualms I had about the life expectation of my undeveloped films were put to rest by the handbook,' Sasha recalls drily. 'First I should seal the cartridges in a condom, then I should bury the condom in a tub of ice cream. Comrades operating in conditions where no refrigerators, ice cream, electricity or condoms are available should presumably consult a different handbook.'

For his memoranda of conversations overheard, he availed himself of the same technique.

'I committed my thoughts to paper in the comfort of my apartment. I photographed the paper with my thirty-five-millimetre domestic camera. I then burned the paper and added the undeveloped film to my collection.'

Then came a golden Friday evening when Sasha was going about his weekly chore of logging visa applications from citizens of non-socialist countries who wished to enter the GDR on official business. Staring up at him were the unmistakable features of Mundy, Edward Arthur, born Lahore, Pakistan, husband of Kate née Andrews, occupation British Council travelling representative. And attached to it, the information thrown up by Stasi Central Records:

1968–69: member Oxford University Socialist Club and Society of Cultural Relations with the USSR, peace activist, various marches . . . while a student of the Free University of Berlin (West) engaged in anti-capitalist, pro-peace demonstrations . . . suffered severe beating at hands of West Berlin police . . . later deported from West Berlin for riotous and anarchistic tendencies (West Berlin police report, source CESAR).

Sasha's breathless account of what he did next will resound in Mundy's memory for evermore. They are crouched in a bar in Dresden during a conference of international agrarians.

'At the sight of your not very beautiful face, Teddy, I experienced a revelation comparable to that of Archimedes. My undeveloped films need not after all spend a thousand years frozen into condoms. On the Monday morning when I took your visa application to the Professor, my hand was shaking. The Professor observed this. How could he not? It had been shaking all weekend. "Sasha," he asked me. "Why is your hand shaking?"

'"Comrade Professor," I replied. "On Friday evening Providence delivered me the opportunity I have been dreaming of. With your wise help I believe I am at last able to repay the trust you have invested in me, and assume an active rôle in the struggle against those who wish to frustrate the advance of socialism. I beg you, comrade: please, as my patron, as the lifelong counsellor and friend of my heroic father, grant me this chance to prove that I am worthy of him. The Englishman Mundy is an incurable bourgeois but he cares for the human condition and makes radical if incorrect perceptions, as his record shows. If you allow me to develop him aggressively under your incomparable guidance, I swear you will not be disappointed."'

'And you didn't mind?' Mundy asks diffidently.

'Mind what?' — Sasha, combative as ever.

'Well — that I was going to be passing your information to the hated capitalists of the West?'

'You are being ridiculous, Teddy. We must fight all evil where we find it. One evil does not justify another, or negate another. As I told you already, if I could also spy on America, I would happily do so.'

The stewardess is telling Mundy to fasten his seat belt. The plane is about to land at Gdansk for his forty-ninth meeting with his secret sharer.

Ted Mundy is these days a seasoned conference animal. Drop him blindfold into any people-packed marquee or congress hall on the East European circuit, give him a few seconds to sniff the tobacco fumes and deodorant and listen to the babble, and he could tell you to the hour which day it was in the five-day rhythm, who of the usual tribe of cultural minders and officials from which countries had shown up, and whether a joint closing statement was likely to paper over the cracks, or were we going to be looking at another bunch of dissenting minority reports and snide speeches at the farewell dinner?

An important variable is the state of hostilities in the Cold War. If the political atmosphere is tense, delegates will be hunting anxiously for common ground. If relaxed: cathartic verbal mud-slinging is likely to break out, resolving itself in frenzied sexual couplings between adversaries who an hour earlier were threatening to tear each other to pieces.

But tonight, the third of the Gdansk Mediaeval Archaeologists' get-togethers, the atmosphere is unlike any he has ever known: rascally, joyous, rebellious and end of term. The conference hotel is a many-gabled Edwardian pile set among sand dunes on the Baltic shore. On the front steps, under the eyes of powerless policemen, students are pressing samizdats on arriving delegates. The bar is a glass conservatory that runs along the seaward side. If Mundy looks between the talking heads, he can see the sea's black horizon and the lights of distant ships. The mediaevalists to his surprise have turned out to be a sparky lot. Their Polish hosts are delirious with their own irreverence, and the glorious names of Lech Walesa and Solidarity are on every tongue. A black-and-white television set and several radios provide competing news flashes. Chants of *Gorby! Gorby! Gorby!* break out periodically round the room.

'If Gorbachev is meaning what he is saying,' a young professor from Lodz is yelling in English to his counterpart from Sofia, 'where will such reforms end, please? Who will restore devils back to box of Pandora? Where please will be one-party State, if right of choice will be officially exercised?'

And if the wild talk of the delegates tells one side of the story, the apprehensive faces of their minders tell the other. With heresies like these springing up all round them, should they side with the heretics or denounce them to their superiors? They will of course do both.

Mundy has so far seen little of Sasha. An embrace, a couple of waves, a promise to grab a drink together. After the ecstatic reunions of the early years, good sense has dictated that they scale down their demonstrations of mutual affection. Neither the intellectual Horst nor the gruesome Lothar is in attendance. They were replaced six months ago by the spectral and unsmiling Manfred. Tomorrow, the last full day, pretty Wendy from our embassy in Warsaw will pop up to press the flesh of the British contingent – not forgetting, of course, the flesh of Ted Mundy, the Council's evergreen representative. But it's a press, nothing more. Mundy has an eye for Wendy and Wendy has an eye for him. But between them stands the iron prohibition of the Edinburgh School of Deportment: no sex in the workplace. Nick Amory, to whom Mundy has rashly confessed his interest, puts it less delicately.

'There are plenty of good ways to commit hara-kiri in your job, Edward, but getting your rocks off in Badland is undoubtedly the best. Wendy is a part-timer,' he adds, by way of further warning. 'She's married to a diplomat, she has two children, and she spies to pay the mortgage.'

A bunch of mediaevalists has joined together in a rendering of the 'Marseillaise'. An abundant Swedish woman with a deep décolleté is conducting. A drunken Pole is playing the piano beautifully. Sasha, fresh from a round of fringe parties, his eyes radiant beneath his beret, is entering at the far end of the bar, slapping backs, shaking hands, embracing anyone within his limited range. On his heels comes spectral Manfred.

Sasha needs a walk on the sand to clear his head. A warm spring wind is rattling off the sea. Ships' lights are strung the length of the horizon. Peaceful fishing boats, or the Soviet Sixth Fleet? It no longer seems to matter. A full moon lights the dunes in black and white. The deep sand is negotiable, but liable to sudden descents. More than once, Sasha is obliged to grab Mundy's arm to save himself from falling, and he's not always successful. On one occasion, as Mundy hauls him to his feet, he feels something soft fall into his jacket pocket.

'I think you have a bad throat, Teddy,' he hears Sasha say severely. 'Maybe with these excellent Communist lozenges you will sing better.'

In return, Mundy passes Sasha a chrome hip flask made in England and remade in the Professor's workshops, then stuffed with fabrications made in Bedford Square and photographed by Mundy Two. A hundred yards behind them, the gloomy sentinel Manfred stands hands in pockets at the water's edge, staring out to sea.

'The Professor is terrified,' Sasha whispers excitedly below the rattle of the wind. 'Fear! Fear! His eyes are like marbles, never resting!'

'Why? What does he think will happen?'

'Nothing. That is why he is terrified. Since all is illusion and propaganda, what can go wrong? The Professor's Great Director himself returned only yesterday from Moscow with the firmest assurances that nothing whatever is happening. *Now* can you imagine how afraid he is?'

'Well, I only hope he's right,' says Mundy doubtfully, concerned that Sasha's high hopes will once more be dashed. 'Just remember Hungary fifty-six and Czecho sixty-eight and a couple of other times when they put the clock back.' He is quoting Amory who is quoting his masters: *Don't let him grab at straws, Edward. Gorbachev may be changing the window, but he's not selling the store.*

But Sasha will not be discouraged:

'There *must* be two Germanys, Teddy. Two is a minimum. I love Germany so much I wish there were ten. Tell this to your Mr Arnold.'

'I think I told him a few times already.'

'There must be no annexation of the GDR by the Federal Republic. As a first condition of constructive coexistence, the two Germanys must expel their foreign occupiers, the Russians and the Americans.'

'Sasha, listen to me, will you? "Her Majesty's Government believes that German reunification should only take place as part of an overall European settlement." That's the official line, and it's been that way for the last forty years. Unofficially it's stronger: who needs a united Germany? Thatcher doesn't, Mitterrand doesn't, a lot of Germans don't, West as well as East. And America doesn't care.'

Sasha might not have heard him. 'As soon as the occupiers have departed, each Germany will call free and fair elections,' he continues breathlessly. 'A key issue in both will be the creation of an unaligned bloc at the heart of Europe. A federation of the two separate Germanys is only possible if there is total disarmament on both sides. With that achieved, we shall offer alliances to Poland and France on the same terms. After so many wars and divisions, Central Europe will become the crucible of peace.' He stumbles and collects himself. 'No Anschluss by the Federal Republic, Teddy. No Grossdeutschland under the domination of either superpower. Then we can finally drink to Peace.'

Mundy is still searching for a soothing answer when Sasha seizes his arm in both hands and stares imploringly up at him. His words come in gulps. His whole body is shaking. 'No Fourth Reich, Teddy. Not before there is disengagement on both sides. Until then, the two halves stay sovereign and separate. Yes? Say yes!'

Sadly, almost wearily, Mundy shakes his head. 'We're talking about something that isn't happening,' he says, kindly but emphatically. 'The glacier's moving, but it's not melting.'

'Is this the ridiculous Mr Arnold you are quoting again?'

'I'm afraid it is.'

'Give him my greetings and tell him he's an arsehole. Now take me indoors and get me drunk.'

Mundy and Kate have agreed to talk the whole thing through as adults. After eleven years, that's the least they owe each other, says Kate. Mundy will take a day off work and make a special trip to Doncaster, Kate has looked up the trains for him. She will meet him with the car, they'll drive to the Troutstream for lunch, which is out of town and private and, unless Mundy's tastes have changed recently, they both like trout. The last thing either of them needs, she says, is to bump into local press people, or worse still someone from local Party headquarters. Quite why she should be so nervous of being caught in flagrante with her husband is obscure to Mundy, but he takes her word for it.

And when they've had their talk, and agreed guidelines, she says, it would be nice if Ted came back to the house in time to kick a ball about with Jake in the garden, and perhaps Philip will drop by casually for a drink, as he often does, to talk Party policy. And, when Philip sees the game going on, he can join in, says Kate. That way, Jake can see for himself that there's no atmosphere. Things may have changed a little, but we're all good friends together and Jake is our first priority. He will have two happy homes instead of one, which is something that rationally, in the long term, he'll learn to accept. Because the one thing we're all totally agreed about, says Kate, is that there will be no tug-of-war for Jake's affections.

In fact, so much is agreed in advance by the time Mundy boards the train at King's Cross that he can't help wondering whether — with all Eastern Europe on the boil and Sasha needing to report twice as often as Mundy can get to him — his journey is strictly necessary. But to his surprise it is. Mulling it all over on the train, he realises that he agrees without reservation to everything she wants.

Adamantly. Passionately.

Jake's love for his mother is more important to him than any love in the world. He will do anything to preserve it.

And as soon as he climbs into the car, that's what he tells her. As ever a useless negotiator in his own interest, he begs her, beseeches her, to allow him to take the entire blame for the failure of the marriage on his own shoulders. If keeping a low profile for the first few months of the separation will help, he'll keep one. If kicking a ball about in the back garden with the Labour Party's latest apostle of the New Direction is going to convince Jake that his mother has made a sound career choice, Mundy will kick it till he drops. And that isn't altruism. That's survival. His own as much as Jake's. No wonder that even before they sit down to lunch, Mundy feels more post-coital than post-marital.

'We're doing it really well,' Kate assures him over the avocado and crab starter. 'I just wish other people could be so civilised.'

'Me too,' says Mundy heartily.

They talk about Jake's schooling. In Jake's case *only*, Kate is *half* decided to waive her objection to private schools. Jake's turbulent nature is crying out for individual attention. She has discussed this with Philip, of course, and with her constituency, and everyone's agreed that provided it's a special need, and there's no obvious local alternative, and no unfortunate publicity, they can live with it. Mundy detests private schools but assures her that, if Jake really wants it, he'll come up with the fees.

'I'm just so sorry about the Council,' she says, over her trout with almonds and green salad. 'It really upsets me, how little they seem to appreciate you.'

'Oh, don't blame the poor old Council,' Mundy exclaims gallantly. 'They've been good to me in their own way. It's not their fault.'

'If you'd just been able to stand up for yourself.'

'Oh, I know, I know,' says Mundy wearily, in their old spirit of togetherness.

They talk about what Kate refers to as *access*, and which to Mundy has a different connotation, but he quickly readjusts.

'Philip's got a book coming out in the spring,' she tells him over apple crumble and custard.

'Super. Marvellous.'

'Non-fiction, of course.'

'Of course.'

They talk *grounds* – or Kate does. As a prospective parliamentary candidate she obviously can't consider admitting to adultery. If Ted thinks he should go that route, she'll have no option but to drag up mental cruelty and desertion. How about settling for irretrievable breakdown?

Irretrievable breakdown sounds great, says Mundy.

'You have *got* someone, haven't you, Ted?' Kate demands a little sharply. 'I mean, you can't have been sitting in London all these years with *nobody*.'

Pretty much, that's exactly what Mundy has been doing, but he is too polite to admit it. They agree it's wiser not to discuss money. Kate will find herself a lawyer. Ted should do the same.

A lawyer is always an arsehole.

'And I thought we'd wait till after Philip's new job has been confirmed, if it's all right by you,' says Kate over a terminal coffee.

'To get married?' Mundy asks.

'To get divorced.'

Mundy calls for the bill and pays it out of Amory's brown envelope. What with the rain and everything, they agree it's probably not the right evening for football with Philip. On the other hand, Mundy wants to see Jake more than he's ever wanted to see anyone in his life, so he says maybe he'll just come back home and give him a game of draughts or something, then grab a taxi to the station.

They arrive at the house and, while Kate puts on a kettle, Mundy waits in the sitting room feeling like an insurance salesman and peering at the places where he would put flowers if he was still resident, and at the clumsy arrangement of the furniture that wouldn't take five minutes to fix if Jake just gave him a hand. And he reflects that he possesses too many of the domestic concerns that Kate manages perfectly well without, but then Kate grew up with a family whereas Mundy was always trying to invent one. His thoughts are still running in this direction when the front door flies open and Jake marches into the room accompanied by his friend Lorna. Without a word he storms past his father, switches on the television and crashes onto the sofa with Lorna at his side.

'What are you doing back from school so early?' Mundy asks suspiciously.

'Sent,' says Jake defiantly, without turning his head from the screen.

'Why? What have you done?'

'Teacher says we're to watch history in the making,' Lorna explains smugly.

'So we're watching it, anything wrong with that? What's for tea, Mum?' says Jake.

Teacher is right. History is indeed being made. The children watch, Mundy watches. Even Kate, who doesn't regard foreign policy as an election winner, watches from the kitchen doorway. The Berlin Wall is coming down, and hippies from both sides are jumping about on what's left of it. Hippies from the West have long hair, Mundy notices in his numb state. Newly liberated hippies from the East still wear it short.

At midnight Mundy's train delivers him to King's Cross. From a phone box he calls the emergency number. Amory's voice tells him to leave his message *now*. Mundy says he hasn't got one, he's just wondering whether there's anything he should be doing. He means, he's frightened stiff for Sasha, but is too well trained to say so. He gets an answer of sorts when he arrives at Estelle Road, but it was left on the machine six hours ago. 'No squash tomorrow, Edward. Courts are being renovated. Sit tight and take lots of water with it. *Tschüss*.' He switches on the television.

My Berlin.

My Wall.

My crowds vandalising it.

My crowds storming Stasi headquarters.

My friend locked inside, waiting to be mistaken for the enemy.

Thousands of Stasi files being flung into the streets.

Wait till you read mine: Ted Mundy, Stasi secret agent, British traitor.

At 6 a.m. he goes to a phone box in Constantine Road

and again calls the emergency number. Where does it ring? In the Wool Factory? Who's bothering to deceive the Stasi any more? At Amory's home – where's that? He leaves another meaningless message.

Back in Estelle Road, he lies in the bath listening to North German radio. He shaves with enormous concentration, cooks himself a celebratory breakfast but has no appetite for it and leaves the bacon on the doorstep for nextdoor's cat. Desperate for exercise, he sets off for the Heath but ends up in Bedford Square. His front-door key works, but when he presses the bell to the inner bailey, no nice English girl wearing her father's signet ring welcomes him aboard. In an unscripted fit of frustration, he gives the door a violent shake, then hammers on it, which sets off an alarm bell. A blue light is flashing in the porch as he steps outside and the din of the bell is deafening.

From a public telephone in Tottenham Court Road tube station he again calls the emergency number and this time gets Amory live. In the background he hears German shouting and assumes his call has been patched through to Berlin.

'What the fuck do you think you were doing at the Factory?' Amory demands.

'Where is he?' Mundy says.

'Disappeared from our screens. Not at his office, not at his apartment.'

'How d'you know?'

'We've looked, that's how. What do you think we've been doing? We've checked his flat and frightened his neighbours. The consensus is, he saw the way the wind was blowing and got out before he was clubbed down in the street or whatever the hell's going on.'

'Let me look for him.'

'Marvellous. Do that. Bring your guitar and come and sing outside the prisons till he hears your golden voice. We've got your passport in case you've forgotten. Ted?'

'What?'

'We care about him too, all right? So stop making a martyr of yourself.'

It's a full five months before Sasha's letter arrives. How Mundy passed them is afterwards unclear to him. Football afternoons with Jake in Doncaster. Football afternoons with Jake and Philip. Ghastly threesome dinners with Philip and Kate which Jake refuses to attend. Dismal weekends with Jake alone in London. Films Jake needs to see and Mundy loathes. Spring walks on the Heath with Jake trailing two paces behind. Hanging around the British Council as the blessed day of Early Retirement by Mutual Consent draws near.

The same old handwriting. Blue airmail paper. Postmarked Husum, North Germany, and addressed to Estelle Road, NW3. How the hell did he know my address? Of course – I put it in my visa application a thousand years ago. He wonders why Husum is familiar to him. Of course – Theodor Storm, author of *The Rider on the White Horse*. Dr Mandelbaum read it to me.

Dear Teddy,

I have reserved two luxurious suites in your name at the Hotel Dreesen in Bad Godesberg for the night of the 18th. Bring everything you possess in the world, but come alone. I wish neither to say hullo nor goodbye to Mr Arnold, who can go fuck himself. I came to Husum in order to confirm that the Herr Pastor is truly buried. I regret so much that

he is not alive to witness the exalting sight of Our Dear
Führer annexing East Germany by means of God's
Almighty Deutschmark.
Your brother-in-Christ,
Sasha

Sasha has lost weight, though he had little enough to lose. The Western super-spy is folded like a starved child into the corner of a winged chair big enough for three of him.

'It was force of nature,' Mundy insists, wishing he didn't sound so apologetic. 'It was all there, banked up, ready to happen. Once the Wall was down, there was no stopping the process. You can't blame anyone.'

'I blame them, thank you, Teddy. I blame Kohl, Reagan, Thatcher and your duplicitous Mr Arnold who gave me false promises.'

'He gave you nothing of the kind. He told you the truth as he found it.'

'Then in his profession, he should know that the truth as he finds it is always a lie.'

They fall quiet again, but the Rhine is never quiet. Though it is night-time, chains of barges charge ceaselessly past the windows, and by their din they could as well be passing through the room. Mundy and Sasha are sitting in darkness, but the Rhine is never dark. The sodium lamps that line the towpath shine upward onto the oval ceiling. The lights of the pleasure boats flit at will across the pilastered walls. On Mundy's arrival, Sasha led him to the window and gave him the tour: across the river from us, Teddy, you will see the mountain-top hotel where your revered Prime Minister Neville Chamberlain resided while he was giving half of Czechoslovakia to Hitler. In this hotel where we are sitting – I dare think these very rooms – Our Dear Führer and his retinue consented to receive Mr Chamberlain's generous gift. 'How the Führer would have adored to be with us here tonight, Teddy! East Germany annexed, Grossdeutschland reunited, the Red Peril put to rest. And tomorrow the world.'

'I have messages for you from Mr Arnold,' Mundy says. 'Shall I convey them to you?'

'Please do.'

'Within reason, it's whatever you want. Resettlement, a new identity, you've only to say. Apparently you told them at the beginning that you didn't want money. They're not expecting to hold you to that.'

'They are the soul of generosity.'

'They'd like to meet you and talk your future through with you. I've got a passport for you in my pocket and a couple of tickets for tomorrow morning's flight to London. If you don't want to go to them, they'll come to wherever you're prepared to meet them.'

'I am overwhelmed. But why are they so anxious for my welfare when I am a spent force?'

'Maybe they have a sense of honour. Maybe they don't like to think of you wandering round like a zombie after all you've done for them. Or maybe they don't want to read your memoirs.'

Another long silence, another infuriating new direction. Sasha has set down his whisky and picked up a mint chocolate. He is fastidiously peeling the silver paper from it with his fingertips. 'I was in Paris, that much is certain,' he recalls, in the practical tones of someone attempting to reconstruct an accident. 'I have a label from Paris attached to my suitcase.' He selects an edge of chocolate and nibbles at it. 'And in Rome I was undoubtedly a night porter. Now *that's* a profession for retired spies. To watch over the world while it's asleep. To sleep while it goes to the devil.'

'I think we can do better than night porter for you.'

'And from Rome, I must have taken a train to Paris and from Paris to Hamburg, and from Hamburg to Husum where, despite my ragged appearance, I persuaded a taxi driver to take me to the house of the late Herr Pastor. The front door was opened by my mother. She had a cold chicken waiting for me in the refrigerator and a bed warmed for me upstairs. We may therefore deduce that I had telephoned her in the course of my travels and advised her of my intention to visit her.'

'Sounds a reasonable enough thing to have done.'

'I have read that there are primitive tribes who believe that someone must die in order for someone else to be born. My mother's renaissance confirms this theory. She nursed me day and night with considerable skill for four weeks. I was impressed.' An anchor chain shrieks and drowns. A ship's horn laments its passing. 'But what will become of *you*, Teddy? Is Mr Arnold equally open-handed with his countrymen? How about footman to the Queen?'

'They're talking of buying me a partnership in a language school. We're discussing it.'

'Here in Germany?'

'Probably.'

'Teaching German to the Germans? It's high time. One half speaks Amideutsch, the other Stasideutsch. Please begin your work as soon as possible.'

'English actually.'

'Ah, of course. The language of our masters. Very wise. Has your marriage failed?'

'Why should it have done?'

'Because otherwise you would have retreated to the bosom of your family.'

If Sasha is hoping to goad Mundy, he has succeeded.

'So we're bereft,' he snaps. 'Great. Washed up. Two Cold War bums on the skids. Is that who we are, Sasha? Is it? So let's have a bloody good cry about it. Let's go all passive and self-pitying and agree there's no hope for anyone. Is that what we're here to do?'

'It is my mother's wish that I escort her back to Neubrandenburg where she was born. There is an establishment for the elderly with which she has been in correspondence. Mr Arnold will please pay the fees until her death, which cannot be far off.' He takes a card from his pocket and lays it on the table. *The Ursuline Convent of St Julia*, Mundy reads. 'Mr Arnold's money may be tainted, but the Herr Pastor's is untouchable and will be given to the wretched of the earth. I wish you to come with me, Teddy.'

The river traffic is so loud at this moment that Mundy does not immediately catch Sasha's last words. Then he sees that he has sprung to his feet and is standing before him.

'What the hell are you talking about, Sasha?'

'Your luggage is still packed. So is mine. We have only to pay the bill and go. First we take my mother to Neubrandenburg. She's a nice woman. Good manners. You want to share her with me, I won't be jealous. Then we go.'

'Where to?'

'Away from the Fourth Reich. Somewhere there's hope at last.'

'Where would that be?'

'Wherever hope's the only thing they can afford. You think the war's over because a bunch of old Nazis in East Germany have traded Lenin for Coca-Cola? Do you really believe that American capitalism will make the world a sweet safe place? It will pick it dry.'

'So what are you proposing to do about it?'

'Resist it, Teddy. What else is there to do?'

Mundy doesn't answer. Sasha is holding up his suitcase. In the darkness it looks larger than he is, but Mundy doesn't move to help or stop him. He remains seated while he runs through a list of extraneous bits and pieces that all of a sudden are very important to him. Jake wants to go glacier skiing in May. Kate wants Estelle Road back. She's proposing to base in London and commute to her constituency so that Philip can be closer to the seat of power. Maybe I should find a crash course somewhere, get myself a degree in something. Amid all the honking and hooting from the river, he doesn't even hear the door close.

And still Mundy remains there, slumped in his armchair, methodically working his way through a glass of nearly neat Scotch, listening to the clatter of a world he is no longer part of, savouring the emptiness of his existence, wondering what's left of him now that his past has walked out on him, and how much of him is usable, if any of him is, or is it better to write off the whole mess and start again?

Wondering also who he was when he did all that stuff he'll never do again. The deceiving and pretending – in the name of what? The Steel Coffin and the army greatcoat on the autobahn – for whom? Wondering whether what he did was worth a busted marriage and a busted career and a child I daren't look in the eye.

Would you do it all again tomorrow, Daddy, if the bugle sounded? Irrelevant. There isn't a tomorrow. Not one like yesterday.

He refills his glass and drinks to himself. Better to be a salamander and live in the flames. Very funny. So what happens when the fire goes out?

Sasha will come back. He always does. Sasha's the boomerang you can't throw away. A couple more minutes and he'll be banging on the door, telling me I'm an arsehole and kindly pour him another Scotch, and I'll pour myself another while I'm about it.

And Mundy does just that, not bothering to add water.

And when we've had a belt or two, as dear old Jay Rourke would say, we'll get down to the real business of celebrating our achievement: Cold War's over, Communism's dead, and we were the boys who made it happen. There'll be no more spies ever, and all the frightened people in the world can sleep peacefully in their beds at night because Sasha and Teddy made the world safe for them at last, so cheers, old boy, well done both of us and here's to the salamander, and Mrs Salamander, and all the little salamanders to come.

And in the morning we'll wake up with a God-awful hangover and think: what the fuck's all this singing and rejoicing and clapping and honking, up and down the river bank? And we'll throw open those double windows and step onto the balcony and the cruise boats and barges will be covered in flags and sounding their sirens at us and the crowds will be waving and yelling, 'Oh *thank* you, Sasha! *Thank* you, Teddy! That's the first good sleep we've had since Our Dear Führer went to his reward and we owe it all to you two boys. Three cheers for Teddy and Sasha. Hip hip!'

And cheers to you too.

Mundy stands up a little too quickly for his head, but makes it to the door and hauls it open, but the corridor is empty. He goes to the top of the stairs and yells, '*Sasha you arsehole, come back!*' But instead of Sasha it's an elderly night porter who appears, and guides him respectfully back to his suite. The door in the meantime has locked itself, but the night porter has a master key. Another retired spy, no doubt, thinks Mundy, handing him fifty marks. Watching over the world while it sleeps. Sleeping while it goes to the devil.

11

Below them at the Bavarian lakeside the merry-go-round is still belching out its honky-tonk and the Silesian matador is still crooning about *amor*. Now and then a surface-to-air rocket bursts ineffectually among the stars, and the surrounding mountains tremble to its red and gold. But there is no answering fire, no plume of black smoke as an enemy plane comes plunging to earth. Whoever they are shooting at has air supremacy. *A terrorist for Karen is someone who has a bomb but no aeroplane*, Mundy hears Judith say in his ear. It's been a long time since he has let Judith into his life, but with a whisky in his hand and an attic ceiling over his head and Sasha's crooked back not ten feet from him, it's hard to control the memories swirling around.

It's Christmas evening in Berlin, he decides, except that no carols play, no church candles flicker on piles of stolen books. And Sasha is cooking, instead of a chunk of bullet-hard venison, Mundy's favourite Wienerschnitzel from the carrier bag that he nursed so carefully up the spiral staircase. The attic apartment has rafters and bare brick walls and skylights, but that's as far as the similarity goes. A modern kitchen of ceramic tile and brushed steel fills one corner of the room. An arched window looks onto the mountains.

'Do you own this place, Sasha?'

When did Sasha ever own anything? But as with any two friends reunited after more than a decade, their conversation has yet to rise above small talk.

'No, Teddy. It has been obtained for us by certain friends of mine.'

For *us*, Mundy notes.

'That was considerate of them.'

'They are considerate people.'

'And rich.'

'You are correct, actually. They are capitalists who are on the side of the oppressed.'

'Are they the same people who own that smart Audi?'

'It is a car they have provided.'

'Well, hang onto them. We need them.'

'Thank you, Teddy, I intend to.'

'Are they also the people who told you where to find me?'

'It is possible.'

Mundy is hearing Sasha's words, but what he is listening to is his voice. It is as intense as it ever was and as vigorous. But what it can never conceal is its excitement, which is what Mundy is hearing in it now. It's the voice that bounced back from whichever genius he had been talking to last, to announce that they are about to reveal the social genesis of human knowledge. It's Banquo's voice when he stepped out of the shadows of a Weimar cellar and ordered me to pay close attention and keep my comments to a minimum.

'So you are a contented man, Teddy,' he is saying briskly, while he busies himself at the stove. 'You have a family, a car, and you are selling bullshit to the masses. Have you as usual married the lady of your choice?'

'I'm working on it.'

'And you are not homesick for Heidelberg?'

'Why should I be?'

'You ran an English-language school there until six months ago, I believe.'

'It was the last of a long line.' How the hell does he know this stuff?

'What went wrong?'

'What always went wrong. Grand opening. Mailshots to all the big firms. Full-page ads. Send us your tired and weary executives. Only problem was, the more students we had, the more money we lost. Didn't somebody tell you?'

'You had a dishonest partner, I believe. Egon.'

'That's right. Egon. Well done. Let's hear about you, Sasha. Where are you living? Who've you got? What are you doing and who to? And why the hell have you and your friends been spying on me? I thought we'd given all that up.'

A lift of the eyebrows and a pursing of the lips as Sasha selects one half of the question and pretends he hasn't heard the other. 'Thank you, Teddy, I am fully extended, I would say. My luck appears to have changed for the better.'

'About time then. Itinerant radical lecturer in the hell-holes of the world can't have been a laugh a minute. What's extending you?'

Another no answer.

The table is laid for two. Fancy paper napkins. A bottle of burgundy on an arty wooden coaster. Sasha lights the

288

candles. His hand is shaking the way he says it shook when it carried Mundy's visa application to the Professor more than twenty years ago. The sight triggers a rush of protective tenderness in Mundy that he has sworn not to feel. He has sworn it in his mind to Zara, to Mustafa and to himself, and to the better life all three of them are leading. In a minute he will tell Sasha exactly that: *If this is another of your great visions that we're about to share, Sasha, the answer is no, no and no, in that order*, he will say. After that they can have a natter about old times, shake hands and go their separate ways.

'I propose that we drink sparingly, Teddy, if that is acceptable to you. It is possible we have a long night ahead of us,' says Sasha.

The Wienerschnitzel, predictably, is undercooked. In his excitement, Sasha has not waited for the fat to heat.

'But you received my letters, Teddy? Even if you failed to answer them.'

'Indeed yes.'

'All of them?'

'I presume so.'

'Did you read them?'

'Naturally.'

'My newspaper articles also?'

'Stirring stuff. Admired them.'

'But you still weren't moved to reply.'

'It seems not.'

'Is this because we were not friends when we parted in Bad Godesberg?'

'Oh, we were probably friends. Just a bit tired. Spying takes the stuffing out of you, I always say,' Mundy replies, and gives a bark of laughter because Sasha doesn't always recognise a joke, and anyway it's not a very good one.

'I drink to you, Teddy. I salute you in these wonderful, terrible times.'

'And to you, old boy.'

'All these years, all over the world, wherever I was, teaching or being thrown out, or locked up, you have been my secret confessor. Without you – there were places, times – I could have believed that the struggle was hopeless.'

'So you wrote. Very kind of you. Not at all necessary,' Mundy replies gruffly.

'And you enjoyed the recent little war, I hope?'

'Every minute. Couldn't get enough of it.'

'The most necessary in history, the most moral and Christian – and the most unequal?'

'It made me sick,' says Mundy.

'And still does, I hear.'

'Yes. Still does.'

So this is what he's come about, thinks Mundy. He knows I've been loosing off about the war and wants to enrol me in some campaign. Well, if he's wondering what got into me, join the club. I was asleep. Shelved. Yesterday's spy boring the ears off the English-Spokens at the Linderhof on an overdraft. My white cliffs of Dover lost in the fog, when suddenly –

Suddenly he's as mad as a hornet, pasting the walls of Zara's flat with press cuttings, telephoning people he hardly knows, fuming at the television set, besieging our beloved British newspapers with letters they don't bloody read, let alone print.

So what had happened to him that hadn't happened before?

He'd weathered Thatcher and the Falklands. He'd

watched British schoolchildren display the Churchillian spirit, bawl 'Rule Britannia!' at hastily commissioned cruise liners and decrepit naval destroyers with the mothballs still rattling inside them sailing away to free the Falklands. He'd been ordered by our Leaderene to rejoice at the sinking of the *Belgrano*. He'd nearly vomited. He was case-hardened.

As a tender schoolboy, aged nine, he had shared the Major's delirium at the sight of our gallant British forces liberating the imperilled Suez Canal — only to see it remain firmly in the hands of its rightful owners, and to discover that the government, then as now, had lied in its teeth about its reasons for taking us to war.

The lies and hypocrisies of politicians are nothing new to him. They never were. So why now? Why leap on his soapbox and rant uselessly against the same things that have been going on since the first politician on earth lisped his first hypocrisy, lied, wrapped himself in the flag, put on God's armour and said he never said it in the first place?

It's old man's impatience coming on early. It's anger at seeing the show come round again one too many times.

It's the knowledge that the wise fools of history have turned us over once too often, and he's damned if they'll do it again.

It's the discovery, in his sixth decade, that half a century after the death of Empire, the dismally ill-managed country he'd done a little of this and that for is being marched off to quell the natives on the strength of a bunch of lies, in order to please a renegade hyperpower that thinks it can treat the rest of the world as its allotment.

And which nations are Ted Mundy's most vociferous allies when he airs these futile opinions to anybody civil enough to listen to him?

The beastly Germans.

The perfidious French.

The barbaric Russians.

Three nations who have the guts and good sense to say no and may they long continue.

In his shining bright anger Mundy *redux* writes to Kate his ex-wife — now, for her sins, tipped for high office in the next government. Perhaps he's not as diplomatic as he should be, but he was married to the woman, for Heaven's sake, we have a child in common. Her four-line typed reply, signed in her absence, advises him that she has taken note of his position.

Well, it's a hell of a long time since she did that.

Mundy *redux* next appeals to his son Jake, after several false starts now in his final year at Bristol, urging him to get his fellow students onto the streets, put up barricades, boycott lectures, occupy the Vice-Chancellor's lodgings. But Jake relates better to Philip these days, and has little time for menopausal offshore fathers who haven't got e-mail. A hand-written reply is beyond his powers.

So Mundy *redux* marches, the way he used to march with Ilse, or with Sasha in Berlin, but with a conviction he never felt before because convictions until now were essentially what he borrowed from other people. It is a little surprising, of course, that the beastly Germans should bother to demon-strate against a war that their government condemns but, bless them, they do. Perhaps they know better than most just how easy it is to seduce a gullible electorate.

And Mundy *redux* marches with them, and Zara and Mustafa come, and so do their friends, and so do the ghosts of Rani, Ahmed, Omar and Ali, and the Kreuzberg cricket club. Mustafa's school marches and Mundy *redux* marches with the school.

The mosque marches and the police march alongside, and it's a new thing for Mundy *redux* to meet policemen who don't want war any more than the marchers do. After the match he goes with Mustafa and Zara to the mosque, and after the mosque they sit sadly over coffee in a corner of Zara's kebab house with the enlightened young imam who preaches the value of study as opposed to dangerous ideology.

It's about becoming real after too many years of pretending, Mundy decides. It's about putting the brakes on human self-deception, starting with my own.

'Your little Prime Minister is not the American President's *poodle*, he is his *blind dog*, I hear,' Sasha is saying, as if he has been looking in on Mundy's thoughts. 'Supported by Britain's *servile corporate media*, he has given *spurious respectability to American imperialism*. Some even say that it was you British who led the dance.'

'I wouldn't be at all surprised,' says Mundy, sitting upright as he recalls something he has read somewhere, probably in the *Süddeutsche*, and repeated.

'And since the so-called coalition, by making an unprovoked attack on Iraq, has already broken *half the rules in the international law books, and intends by its continued occupation of Iraq to break the other half*, should we not be insisting that the principal instigators be forced to account for themselves before the International Courts of Justice in The Hague?'

'Good idea,' Mundy agrees dully. If not exactly his own, it's certainly one he has lifted, and used to stunning effect.

'Despite the fact, of course, that America has *unilaterally declared itself immune from the jurisdiction of such courts*.'

'Despite it.' He has made the same point to a packed meeting at the Poltergeist just two weeks ago, after something he heard on the BBC World Service.

And suddenly that does it for Mundy. He's had enough and not just of this evening. He's sick to death of sly games. He doesn't know what Sasha's up to, but he knows he doesn't like it nor the superior grin that goes with it. And he's about to say some of this and perhaps all of it when Sasha barges in ahead of him. Their faces are very close and lit by the Christmas candles from the Berlin attic. Sasha has grasped him by the forearm. The dark eyes, for all their pain and desperation, radiate an almost pathetic enthusiasm.

'Teddy.'

'What the hell is it?'

'I have only one question for you. I already know the answer but I must hear it from you personally, I have promised. Are you ready?'

'I doubt it.'

'Do you believe your own rhetoric? Or is all your huffing and puffing some kind of self-protection? You are an Englishman here in Germany. Perhaps you feel you must strike an attitude, speak louder than you feel? It would be understandable. I don't criticise you, but I'm asking you.'

'For Christ's *sake*, Sasha! You wear the beret. You drag me out here. You smirk at me like Mata Hari. You throw my own words in my face. Now will you kindly lay your egg and tell me what the fuck is going on?'

'Teddy, please answer me. I bring unbelievable hope. For both of us. An opportunity so great you cannot imagine. For you, immediate release from your material worries. Your rôle as teacher restored, your love of the multicultural community made real. For me – a platform greater than I ever dreamed of. And nothing less than a hand in the making of a new world. I think you are going to sleep.'

'No, Sasha. Just listening without looking at you. Sometimes it's a better way.'

'*This is a war of lies*. Do you agree? *Our politicians lie to the press, they see their lies printed and call them public opinion*.'

'Are these your words or something I stole?'

'They are the words of a great man. Do you agree with them? Yes or no.'

'All right: yes.'

'*By repetition, each lie becomes an irreversible fact upon which other lies are constructed. Then we have a war. This war*. These are also his words. Do you agree with them? Please, Teddy! Yes or no?'

'Yes again. So what?'

'*The process is incremental. As more lies become necessary, more wars are needed to justify them*. Do you still agree?'

With the anger rising inside him Mundy waits with seeming impassivity for the next salvo.

'*The easiest and cheapest trick for any leader is to take his country to war on false pretences. Anyone who does that should be hounded out of office for all time*. Am I being too strident for you, Teddy, or do you agree with this sentiment also?'

Mundy finally explodes. '*Yes, yes, yes*. All right? I agree with *my* rhetoric, *your* rhetoric and your latest *guru*'s rhetoric. Unfortunately, as we have learned to our cost, rhetoric doesn't stop wars. So goodnight and thank you, and let me go home.'

'Teddy. Twenty miles from here sits a man who has pledged his life and fortune to the Arms Race for Truth. That expression also is his own. To listen to him is to be inspired. Nothing you hear will alarm you, nothing will be to your peril or your disadvantage. It is possible he will make a proposal to you. An amazing, unique, completely electrifying proposal. If you accept it, and he accepts you, you will come away with your life immeasurably enriched, spiritually and materially. You will enjoy a renaissance as never before. If no agreement is achieved, I have given him my word that his secret will be safe with you.' The grip on Mundy's forearm tightens. 'Do you want me to flatter you, Teddy? Is that what you are waiting for? Do you want me to woo you the way our beloved Professor wooed you? Hours of foreplay over expensive meals? Those times are over too.'

Mundy feels older than he wants to feel. Please, he thinks. We've been here. We've done this stuff. At our age there are no new games any more. 'What's his name?' he asks wearily.

'He has many names.'

'One will do fine.'

'He is a philosopher, a philanthropist, a recluse and a genius.'

'And a spy,' Mundy suggests. 'He comes and listens to me at the Poltergeist and he tells you what I said.'

Nothing can prick Sasha's enthusiasm. 'Teddy, he is not a spy. He is a man of huge wealth and power. Information is brought to him as a tribute. I mentioned your name to him, he said nothing. A week later he summoned me. "Your Teddy is at the Linderhof, spouting bullshit to English tourists. He has a Muslim wife and a good heart. First you will establish whether he is as sympathetic as he claims. If he is, you will explain to him the principle. Then you will bring him to me."'

The *principle*, Mundy repeats to himself. There will be no war, but in the pursuit of principle not a stone will be left standing. 'Since when have you been attracted to rich and powerful men?' he asks.

'Since I met him.'

'How? What happened? Did he jump out of a cake?'

Impatient of Mundy's scepticism, Sasha releases his arm. 'At a Middle Eastern university. Which one is unclear to me and he will not reveal it. Perhaps it was Aden. I was in Aden for a year. Maybe Dubai or Yemen, or Damascus. Or further east in Penang, where the authorities promised to break my legs if I wasn't gone by morning. He tells me only that he slipped into the Aula before the doors closed, that he sat at the back and was profoundly moved by my words. He left before questions but immediately ordered his people to obtain a copy of my lecture.'

'And what was the subject of this lecture?' Mundy wants to suggest the social genesis of knowledge, but a merciful instinct restrains him.

'It was the enslavement of the global proletariat by corporate-military alliances,' Sasha declares with pride. 'It was the inseparability of industrial and colonialist expansion.'

'I'd break your legs for that one. How did He of Many Names make his money?'

'Disgracefully. He is fond of quoting Balzac. "Behind every great fortune lies one great crime." Balzac was talking bullshit, he assures me. It requires many crimes. Dimitri has committed all of them.'

'So that's his name. Or one of them. Dimitri.'

'For tonight, for us, it is his name.'

'Dimitri who?'

'Mr Dimitri.'

'From Russia? Greece? Where else do Dimitris come from? Albania?'

'Teddy, you are being irrelevant. This man is a citizen of the entire world.'

'We all are. Which bit of it?'

'Would it impress you if I told you he had as many passports as Mr Arnold?'

'Answer my question, Sasha. How did he make his bloody money? Arms dealing? Drugs? White-slaving? Or something really bad?'

'You are charging through open doors, Teddy. I exclude nothing. Neither does Dimitri.'

'So this is penance. Guilt money. He's fucked up the globe, and now he's going to rebuild it. Don't tell me: he's an American.'

'It is not penance, Teddy, it is not guilt, and so far as I know he is not American. It is reform. We do not have to be Lutherans to believe that men can be reformed. At the time he chanced to hear me speak, he was a pilgrim in search of faith, as you and I have been. He questioned everything and believed in nothing. He was an intellectual animal, brilliant, bitter and uneducated. He had read many books in order to inform himself, but he had not yet defined his rôle in the world.'

'But you were the boy. You showed him the light,' says Mundy roughly and, resting his head in his hand, closes his eyes for a bit of quiet, and realises that his body is gently shaking from head to toe.

But Sasha allows him no quiet. In his zeal, he is unrelenting. 'Why are you so cynical, Teddy? Have you never stood in a bus queue and overheard ten words that expressed something in your heart that you didn't know was there? It was my good luck to speak the ten words. He could have heard them anywhere. Today he knows that. Already at the time I spoke them, they were being spoken in the streets of Seattle, and Washington DC, and Genoa. Wherever the octopus of corporate imperialism is attacked, the same words are being spoken.'

Mundy remembers something he once wrote to Judith about having no firm ground. He has none now. This is Weimar all over again. I'm an abstraction, talking to another about a third.

'So Mr Dimitri heard you,' he says patiently, in the tone of somebody reconstructing a crime. 'He stood in your bus queue. And he was knocked out by your eloquence. As we all are. So now let me ask you again. How did you *meet* him? When did he become flesh and blood for you? Or are you not allowed to say?'

'He sent an emissary. Exactly as he sent me to talk to you today.'

'When? Where? Whom did he send?'

'Teddy, we are not in the White Hotel.'

'And we're not deceiving anyone either. That's over. We can talk like human beings.'

'I was in Vienna.'

'What for?'

'A conference.'

'Of?'

'Internationalists and libertarians.'

'And?'

'A woman approached me.'

'Anyone we know?'

'She was a stranger to me. She evinced a familiarity with my work, and asked whether I would be willing to meet an illustrious friend of hers, a man of distinction who shunned the limelight.'

'So she didn't have a name either.'

'Kolbach. Maria Kolbach.'

'Age?'

'It is not relevant. She was not desirable. Perhaps forty-five.'

'From?'

'It was not revealed. She had a Viennese accent.'

'Working for whom?'

'Maybe Dimitri. It is not known.'

'Was she part of the conference?'

'She did not say so, and her name was not on the list of delegates or organisers.'

'Well, at least you looked. Was she Fräulein or Frau?'

'It was not revealed.'

'Did she give you her card?'

'No. And I did not request it.'

'Show you her driving licence?'

'Teddy, I think you are actually full of shit.'

'Do you know where she lives, if she lives anywhere? Did you look her up in the Vienna telephone directory? Why are we dealing with a bunch of fucking *ghosts*?' He catches sight of Sasha's crestfallen expression, and reins himself in. 'All right. She accosts you. She pops the question. And you say, yes, Frau or Fräulein Kolbach, I would like to meet your illustrious friend. *Then* what happened?'

'I was received in a substantial villa in one of the best quarters of Vienna, the name of which I am not at liberty to reveal. Nor may I reveal the burden of the discussion.'

'She took you there, presumably.'

'A car was waiting outside the conference hall. A chauffeur drove us. It was the end of the conference. There were no further engagements. When we arrived at the villa she rang the bell, presented me to a secretary and removed herself. After a short wait I was admitted to a large room, occupied only by Dimitri. "Sasha," he says to me, "I am a man of great and illicit wealth, I am an artist of the unobserved life, also your devoted disciple. I have a mission of immense importance to offer you, but if the knowledge is too great for you to bear alone, kindly inform me immediately and leave." I asked him: is the mission legitimate? He replied, it is more than legitimate, it is essential to the benefit of all mankind. I then made him a vow of secrecy. In return, over several hours, he described to me the nature of his vision.'

'Which was — ?'

Sasha the great double agent has disappeared. In his place sits the credulous and impassioned dreamer of the Berlin attic.

'It was a vision for which I personally and my saviour and friend Ted Mundy are perfectly equipped in all respects. It was a vision that could have been deliberately crafted to accommodate our every need.'

'And that's all you're telling me.'

'The rest you must hear from Dimitri himself. In Vienna, he asked me whether, after all that I had endured, I still had faith in life.'

'And you of course said yes.'

'With conviction. And now that I have heard him describe his vision, with passion.'

Mundy has risen from the table and with his back to Sasha is standing at a wide window. Far below him glow the last embers of the fair. The lake is black and still, the mountains beyond it shadows on a clouded sky.

'When did you last see him?'

'In Paris.'

'In another villa?'

'An apartment. It was so big I wished for a bicycle to go to the bathroom.'

'And before that?'

'Only Vienna.'

'So how do you communicate? Leave each other notes under rocks?' Sasha declines to reply to such a facetious question, so Mundy asks another. 'Does he know we worked together?'

'He knows that in Berlin you were a radical who was beaten by fascists as he too in his time has been beaten by fascists. He knows you sacrificed yourself for a comrade.'

'How about you?'

'Please?'

'Does he know you did a little of this and that for Mr Arnold?'

'He is aware that all my life I have fought the tyranny wherever I have found it, with whatever weapons were available to me. *Teddy!*'

Now it is Sasha's turn to be exasperated. Leaping to his feet he has hobbled down the room to join Mundy at the window, and is staring up at him, holding out his hands in angry supplication. '*Fuck* this, actually, Teddy! Do you not understand how I have spoken for you? When Dimitri asked me whether I knew of other good men or women from my past, people of integrity, of like mind, courage and sound sense – who did I first think of, but Teddy? When he described to me, in glowing words, how together we may help to change the world – it was you, it was nobody but you, that I saw marching at my side!' He pulls back, lets his hands flop and waits for Mundy to speak, but Mundy is still staring at the black lake and the shadows of the mountains behind it. 'We are indivisible, Teddy. That is my conviction. We have endured together. Now we can triumph together. Dimitri is offering us everything you need: money, a purpose, a fulfilment of your life. What have you to lose by hearing him?'

Oh, nothing much, thinks Mundy. Zara, Mustafa, my happiness, my debts.

'Go back to Munich, Teddy,' Sasha suggests scathingly. 'Better to be afraid of the unknown and do nothing. Then you will be safe.'

'What happens if I listen to him and say no?'

'I have assured him that, like myself, you are an honourable man, capable of keeping a secret. He will have offered you a kingdom. You will have declined it, but will not speak of it.'

Only the detail matters, Mundy is reflecting. Sasha does the grand thoughts, I do the little ones. That's how we get along. So let's think of getting Zara's teeth fixed, and buying Mustafa the computer he's pining for. He might even teach me to send e-mails to Jake.

'Snake oil,' he says suddenly in English, and breaks out laughing, only to find Sasha scowling at him. 'Snake oil,' he repeats, now in German. 'It's what confidence tricksters sell to gullible people. It's what I sold to the Professor, come to think of it.'

'So?'

'So maybe it's time I bought a little. Who's driving?'

Not daring to reply, Sasha takes a breath, squeezes his eyes shut, opens them and hobbles eagerly back across the room. At the telephone, tapping out a number from memory, he pulls back his shoulders, Party-style, as a prelude to addressing authority.

'At the lodge in one hour!' he reports, and rings off.

'Will I pass like this?' Mundy enquires facetiously, indicating his workaday clothes.

A stranger to irony as so often, Sasha gives Mundy a quick up-and-down. His eye settles on the velcro Union Jack stuck to the handkerchief pocket of his elderly sports coat. Mundy tears it off and shoves it in his pocket.

Driving a car takes up all Sasha's attention. He is an eager schoolchild, straining upward, eyes just making it over the steering wheel as he hammers his horn or flashes his lights at whatever offends him.

He also knows the way, which is fortunate because within minutes of leaving the lay-by Mundy the topographical cretin has as usual lost all sense of direction. At first he reckons they are heading south, but soon they are following a skimpy, twisting path at the foot of great mountains. The moon that had earlier deserted them is back at full strength, lighting meadows and making white rivers of the roads. They enter forest and bump down a pitted alley of fir trees. Deer stare into their headlights, zigzag ahead of them into the blackness of the trees. An owl with a snow-white underbelly glides over the bonnet.

They make a right turn, start to climb and after ten minutes reach a clearing stacked with felled logs. Mundy remembers the forest clearing outside Prague on the day Sasha told him about his father the Stasi spy. They mount a concrete ramp and enter a barn big enough to house a Zeppelin. Half a dozen smart cars, German and Austrian, are parked in an orderly row as if for sale. Set apart from them stands a black Jeep. Sasha pulls up beside it.

It's a new Jeep, a big American one with a lot of chrome

and lights. A scrawny, middle-aged woman in a headscarf sits motionless in the driving seat. It crosses Mundy's mind that she could be the same woman in the Sherpa coat who was fumbling for her door key when he climbed the spiral staircase three hours ago, but for Sasha's sake he dismisses the idea. There is no greeting. Sasha clambers out of the Audi and beckons to Mundy to do the same. The woman continues to glower ahead of her through the windscreen of the Jeep. Mundy calls good evening to her but she ignores him.

'Where are we going?' he asks.

'We have another short journey to make, Teddy. Our friend prefers the hospitality of Austria. It is irrelevant.'

'I haven't got my passport.'

'A passport will not be necessary. The border here is anyway a technicality.'

I am an artist of the unobserved life.

Sasha hauls himself into the Jeep. Mundy climbs after him. Without putting on her lights, the woman drives out of the barn and down the ramp. She is wearing leather gloves. So was the woman on the staircase. She switches off the engine, listens for something, doesn't hear it, apparently. Then with headlights blazing she plunges the Jeep into the blackness of the mountain and at a giddy speed begins the climb.

The wooded hill is a wall of death and she is mad to attempt it. Mundy clutches the grab handle in front of him. The trees are too close together. She can't possibly squeeze the Jeep between them. The path is too steep, she's going too *fast*! Nobody can hold this speed, but she can. She can do all of it. The Edinburgh academicians would be proud of her. Her gloved hand whips the lever through the low gears and the Jeep doesn't falter.

They have scaled the wall. By the half-moon Mundy sees four valleys stretched below him like the spokes of a white wheel. She weaves the Jeep between rocks strewn over a wide grass plateau. They are on tarmac, descending a gentle slope towards a large converted farmhouse surrounded by barns and cottages. Smoke is coming out of the chimney of the main house. There are geraniums in the window boxes. The woman hauls on the handbrake, slams her door open and strides off. Two fit young men in anoraks step forward to receive them.

In Estelle Road, thinks Mundy, I opened the door to a couple of kids like these, and they turned out to be Mormon missionaries from Missouri wanting to save my soul. Well, I didn't believe them then, and I don't believe them now.

The room where they are made to wait is long and timbered and smells of resin and honey. It has flowered sofas and a coffee table strewn with brand-new art magazines. Mundy sits and tries to interest himself in an article on the post-modernists in architecture while Sasha prowls. It's like taking Mustafa to the nice Turkish doctor, he thinks, watching him: in a minute he's going to tell me he feels all right now, and he'd like to go home.

'Been here before, Sasha?' Mundy asks conversationally.

Sasha puts his hands over his ears. '*No,*' he hisses.

'Just Vienna and Paris then?'

'Teddy, please. It is not appropriate.'

Mundy is reminded of a truth he has learned about people constantly at war with authority: they're also in love with it. An aseptic blonde in a business suit is standing in the doorway.

'Mr Mundy?'

'The same,' he agrees cheerfully, clambering to his feet because he's in the presence of a lady.

306

'Richard would like to speak with you, please. Will you come this way?'

'Richard? Who's Richard?'

'Richard handles the paperwork, Mr Mundy.'

'What paperwork's that?' He wants to hear her more, place her voice.

'It's no big deal, sir. Richard will explain it to you, I'm sure.'

Vassar with a German accent, he decides. Air hostess courtesy. One more question, sir, I'll break your fucking neck. He glances at Sasha in case he's proposing to come along too, but he has his back to both of them and is examining a print of peasants in Tyrolean dress. The Vassar blonde leads him down a corridor lined with antlers and up a narrow back staircase. On the walls, muskets and racks of pewter plates. An old pine door stands ajar. She knocks, pushes it open and steps aside for Mundy to brush past her. I'm in a movie, he's thinking, as their hips graze each other: James Bond visits the ogre's castle. In a minute she's going to inject me with a truth drug.

'And *your* name?' he asks.

'Janet, sir.'

'I'm Ted.'

Richard is blond too, and just as clean. His hair is cropped short. He has body-built shoulders, wears a blue blazer and an airline steward's blue tie. He sits in a square wooden room scarcely larger than a sauna, at a small red desk. His handshake is practised and wholesome and he is an athlete of some kind. Perhaps the girl is too. There is no telephone on the desk, no computer or other temptation. There is one buff file and it is closed. Nobody has written FILE on it. Richard sets his fingertips either side of it as if he is about to levitate.

'May I call you Ted, please? Some Brits, they are so formal!'

'Not this one, I assure you, Richard!' He has placed Richard's accent too: Scandinavian declamatory, every sentence a complaint.

'Ted. It is Mr Dimitri's policy to pay an appearance fee to all his potential employees, whether or not the interview has a successful outcome. The fee is one thousand dollars cash, payable on signature of a contract of service for one day. Is this acceptable to you, Ted?'

Confused as always when he is offered money, Mundy lets out one of his embarrassed barks and shoves his wrist against his mouth. 'I suppose I might force myself,' he concedes. And barks again.

'The contract is short, Ted. The key element here is *confidentiality*,' says Richard, who has clearly learned his lines to perfection. 'Under its terms, you are forbidden to disclose the content of your discussion with Mr Dimitri and his staff. That means also the fact that such discussions took place at all. Okay? You can go along with this condition? Take a good look, please. Don't sign till you have read. In life, we say this is an axiom.'

Do we really? Well, well. In *life*, no less. Plain, high-quality paper, no address, the date. Three paragraphs of electronic type. Something called the New Planet Foundation is about to own Ted Mundy for a day. In exchange Mundy will undertake not to talk, write, or by any means describe, relate, impart, disclose or otherwise divulge – and any other stupid verb that lawyers who are always arseholes can think of to turn an honest sentiment into an unintelligible piece of junk – whatever may or may not have passed between them in the ogre's castle.

Mundy signs, they shake hands again. Richard's is dry and hard. When he has shaken Mundy's hand for long enough, he reaches inside his blazer and produces a yellow envelope, sealed. Not from a drawer, note well, not from a safe, not from a cashbox but from his pocket, next to his heart. And he doesn't even want a receipt for it.

Richard opens the door, they shake hands once more for the cameras, except that, as far as Mundy knows, there aren't any. Two more anoraks are waiting in the corridor. White faces, black anoraks, dead faces. Offcuts of the Mormon guards.

'Sir, Mr Dimitri will see you now,' says one of them.

Two blazers guard a pair of richly carved doors, but these blazers, unlike Richard's, are green. Somebody's *really* thought about wardrobe, Mundy thinks. One pats him down while the other fills a shallow basket with the prisoner's embarrassing possessions: a battered pewter hip flask, a velcro Union Jack, a dog-chewed copy of the *Süddeutsche*, a mildewed cellphone, a pocketful of collection money in assorted currencies taken at the Linderhof departure door, a bunch of keys to his apartment, a thousand-dollar envelope.

The carved doors fly open, Mundy steps forward and waits for his first sight of the billionaire philosopher, philanthropist, recluse and genius who has pledged his life and fortune to Sasha and the Arms Race for Truth. But all he sees is a roly-poly fellow in a baggy tracksuit and trainers, wading down the room at him while two men in suits look on from the sidelines.

'Mr Mundy, sir, I have had it said to me that your views on recent events in the world coincide remarkably with Sasha's and my own.' If Mundy is expected to answer, he needn't worry: Dimitri gives him no time. He has grabbed him by the left biceps and is wheeling him from point to point around the room.

'This is Sven, this is Angelo,' he declares, dismissing the suits rather than introducing them. 'They pick the fly shit out of the pepper for me. Detail bores me these days, Mr Mundy. Like Sasha I'm a man of the broad brush. That war on Iraq was illegitimate, Mr Mundy. It was a criminal and immoral conspiracy. No provocation, no link with Al Qaeda, no weapons of Armageddon. Tales of complicity between Saddam and Osama were self-serving bullshit. It was an old Colonial oil war dressed up as a crusade for Western life and liberty, and it was launched by a clique of war-hungry Judaeo-Christian geopolitical fantasists who hijacked the media and exploited America's post-Nine Eleven psychopathy.'

Mundy again wonders whether he is supposed to add anything to this, and again Dimitri relieves him of the choice. His voice is as violent as his gestures: a rasping, pounding mongrel of a voice even in repose. In Mundy's imagination it is sired in the Levant, trained in the Balkans and finished off in the Bronx— or so he tells himself as he strives to keep his mental distance from it – now Greek, now Arab, now American-Jewish, now all of them thrown together in a pilfered, semi-literate English cocktail that has never mixed. Does Dimitri have a mother tongue? Mundy doubts it. There is a fellow orphan in Dimitri, Mundy can feel it: a docklands kid, a knife child, an inventor of his own rules.

'All it takes for a war like that to start, Sasha tells me, is for a few good men to do nothing. Well, they *did* nothing. Whether they're good men, that's another thing. The Democratic opposition did fuck all. Stay home, sing patriotic songs till it's safe to come out, was their policy. Jesus Christ, what kind of opposition is that? What kind of moral courage? Do I go too fast for you, Mr Mundy? People tell me I give them no time to think. You want time to think?'

'Oh, I can manage, thanks.'

'I believe you can. You have an intelligent head, a good eye, I like you. Iran is next in line, Syria, Korea, take your pick. Forgive me, I am failing as a host. I was forgetting the vital rôle played by your British Prime Minister, without whom there might have been no war.' A quick turn as they pursue their Palais Glide. 'Mr Mundy will take tea, Angelo. He's married to a Turk, he should drink apple tea or coffee, but he takes a strong Indian tea with cow's milk in it and a bowl of brown cane sugar on the side. The Turks had an honourable rôle in this war, Mr Mundy. You should be proud of your lady, as you surely are.'

'Thank you.'

Turn again.

'My pleasure. Turkey's Islamist government refused to assist the American aggressor, and their military for once restrained their customary impulse to beat the shit out of the Kurds.' A half-step, and thank God we're moving towards the sofa because Mundy's head is swimming, he has the sensation of taking part in three conversations at once, yet he's scarcely uttered a word. 'A man has to inform himself, Mr Mundy. And I do that, as you will notice. The world is knee-deep in lies. Time the lambs ate the lion. Sit down, please, sir. Here on my right side. I have a bad left ear. Some arse-hole put a meat hook in it a while back, and all it gives me is the sound of the sea. Well, I don't like the fucking sea. I sailed it seven years, then I bought the ship and went ashore and bought some more ships, and I never went to sea again.'

In sideways glances, Mundy has managed to assemble an image of his host to go with the voice. He is seventy if a day. He has a wide, rolling body and a bald, liver-spotted head with criss-cross lines on it and deep creases between the cushions of his face. He has a child's sweet blue eyes, very liquid, and the quicker he talks the quicker they move. Mustafa has a wind-up toy that does the same and perhaps that's why Mundy is finding it hard to take Dimitri seriously. He has the feeling of sitting too close to the stage, and seeing the cracks in Dimitri's make-up, and the pins in his wig, and the wires when he spreads his wings.

Angelo has brought Mundy's tea, and for Dimitri a glass of soya milk. Mundy and Dimitri are turned sidesaddle to one another on the long sofa, like a television host and his guest. Sven roosts on a tall-backed leather chair outside their eyeline. On his lap he clutches a notebook to take minutes. The notebook is brand new. The pen is a streamlined black-and-gold affair, pride of the executive classes. Like Angelo, who prefers the fringes, Sven is gaunt and severe. Dimitri likes men about him who are thin.

'So who are you, Mr Mundy?' Dimitri demands.

He is leaning back in the cushions, his stubby hands linked over his stomach. His sneakers are turned inward to avoid giving unintentional offence. Perhaps, like Mundy, he has learned his manners in the East. 'You're a Pakistani-English-born gentleman who played student anarchist in Berlin,' he is intoning. 'You're a lover of the German soul who sold Shakespeare for the Queen and you're shacked up with a Turkish Muslim. So who the fuck are you? – Bakunin, Gandhi, King Richard or Saladin?'

'Ted Mundy, tour guide,' Mundy replies, and laughs.

Dimitri laughs with him, and claps him on the shoulder then kneads it, which Mundy could do without, but never mind, they're such good pals.

'Every war is worse than the last one, Mr Mundy. But this war is the worst I ever saw if we're talking about lies, which I am. Lies happen to be something of a speciality of mine. Maybe because I told so many in my time, they piss me off. Makes no difference the Cold War's over. Makes no difference we're globalised, multinational or what the hell. Soon as the tom-toms sound and the politicians roll out their lies, it's bows and arrows and the flag and round-the-clock television for all loyal citizens. It's three cheers for the big bangs and who gives a fuck about casualties as long as they're the other guy's?'

He seems not to need to breathe between sentences.

'And don't give me that horseshit about Old Europe,' he warns, though Mundy has not opened his mouth. 'We're looking at the oldest America in the book. Puritan zealots butchering savages in the name of the Lord – how do you get older than that? It was genocide then, it's genocide today, but whoever owns the truth owns the game.'

Mundy considers speaking up for the largest anti-war demonstrations the world has ever seen, but it is clear by now that interrupting Dimitri is not part of the interview. Dimitri's voice, whatever his peaceful intentions, rules by force. It neither rises nor falls. It could advise you of the Second Coming or the imminent extinction of the human race, and you would question it at your peril.

'March, you get sore feet. Protest, you get a bad throat and a policeman's boot in your teeth. Anybody who nails the lies is a radical malcontent. Or he's an Islamist anti-Semite. Or he's both. And if you're worried about the future, please don't be, because there's a new war just around the corner, and you won't have to bother about a thing, just switch on the TV and enjoy another virtual war brought to your screens courtesy of your favourite feel-good junta and its corporate parasites.' There is no pause, but one thick hand opens and offers the question: 'So what the fuck do we *do*, Mr Mundy? How do we make it impossible for your country, or America, or any damn country, to take the world to war on the strength of a bunch of cooked-up lies that in the cold light of day look about as plausible as the pixies in your fucking garden? How do we get to protect your children and my grandchildren from being suckered into war? I am speaking, Mr Mundy, of the corporate state and its monopoly of information. I am speaking of its armlock on the objective truth. And I am wondering how the fuck we turn back the tide. Would you be at all interested in that? Of course you would' – answering before Mundy can – 'and so would I. And so would every sane citizen of the world. I ask you again: what the *fuck* do we do to bring sanity and reason back into the political arena, if it was ever there in the first place?'

Mundy is whisked fleetingly to the Republican Club where similar discussions raged nightly, and with similar epithets. Now, as then, no easy answer springs to mind. But that is not entirely because he is bereft of words. It is more because he feels he has landed in the middle of a play where everybody knows the plot except himself.

'Do we need a new electorate? The fuck we do. It's not the people's fault they can't see straight. Nobody gives them a chance. "Look *this* way, don't look *that* way. Look *that* way, and you're an un-citizen, an anti-patriot, a schmuck." Do we need new politicians? Sure we do, but it's the electorate that has to find them. You and me, we can't do that. And how the hell can the electorate do its job when the politicians refuse to step up to the discussion? The electorate is screwed before it gets into the polling booths. If it ever does.'

For a moment Dimitri allows it to seem that he is as short of solutions as Mundy is. But it is quickly apparent he is only making a dramatic pause before ascending to a higher plane. In theatre, we call it a beat. To herald it, Dimitri has pointed a stubby finger at Mundy's face, and is looking straight down its sights into Mundy's eyes.

'I am speaking, Mr Mundy — I am speaking of something even more important to the development of Western society than the ballot box. I am speaking of the deliberate corruption of young minds at their most formative stage. Of the lies that are forced on them from the cradle onwards by corporate or State manipulation, if there's a difference any more between the two which I begin to doubt. I am speaking of the encroachment of corporate power on every university campus in the first, second and third worlds. I am speaking of educational colonisation by means of corporate investment at faculty level, conditional upon the observation of untrue nostrums that are advantageous to the corporate investor, and deleterious for the poor fuck of a student.'

You're great, Mundy wants to tell him. You get the part. Now put your finger back in its holster.

'I am speaking of the deliberate curtailment of free thought in our society, Mr Mundy, and how we may address it. I am an urchin, Mr Mundy. Born one, stayed one. My intellectual processes are untutored. Scholars would laugh at me. Nevertheless I have acquired many books on this subject.' So Sasha said, Mundy is thinking. 'I have in mind such thinkers as the Canadian Naomi Klein, India's Arundhati

Roy who pleads for a different way of seeing, your British George Monbiot and Mark Curtis, Australia's John Pilger, America's Noam Chomsky, the American Nobel Prize winner Joseph Stiglitz, and the Franco-American Susan George of World Social Forum at Porto Alegre. You have read all of these fine writers, Mr Mundy?'

'Nearly all.' And nearly all Adorno, nearly all Horkheimer and nearly all Marcuse, Mundy thinks, recalling a similar interrogation in Berlin a few lifetimes ago. I love them all, but I can't remember a word any of them said.

'From their varying perspectives, each of these eminent writers tells me the same story. The corporate octopus is stifling the natural growth of humanity. It spreads tyranny, poverty and economic serfdom. It defies the simplest laws of ecology. Warfare is the extension of corporate power by other means. Each thrives off the other and the recent war proves the point in spades. Does this urgent message cut any ice with you, Mr Mundy, or am I conducting a dialogue with myself?'

'It rings a lot of bells, actually,' Mundy politely assures him.

Dimitri is evidently approaching the summit of his oration, as he has no doubt approached it many times before. His face darkens, his voice lifts, as he leans confidingly towards his audience.

'How do these corporations achieve their stranglehold on our society? When they're not shooting, they're buying. They buy good minds, and tie them to their wagon wheels. They buy students wet from their mothers, and castrate their thought processes. They create false orthodoxies and impose censorship under the sham of political correctness. They build university facilities, dictate university courses, over-promote the professors who kiss ass and they bully the shit out of heretics. *Their one aim is to perpetuate the insane concept of limitless expansion on a limited planet, with permanent conflict as its desired outcome*. And their product is the zero-educated robot known otherwise as the corporate executive.'

He has reached the summit and is starting down the hill.

'Mr Mundy, twenty years from now there will not be a place of learning in the Western Hemisphere that hasn't sold its soul to corporate bigotry. There will be only one permitted opinion on every subject from the Garden of Eden to pink stripes in toothpaste. There won't be a contrary voice that's worth a whore's embrace unless somebody turns the river round and gets it flowing in the opposite direction. Well, I am one of those somebodies, and so is Sasha, and I am inviting you to be another.'

The mention of Sasha rouses Mundy from his trance. Where on earth is he? Is he still working on that print of Tyrolean peasants, or has he graduated to post-modern architecture? Dimitri has taken to the floor. Other men of power, when describing their plan to redesign mankind, might fling their arms about, but Dimitri is a master of the economic gesture. His walk is measured, hands clasped behind his navvy's back. Only occasionally does he release an arm to make the short, emphatic point.

The purpose of his great plan is to create *corporation-free academic zones*.

It is to foster *seminaries of unbought opinion*, Mr Mundy, open to students of any age, nationality and discipline who are interested in reinventing human incentive in the twenty-first century.

It is to establish nothing less than a *rational market place of free opinion*, where the true causes of war, and the means of preventing it, can be aired.

And finally his plan acquires a name – not several names, like its author, but one resounding name to echo down the ages: the Counter-University, no less, a global venture, Mr Mundy, as multinational and elusive as the corporations it seeks to counter, untainted by vested, religious, State or corporate interest, and financed by Dimitri's own immense, larcenous resources.

'The Counter-University has no dogma,' he declares, swinging round on one heel to address Mundy down the room. 'We offer no doctrinal front for our corporate adversaries to piss on. Like them, we shall be offshore and responsible to nobody. We shall use stealth. We shall be intellectual guerillas. We shall install ourselves wherever the enemy is encamped, and subvert him from within. Think your own fine University of Oxford. Imagine a student of science. He walks out of the bio lab. He comes a couple of hundred yards down the road. It's been a long day. He sees our sign, the Counter-University. He's had his head up some corporate test tube all day. He walks in, sits down, listens. "They're inviting *me*, as an individual, to live up to my duties as a responsible citizen of an endangered globe? What the fuck's happening to me?" he says to himself in perplexity. "These guys are off the wall. This is not what my corporation sponsors me for. I'm not paid to have a conscience, I'm paid to find new ways to fuck up the planet." Then he listens a little longer, and he begins to get the idea. "Hey. I'm somebody after all. Maybe I don't have to prove what a big guy I am by fucking up the planet. Maybe I should reconsider my relationship with it, love it even." Know what he does then? He takes our card. And he goes home. And he visits a certain website we have discreetly recommended to him. This website will further awaken the sense of discovery in him. Soon he will see himself as a pioneer of disrespectful thinking. He will have a dozen such websites, each one of them a stepping stone to spiritual freedom. Websites for our Counter-University. Websites for our Counter-Libraries. Websites for scurrilous but informed debate among our ever-growing army of renegades.'

He stops dead, turns, tilts his body so that Mundy has to meet his gaze. *I've got it*, Mundy thinks. *You're Erich von Stroheim in* Sunset Boulevard.

'It sucks, okay, Mr Mundy? An old crackpot with money coming out of his ass thinks he can redesign the world.'

'I didn't say that.'

'Well, say something. You're making me nervous.'

Mundy finally manages to: 'Where do I come in?'

'You were until recently the joint owner of a language school in Heidelberg, I believe, Mr Mundy?'

Sven speaking. Sven who picks fly shit out of pepper. Behind Sven sits Angelo, arms folded in the shadows. Exhausted by his performance, Dimitri has collapsed onto the sofa.

'Guilty,' Mundy agrees.

'And the purpose of the school was to teach advanced English to business professionals?'

'Correct,' says Mundy, thinking that Sven speaks exactly like one of his best pupils.

'And this school is now closed, sir? Pending legal proceedings?'

'It is quiescent. It is, at present, an ex-school,' Mundy says blithely, but his wit, if such it is, finds no acknowledgement in Sven's unyielding eyes.

'But you are still co-owner, together with your former partner, Egon?'

'Technically, maybe I am. Practically I'm sole owner by default. Along with the bank, six mortgage companies and sundry creditors.'

'Sir, how would you describe the status of the school building, please, at this moment in time?' Sven opens a folder that looks as though it knows more about Mundy's affairs than Mundy does. *Moment in time*, I'm not sure about, thinks Mundy the pedant. How about just *at this moment*, or even plain *now?*

'Boarded up and padlocked, basically,' he replies. 'Can't be used, can't be rented, can't be sold.'

'You have seen it recently, the school, sir?'

'I tend to keep my head down. Lots of writs still flying about. I drove past it a month ago and the garden was a jungle.'

'What is the capacity of the school, please?'

'In numbers? Teachers? What do you mean?'

'How many persons may be seated at one time in the main room?'

'Sixty, probably. That would be the old library. Sixty-five at a pinch. We didn't work that way. Well, we did for the odd lecture. It was small classes in small rooms. Three teachers – me, Egon and one other – six to a class, maximum.'

'And in income terms? Cash? What were you taking, if I may enquire, sir?'

Mundy pulls a face. Cash is not his best subject. 'That was Egon's side of the house. Top of my head, reckoned in teaching hours, twenty-five euros a pop, per hour per student, three teachers working on demand – it was made-to-measure stuff, mind you, six in the morning some of it – grab 'em on their way to work –'

'Sure,' says Sven, bringing him down to earth.

'Say three, three and a half grand a day if we're lucky.'

Dimitri comes suddenly alive again. 'Your students, they came from *where*, Mr Mundy?'

'Wherever we could get them. We targeted the young managerial class. Some from the university but mostly local business. Heidelberg's the high-tech capital of Germany. Biochem, IT, software, media, print technology: you name it. We've got a whole satellite town down the road that does nothing else. And the university to back it up.'

'I heard people of all nations.'

'You heard right. French, German, Italian, Chinese, Spanish, Turkish, Thai, Lebanese, Saudis and black Africans, the whole caboosh, male and female. And a lot of Greeks.'

But if Mundy is fishing for Dimitri's nationality, he's wasting his time.

'So the money came from all over the world,' Sven suggests, as Dimitri again lapses into silence.

'Just not enough of it.'

'Did any go out, sir?'

'Too much.'

'All over the world?'

'Only with Egon. Otherwise we just paid ourselves and the bills.'

'Did you work weekends in this school, sir?'

'Saturdays all day and Sunday evenings.'

'So the students came and went all days, all hours? Foreigners of all kinds? In and out?'

'In our heyday.'

'How long was your heyday?'

'A couple of years. Till Egon got greedy.'

'You had lights in the windows all night long? Nobody was surprised?'

'Only till midnight.'

'Who says?'

'The police.'

'What the hell do the police know about anything?' Dimitri cuts in sharply from the sofa.

'They're authorities on peace and quiet. It's a residential area.'

'Did you have, like, school *terms*?' Sven resumes. 'Like "this is vacation time, this is term time"?'

Thank you for explaining what a school term is, Mundy thinks. 'In theory we were open all year. In practice we followed the established pattern. High summer was no good because pupils wanted to go on holiday, Easter and Christmas the same.'

Dimitri sits suddenly upright like a man who needs to hear no more of this. He slaps his hands on his thighs. 'Okay, Mr Mundy. Now you listen to me, and listen hard because here it is.'

Mundy is listening hard. He is listening, watching and marvelling. Nobody could ask more of his powers of concentration.

'I want your school, Mr Mundy. I want it back in business, up and running, chairs, desks, library, all appropriate equipment. If the furniture's been sold, buy new. I want it looking and talking like it was before it went belly-up, but better. You know what is a *mystery ship*?'

'No.'

'I saw the movie. A crappy cargo ship like a tanker is rusted to hell. It's a sitting duck on the horizon for the German submarine. All of a sudden the crappy cargo ship hoists the British ensign, drops its side and has like a sixty-pounder stashed in its guts. It shoots the shit out of the submarine and the Nazis all drown. That's what your little language school is going to do on the day the Counter-University hoists its flag and tells the corporations they are no longer running the fucking world their way. Give me a date, Mr Mundy. If St Nicholas came through with a bag of gold tomorrow, how soon would you be able to open for business?'

'It would have to be a pretty big bag.'

'I heard three hundred thousand dollars.'

'It depends how much interest they calculate. Over how far back.'

'You're a Muslim. You shouldn't talk interest. It's against your religion.'

'I'm not a Muslim. I'm just learning the ropes.' *Why do I bother to say this?*

'Three fifty?'

'I wasn't able to pay the staff for the last three months. If I'm ever going to show my face in Heidelberg again I'd have to pay them first.'

'You're a hard bargainer. So it's half a million. When d'you open?'

'You said for business.'

'I said *when.*'

'Technically, as soon as we've cleaned the place up. We might be lucky and get a few walk-ins, we might not. To be functioning in any way that makes sense – September. Mid.'

'So we open early and we open small, why not? If we open big, they'll get us thrown off the campus. Open small and look busy, two cities only, and they'll think we're not worth the hassle. We open in Heidelberg and the Sorbonne and fan out from there. Do you have signs on the door?'

'Brass plates. Did have.'

'If they're there, clean them up. If they've gone, make new. It's business as usual, the same old crap. September, when we bring in the big lecturers, we'll drop our side and start shooting. Sven, see he takes an ad somewhere. "Mr Edward Mundy will resume his former post as Principal of his school with effect from whenever."' The baby-blue eyes hold Mundy in some kind of painful, almost pitying stare. 'You don't look right to me, Mr Mundy. Why aren't you waving your bowler hat in the air? Are you depressed or something that a guy you don't even have to fuck is getting you out of hock for half a million bucks?'

Being told to change your expression is never easy, but Mundy does his best. The sense of dislocation he experienced moments earlier has returned. His thoughts are the same as Dimitri's: why am I not rejoicing?

'Where does Sasha come in?' he says, which is all he can think of to ask.

'The Counter-University will have a fine lecture circuit. My people in Paris are in the process of assembling a stable of incorruptible academics, men and women who regard orthodoxy as the curse of free thought. I intend that Sasha assist in this process, and be one of the lecturers. He's a fine mind, a fine man, I heard him and I believe in him. He will have the title of Director of Studies. In Heidelberg, he will supervise the creation of your library, advise you on your future academic schedule and assist you in the recruitment of human resources.'

Dimitri stands up with a speed and decisiveness that brings both Sven and Angelo leaping to their feet. Mundy unwinds himself from the sofa and stands too. It's like my first time in the mosque, he thinks. When they stand, I stand. When they kneel down and put their heads on the rush matting, I kneel down too and hope someone's listening.

'Mr Mundy, we have done our business. Sven will discuss your administrative concerns with you. Angelo will take care of your remuneration. Richard upstairs has a short contract for you to sign. You will receive no copy of your contract, you will receive no confirmation in writing of anything we have agreed here tonight.'

Grappling with Dimitri's iron grasp, Mundy again fancies he is reading a hidden signal in the moist, unblinking gaze. *You came here, you wanted it and now you've got it*, it seems to be saying. *You have nobody to blame but yourself.* A side door opens, Dimitri is gone. Mundy hears no departing footstep, no thunderous applause as the final curtain falls. One of the blazers is standing at Mundy's elbow, waiting to give him back his toys

The blonde woman in the business suit once more leads the way. The same anoraks watch from the shadows. Richard upstairs is sitting at his desk as before. Is he made of wax? No, he smiles. Has he been waiting up here all evening in his nice new blazer and tie, hands pre-spread either side of the leather folder that opens from the centre like a double window?

The blonde woman departs. They are alone again, two fellows across a desk. Secrets may be traded, except that Mundy is keeping his secrets to himself:

I believe none of it, but that doesn't mean it isn't true.

I am in a madhouse, but half the world is run by madmen and nobody complains.

If mad kings, mad presidents and mad prime ministers can wear the mask of sanity and still function, why not a mad billionaire?

In the battle between hope and scepticism that is being fought inside me, it is increasingly clear I stand to gain everything and lose nothing.

If the Counter-University turns out to be somebody's sick dream, I remain what I was before I walked through the door: poor but happy.

If against all odds the dream comes true, I'll be able to look my creditors in the eye, reopen the school, move us all up to Heidelberg, put Zara through nursing college and Mustafa into a good school and sing *The Mikado* every morning in my bath.

So how often does *that* little possibility present itself? we ask ourselves. Did it ever? No. Will it ever again? No.

And if I need another reason for saying yes, which I don't, there's Sasha, my one-man chaos theory.

Why I should feel responsible for him is a question to be answered in another life. But I do. A happy Sasha is a joy to me, and a wretched Sasha is a rock on my conscience.

The contract is six pages long and by the time Mundy reaches the end of it he has forgotten the beginning. However, a few stray points have lodged in his head, and in case they haven't, Richard is sitting across the desk to count them off on his athletic fingers:

'The house will be legally yours, Ted, unencumbered from the day you complete your first full year of tuition. Your basic outgoings, Ted, that's heat, light, local taxes, house maintenance, will be carried by one of Mr Dimitri's many foundations. For this purpose we will create a cash float, payable in advance, accounted for retrospectively on every quarter-day. Here are your bank details as we presently have them. Kindly check and confirm they are correct. Vacations we leave to your discretion, but Mr Dimitri is adamant that all of his employees enjoy their full allocation of leisure. Do you have further questions? Now's your chance, Ted. Any later is too late.'

Mundy signs. The pen is the same model as Sven's. He initials each page bottom right. Richard folds the signed contract and feeds it into the pocket where he kept the thousand dollars' cash. Mundy stands. Richard stands. They do some more handshaking.

'Allow five working days for the money to come through, Ted,' Richard advises, just like the advertisements.

'The whole sum?' Mundy asks.

'Why not, Ted?' says Richard with a smile of spiritual mystification. 'It's only money. What's money beside a great ideal?'

12

Not for the first time in his life by any means, Ted Mundy has lost touch with who he is. A credulous fool, caught yet again in Sasha's slipstream? Or the luckiest man on earth?

Making breakfast, making love, taking Mustafa to school and himself to the Linderhof, playing the loyal servant of the late King Ludwig, hurrying home again for Zara's night off, adoring her, protecting her in her enormous and intelligent vulnerability, bringing her library books on nursing and enjoying a kick-about with Mustafa and the gang, he relives without pause his night visit to the mountain top, says nothing to anybody, and waits.

If now and then he tries to persuade himself that the entire adventure is the wish-child of his hyperactive imagination, then how does he explain, please, the one thousand dollars he secreted under the driver's floor-mat of his Beetle for the return journey to Munich, and which he next day transferred to the safety of the plant room, where it now keeps company, appropriately, with Sasha's letters?

The long night's unreality began with Sasha's ghostly reappearance, and ended with his departure. After a further promenade with Sven, Angelo and Richard through the technicalities of his resurrection, Mundy is returned to Sasha who greets him with such effusive joy as puts to shame whatever reservations he may be harbouring. The news of Mundy's recruitment to the Cause has reached him in advance. Seeing Mundy enter, Sasha seizes his hand in both his own and, to Mundy's confusion, presses it to his damp forehead in a gesture of Oriental obeisance. In awed silence they board the Jeep and, with the same scraggy woman at the wheel, make an unexpectedly stately descent of the forest track.

Reaching the barn, she parks and waits while they transfer themselves to the Audi, where Sasha once more takes the wheel. But they have not driven two hundred yards before the Audi skids to a halt and Sasha staggers onto the grass verge, hands pressed to his temples. Mundy waits, then goes after him. Sasha is retching his heart out in rhythmic heaves. Mundy touches his shoulder but he shakes his head. The retching subsides. They return to the car.

'Want me to drive?' Mundy asks.

They change seats.

'Are you all right?'

'Of course. A matter of digestion.'

'What's your next move?'

'I am required immediately in Paris.'

'What for?'

'Did Dimitri not tell you I am personally charged with the composition of our college libraries?' He has put on his Party voice. 'In Paris, a committee of illustrious French and

German academics under my supervision will compose a list of works that will be common to all libraries of the project. Once the core volumes are in place, each library will be invited to augment its collection. Librarians will of course be guided by the popular will.'

'Is Dimitri on this illustrious committee?'

'He has expressed certain wishes, and these have been placed before us for our consideration. He asks no preferential treatment.'

'Who picks the academics?'

'Dimitri made certain recommendations. I was graciously invited to add my own.'

'Are they all liberals?'

'They belong to no category. The Counter-University will be celebrated for its pragmatism. I am told that in American neo-conservative circles, the beautiful word *liberal* is already a term of abuse.'

But when they reach the lay-by where Mundy's Beetle is parked, the Party voice gives way to another outburst of emotion. In the pre-dawn light, Sasha's eager face is glistening with sweat.

'Teddy. My friend. We are partners in an historic enterprise. We shall do nothing to harm, nothing to destroy. Everything we dreamed of in Berlin has been delivered to us by Providence. We shall stem the advance of ignorance and perform a service of enlightenment for all humanity. On the balcony, after you had signified your acceptance, Dimitri invited me to name the stars in the firmament. "That is the Plough," I said. "And over there you can just make out the Milky Way. And here is Orion." Dimitri laughed. "Tonight, Sasha, you are right. But tomorrow we shall draw new lines between the stars."'

Mundy climbs into his ancient car, Sasha moves to the driving seat of the Audi. For a while they maintain a companionable distance on the empty road, but as Sasha begins to outstrip him, Mundy has the momentary sensation that the car ahead of him is empty. But Sasha always comes back.

Thrown once more upon the banalities of his daily life, Mundy struggles to put himself in the position of the owner of a lottery ticket that may or may not have won the jackpot. If it happens, it will be true. If it doesn't happen, nobody but myself needs to be disappointed. At the same time, the events of the long night circulate in his memory like a movie he can't switch off, whether he's pointing out the glories of the Italian waterfall descending the slopes of the Hennenkopf, or explaining to Mustafa, in the great tradition of Dr Mandelbaum, that to possess another language is to possess another soul.

That woman in the headscarf who drove the Jeep, now — he asks himself. She drove like Jehu when I didn't know where we were going, and like an undertaker when I did. Why?

Or take gloves — he asks himself. The woman in the Sherpa coat who was standing on the spiral staircase fumbling in her handbag for the door key: she wore gloves. Strong, new, yellowy, spotty, tight-fitting pigskin jobs with heavy stitching. Mrs McKechnie had a pair, and I hated them.

But the woman who drove the Jeep was also wearing a new pair of Mrs McKechnie's gloves. And she had exactly the same resistance to eye-contact as the woman on the spiral staircase. The woman on the spiral staircase kept her head down while she was fumbling. The woman in the Jeep wore a headscarf because when you drive you can't keep your head down.

The same woman, then? The same head, with or without the scarf? Or only the same gloves?

Or take Richard's carpet — he thinks. Everything in Richard's upstairs lair was new, including Richard: new haircut, new blue blazer, new airline steward's tie. But the newest thing of all was that deep-pile carpet. It was so new that when I stood up to shake Richard's hand and looked down, I saw bubbles of fluff where our feet had been. And everybody knows that you can't vacuum a new carpet, you can only brush it.

So was the carpet purchased in Dimitri's honour? Or ours? And how about the blazer?

That carpet altogether — now that Mundy thinks about it — is a puzzle in its own right, whether it's new or old. Or it's a puzzle to Ted Mundy, the do-it-yourself homebuilder. Deep-pile wall-to-wall in an old chalet with lovely wooden floors? It's daylight vandalism, ask Des.

All right, it's a matter of taste. But that doesn't take care of the feeling that everything in the room, including Richard, has come out of the showroom on the same day.

Or put another way: the feeling that this was a first night; and that as usual the props and costumes had only just made it through the lines.

And if these quibbles seem trivial beside the splendour of Dimitri's Grand Vision, perhaps that's because I'm trying to bring it down to scale. If I don't believe in the carpet — in other words — why should I believe in Dimitri?

But I *do* believe in Dimitri! When Mad King Dimitri builds his castle in the air, I believe every golden word. Becoming his loyal servant and getting my debts paid looks like a contract made in Heaven. It's only when Dimitri stops talking that the doubts come creeping to the surface.

Back and forth, night and day, while Ted Mundy waits to hear whether he's won the jackpot.

And while he waits, he watches.

Ever since his undignified retreat from Heidelberg, he has put every possible inconvenience in the way of his mail. When an address has proved abusive he has changed it. The Munich apartment remains firmly on the secret list. At the Linderhof he is more vulnerable, but he has taken precautions. The staff pigeonholes are situated in the administrative offices. The letter M, being halfway down, is below the eye level of the casual passer-by. It is perfectly reasonable that a diligent tour guide, hastening past the window on his way to quell a restless group of English-Spokens, should neglect to check his mail. A whole week can go by easily – longer – before the equally diligent Frau Klamt pops out of her box and presses an ominous-looking envelope into his hand.

Overnight, all that has changed. From defence, Mundy has moved to attack.

Until now, he has observed the passage of mail vans in and out of the Linderhof much as he might log the manoeuvres of enemy vehicles. No longer. A mail van is hardly out of the castle gates before Mundy is poking his head round Frau Klamt's door, asking her whether there's anything for him.

Which is how it comes about that, eight days after his descent from the mountain top, in the ten minutes' grace allowed to him between his third and fourth tours of the day, a breathless Ted Mundy learns that he is *invited* to call his bank manager in Heidelberg *at his convenience* to arrange a meeting at which will be discussed the disposal of credit payments received by wire transfer and amounting between them to 500,000 US dollars.

The bank has fielded no fewer than three executives, which strikes Mundy as pretty rich, considering how many times he has had to listen to the incredibly boring Herr Frinck on the subject of paying people to sit around and watch other people work.

Herr Frinck himself sits at the centre, Brandt and Eisner roost either side of him. Herr Doktor Eisner is from our insolvency department. Herr Brandt, a mere commoner, is a senior manager from our Head Office. Sometimes, Head Office likes to slum it, says Frinck – or, as he prefers to put it, *participate proactively at client level*: has Mundy any objection to his presence? Mundy couldn't be happier with Herr Brandt's presence. He feels like the boy in the painting, waiting to be asked when he last saw his father. He has put on his suit for the occasion. It's too heavy and he is puzzled to find that it has shrunk: the sleeves keep riding up to his elbows. Inside it, he feels stupid, sticky and nervous, which is how he always feels when money is the only subject on the agenda. Herr Frinck enquires after the health of – he offers a broad-minded smile – *Frau Mundy*. In accordance with bank protocol, the lingua franca today is English. When three German bankers face one penurious English client, it is self-evident that their English will be superior to his German.

'She couldn't be better, thank you,' Mundy replies heartily to Frinck's question. 'Well, at *her* age, what else would you expect?' – bark.

The reminder that the bank's client is supporting a young and doubtless extravagant common-law wife brings no joy to the faces of Herr Frinck or Herr Doktor Eisner. Herr Brandt from Head Office, on the other hand, seems to think it rather sporting of him. Herr Frinck laments the war. Deeply disturbing, he says, prodding the bridge of his spectacles with his fat forefinger. The consequences totally unforeseeable, puff, puff. It was all fine and well for Berlin to take the high moral ground, but America has made it clear there would be a price to pay, and now we are waiting for the bill. Mundy says, however much it is it will be a price worth paying. He practically offers to pay it himself. His generous instincts are grimly noted.

Herr Frinck has prepared a list of Mundy's many creditors. Herr Doktor Eisner has run his eye over it. Herr Frinck wishes to make a statement in view of the presence of sleek Herr Brandt from Head Office. The behaviour of Mr Mundy throughout this whole matter has been exemplary. Mr Mundy had every opportunity and indeed encouragement to declare himself legally bankrupt. To his credit he resisted. Now everybody, including the bank, can be paid in full. It is most gratifying, says Herr Frinck. It is admirable. Interest may safely be charged at the full rate, a most rare outcome in these circumstances.

Herr Doktor Eisner declares Mr Mundy to be a true English gentleman. Herr Frinck seconds this. Mr Mundy says, in that case he's the last of a breed. The joke is either not appreciated or not understood – except by handsome Herr Brandt who is moved to enquire, in the lightest possible of tones, where in Heaven's name Mr Mundy got all this money from.

'We are looking at three transfers,' Herr Brandt announces. He has them among the papers before him as he speaks, in three separate folders of transparent plastic which he now passes to Mundy for his inspection. 'From United Chemical of Guernsey, two hundred thousand, per order of client. *Voilà!* From Crédit Lyonnais in Antigua, two hundred thousand per order of client. *Voilà!* From Morgan Guaranty Trust, Isle of Man, one hundred thousand, also per order of client. Big banks in small places. But who are the clients, Mr Mundy?'

Grateful that Sven, Richard and Angelo have briefed him for this eventuality, Mundy pulls a regretful and, he hopes, convincing smile. 'Don't think I can entirely answer that one, Herr Brandt. The negotiations are at a rather delicate stage, to be frank.'

'Ah,' says Herr Brandt, disappointed, and inclines his handsome head to one side. 'But a little bit, maybe? Off the record,' he suggests. Winningly.

'The money's by way of an advance. Start-up money,' Mundy explains, using Sven's term.

'Against what exactly, Mr Mundy?'

'Reopening the school on a profitable basis. I've been conducting some rather confidential talks with an international foundation. I didn't want to tell the bank till it was pretty much a done thing.'

'Wonderful. Well done. So what is actually the *remit* of this foundation? This is really *most* interesting, I must say,' Herr Brandt adds aside to his two colleagues, with the enthusiasm appropriate to a man from headquarters visiting his troops on the ground.

'Well, *one* thing it does is foster the spread of English,' Mundy replies, drawing again on his briefing. 'English as Esperanto, basically. Giving the world a common language as a means to international understanding. They've got big institutional money riding on it.'

'Excellent. I'm impressed.' And Mundy can tell from Herr Brandt's sunny smile that he really is. 'And they have selected your school here for development? As part of their scheme?'

'Among others, yes.'

'How far have your talks progressed, if I am not being indiscreet?'

Mundy is aware that his briefing has about run its course. All the same, he hasn't endured ten years of the Professor's probings, not to mention months of hard sweat at the Edinburgh School of Deportment, without acquiring a few skills.

'Well,' he begins boldly. 'I'd say, give or take a bit – you can never be sure of anything, of course – we've just about arrived in clear water. We're not talking about what you'd call hard-nosed professional negotiations, obviously, but even a non-profit-making foundation has to satisfy its own criteria.'

'Naturally. And what criteria are we considering here, if I may be so curious?'

Never hesitate. 'Well, for openers, the proportion of non-Caucasian students we take. It's a global foundation, so naturally they're looking for diversity.'

'Naturally. And what else, please?'

'Criteria?'

'Yes.'

'The syllabus, clearly. The culture content. The level of attainment we hope to reach after a specific period of instruction. Performance generally.'

'Religion?'

'What?'

'You are not a Christian organisation?'

'Nobody's talked to *me* about religion. If we're multi-ethnic, presumably we're multi-faith.'

Herr Brandt has flipped a file open with a smack and is peering into it with an expression of cheerful confusion.

'Listen. I tell you what we did, okay?' He treats Mundy to a radiant smile. 'You let us into your secret, we let you into ours, okay? We mounted a little exercise. Sometimes we do that. We traced one of these payments back to its roots – only one – not always easy, okay? All the way back to the bank behind the bank behind the bank. It took a lot of guess-work at first, but we did it. From Guernsey we went to Paris. From Paris to Athens. And from Athens to Beirut and from Beirut to Riyadh. End-station was Riyadh. Maybe you see now why I ask you about religion.'

If they try to put you in the dock, slam back at them. The truth is what is demonstrable.

'I've no doubt these people bank all over the world,' Mundy retorts testily. 'For all I know they've got Arab backers, why not?'

'Arab backers who support the spread of *English*?'

'If they're interested in furthering international dialogue, why not?'

'And use such complicated banking routes?'

'Shy, probably. You can hardly blame them these days, can you, when every Muslim is by definition a terrorist.'

Herr Frinck is clearing his throat and Herr Doktor Eisner is fidgeting ostentatiously with his papers, lest Herr Brandt from Head Office has forgotten that Mr Mundy's common-law wife is a Turk. But Herr Brandt's handsome smile takes care of everything.

'And you have a contract, obviously, Mr Mundy,' he says comfortably.

'I told you already. We're still negotiating the small print,' Mundy replies, by now on the edge of indignation.

'Indeed you did. But in the meantime you have a short-term contract, no doubt. Not even the most benevolent foundation would provide so much money without a contract of some sort.'

'No.'

'Then, an exchange of letters.'

'Nothing concrete that I'm able to show you at this stage.'

'Is the foundation paying you a salary?'

'They've costed in an initial fifty thousand dollars for staff fees. I get ten thousand of them. That's two months' pay in advance. Once the school reopens, they'll raise me fifty per cent.'

'And your appointment is residential?'

'Eventually. Once the house is ready.'

'Plus expenses?'

'Presumably.'

'And a car?'

'Down the line. If it's necessary.'

'So not a bad salary for a teacher with your financial record. I congratulate you. You are clearly a very tough negotiator, Herr Mundy.'

Suddenly everybody is standing. There is work to be done: cheques to be signed, securities to be released and pledges redeemed. Herr Doktor Eisner's department has everything prepared. Shaking Mundy's hand and gazing reverently into Mundy's eyes, Herr Brandt is anxious to reiterate his heart-felt admiration for Mundy's acumen. It was purely a Head Office exercise, nothing personal; a bank these days lives with one foot in the law courts. Herr Frinck confirms this. So does Herr Doktor Eisner. Speaking as a lawyer, Eisner confides to Mundy as he leads him upstairs, he has never known a time when the banking industry was so beset with legal pitfalls.

*　　*　　*

The schoolhouse is still there. It hasn't, like Number Two, The Vale, disappeared; no builder's board offers family homes on a ninety per cent mortgage. It's the same faithful old aunt it always was, frowning down at him from its ivy-clad bay windows and slate-clad turrets and bell tower with no bell. The same arched front door with coach bolts like cardigan buttons awaits him. He advances shyly. First, he must open the padlock on the front gate with its wishing-well canopy. He does so, then walks slowly up the brick path to the six steps leading to the porch, where he stops and turns, and confirms as if he doubted it that the same magical view is also intact – across the river to the old city with its spires, then upwards, and upwards again, to the red ruined castle stretched along the Kaiserstuhl.

The house had been an idiotic choice from the start. He knows that now. Half of him knew it at the time. A commercial *school*, stuck on a hillside – parking for three cars only, the wrong side of town, convenient for nobody? Yet it was a fine roomy house. And a snip at the price, as Des would say, provided you were prepared to roll your sleeves up, which Mundy was, even if Egon preferred to sit and fiddle the books in the conservatory. The front garden had four good apple trees – all right, you don't buy a house for its apple trees. But there's a vineyard at the back, and once the school took off, he was going to make his own Château Mundy and send a few bottles to old Jake to put down.

And above the vineyard runs the Philosophers' Path – he can see it now through the apple trees. And above the path, the Heiligenberg, and some of the best woods in Germany to walk in – if you walked, which admittedly not all mature students do.

Or look at the literary associations – weren't *they* worth

anything? Hadn't Carl Zuckmayer and Max Weber lived a couple of hundred yards from here? The very street named after Hölderlin? What more does today's upwardly mobile young executive want from a language school, for Heaven's sake?

Answer, unfortunately, a great deal.

The latchkey turns, and when he puts his weight against the door it yields. He steps inside and is ankle-deep in junk mail. He closes the door and stands in three-quarter darkness because of the ivy over the windows, and for the first time in months allows himself to remember just how much he loved the place, and how much of himself he invested here only to look on helplessly while it all slipped away from him: the money, the friend he trusted, the dream of getting it right at last.

Lost in marvel at his own folly, he picks his way through the wreckage of his too-recent past. In the central hall where he is standing, the pupils assembled for classes and were sorted according to need into four tall rooms. The splendid staircase got its light from the art nouveau skylight and if the sun was up as you crossed the hall, coloured shards of red and green and gold slid over you. His old classroom is bare: desks, chairs, coat-racks, all gone, sold. But his writing is still on the blackboard, and he can hear his own voice reading it:

As a valued customer of British Rail, we would like to apologise to you for the presence of the wrong kind of snow on the line.
Question: Who is the customer?
Question: Who is the subject of the sentence?
Question: Why is this the wrong kind of sentence?

He is perching as if by magnetic power on his old spot in the window bay: just the right height for a beanstalk like me, and a nice bit of evening sun while you're waiting for your last class to arrive.

End of reverie. The past isn't what you came for.

Dimitri told you his money stinks. So now it does. Does that make him a liar?

All right, slipping half a million bucks to a washed-up language tutor may not be normal business practice to some anally oriented apparatchik from Head Office. But it could be all part of the day's work for a fellow who buys and sells ships out of his back pocket.

Assuming Herr Brandt *is* a senior executive from Head Office, of course. That quick confiding eye and over-ready smile of his could come out of quite a different stable. There was more than one occasion, during our uncomfortable pas de deux, when I wondered whether I might be back in the Presence.

For twenty minutes or more Mundy lets his thoughts drift free-range through his head. Many surprise him, but they often do. For instance, that he is mysteriously under-impressed by his new-found affluence. If he could transfer himself by magic wand to anywhere in the world just now, he'd either be in bed with Zara in the flat, or closeted in the woodshed with Mustafa, helping him finish off a chaotic model of the Dome of the Rock in time for his mother's birthday.

Mundy jumps to his feet and swings round. A thunderous banging has broken out behind his right ear.

Recovering his composure he is delighted to find himself staring at the gnomic features of old Stefan, his former gardener and boilermaster floating six inches away from him on the other side of the glass. It is a sash window. In a trice, Mundy has prised open the central lock, stooped, grabbed the brass handles and with a great unfolding of his body sent the lower half of the window rattling up its ropes. He stretches out his hand, old Stefan seizes it and, with the agility of a gnome half his age, vaults into the room.

A tumult of breathless small talk follows. Yes, yes, Stefan is fine, his wife Elli is fine, the *Söhnchen* – he means his hulk of a fifty-year-old son – is *excellent* – but where has Herr Ted *been*, how is *Jake*, is he still studying in Bristol? And why has it taken Herr Ted so *long* when we all *miss* him, nobody in Heidelberg bears him a grudge, for God's sake, the little matter of Herr Egon is *long forgotten*! . . .

And it's while all this is being thoroughly gone over that Mundy realises that old Stefan was not hanging around the garden by chance.

'We have been *expecting* you, Herr Ted. We knew two weeks ago that you would soon be here.'

'Nonsense, Stefan. First I heard of it myself was ten days ago.'

But old Stefan is tapping the side of his nose with his crooked finger to show what a shrewd old gnome he is. 'Two weeks ago. Two weeks! I told Elli. "Elli," I said. "Herr Ted is coming home to Heidelberg. He will pay his debts like he always said he would, and he'll take back the villa and start the school again. And I'll work for him. It's all agreed."'

Mundy keeps his tone light. 'So who slipped you the news, Stefan?'

'Your surveyors, naturally.'

'Which surveyors are they? I've got so many.'

Old Stefan is shaking his head and squeezing up his twinkly eyes while he tut-tuts in disbelief.

'From your mortgage company, Herr Ted. The people who are giving you your loan, of course. Today, nobody can keep anything secret, it's well known.'

'And they've been here already?' Mundy says, managing to sound as if he was expecting them, and is perhaps a little irritated to have missed them.

'To look round, naturally! I was passing, I saw some figures in the window, a little light moving about, and I thought, ahah! Herr Ted's back. Or maybe he's not back and we've got some burglars. I am too old to die, so I banged on the door. A nice young fellow, a good smile, overalls. A torch in his hand. And in the background some other fellows I didn't see, maybe a woman. Women these days are everywhere. "We are surveyors," he tells me. "Don't worry. We are nice people." "For Herr Ted?" I say. "You are surveying for Herr Ted?" "No, no. For the mortgage company. If the company lends him money, your Herr Ted will come back."'

'What time of day was this?' Mundy asks, but the person he is really listening to is Kate, the day she came home early from school and saw shadows in the window at Estelle Road: *Light on their feet . . . moving back and forth across the doorway.*

'Morning. Eight o'clock. It was raining. I was on my way to Frau Liebknecht's garden on my bicycle. In the afternoon, on my way back, five o'clock like now, they were still here. I'm so nosy it's ridiculous. Ask Elli. I'm incorrigible. "What takes you so long?" I ask them. "It's a big house," they said. "It will cost a lot of money. A lot of money takes a lot of time."'

*   *   *

He has done walks like this in Edinburgh. They went this way:

All right, Ted, in a minute you're going to step out of the front door of this house and you're going to the main railway station. You can use any public transport you like barring taxis, because we never take taxis, do we? — not the first one that comes along, not the second nor the third nor the thirteenth. Not when we've got our ears up. And by the time we reach the railway station, I'll want to know whether we're being followed and who by, and I don't want to know they know you know. Are we clear on that? And I want you at the station within half an hour because we've got a train to catch. So don't start giving me the scenic route by way of Edinburgh Zoo.

He walks and lets Heidelberg take him into its protection. Back into the lane, and a careless look at the surrounding cars and windows: oh how I love this little square with its leafy villas and secret gardens! Across the main road, down to the river's edge, and are those the same lovers who were canoodling on that bench when I came up here? Then over the Old Bridge that was blown to smithereens in 1945 in a vain effort to halt the advancing American army, but everyone's forgotten that, and a lot don't even know it, least of all the schoolkids and tour groups that walk up and down it, admiring the barges and the statues, much as Mundy does as he leans over the parapet waiting to see who stops behind him to light a cigarette, study a guidebook or take a photograph. The day is hot, the Hauptstrasse, which is a pedestrian precinct, is as usual jammed with slowly moving crowds, so Mundy improves his speed as if he has a train to catch, which indeed he has, but not quite yet, and keeps an eye on shop windows for anyone who might recall a forgotten engagement and similarly accelerate. He keeps going fast, cycles overtake him, and perhaps his followers called for them because following a six-footer going at full throttle when you are a few sizes shorter and also a pedestrian is a mug's game. He leaves the old town and enters the flat industrial ghetto of grey-block houses and logo cafés. But by the time he reaches the station, all he can tell his absent Edinburgh instructors is that, if he is being followed, he's being given the VIP coverage, which comprises everything from road sweepers to satellites, and the squirt of all-day hairspray on your shoulder that in the words of one eloquent instructor makes you glow like a fucking firefly on their grubby little television screens.

In the station concourse he goes to a public phone and with his head stuffed inside an enlarged helmet calls home. Zara has left for work. She will be at her café in an hour. He gets Mustafa, who howls. What – about – Dome – of – Rock – Ted? You – very – bad!

'We'll give it a double dose tomorrow night.' He does the banter. Yes, yes, I'm tucked up with my girlfriend.

Zara's cousin Dina comes to the phone. Dina, I've got to spend the night in Heidelberg, there's another meeting with the bank tomorrow. Can you explain to Zara, please? Can you try and get Mustafa into bed before midnight, please? Don't let him use the Dome as an excuse. Dina, you're a brick.

He calls the Linderhof, gets the machine, pinches his nose and leaves a message saying he won't be in tomorrow: flu.

The train to Munich leaves in forty minutes. He buys a newspaper, sits on a bench and watches the world go by while he wonders whether the world is watching him.

What were they doing in the schoolhouse all day? Measuring it for deep-pile carpets?

Nice. Young. Good smile. Overalls. Torch in his hand. No, we are only surveyors.

It's a stopping train and takes for ever. It reminds him of the stopping train from Prague the time he sat with Sasha in the guard's van with their bicycles. At a tiny station in a flat field he alights and moves back two carriages. A couple of stations later he moves further back. By the time he reaches Munich there are six people left on the train, and Mundy is the last by fifty yards to leave it.

The high-rise car park has a lift but he prefers the stairs, although they stink of piss. Men in leather haunt the half-landings. A black prostitute says twenty euros. He remembers Zara joining him for breakfast at the outdoor café on the day his life began again. *Please, sir, would you like to go to bed with me for money?*

His Volkswagen Beetle is on the fourth floor, in the corner bay where he left it this morning. He walks once round it, checking the doors for smear marks; and for clean patches where smear marks have been wiped off; and for new scratch lines on the fascias of the locks. *Good lad, Ted. We always said you were a natural and you are.*

Affecting to look for oil leaks, he crouches front and back, gropes for clever boxes, homers, and whatever else he can think of that was in fashion thirteen years ago. *Always try to focus your fear, Ted. If you don't know what you're scared of, you'll be scared of everything.*

Fine, I'll focus it. I'm afraid of bankers who aren't bankers, money launderers, crooked billionaire philanthropists who send me half a million dollars I don't trust, wealthy Arabs who pay for the spread of the English language, fake surveyors and my own shadow. I'm afraid for Zara, Mustafa and Mo the dog. And for my ever-tenuous hold on human love.

He unlocks the car and when it doesn't explode he makes a long arm into the back and unearths a gangrenous khaki waistcoat with kapok padding and poacher's pockets. Hauling off his suit jacket, he slips on the waistcoat and changes over the contents of his pockets. The car starts first time.

To descend to earth he must enter a hellish iron car-lift that reminds him of the Steel Coffin. For half the official parking price in cash, an old attendant unlocks the doors for him with a prison-sized key and consigns him to the nether world. Emerging in free air, Mundy takes a right and another right to avoid passing Zara's café because he knows that if he caught sight of her, he would scoop her up and drive her home and cause a lot of unnecessary confusion in everybody's minds including his own.

He reaches a roundabout and heads south. He is watching his mirrors but sees nothing to focus his fear on – but then if they're any good, I wouldn't, would I? It's midnight. A pink moon is shining, the road in front of him is as empty as the road behind him and there's a brave showing of stars. *Tomorrow we shall draw new lines between the stars.* Dimitri may have pillaged the globe in order to save it, but along the way he found time to take a course in kitsch.

He is heading south down the road he drives every day and in forty minutes he will reach the first of the two intersections and filter left. He does. No blue Audi with Sasha crouched ape-like at the wheel shepherds him, but he doesn't need one. In defiance of the lousy sense of direction that he shares with Trotsky, he knows the way. On the drive back with Sasha he made a mental record of the lefts and rights, and now he's following them in reverse order.

He passes the lay-by where he left his car in order to pursue Sasha up the spiral staircase and keeps driving until he reaches the skimpy path that ran along the foot of the mountains. His petrol tank is a quarter full, but it won't stop him getting there. Soon he's driving through forest, down the same pitted alley, though the pits are deeper because the moon is brighter. He enters the forest clearing that was like the clearing outside Prague, but instead of crossing it he scans the trees for another opening, spots one below him and, switching off his headlights then his engine, coasts quietly towards it, cursing the twigs for snapping under his tyres and the birds for screaming murder.

He rolls the car under the fir trees until he feels the weight of foliage on the roof, parks and picks his way between the boulders towards the concrete ramp.

Distances are real now. He's entering Badland and the rat is gnawing at his stomach. The barn looms ahead of him. Without the Audi's headlights shining on it, it's bigger than he remembers: two Zeppelins' worth at least. Its doors are shut and padlocked. He edges along one side. Unlike the all-day surveyors in Heidelberg, he has no flashlight and no assistants.

He is handing himself along the barn's wooden wall, using its stone footings as a walkway, waiting for a window or a gap in the timber. There isn't one. He finds a loose plank and eases it. He needs his tool bag. Mustafa's got it. He needs Des. We're divorced.

The plank is warped. He warps it a little more. It writhes, bends back on itself and comes free. He peers through the gap. Shafts of moonlight show him what he needs to know. No shiny Jeep, no rows of quality cars for sale. In their place, three businesslike tractors, a wood saw and a pyramid of baled hay.

Have I come to the wrong address? No, I haven't, but the tenants have changed.

He walks back to the front of the barn and sets off along the track towards the wall of death. The Jeep's ascent by his reckoning took ten to twelve minutes. The walk will take him an hour. Soon he wishes it could be longer. He wishes it could take all his life, with Zara and Mustafa, and Jake if he's not too busy, because in Mundy's book there's nothing in the world to beat plodding through pine forest by the light of the moon with mist in the valley and the first pale flush of dawn coming up ahead of you, and the clatter of spring streams half deafening you, and the scent of resin bringing tears to your eyes, and the deer playing hide-and-seek as you trot along.

It's not the same farmhouse.

The house I came to was enormous and hospitable, with merry lights in the windows and geraniums in the window boxes and Hansel and Gretel smoke coming out of the chimney.

But this farmhouse is low, grey, shuttered and sullen. It is surrounded by a previously unobserved high-wire perimeter fence and backed against a blue rock face, and everything about it – but particularly the painted signs – says private, dangerous dogs, forbidden, one step further and you'll be prosecuted so fuck off. And if anyone is asleep in the rooms upstairs, they're sleeping with their windows bolted and their curtains open and they've padlocked themselves in from outside.

The fence is neither electrified nor new, which at first makes him feel a fool. But then he tells himself that not even the smartest Edinburgh graduate can be expected to notice everything on a first flying visit. And certainly not when he's being driven at breakneck speed at dead of night by a pigskin-gloved Amazon with Sasha in the back breathing down his neck.

There is razor wire at the top of the fence and conventional barbed wire below. There is a locked iron gate, but inside the perimeter there are also two roe-deer that want badly to get out.

So somehow they got in. Maybe they jumped. No, they didn't, it's too high, even for them.

What they did – Mundy discovers, as he follows the fence round and searches the barns and outbuildings for signs of life and sees none – is cross a flattened stretch five feet wide where a tractor or other farm vehicle has ignored the warning signs and smashed its way in or out, and now the deer can't find it again.

But Mundy can find it and, better than that, he has discovered in his state of febrile agility an easy passage up a low-pitched slate roof to a window on the upper floor. And he has the wit, before he attempts the climb, to equip himself with a bit of rock. It's solid slate, weighs a ton, but for smashing open windows can't be bettered.

What have I come here for?

To make sure they're all as beautiful in the morning as they were at night.

To take a second look at the hidden signal in Dimitri's baby-blue eyes, the one that said, *You asked for this*.

To enquire, in the most casual way, what they think they're doing, at this extremely delicate point in all our histories, fooling around with funny money out of Riyadh.

And what caused them to conduct a day-long survey of my insolvent schoolhouse two weeks *ahead of* asking me how much space it has.

Assuming it was a survey, which we don't.

In short, we are here to shed a little healthy light on an increasingly perplexing experience, my dear Watson.

Only to discover that he has arrived on the scene too late. The troupe has packed up its props and costumes and moved on.

Next gig Vienna. Or Riyadh.

It is a well-worn dictum, and not only of the spy business, that you can tell who people are by what they throw away.

In a long moonlit bedroom, six bunk beds, slept in and abandoned. No pillows, sheets or blankets. Bring your sleeping bag.

Spread round the beds, the sort of waste the rich leave for the maid – to use, dear, or to give to somebody you like.

A can of fashionable men's deodorant, half full. One of the Mormons? An anorak? A suit? A blazer?

Unisex hairspray. Richard?

A pair of Italian court shoes that weren't comfortable after all. Tights, lightly snagged. A high-necked silk blouse left hanging in a wardrobe. The aseptic blonde? Her chastity kit?

Three-quarters of a litre of good Scotch. For Dimitri, to mix with his soya milk?

A six-pack of Beck's beer, two left. A part-used carton of Marlboro Lite. An ashtray full of stubs. Angelo? Sven? Richard? You'd think all three had sworn on their mothers' knees never to touch nicotine or liquor.

Or is Ted Mundy, super-sleuth, chasing his usual wild goose? Has a new crowd moved in here since the old one left, and I'm reading the wrong entrails?

* * *

Mundy gropes his way along a corridor, descends a couple of steps and makes a soft landing in carpet. There are no windows. He pats the walls around him and discovers a light switch. Billionaire philanthropists don't bother to switch off the power when they leave. He is standing opposite the door to Richard's office. He steps inside, half expecting to see Richard with his new haircut sitting at his brand-new desk, dressed in his brand-new blazer and airline steward's tie, but the desk is all that remains of him.

He pulls open the drawers. Empty. He drops to his knees on the deep-pile carpet and lifts the edge. No tacks, no Smooth Edge, no easy-grip or underlay: just deep, expensive, crudely cut carpet to cover the wiring underneath it.

What wiring? Richard had no telephone and no computer. Richard was sitting at a bareback desk. The ends of the wires are taped off. He follows the wires under the carpet to a painted chest of drawers beneath the window. He pulls out the chest. The wires run up the wall and across the sill and through a freshly drilled hole in the window frame.

To Mundy the homebuilder, the hole is cowboy work. The window frame is of fine old wood. The bastards might as well have shot a bullet through it. He opens the window and leans out. The wire goes down the wall for six feet and ducks back into the house: *there*. No staples, of course, which is typical. Just let it dangle till the next foehn wind slings it into the forest.

He returns to the staircase, descends a flight and makes for the living room where the philanthropist and his acolytes received their latest novice. Early dawn light is filling the windows on the valley side. At the spot where he watched Dimitri in his tracksuit bearing down on him, Mundy pauses. Dimitri came in through that door and went out through it.

Making the same diagonal traverse, Mundy reaches the

door, shoves it open and enters not a Green Room but a glazed lean-to kitchen tacked onto the north side of the house. It is part of a covered balcony – the same balcony, no doubt, where Dimitri invited Sasha to name today's stars.

The wires from upstairs are poking through the window. This time, instead of putting a bullet hole through the window frame, the cowboys have bashed out a pane of glass. The wire's ends are once more taped.

So this is where Dimitri hid after delivering his great soliloquy. This is where he held his breath and waited till I'd left the auditorium. Or did he amuse himself by playing with some clever piece of machinery, something that connected him with Richard upstairs? What for, for Heaven's sake? Why stoop to humble wires in our modern high-tech age? *Because low-tech wires that aren't tapped are a bloody sight safer than high-tech signals that are, Ted*, the sages of Edinburgh reply.

With a sense that he is outstaying his welcome Mundy returns upstairs and climbs down the slate roof to hard ground. He remembers the dangerous dogs and wonders why they haven't bitten him yet, and why they have left the roe-deer in peace. Perhaps they decamped with the rest of the philanthropists. At the bit of flattened perimeter fence he makes a half-hearted effort to persuade the deer to come with him, but they dip their heads and eye him reproachfully. Maybe when I've gone, he thinks.

Flare-paths of orange cloud sweep across the sky. Mundy bounds down the steep track, trusting in physical exertion to produce some kind of enlightenment. With each stride the voices in his head grow more emphatic: abort, send the money back, say no – but who to? He needs to talk to Sasha, but has no route to him: *I am required immediately in Paris . . . I am personally charged with the composition of our college libraries . . .* Yes, damn you, but what's your phone number? I didn't ask.

'Checkpoint,' he says aloud, and feels the rat give a bite at his abdomen.

A line of frontier guards or policemen – he can't tell which – is strung across the track twenty yards below him. He counts nine men. They wear blue-grey trousers and black jackets with red piping, and Mundy guesses they are Austrian not German because he's never seen uniforms like that in Germany before. They are aiming their rifles at him. Plainclothes men are hovering behind them.

Some of the guns are aimed at his head, the rest at his midriff, all with a marksman's concentration. A loudspeaker is booming at him in German to put his hands on his head *now*. As he does so, he sees more men to his left and right, as many as a dozen on each side. And he notes that they have had the sense to stagger their positions so that when they shoot at him they won't shoot each other by mistake. The loudspeaker belongs to the group below him, and its voice is bouncing all over the valley like a ricochet that won't lie down. Deep Bavarian accent, could be Austrian.

'Take your hands off your head and stretch your arms above you.'

He does as he is told.

'Shake your hands around.'

He shakes them.

'Take off your watch. Drop it on the ground. Roll back your shirtsleeves. Further. All the way to the shoulders.'

He pushes his sleeves up as far as they'll go.

'Keep your hands in the air and turn round. Keep turning. Stand still. What have you got in your waistcoat?'

'My passport and some money.'

'Anything else?'

'No.'

'Anything inside the waistcoat?'

'No.'

'No gun?'

'No.'

'No bomb?'

'No.'

'Sure?'

'Positive.'

Mundy has pinpointed him. He's the odd one out in the middle of the nine. Peaked cap, mountain boots. No rifle, but a pair of field glasses. Each time he speaks he has to drop the glasses and pick up the microphone.

'Before you take off your waistcoat, I'm going to tell you something. Are you ready?'

'Yes.'

'If you touch the pockets of the waistcoat or put your hand inside it, we'll kill you. Understood?'

'Understood.'

'*With one hand only* you take off the waistcoat. Slowly, slowly. No fast movements or we shoot you. It's not a problem. We kill people. We don't mind. Maybe you kill people too, yes?'

Using his left hand and punching his right stiffly in the air, Mundy finds the zipper at his neck and draws it gingerly downward.

'Okay. *Now*.'

He slithers out of the waistcoat and lets it flop to the ground.

'Put your hands back on your head. Good boy. Now you take five big paces to your left. Stop.'

Mundy takes his five paces and sees out of the side of his right eye a brave young gendarme approach his waistcoat, prod it with the barrel of his rifle, then turn it over.

'All clear, captain!' he reports.

As a supreme act of courage, the boy shoulders his rifle, picks up the waistcoat and takes it down the hill to his leader where he dumps it like dead game at his feet.

'Take off your shirt.'

Mundy takes it off. He wears no vest. Zara says he's too thin. Mustafa says he's too fat.

'Take off your left shoe. *Slowly!*'

He takes off his left shoe. Slowly.

'Right shoe.'

He stoops and takes off his right shoe. Equally slowly.

'Now socks. Good boy. Now take five paces to your right.'

He's back where he started, standing barefoot in thistles.

'Unbuckle your belt. *Slowly*. Put it on the ground. Strip naked – yes, your underpants too. Now put your hands back on your head. What's your name?'

'Mundy. Edward Arthur. British subject.'

'Born?'

The captain is holding Mundy's passport in the hand that doesn't hold the field glasses, and he is checking Mundy's answers against it. He must have fished it out of the pocket of the waistcoat.

'Fifteenth August 1947.'

'Where?'

'Lahore, Pakistan.'

'Why do you have a British passport if you're from Pakistan?'

The question is too large for one unarmed naked man to answer. When my mother began her labour the sun was still

Indian. By the time she was dead it was Pakistani, but you wouldn't understand that.

'My father was British,' he replies. And my mother was Irish, he might add, but he doesn't feel the need.

An old trooper with Father Christmas eyebrows is waddling up the hill to him, pulling on a pair of rubber gloves. He is accompanied by the brave young gendarme carrying a pair of crimson pyjamas.

'Bend over, please, son,' the old trooper says quietly. 'You make any problems, they'll shoot us all, so be a good fellow.'

The last time anyone did this to me was in the early days of my recruitment to the secret flag. Kate decided I had prostate cancer because I was peeing too often, but it was nerves. The old trooper has his fingers so far up Mundy's arse he wants to cough, but he doesn't find whatever he is looking for, because he shouts 'Nix' to the captain. The crimson shirt has no buttons so Mundy must haul it over his head. The trousers are too big for him, even after he has drawn the tapes as tight as they'll go.

Two men have grabbed his arms and are pinning them behind his back. Leg-irons snap round his ankles. A gumshield forces his teeth apart. Blackened goggles descend over his eyes. He would like to shout but he can only gurgle. He would like to fall over but he can't do that either, because a dozen hands are toppling him crab-like down the hill. His mouth fills with exhaust fumes as more hands shove him face down on a throbbing steel floor between a gauntlet of toecaps. He is back in the Steel Coffin, heading for the marshalling yards, but without Sasha's monkey-wrench to look forward to. The floor jerks forward and his feet crash against the rear doors. This act of indiscipline earns him what, despite the darkness, is a blinding kick over the left eye. Change of reference: he is Sasha in the dog van on his way to lunch with the Professor. Then he's Ted Mundy again, in the *grüne Minna*, being driven to the police station to make another voluntary statement.

The van bumps to a halt. He is hopping up an iron ladder under the churning rotaries of an unseen helicopter. He is flat on the floor again, this time chained to the deck. The helicopter lifts off. He feels sick. The helicopter flies, he doesn't know for how long. It lands, he is grappled down more steps, across tarmac and through a succession of clanging doors. He is chained to a dunce's chair in a grey-brick room with no windows and a steel door, but it takes him a while to realise he can see.

After that, in his later memory, it is only a matter of a few hours and several lifetimes before he is a free man again, wearing his own clothes and sitting in a flowered armchair in a pleasantly furnished office with rosewood furniture and regimental trophies and photographs of heroic pilots waving from their cockpits and an eternal gas-fired log burning cheerfully in the grate. With one hand he holds a warm poultice to his eye. In the other, a king-sized dry Martini cocktail. And across the room from him sits his old friend and confidant Orville J. Rourke – call me Jay – of the Central Intelligence Agency in Langley, Virginia – and dammit, Ted, you don't look a day older than when you and I took those crazy walks through darkest London all those years ago.

Mundy's return to life, now that he is able to reconstruct it, came in three set pieces.

There was Mundy the Terrorist Prisoner, chained to a chair and being asked a lot of aggressive questions about his movements by two young American men and one matronly

American woman. The matronly woman kept gabbling Arabic at him, presumably in the hope of catching him out.

Then there was Mundy the Object of Concern – initially to a young male doctor, also American and by his demeanour military. This doctor was accompanied by an orderly bearing Mundy's clothes on a hanger. The doctor needed to *take a look at this eye of yours, if I may, sir.*

The orderly also called Mundy sir. 'Sir, there's a restroom right across the corridor here, also a razor for your convenience,' he said, hanging Mundy's clothes on the handle of the open cell door.

The doctor advised Mundy that the eye was nothing to worry about. Just rest it. If it gets sore, put a patch over it. Mundy, ever the wag, said thanks, he had one over it not long ago.

And after that there was Mundy the Magnanimous, holding court in the same room where he is now sitting, being plied with hot coffee and cookies, and Camel cigarettes he didn't want, while he received the apologies of people he didn't recognise and assured them that he had no hard feelings, everything's forgiven and forgotten. And these embarrassed young men and women had names like Hank and Jeff and Nan and Art, and they wanted Mundy to know that our Chief of Ops was on his way from Berlin *right now*, and meanwhile – well – Jeez, sir – all we can say is, we're so sorry, we had no idea who you were and – this is Art speaking now – *I am truly proud to meet you, Mr Mundy, sir, they taught your fine record on my training course* – by which was meant, Mundy assumed, his fine record as a Cold War spy rather than as a language tutor on the skids or a loyal servant of the late King Ludwig. Though how on earth Art was able to put Mundy's name to a standard case history taught at his CIA training school was another mystery, unless Jay Rourke in his outrage had used it to rub their noses in the mess they'd made. Because Mr Rourke is really pissed with us, sir, and he needs Mr Mundy to know that before he gets here.

'I guess the best we can say for those kids is, they were obeying orders,' Rourke is summing up, with a doleful shake of his head, an hour later.

Mundy says he knows, he knows. Rourke hasn't changed either, he's thinking. Which is a pity. With people, you see in them what you think you already know, so Mundy sees the same droll, spare, good-looking, lazy-spoken Bostonian shit that Rourke always was, with his Dublin suit and Harvard shoes with heavy treads and easy Irish charm.

'Just too bad we never got to say a decent goodbye,' Rourke recalls, as if he feels there is something else he needs to get off his chest. 'Some bushfire crisis blew up so fast there wasn't time to pack my toothbrush. And dammit, for the life of me, Ted, I don't believe I remember what it was. Still, I guess hullo is always better than goodbye. Even in *these* circumstances.'

Mundy guesses it is too, and takes a pull of his Martini.

'We tell Austrian Liaison we're interested in a certain house — we suspect a terrorist connection and we want first look at anybody acting suspiciously around the place — well, I guess that's what we asked for and that's what we have to live with these days. Over-compliance from our friends and allies, and a disregard for innocent people's human rights.'

And you're still peddling the same spurious sedition, Mundy notes.

'Enjoy the war?' Rourke asks.

'Hated it,' Mundy retorts, whacking the ball back as hard as his weightless condition allows.

'Me too. Agency never gave those fucking Washington evangelists one scrap of encouragement, you have my word.'

Mundy says he can well believe it.

'Ted, can we stop pissing around?'

'If that's what we're doing.'

'Then why don't you just explain what you were doing up there, Ted, four in the morning for Christ's sakes, taking bearings in an empty house that we have a certain very specific interest in? I mean, frankly, between you and me, getting on that plane and flying down here, I couldn't help asking myself whether we weren't right to pull you in.'

13

Mundy has been giving a lot of thought to how he will answer Rourke's questions, and has come to the reluctant conclusion that he must tell him the truth. He has examined the problem from Sasha's point of view, and from his own. He has carefully considered Sasha's exhortation to confidentiality and Richard's thousand-dollar contract, but he has decided that in the circumstances neither is binding. It's only on the matter of Dimitri's grand design, and his declared war on the corrupting power of corporate America, that he feels any compunction to sweeten his story. For the rest, he is happy to fall back on his old confessive ways.

After all, what's a bit of burning joss between old pals?

And Rourke, exactly as in their Eaton Place days, hears him out with just that blend of broad tolerance and disrespect for authority that made frank talking with him such a pleasure. And when Mundy has finished his narrative, Rourke remains motionless and chin in hand for quite some while,

363

staring ahead of him and allowing himself only the odd little nod now and then and a grim pursing of the lips, before he rises from his chair and, headmaster-like, patrols the room with his hands jammed deep into the pockets of his gabardine trousers.

'Ted, do you have any *idea* what Sasha got up to in the last ten years?' he asks, placing so much emphasis on the word *idea* that Mundy can only have the worst expectations. 'The people he rode with, the bad places he was in?'

'Not a lot.'

'Sasha didn't tell you where he'd *been*? Who he'd *played* with?'

'We haven't talked that much. He wrote to me a bit while he was in the wilderness. Nothing very revealing.'

'Wilderness? He used that word?'

'No, I did.'

'Up there in the safe flat at the lakeside – he told you Dimitri was this great, good man?'

'He's pretty smitten with him.'

'And you find no *change* in him, after all these years of separation – no quantum change, no feeling he's moved on, moved *away* from you, in some intangible sense?'

'Same weird little bugger he always was, far as I can see,' says Mundy awkwardly, beginning not to like the trend of this conversation.

'Has Sasha given you any indication at *all* of how he feels about Nine Eleven, for instance?'

'He thought it was a foul act.'

'Not even "they had it coming to them" kind of thing?'

'Not a murmur of it, rather surprisingly.'

'Surprisingly?'

'Well, given the stuff he used to chuck at America, and

the stuff he's seen while he's been out on the stomp, it wouldn't exactly have surprised me if he'd said, "Serves the bastards right."'

'But he didn't?'

'Quite the reverse.'

'And this was in a letter?'

'Sure.'

'A solus letter – dedicated to the subject?'

'One of a long line.'

'Written when?'

'A couple of days after the event. Maybe one day. Don't think I noticed.'

'From where?'

'Sri Lanka, probably. He had some kind of lectureship in Kandy.'

'And you found the letter totally convincing? You didn't feel it was – like –'

'Like what?'

Rourke gives one of his sophisticated shrugs. 'That it was written for the record, maybe. In case his pal Teddy was thinking of passing it to any of his connections in British Intelligence.'

'No, I didn't,' Mundy says hotly to Rourke's back, and waits for him to turn round, but he doesn't.

'Ted, when you were in Berlin with Sasha all those years ago, did he have explicit views on *direct action*?'

'He was dead against it. All the way.'

'Did he have a reason?'

'Sure he did. Violence plays into the hands of the reactionaries. It's self-defeating. He said it over and over again. Dozen different ways.'

'So he was practical. Violence doesn't work, so let's go

365

for something that does. If it had worked he'd have gone for it.'

'You can call it practical. You can call it moral. It was an article of faith for him. If he'd believed in bombs, he'd have thrown bombs. That's who he is. He didn't believe in them, so the bomb-throwers hijacked the protest movement and he made the mistake of a lifetime and jumped over the Wall the wrong way.'

Mundy is protesting too much and knows it, but Rourke's insinuations are setting off alarm bells in him that need shouting down.

'So if I told you he'd jumped over *another* wall, would you really be so surprised?' Rourke asks languidly.

'Depends which one you're talking about.'

'No, it doesn't. You know damn well, Ted Mundy' – more languidly still. 'We're talking about going the black road. We're talking about a crippled obsessive who must either play in the Super Bowl, or he's a nobody.' Rourke opens his hands and appeals to the eternal gas-fired log. *'I'm Sasha, fundamentalist. Fly me! I divert rivers and move mountains. I sit at the feet of great philosophers and turn their words into deeds.* Know who Dimitri is, when he's not being Dimitri?'

Mundy's fingers are mangling whatever facial expression he might otherwise have. 'No. I don't. Who?'

Rourke has come close: so close that he is able to put his hands on the two arms of Mundy's chair and lean down on him and peer into his face with awe at the secret he is about to unveil.

'Ted, this isn't just off the record. That plane I came in. It came here empty. I never left my fucking desk in Berlin and I have six witnesses who will swear to that. Did Dimitri tell you he is an artist of the unobserved life?'

366

'Yes.'

'I'd sooner trail Lucifer. He doesn't use telephones worth a fuck, won't touch a cellphone. Computers, e-mails, electronic typewriters, the humble post, forget it.' Mundy remembers the low-tech wiring in the farmhouse. 'He'll travel five thousand miles to whisper into a man's ear in the middle of the Sahara desert. If he sends you a postcard, look at the picture, because that's where the message is. He lives big or small, he doesn't give a shit. He never sleeps two nights running in the same bed. He'll take a house in someone else's name – in Vienna, Paris, Tuscany or up in the mountains – move in, make like he's going to live there for the rest of his life and the next night he's sitting in a cave in fucking Turkey.'

'In aid of what?'

'The bomb in the market place. He bombed for the Spanish anarchists against Franco, the Basques against the Spanish and the Red Brigades against the Italian Communists. He ran with the Tupamaros and all fifty-seven varieties of Palestinian, and played both sides of the net for Ireland. May I tell you, please, what his message to the faithful of Old Europe is, right now? You'll love this.'

Waiting for the pay-off, Mundy reflects that Rourke takes private pleasure in contrasting life's obscenity with his own elegance. The more disgraceful a proposition, the more courtly his manner. As if to demonstrate this, he has reclaimed his armchair and stretched out his legs and treated himself to another little sip of dry Martini.

'"Folks," he's saying, "it's time for us Euro-angries to stop all being so damned squeamish. How's about a little solidarity for a change with the perpetrators of the most sensational act of anti-capitalism since the invention of gunpowder? How's about extending the hand of friendship to our brothers and sisters in arms around the globe, instead of muttering about certain little hang-ups they may have about democracy? Are we not all united in our hatred of the common enemy? These Al Qaeda boys have brought off just about everything Mikhail Bakunin dreamed of. If anti-fascists can't accept human diversity within their ranks, tell me who can!"'

He sets down his glass, catches Mundy's eye, and smiles.

'That's who Dimitri is, Ted. When he's being himself and not Dimitri, of course. And that's Sasha's latest Svengali. So let us proceed to my next question, Ted: who is Ted Mundy in this equation?'

'You know bloody well who I am,' Mundy bursts out. 'You spent months sniffing through my underclothes, damn you.'

'Oh, *come on*, Ted! That was *then*. This is live ammunition time. Are you for us or against us?'

Now it is Mundy's turn to stalk around the room and bring his temper back under control.

'I still don't understand what Dimitri wants,' he says.

'You tell me, Ted. We know everything and we know zilch. He's in touch with people who are in touch with anarchist groups around the European circuit. Big deal. He flirts with the leading European professors of anti-American studies. He's talking up a storm about nailing the Big Lie. He has a retinue. He insists they dress like the enemy. It's an old saw of his: fascists think twice before they shoot a hole in a good suit. Did he tell you that story?'

'No.'

Settling back in his armchair, Rourke permits himself a diversion. 'It's too amusing. He got caught in a firefight with the Greek police one time, and he's wearing this seven-hundred-dollar suit. He was out of ammo, standing in this open square in the middle of Athens with an empty gun in his hand and he's looking straight into the barrel of this sniper up on the roof who's taking a bead on him. He puts a fedora on his head and walks out of the square before the sniper gets up the nerve to put a bullet through his seven-hundred-dollar suit. Sure he didn't tell you that one?'

'Where does he get his money from?' Mundy wants to know, staring into the whited-out window.

'All around. Small parcels, no two the same. Coming in from everywhere. It bothers us sick: the too-much money. This time round it was the Middle East. Last time it was South America. Who gives it to him? What for? What the fuck does he want with it? Everybody in the world will tell the *truth* suddenly? – like bears eat candy in the forest. He's getting old. He's calling in the promises he's owed from everywhere. Why? What's his endgame? We think he wants to go out with a bang.'

'What kind of bang?'

'What other kind is there? Heidelberg's where Germany meets America. It's the pretty city we didn't bomb in forty-five so that America would have somewhere to put her headquarters when the war was over. Mark Twain went nuts about the place; America began its post-Hitler, anti-Soviet existence there. It has the US Mark Twain Village and the US Patrick Henry Village with a population of God knows how many thousands of US personnel. It's home to Headquarters US Army Europe, and a bunch of other major commands. Back in seventy-two, the Baader-Meinhof crowd killed some US soldiers and wiped out the staff car of a US NATO general with a bazooka, and they damn near wiped

369

out the general with it. If you want to blow America and Germany apart, Heidelberg's not a bad place to make your point. You like the city?'

'Love it.'

'Then maybe you'd like to help us save it.'

Mundy has decided what it is he feels about Rourke. There is something fundamentally untouched about him, something offensively virginal. The lines Mundy previously mistook for life-experience are the lines of an over-indulged child who has never been beaten up by anybody's police, or crossed bad borders, or been locked away in the White Hotel, or hog-tied and chained to the floor of a helicopter. In this respect he embodies what Mundy considers the least attractive characteristic of both our Western leaders and their spokesmen: a levitational self-belief that nimbly transcends the realities of human suffering.

He wakes to discover that Rourke is recruiting him. Not desperately like Sasha, or subliminally like Amory, or blatantly like the Professor, and not with any of the Messianic flair of a Dimitri. But eloquently, nonetheless.

'You do what you did before, Ted. You become our man. You pretend to be their man. You stay aboard. You wait. You watch and listen. You make nice to Sasha and Dimitri and whoever else comes into your life. And you find out what the fuck everybody is *at*.'

'Maybe Sasha doesn't know.'

'Oh, he *knows*, Ted. Sasha's a traitor, remember.'

'Who to?'

'Didn't he spy on his own people? Maybe you have a sweeter word for that. Wasn't his father a turncoat twice over? Sasha's been a prominent person to us these last few years. We don't lose sight of people like that. Not even when they go wandering in the wilderness looking for some new god to put the sparkle back into their eyes.' He pauses to allow Mundy to dispute this, but Mundy doesn't oblige. 'And when you've done waiting, you wait again. Because that's how this game is played: by seeing it all the way through, until the magic moment when Special Agent Ted Mundy jumps up on the table and flashes his badge, and says, "Okay, boys, we've all had a good time, but now it's curtains. So drop your guns and put your hands in the air because we have you surrounded." Ted, you wish to ask a question.'

'What guarantees do I get?'

Rourke does his most hospitable smile. 'If this thing breaks the way we think it will, total witness protection for you and yours, resettlement, a cash sum in millions and you get to keep the real estate. Retraining, but you're a little far gone for that. Want to talk numbers?'

'I'll take your word for it.'

'You'll be saving lives. Maybe a lot. Want time to think it over? I'll count to ten.'

'What's the alternative?'

'I don't see one, Ted. I try, I rack my brains, I search my heart. You could go to the German police. They might help. They did before. You're a British expatriate and former Berlin anarchist living with a retired Turkish hooker: I can see you engaging their concern.'

Does Mundy speak? Probably not.

'Basically, my guess is the German police would push you straight over to the German spooks, who would push you on to us. I don't think anybody's going to leave you alone. That's not what we're in business for. You're just too, too desirable.' He cocks his ear. 'Do I hear a yes? Is that a nod I see?'

Apparently, it is. But a distracted one, naturally, because Mundy's mind, or what's left of it, is far away in Paris with Sasha and his fellow scholars of the library committee. *We are indivisible, Teddy. That is my conviction. We have endured together . . . Long ago you saved me. Allow me at least the chance to be the road to your salvation.*

Mundy waits.

And having waited, he waits again.

No two things happen simultaneously. Everything is linear while he waits. He waits at the Linderhof and at home: for the envelope in Sasha's familiar spiky handwriting, for Sasha's clotted voice on the phone.

He makes a day-trip to Heidelberg, three hours in the train each way, and talks to cleaners, builders and decorators, but no message from Sasha greets him, and when he returns home at midnight he discovers that Zara has broken bounds and come home early.

She knows he knows something that he's not telling her. Her suspicions were aroused when he stayed in Heidelberg that night. She doesn't believe he had a second meeting with the bankers next morning. And look at his black eye.

It was just a bit of builder's scaffolding, he tells her, not for the first time. I was walking down a narrow street when this bit of plank jumped out and hit me in the eye. It's the price I pay for being tall. I should have looked where I was going.

What do they want you for, those bankers that I don't believe in? she demands. Stay away from them. They're worse than the police.

He tries telling her a little of what they want. These bankers are all right, he assures her. They're trying to help

372

me. They're putting up some money, and if I can get the school back on its feet, they may even let me run it again. Anyway, it's worth a shot.

Her German is serviceable at best, his Turkish non-existent. They can trade facts, and they can call in Mustafa who is always proud to interpret. For their feelings however they must consult each other's faces, eyes and bodies. What Zara rightly reads in him is evasion. What Mundy reads in her is fear.

Next morning at the Linderhof he makes a sortie to the plant room and unearths Richard's thousand dollars' cash. The same evening, in controlled desperation, he hands the money to the dental clinic. Her broken teeth may finally be capped. But when he shows Zara the receipt she is at first radiant, then relapses into her former gloom. Through Mustafa she accuses Mundy of stealing the money. It takes all his wits to dissuade her. They've paid me a *bonus*, Zara. It's for the extra tours I did when people were away, a sort of tip. For an experienced liar he makes a lousy job of it, and when he reaches out to her in bed she shrinks away from him. *You don't love me any more*, she says. A day later Mustafa teases him about his non-existent girlfriend once too often. Mundy snaps at him and is ashamed. By way of reparation he slaves at their Dome of the Rock and places an order for Mustafa's longed-for computer.

Rourke rings his new agent daily on the mildewed cell-phone prompt at twelve-thirty, Mundy's lunch break. During their post-recruitment discussion, Rourke tried his damnedest to persuade Mundy to accept the Agency's latest super-secure, hot-and-cold-running model, but Mundy wasn't having any of it. I'm the last Luddite in the spy trade, Jay. Awfully sorry. He has read, but does not say so, that cellphones in the wrong hands can blow people's heads off. As usual, Rourke starts straight in: no *Hi, Ted,* or *This is Jay.*

'Michael and his friends have about finished their homework,' he announces. Michael is Sasha. 'He could be heading your way in a couple of days from now.'

So wait. For Michael.

A couple of days become four. Rourke says relax, Michael bumped into some old friends.

On the fifth, strolling past the administrative offices, Mundy observes a white envelope addressed to him in electronic type, postmark Vienna. The letter is on plain paper, dated but unsigned. No sender's address. The text is in English.

Dear Mr Mundy,
   An important consignment of books will be delivered to your school on Wednesday, 11 June between 17.00 and 19.00 hours You should kindly make yourself available to receive them. Our representative will be in attendance.

No reply required, none possible. Rourke says relax, Michael will be your representative.

Standing obliquely to the first-floor bay window of the Heidelberg schoolhouse and peering down the brick path towards the iron front gates, Mundy feels profound relief that his thoughts and actions are at last one. He is in the place where his mind has been for the last two weeks. *Michael is on his sweet way*, Rourke has confirmed over the cellphone. *Michael's train is suffering a minor delay, he expects to be with you in half an hour.* Rourke's disembodied bulletins are snide and imperious. Mundy hates them. He is wearing an old leather jacket and corduroys: nothing that he wore or took off during his captivity. He is assuming saturation surveillance but has no desire to be a walking microphone. The time is coming up to five-twenty. The last workman left ten minutes ago. Those Counter-University chaps think of everything.

In his days of waiting Mundy has gone over his predicament from every angle he can think of, and come to no conclusion. As Dr Mandelbaum would say, he has assembled the information, but where is the knowledge? Spurred by the imminence of Sasha's arrival, he once more reviews the possibilities, starting with the most attractive.

Rourke and his Agency are deceiving themselves, and me. In the great tradition of their trade, they are turning fantasy into self-fulfilling prophecy. Dimitri has a shady past, as he admits, but he is reformed and his noble intentions are as he describes them.

In support of the above argument: Rourke is the same idiot who spent four months trying to prove that Sasha and Mundy were working for the Kremlin.

Against the above argument: the fly-by-night nature of Dimitri's circus, his murky money, the improbability of his Grand Vision, and his alleged advocacy of an alliance between Euro-anarchists and Islamic fundamentalists.

Rourke and his Agency have got it right, Dimitri is bad to very bad, but Sasha is his innocent dupe.

In support of the above argument: Sasha's gullibility is well attested. He is intelligent and perceptive, but as soon as his ideals are appealed to, he abandons his otherwise well-developed critical faculties and goes barmy.

Against the above argument: unfortunately, very little.

Dimitri is as bad as Rourke says he is, and — to quote the sages of Edinburgh — Sasha is complicit, conscious and aware.

Dimitri and Sasha together are taking me for a ride because they want my school for their own nefarious purposes.

In support: during Sasha's thirteen years in the wilderness he has witnessed at first hand the rape of the earth and the destruction of indigenous cultures by Western-led industrialisation. He has suffered great personal humiliation, and kept some pretty steamy company. In theory, these are all good reasons why Sasha should sign up to what Rourke calls the black road.

Against: Sasha never lied to me in his life.

Mundy has carried these unresolved arguments around like warring children inside his head for every unsleeping hour of the last fortnight, on his walks with Mo, or while earnestly helping Mustafa with his Dome, or striving to calm Zara's apprehensions, or marching his English-Spokens round Mad Ludwig's castle. And they are in his head now as he watches the white, unmarked van pull up outside the gates.

Nobody gets out. Like Mundy, the men are waiting. One has his head in a book. The other is talking on his cellphone. To Dimitri, Richard? Or to Rourke? The van has a Viennese registration. Mundy makes a mental note of it. *You're a proper wizard for the memorising, Ted, says a sycophantic Edinburgh instructor, I don't know how you do it, I'm sure.* Simple, old boy, nothing else in my head. A sleek Mercedes limousine drives past. Black woman driver, white male passenger, the city flag flying from the wing, police motorcyclist riding point. Some city bigwig has his residence just up the road. The limousine is followed by a humble station taxi, the property of one Werner Knau, who likes to inscribe his name in gold Gothic lettering. A rear door opens, Sasha's left sneaker emerges, then the leg. A pianist's fingers enfold the door pillar. Now the whole man has hauled himself out, his Party briefcase after him. He stands but, unlike Mundy, does not have to beat his pockets to discover which one has the money in it. He has his purse, and he is methodically counting out the change from one palm to the other, just as he counted it in Berlin, or Weimar, or Prague, or Gdansk and any of the cities where East met West in a spirit of peace, friendship and cooperation. He pays the taxi and exchanges a couple of words with the men in the van while he points imperiously up the brick path.

Forsaking his post at the bay window, Mundy makes his way downstairs to meet him. It's our first day again, he is thinking. Do I embrace him, Judas style? Or shake his hand, German style? Or go all English and do nothing?

He opens the front door. Sasha is hobbling jubilantly up the path towards him. The evening sun lights one side of his face. Mundy is standing on the step. Sasha arrives three feet below him. He drops his briefcase and flings out his arms, but to embrace the whole world rather than just Mundy.

'Teddy, my God,' he cries. 'Your house, this place – we are fantastic! Now Heidelberg is famous for three things: Martin Luther, Max Weber and Teddy Mundy! You can stay in Heidelberg tonight? We can talk – drink – play? You have time?'

'How about you?' says Mundy.

'Tomorrow I go to Hamburg to interview certain important academics, each one separately. Tonight I am an irresponsible Heidelberg student. I shall get drunk, challenge you to a duel, sing "Wer soll das bezahlen" and land up in the students' cells.' He has put his hand on Mundy's shoulder and is about to use him as a walking stick when he dives away again to extract something from his briefcase. 'Here.

For you. A gift from decadent Paris. You are not the only one who gets a good salary these days. Do we have a refrigerator? Power? We have everything, I am sure.'

He shoves it into Mundy's hands: a bottle of vintage champagne, the best there is. But Sasha is not interested in Mundy's thanks. He is pushing past him into the hall to make his first inspection of their new domain while Mundy hates himself for the dark suspicions that Rourke planted in his head.

First they must stand in the hall while Sasha feasts his gaze on the moulded ceilings, the grand staircase and mahogany rotunda of curved doors leading to the separate classrooms. And Mundy must watch how the diamonds of colour from the great art nouveau skylight make a pierrot of him, but a happy one.

Gradually they proceed – by magnetic attraction evidently, since Mundy has not pointed him the way, but perhaps the sinister surveyors have – to the old library, formerly divided into cubicles but now restored to its full glory, with new battens for adjustable bookshelves already fitted to the walls. Shoulders pressed back, the Schiller head revolving in marvel, Sasha attains by stages the far end of the room and unlocks a glazed door onto a courtyard.

'But good heavens, Teddy! I thought you were a master at this kind of thing! We can add this whole area to our library! Throw a glass roof over, a couple of steel pillars, and you can accommodate another thousand volumes. Expand now, it's no problem. Later, it will be a nightmare.'

'Reason number one: books don't like glass. Reason number two: you're standing in the new kitchen.'

On every floor, Sasha's satisfaction grows. The top floor pleases him particularly.

'You propose to live up here, Teddy? With your family, did I hear?'

Who from? Mundy wonders. 'Maybe. It's an option. We're thinking it over.'

'Is it absolutely necessary for you to be resident?'

'Probably not. Have to see how the project works.'

Sasha puts on his Party voice. 'I think you are actually being a little bit self-indulgent, Teddy. If we knock out the partition walls we can make a mattress dormitory and accommodate twenty poor students at least. We did it in Berlin, why not here? It's important you don't give the accidental impression of being a landlord. Dimitri is most concerned we do not create the semblance of an authoritarian structure. We must present a *contrast* to the university. Not imitate it.'

Well, let's hope the walls heard that too, Mundy is thinking. He is spared a reply by halloos from the stairwell. The delivery men have fork-lifted their load as far as the front door and need to know where they should put it next.

'Why, in the library, obviously!' Sasha shouts gaily down the stairs. 'Where else do books go, for God's sake? These fellows are ridiculous.'

But Mundy and the foreman have already agreed that the best place for the books is the hall: make an island at the centre and cover it with dust-sheets until the library's finished. The delivery men are venerable and wear white coats. To Mundy they look more like cricket umpires than removal men. Undeterred, Sasha launches on a ponderous description of his wares.

'You will discover on inspection that each box carries a plastic envelope tacked to its lid, Teddy. The envelope contains a list of titles inside the box and the initials of the packer. The volumes are assembled in alphabetical order by author. You will see that each box is numbered in the sequence in which it will eventually be opened. Are you listening to me, Teddy? Sometimes I fear for your concentration span.'

'I'm getting the idea.'

'We are speaking *in toto* of a core library of four thousand volumes. Books that we anticipate will be heavily in demand are supplied in multiples. Clearly no box must be opened until all building work has ceased. Books that are placed prematurely on their shelves will gather dust and will only have to be removed and cleaned at a cost of valuable time and money.'

Mundy promises to give the matter his close attention. While the men cart the boxes into the hall, he guides Sasha to the garden where he can do no harm, and sits him on an old swing seat.

'So what kept you in Paris?' he asks casually, thinking that whatever it was hasn't hurt his self-esteem.

The question pleases Sasha. 'I had a stroke of good fortune, actually, Teddy. A certain lady whose acquaintance I had enjoyed in Beirut happened to be passing through the city, and we were able to have what diplomats I believe describe as a full and frank exchange of views.'

'In bed?'

'Teddy, I think you are being indelicate' – with a smirk of satisfaction.

'What does she do for a living?'

'She is formerly an aid worker, now a freelance journalist.'

'Of the radical variety?'

'Of the truthful variety.'

'Lebanese?'

'French, actually.'

'Is she working for Dimitri?'

Sasha pulls in his chin to indicate his disapproval.

So yes, she is working for Dimitri, thinks Mundy.

At the same moment they hear the van's engine start. Mundy jumps to his feet but he's too late. The umpires have departed, leaving nothing to sign and nobody to tip.

Sasha is delighted by Teddy's great idea. After his exertions in Paris, an outing is just what he needs. It's what Mundy needs too, but for different reasons. He wants the woods outside Prague on the day you told me the Herr Pastor was a Stasi spy. He wants the bucolic intimacy of shared confession. He has borrowed the bicycles from old Stefan. The small one, Stefan's own, is for Sasha, and a big one, which belongs to Stefan's hulk of a son, for Mundy. He has bought sausage and hard-boiled eggs and tomatoes and cheese and cold chicken, and pumpernickel bread which he detests and Sasha loves. He has bought whisky and a bottle of burgundy to help loosen Sasha's tongue and, no doubt, his own. They have agreed by now that Mundy will keep Sasha's bottle of champagne for Opening Day.

'But do you know where we are going, my God?' Sasha asks in fake alarm as they set off.

'Of course I do, idiot. What do you think I've been doing all day?'

Should I pick a row with him? Yell at him? Mundy has never conducted an interrogation before and friends are certainly the wrong people to begin with. Think Edinburgh, he tells himself. *The best interrogations are the ones the suspect doesn't know are happening.* He has marked down a secluded spot a few miles out of town. Unlike Prague it has no hummocks to sit on, but it's a quiet, leafy place set low on the river bank, and impossible to overlook. It has a bench, and willow trees trailing in the swift clear water of the Neckar.

Mundy is being mother, pouring the wine, setting out the picnic. Sasha, spurning the bench, is stretched flat on his back with his bad leg tossed over his good one. He has unbuttoned his shirt and bared his skinny chest to the sun. On the river, earnest oarsmen wrench themselves a path against the current.

'So what else have you been up to in Paris apart from choosing books and sleeping with journalists?' Mundy enquires, by way of an opening bid.

'I would say I have been mustering the troops, Teddy,' Sasha replies airily. 'Has your Zara been beating you again?' – Mundy's black eye not being fully recovered.

'Young troops, old troops? People you know from other lives? What sort of troops?'

'Our lecturers, of course. Our visiting lecturers and intellectuals. What troops do you suppose? The best unbought minds in every major discipline.'

'Where do you dig them up?'

'In principle from all the world. In practice, from so-called Old Europe. That is Dimitri's preference.'

'Russia?'

'We try. Any country that was not a member of the Coalition of the Willing has pride of place in Dimitri's selections. In Russia unfortunately it is difficult to recruit from the uncompromised left.'

'So the lecturers are Dimitri's selections, not yours.'

'They are the result of a consensus. Certain names are put forward – many by myself, if I am immodest – a list is agreed, and placed before Dimitri.'

'Any Arabs on the list?'

'It will happen. Not at once, but in the second or third stage. Dimitri is a born general. We declare our limited aim, we achieve it, we regroup, we advance on the next aim.'

'Was he present with you in Paris?'

'Teddy, I think you are being a little indiscreet actually.'

'Why?'

'Please?'

Mundy hesitates. A barge slips by, its washing flapping in the evening sun. A green sports car is lashed to its forward deck.

'Well, don't you feel it's all getting a little bit damned stupid — all this secrecy about what everybody's up to?' he suggests awkwardly. 'I mean we're not mounting a putsch, are we? Just creating a forum.'

'I think you are being unrealistic, Teddy, as usual. Western teaching institutions that refuse to acknowledge today's taboos are by definition subversive. Tell the new zealots of Washington that in the making of Israel a monstrous human crime was committed and they will call you an anti-Semite. Tell them there was no Garden of Creation and they will call you a dangerous cynic. Tell them God is what man invented to compensate for his ignorance of science and they will call you a Communist. You know the words of the American thinker Dresden James?'

'I can't say I do.'

'"When a well-packaged web of lies has been sold gradually to the masses over generations, the truth will seem utterly preposterous and its speaker a raving lunatic." Dimitri will display this quotation in the entrance hall to every one of our colleges. It was in his mind to name the project the University of Raving Lunatics. Only prudence restrained him.'

Mundy passes Sasha a leg of chicken but Sasha, lying on his back, has his eyes closed, so Mundy waves it in front of his face until he smiles and opens them. Not in Berlin, not in Weimar, not in any of their other trysting places, has Mundy witnessed such contentment in his friend's face.

'Are you going to see her again?' he asks, struggling for small talk.

'It is questionable, Teddy. She is at a dangerous age and showed distinct signs of attachment.'

No change there then, Mundy notes a little sourly, momentarily recalling Judith. He tries again.

'Sasha, on your great safari – during those missing years when you were writing to me –'

'They are not missing, Teddy. They were my *Lehrjahre*, my years of instruction. For this.'

'During those years, did you find yourself' – he was going to say *riding with*, but that was Rourke's expression – 'did you rub shoulders with the far-out people – the ones who advocated armed resistance – indiscriminately – terror, if you like?'

'Frequently.'

'Were you influenced – persuaded by them?'

'What do you mean?'

'We used to talk about it. You and I. Judith did. Karen did. It was all the rage at the Republican Club. How far is it permissible to go? With the drama of the act, and so forth. What's a fair price, in what circumstances? When can the shooting legitimately begin? You used to say Ulrike and her kind were giving anarchism a bad name. I wondered whether anything had changed your mind.'

'You wish for my views on this subject – *here* – *today* – while we drink this excellent burgundy? I think you are being a little Teutonic, Teddy.'

'I don't think so.'

'If I were a Palestinian living in the West Bank or Gaza, I would shoot every occupying Israeli soldier in sight. However, I am a poor shot and have no gun, so my chances of success would be small. A planned act of violence against unarmed civilians is in no case permissible. The fact that you and your American masters drop illegal cluster bombs and other repulsive weaponry on an unprotected Iraqi population consisting sixty per cent of children does not alter my position. Is this what you are asking me?'

'Yes.'

'*Why?*'

It appears that the interrogation has turned itself round. It is Sasha not Mundy who is keeping his anger at bay, and Sasha who is sitting bolt upright on the grass, glowering at him, demanding an answer.

'It just occurred to me that we might have different agendas, that's all.'

'In what sense different? What are you talking about, Teddy?'

'Whether you and Dimitri are looking to do more than just *challenge* the prevailing cant – or challenge it by different means.'

'Such as what?'

'Raising a storm of some kind. Sending out a signal to the real forces of anti-Americanism.' Rourke's words are winging back to him and this time he is reduced to using them. 'Extending the hand of friendship to the perpetrators of the most sensational act of anti-capitalism since the invention of gunpowder.'

For a while Sasha appears to doubt his hearing. He inclines his head in question, and puts on his Party frown. With his small hands spread before him in a gesture to command silence, he consults the objects around him for enlightenment: the nearly empty bottle of burgundy, the hard-boiled eggs, cheese, pumpernickel bread. Only then does he lift his dark brown eyes, and Mundy to his alarm sees that they are brimming with tears.

'Who the fuck have you been talking to, Teddy?'

'Am I right, Sasha?'

'You are so wrong it makes me sick. Go and be an Englishman. Fight your own fucking wars.'

Sasha has dragged himself to his feet and is buttoning up his shirt. His breath is coming in retches. He must have an ulcer or some bloody thing. It's the Dreesen Hotel all over again, Mundy thinks, as Sasha peers round him for his jacket. It's the same bloody river going by, and the same impossible gap between us. In a minute he's going to ride into the sunset and leave me looking like the unfeeling oaf I always was.

'It's my bloody bank, Sasha,' he pleads. 'For Christ's sake, sit down and drink some wine and stop behaving like a drama queen. We've got a problem. I need your help.'

Which is how he planned to play it if he didn't extract the sobbing confession he was counting on.

Sasha is sitting again but he has drawn up his knees and locked his hands round them and the knuckles are white with tension. His jaw is set the way it used to be when he talked about the Herr Pastor, and he refuses to take his eyes off Mundy's face whatever Mundy does. The food and wine have ceased to interest him. All that matters to him are Mundy's words and Mundy's face while he speaks them. And this scrutiny would be about as much as Mundy could take, if it weren't for the hard school he'd been through, and his years of glib lying to the Professor and his acolytes.

'My bank just can't get over where the money came from,' Mundy complains, wiping his wrist across his brow in agitation. 'They have all these regulations about unexpected sums of money these days. Anything over five thousand euros sets their alarm bells ringing.'

He is approaching the fiction, but with fact at his elbow.

'They've backtracked on the money orders and don't like what they've found. They're thinking of going to the authorities.'

'Which authorities?'

'The usual, I suppose. How should I know?' He bends the truth a little further. In a minute it's going to snap. 'They had an extra man there. He said he was from Head Office. He went on asking me who was behind the payments. As if they were criminal somehow. I said what Dimitri's people had told me to say, but that wasn't good enough for him. He kept complaining that I hadn't anything to show them – no contract, no correspondence. I couldn't even tell him the name of my benefactor. Just half a million dollars from some pretty odd places, recycled through big-name banks.'

'Teddy, this is total fascistic provocation. You have been at the bastards' mercy for so long they can't bear you to slip out of their grasp. I think you are being a little naive, actually.'

'Then he asked me whether I'd ever had anything to do with anarchists at any point in my life. Or their supporters. He was talking about Euro-anarchists. People like the Red Army Fraktion and the Red Brigades.' He allows time for this disinformation to have its effect, but it has none at all.

Sasha is watching him with the same shocked, straight stare that he adopted from the moment Mundy started down this road.

'And you?' Sasha enquires. 'What did you say?'

'I asked him what the hell that had got to do with anything.'

'And he?'

'Asked me why I was expelled from Berlin.'

'And you?'

Mundy would like to tell Sasha to shut up prompting him and just listen. I'm trying to sow alarm in you, damn you – draw you out, force an admission from you, and all you do is glower at me as if I'm the villain in this, and you're the lily-white one.

'I said that in my youth I had been a rebel, just like anybody else, but I didn't think that fact had much to do with my present standing at the bank, or my fitness to receive cash from a reputable Trust.' He flounders on. 'They haven't left me alone since. They gave me a whole bunch of forms to fill in, and yesterday I got a call from somebody describing herself as the bank's Special Enquiries Officer, asking me if I could name referees who could vouch for me over the last ten years. Sasha, listen to me, please –'

He is doing a Sasha in reverse: eyes wide, hands open, appealing to him the way Sasha did when he was begging him to go with him to the mountain top.

'Is there really nothing more you can tell me about Dimitri? I mean, just his real name would be a help, for Christ's sake – a few scraps about his past – only the reputable bits, naturally – some idea of who he is and how he made his money – where he's coming from politically?' And for good measure: 'I'm in the hot seat, Sasha. This one isn't going away.'

Mundy is standing and Sasha, in his beggar's crouch, is

still staring up at him. But instead of fear and guilt or tears, his eyes are filled with pity for a friend.

'Teddy. I think you are right. You should get out of this before it's too late.'

'Why?'

'I asked you before we went up to see Dimitri. I ask you again now. Do you truly believe your own rhetoric? Are you really prepared to return to the intellectual barricades? Or are you like the little pipers when they march to war? The first sound of gunshot, they want to go home?'

'Just as long as the barricades are intellectual and nothing else. What do I tell the bank?'

'Nothing. Tear up their forms, don't answer their calls. Leave them with their fantasies. You receive money from an Arab charity and when you were a beardless child, you were a pseudo-militant in Berlin. For their poor sick minds, that's already enough. You are clearly a Euro-terrorist with pro-Islamist sympathies. Did they mention that you were a comrade of the notorious rabble-rouser Sasha?'

'No.'

'I am disappointed. I thought I would have star billing in their ridiculous scenario. Come, Teddy.' He is scrabbling busily about, gathering up food, putting it in the plastic boxes. 'We have had enough of ill humour. We go back to your beautiful school, we drink a lot, we sleep in the attic like old times. And in the morning before I go to Hamburg you tell me whether you want me to find someone else to do the job, no problem. Or maybe by then we have our courage back, okay?'

And with the *okay*, Sasha slings his arm round Mundy's shoulders to cheer him up.

*　*　*

They are cycling side by side the way they learned to cycle together: Mundy soft-pedalling, Sasha precariously at his own speed. Evening dew is falling. The river runs beside them, the red castle observes them darkly in the failing light.

'You know what is bad about those bankers – actually wicked, I would say?' Sasha demands breathlessly, swerving into Mundy and righting himself in the nick of time.

'Greed,' Mundy suggests.

'Worse. Much worse.'

'Power.'

'Even worse than power. They are trying to put us into one bed. Liberals, socialists, Trotskyists, Communists, anarchists, anti-globalists, peace protesters: we are all *Sympis*, all pinkos. We all hate Jews and America and we are the secret admirers of Osama. You know what they dream of, your bankers?'

'Sex.'

'That one day a worthy policeman will walk into the offices of the anti-globalisation movement in Berlin or Paris or London or Madrid or Milan and find a big box of anthrax with a label on it saying, *From all your good friends in Al Qaeda*. The liberal left will be exposed as the closet fascist bastards they've always been, and the petit bourgeoisie of Europe will go crawling to its American Big Brother, begging it to come to its protection. And the Frankfurt stock exchange will go up five hundred points. I'm thirsty.'

A pit stop while they finish the red burgundy and Sasha waits for his chest to calm down.

From the attic of the schoolhouse, if you stand in the man-sized dormer window, you can watch the early summer's dawn steal along the red castle walls and down the river and over the bridges until the whole of Heidelberg has been taken without a shot fired.

But if Mundy must as usual be up and doing, Sasha who could never rise early is sound asleep inside the heap of sofa cushions and blankets and dust-sheets that Mundy put together for him when they had drowned their differences in a second bottle of burgundy. The Party briefcase lies at Sasha's feet beside his jeans and sneakers, he has one thin arm crooked beneath a cushion and his head on top of it, and if Mundy didn't know him better he might wonder whether he was dead because of the discretion of his breathing. On the floor beside him sits Mundy's alarm clock set for ten as Sasha asked, and beside the clock Mundy's note saying, *Cheerio, gone to Munich, give Hamburg a kiss from me, see you in church*. And as a PS: *Sorry to have been an arsehole*.

Carrying his shoes in his hands he pads down the big staircase and across the hall to the front door and sets off at a smart pace for the old town. It is by now half past eight. The tourist traps in the Hauptstrasse are still asleep and will remain so for another hour. But his business is not in the Hauptstrasse. In a glass and concrete side street not far distant from the railway station stands a Turkish travel agency that he has noticed on his wanderings. It seemed to be always open, and is open now. With cash that he has taken from a machine with the aid of his new bank card, he buys two excursion tickets from Munich to Ankara for Zara and Mustafa and, after a moment's deliberation, a third for himself.

With the tickets in his pocket, he walks again beside a busy road until he is the only pedestrian. He enters half-countryside. A paved footpath across a wheat-field brings him to a shopping complex where he finds what he is looking for: a line of public payphones in semi-cubicles. In his pocket he has thirty euros in coin. He dials first to Britain, then to central London, then to God knows where, because never in his life has he dialled such an unlikely set of digits, or so many of them.

And this is Edward's panic button for a rainy day, Nick Amory is saying quietly over a farewell luncheon at his club, handing him a bit of card with a number to memorise. *Whistle and I'll come to you, but you'd better make it bloody good*.

Holding a fountain pen at the ready, he waits for the dialling tone. It is interrupted by a woman's electronic voice saying, *Leave your message now*. With the fountain pen he begins tapping on the mouthpiece: this for who I am, this for who I want to talk to, because why announce yourself to half the listening world by using your own stupid voice?

The woman wants binary answers.

Is your problem immediate?

Tap.

Can it wait twenty-four hours?

Tap.

Forty-eight hours?

Tap.

Seventy-two hours?

Tap tap.

Now select one of the following options. If the meeting you require may safely occur at your last recorded residence, press five.

By the time she's finished with him, he's so exhausted that he has to sit on a bench and let himself dry out. A Roman Catholic priest eyes him, wondering whether to offer his services.

14

On the train back to Munich Mundy has offered up prayers of thanks to Zara's beloved youngest sister, whose wedding will take place in her home village one week from today. He has also noted that tomorrow is Zara's day off and, because it's a Thursday, Mustafa will be home at lunchtime.

The charter flight leaves two days from now at crack of dawn. Arriving at Munich's main station Mundy seeks out a luggage shop and buys a new suitcase – green, Zara's favourite colour – and, from a department store close by, a long grey dress and matching headscarf that according to her cousin Dina, mother to Kamal, she has long coveted. Since living with Mundy, Zara has taken to locking herself up from head to toe as a sign that she has returned to her tradition; but also she is demonstrating her pride that Mundy alone has the key to her. For Mustafa, also on Dina's advice, he buys a flash blue jacket and white trousers like Kamal's: the boys are the same size. Dina,

393

he has established, will also take charge of the dog Mo for the duration.

He next calls on Zara's kebab café. At eleven in the morning business is quiet. The manager, a tubby man in a skull cap, is at first disconcerted by the sight of Mundy bearing down on him with a green suitcase. Has Zara some complaint about her treatment? he enquires anxiously, from behind the safety of the counter. No, Mundy says, she has none. Now that you've learned to keep your hands off her, she's happy in her work, he might have added, but he doesn't. The manager insists Mundy accept a coffee on the house, and how about a slice of chocolate cake? Mundy accepts the coffee, declines the cake and proposes a deal: a month's unpaid leave for Zara with immediate effect, and Mundy will subsidise a temporary replacement to the tune of five hundred euros. They settle for seven hundred.

From a public phone box he calls Zara's Turkish doctor. I'm a bit worried about Mustafa, he says. Adolescence seems to be weighing him down. He's doing all right in class, no truancy, but he's gone solitary, he's sleeping ten hours a day and looking very grey. 'It is the dusk of puberty,' says the doctor knowingly. So what Mundy is wondering, doctor, is this. If I can rustle up the money to send Mustafa and his mother back to Turkey for a big family beanfeast, could you see your way to providing a medical certificate that will satisfy the school authorities?

The good doctor believes he can reconcile this with his conscience.

Mundy calls the Linderhof and makes yet another excuse for not coming in, but it is not well received. He feels badly, but knows no remedy. Returning home, he lets Zara sleep until Mustafa comes back from school, then leads her by the hand to the tiny living room where he has set the stage. The softness of her palms always amazes him. He has placed her youngest sister's photograph prominently on the sideboard, and the green suitcase on the floor below it with the new dress and scarf draped over one corner. Mustafa wears his new blue jacket. Zara's front teeth are repaired but in her apprehension she runs her tongue across them to make sure they are there.

He has laid the tickets side by side on the table together with the written release in Turkish from the manager of the café. She sits down straight as a schoolgirl on the centre chair, arms to her sides. She stares at the tickets, then at Mundy. She reads the letter from her Turkish employer, and without expression replaces it on the table. She takes up the nearer ticket, her own. She studies it with severity and only brightens when she discovers that she may return in three weeks. She seizes Mundy roughly by the waist and presses her forehead against his hip.

Mundy has one more card to play. It's the air ticket for himself. It takes him to Turkey for the last week of their trip, and brings him back with them on the same plane. Zara's happiness is complete. The same afternoon, they make ecstatic love and Zara weeps with shame that she ever doubted him. Mundy's shame is of a different order, but eased by the knowledge that she and Mustafa will soon be out of harm's way.

Driving Zara and Mustafa to Munich airport in the small hours, he at first fears ground fog but by the time they arrive it's lifting and there are few delays. Shuffling down the check-in queue, Zara keeps her eyes down and clings so hard to Mundy that he imagines she is his daughter and he is sending her off to boarding school against her will. Mustafa holds her other arm and makes jokes to keep her spirits up.

At the counter there is business about the trolley-load of gifts that Zara has bought for her sisters, brothers and cousins out of her savings. A container is found. Some of the parcels must be repacked. The distraction is helpful. In his last sight of her, Zara is standing at the passenger departure doors as they close on her. She is bent double like Rani at the roadside, choking over her folded arms, and Mustafa is trying to console her.

Alone with his thoughts on the autobahn, heading north and isolated by a deluge of heavy rain, Mundy is brought back to time present by the trilling of his cellphone. That bloody man Rourke, he thinks, as he shoves it to his ear, and he is preparing to be short with him when to his astonishment he hears Amory, *en clair*, on an open line, chatting to him as if neither of them had a care in the universe.

'Edward, dear boy. Have I woken you from your slumbers?'

But he knows he hasn't.

'Received your message, and of course I'd love to,' he is saying breezily, in the manner of an old friend passing through town. 'How would today suit?'

Mundy considers asking Amory where he's speaking from but sees no point since Amory wouldn't tell him.

'Sounds great,' he says instead. 'What sort of time d'you have in mind?'

'How about one-ish?'

'Fine. Where?'

'How about your place?'

'In Heidelberg?'

'The school. Why not?'

Because it's bugged from ear to ear is why not. Because it's been surveyed for a whole day by polite young men and women. Because Rourke believes it's being prepared as a terrorist nest for Euro-anarchists who would like to split Germany from America.

'Our chum's in Hamburg, isn't he?' Amory continues, when Mundy still doesn't answer.

'Yes. He is.' If he's still our chum, thinks Mundy.

'Until late tonight, right?'

'So he says.'

'And today's Saturday, right?'

'So I'm told.'

'So there are no workmen tearing the place apart.'

'No.' Or putting it back together.

'So what's wrong with meeting at the school?'

'Nothing.'

'Family get off all right?'

'Like a breeze.'

'See you around lunchtime then. Can't wait. Masses to talk about. *Tschüss*.'

A salvo of torrential rain sets his car shuddering. Long bursts of summer lightning fill the sky. The Beetle needs time out, and so does Mundy. Crouched head in hand at a roadside restaurant, he picks the hidden signals out of Amory's message or – as Dimitri would have it – the fly shit out of the pepper. In his laborious dialogue with Amory's electronic lady Mundy had suggested they meet at a remote service station ten miles out of Heidelberg. Instead they are to stage a jolly reunion at the scene of the crime, with Rourke listening to their every word.

So what has Amory told me so far – Amory who never says anything without a purpose?

That he is speaking for the record, over an open line, with nothing up his sleeve. But whose record is he speaking for?

That he is being kept informed of my movements, and Sasha's, and my family's. But who by?

That he has masses to report to me, but only within the hearing of the people he got it from. Amory like Dimitri is an artist of the unobserved life. But this time he's telling me that he's observed.

Mundy returns his thoughts to where they were before Amory interrupted them. Where is she now? Overflying Romania, headed for the Black Sea. Thank Heaven for Mustafa. He longs for Jake but can't reach him. He never could.

Mundy is back at his place in the bay window on the first floor of the schoolhouse staring down the brick path the way he stared down it when he was keeping an eye out for Sasha and his consignment of core library books. He has parked his Beetle outside the front gates, the time is twelve-thirty of the same Saturday and, yes, Sasha is in Hamburg: amazingly for him, he has actually called Mundy to enquire whether he is still of stout heart, or would he after all prefer Sasha to find a replacement for him, because 'Look here, Teddy, we are both completely adult, I would say.' And Mundy for his part has assured Sasha that he is one hundred per cent committed to the great project, he believes in it. And perhaps in a way he does, since he has no option. To walk out on Sasha is to leave him to Dimitri and Rourke, whatever that means.

While he is waiting, Mundy has also done the stupid, anxious things that joes do when they're waiting for their case officers to show up: shaved and showered and pushed his dirty clothes behind a curtain, and prepared a sitting area in one of the classrooms, and put a hand towel and a cake of new soap beside the handbasin, and made a thermos flask of coffee in case Amory no longer drinks Scotch the way he used to. He had actually to stop himself going into the garden and picking wild flowers to put in a jam jar.

And he is still going through these ridiculous acts of over-preparation in his mind, while at the same time picturing the arrival of Zara and Mustafa at Ankara airport and the vast reception committee of her ecstatic relations, when he realises that a tan-coloured BMW with a Frankfurt registration has parked itself behind the Beetle, and that Nick Amory, younger by far than the years between that should have aged him, is emerging from the driver's side, locking the car, opening the gate and setting course for the front door.

Mundy gets only one quick look at him before bounding down the stairs, but it's enough to tell him that Nick's nearly-sixty years sit well on him, that the old shagginess has acquired an unmistakable air of authority, and that the habitual smile, if that's what it ever was – though magically resurfacing the moment Mundy opens the door to him – was not on parade when he started up the path.

The other thing Mundy has noticed, and continues to notice as they square up to greet each other, is Amory's cap, which is a flat cap, green tweed, sporting, and certainly of a better cut than the cap favoured by the Major when he was roaring at Mundy from the touchline, or Des when he was carving the beef for Sunday lunch, or Sasha when he was wearing his *Tarnkappe*.

But a cap for all that.

And since Mundy has never seen Amory wear a cap or any other sort of headgear, let alone one that smacks so offensively of the rural English classes who are his professed aversion – largely, Mundy suspects, because they are where he springs from – it can't fail to excite his attention, even if he's too polite or too Edinburgh-trained to remark on it.

Stranger still, to anybody familiar with English manners, he doesn't take it off when he steps inside the house. He pats Mundy's shoulder. He does a cheerful 'How are you, cobber?' Australian style, and confirms in a quick question that nobody else is in the house or expected – 'And if we're disturbed, I'm your first pupil for September,' he adds, for cover. And then, like Sasha, he sweeps past Mundy and takes up a command position directly beneath the art nouveau skylight, a yard away from the island of packing cases and dust-sheets that, like a statue waiting to be unveiled, dominates the main hall.

But the cap stays put, even while Mundy gives Amory his desired tour of the property. And that's not because Amory has forgotten he's wearing it. To the contrary, he gives it a tweak now and then to make sure it's still there, in much the way Sasha used to tweak his beret; or a shove from behind as if he hasn't got the angle quite right; then a tug at the peak to keep the sun out of his eyes, except that there isn't any: the rain may have stopped, but the sky is black as soot.

Their tour of the property is perfunctory. Perhaps Amory feels as uneasy about his presence here as Mundy does. And as always with Amory, though you forget it between times, he says nothing without purpose.

'Has our chum still not given you any clear picture of what he got up to in the Middle East?' he demands, as he peers down at the pile of soft goods that was Sasha's temporary bed.

'Not really. Travelling lecturer. The odd short-term

contract where they needed a spare professor. Whatever came along, as far as I can see.'

'Not what we'd call a full life then, was it?'

'Plus a bit of aid work. Aid work was hard to come by because of his legs. Basically he was – well, just some kind of wandering academic bum, from the little he's told me.'

'A wandering *radical* academic bum,' Amory corrects him. 'With *radical* and not so academic chums, perhaps.'

And Mundy, instead of attempting to moderate this, says he supposes so, because by now it's becoming clear to him that Amory, for whatever reasons, is playing to the gallery, and that Mundy's job is to support him and not try to take over the scene. It's the same rôle he used to play for Sasha when they were performing for the dread Lothar or the Professor, he thinks. Not every line has to be a master-piece, he used to tell himself: just play it straight and the audience will come to you. He's telling it to himself now.

'And this will be the library,' Amory comments, examining the long room with its builders' ladders and buckets.

'It will.'

'The shrine to objective truth.'

'Yes.'

'Do you seriously believe that crap?'

Mundy has asked himself the same question a few hundred times by now, and is no nearer to a satisfactory answer.

'When I listened to Dimitri, I believed it. When I got out of the room, it began to blur,' he replies.

'And when you listen to Sasha?'

'I try.'

'And when you listen to yourself?'

'It's a problem.'

'It is for all of us.'

They are back in the hall, contemplating the veiled statue of library books.

'Looked inside any of this stuff?' Amory asks, giving his cap another shove.

'I've read a couple of the inventories.'

'Got one handy?'

Mundy pulls back the dust-sheet, picks a plastic envelope from the lid of a packing case and hands it to him.

'Standard stuff then,' Amory remarks, when he has run his eye down the list. 'Available in any lefty library.'

'The strength of the library will be in its concentrated message,' Mundy says, quoting Sasha and sounding hollow to himself. He is preparing to trot out more of the same when Amory thrusts the inventory back at him to say he's seen enough.

'It stinks,' he announces to the house at large. 'Specious, unreal and bloody suspicious. My only problem is, why are you working for that layabout Jay Rourke instead of a decent intelligence officer like me?'

Then he gives Mundy a fat wink, and another buffet on the shoulder, before proposing they get the hell out of here and go somewhere foully expensive for lunch.

'And we'll take my car, if you don't mind,' he murmurs as they set off down the path. 'It's cleaner than yours.'

Inside the BMW, Amory keeps his cap on, but the levity he displayed indoors deserts him and lunch is no longer the first thing on his mind.

'Do you know this town well, Edward?'

'I lived here for three years.'

'I'm a glutton for mediaeval castles. Places with very thick walls and maybe a band playing. I rather think I spotted something of the kind as I drove here. We'll pick up a Wurst as we go.'

They park in the old university square. Mysterious as ever, Amory has got himself a permit.

For half his life, Mundy has been a witness to Amory's facial mannerisms. He has known him resolutely impassive under strain; and resolutely indifferent in success. He has watched the shutters come down when he has attempted to penetrate Amory's private life: to this day he is not sure whether Amory is married or single, or has children. Once or twice, in a supposed moment of confidence, Amory has referred to an infinitely forbearing wife and two achieving children at university, but Mundy is never certain that he hasn't lifted the scenario from the pages of John Buchan. Otherwise, he has remained what he was when he first appeared at Mundy's bedside in the military hospital in Berlin: a dedicated professional who never crosses the white line, and doesn't expect you to cross it either.

It is therefore disturbing to Mundy, as they tramp with the crowds up the steep cobbled lane towards the castle ruins, to see signs of indecision in his old mentor. Nothing has prepared Mundy for this loss of sureness in his last remaining adult. It is not till they reach the castle's apothecary museum, and are standing on the wobbly red-brick floor, bowed over a glass case of *materia medica*, that Amory at last removes his cap and, taking a deep breath through his nose with his lips pressed together, speaks the first small part of what is on his mind.

'My instructions are unequivocal. You take Rourke's shilling. You stay with the operation to the end and beyond. You work for Rourke exactly as you would work for us. Got it?' He has transferred his attention to a wooden effigy of the healing St Roch, and the dog that brought him his daily bread while an angel cured him of the plague.

Mundy stoops obediently beside him. 'No,' he replies, with a firmness that surprises him. 'I haven't got it at all. Not any part of it.'

'And neither have I. And so far as I can read it from what I'm not being told, neither has anyone in the Service.'

Not *shop* any more. Not *firm, office* or *outfit*. Amory may be speaking softly but he is speaking in clear text.

'So who gave you your orders if the Service didn't?' Mundy asks stupidly, as they head back into the crowded courtyard.

'Our masters, who d'you think?' Amory retorts, as if it is Mundy, not he, who is speaking out of turn. 'The advisor to the advisor to the Highest in the Land gave the orders. Whoever makes his Ovaltine at night. "Do as you're told and shut up and this conversation never took place." So I'm doing as I'm told.'

But you're not shutting up, thinks Mundy as they follow a group of plump Frenchwomen down a steep stone staircase.

'Do you happen to know the great Dimitri's real name by any chance?' Amory murmurs, very close to Mundy's ear.

They have reached the cellar darkness of the Big Barrel and are surrounded by tour groups of French, Japanese and Germans, but apparently no English-Spokens. Amory is talking under the cover of their polyglot chatter.

'I thought you might,' Mundy replies.

'What I know about Dimitri, or any other part of this so-called operation, would go on the back of a very small water-beetle,' says Amory.

'Well, Rourke must know his name, for Heaven's sake!'

'You'd have thought so, wouldn't you?' Amory agrees, gazing up admiringly at the Big Barrel's monstrous belly. 'It would be logical, in the normal scheme of things, if one is pursuing the greatest villain of the moment, night and day, to know the fellow's name.'

'Well, have you asked him?'

'Not allowed to. Haven't spoken to dear old Jay – not since he paid his State visit to Bedford Square. He's *far* too secret these days. All dialogue with the dear man has to go through channels.'

'*Which* bloody channels?' Mundy demands, surprised by Amory's lack of reverence for the old mystique, and his own.

'Some Born Again marvel in the US Embassy in London who calls himself Special Defense Liaison Officer and is so grand he doesn't bother to speak to his ambassador,' Amory replies in one long, carefully pointed expletive, as they clamber back up the steps and into the sunlight.

It has not occurred to Mundy – and why should it since it has never happened before? – that Amory's perplexity might exceed his own. Nor that Amory's anger might one day get the better of his discretion.

'There's a new Grand Design about in case you haven't noticed, Edward,' he announces, loudly enough for anyone who cares to hear him. 'It's called *pre-emptive naivety*, and it rests on the assumption that everyone in the world would like to live in Dayton, Ohio, under one god, no prizes for guessing whose god that is.'

'Where does Dimitri get his money from?' Mundy demands, desperate for hard ground, as they start back down the path towards the town.

'Oh my dear fellow, all those bad Arabs, who d'you think?

He's doing their dirty work in Europe for them, rallying the Euro-anarchists to the flag, so he's worth every penny,' Amory replies airily. 'Red squirrels,' he goes on, pausing to peer into the branches of an oak tree. 'How nice. I thought the greys had eaten them all up.'

'I don't believe Sasha knows any part of this,' Mundy urges, forgetting in his perturbation the conventional *our chum*. 'I don't believe he's the man Rourke says he is. If anything, he's mellowed. Grown up. Rourke's talking up a storm.'

'Oh, Jay's talking up a storm all right. It's whipping down the corridors of Whitehall and Capitol Hill at a splendid rate.' Amory again breaks off, this time to allow two lanky boys in lederhosen to clatter past them. 'No, I don't expect our chum – your chum – knows a damn thing about any of it, poor soul,' he resumes reflectively. 'He was never much of a one to see round corners at the best of times, was he? He's fallen for Dimitri hook, line and sinker by all accounts. Besides, he's too busy signing up all those lefty academics and producing core libraries of counterculture. Lot of interesting books there, by the way, Edward. You should take a look at them sometime.'

Which to Mundy's ear makes a thunderous contrast to his earlier dismissal of them. They are entering the Corn Market. At its centre, a bronze Mother of Christ proudly displays her child, while her foot tramples the fallen beast of Protestantism.

'Rourke isn't Agency any more, by the way,' Amory is saying. 'Did I happen to mention that? He signed up with a politically motivated group of corporate empire-builders four years ago. Oil chaps, most of them. Strong attachment to the arms industry. And all of them very close to God. In those days they were fringe but today they're playing to packed houses. Good people, mind. Just like we gung-ho British imperialists used to be, and I'd rather hoped we weren't any more.' They are close to the town centre. Amory seems to know the way. 'Unfortunately, I never took much interest in politics before. Now it's a bit late,' he remarks through his all-weather smile. 'However, *please* don't let that discourage you. The fact that this or that improbable rumour has come my way should not deter either of us from serving our country *exactly* as we are commanded' – his voice now heavy with sarcasm – '*all* that matters as far as our lords and masters are concerned – whether they're sitting in Washington or Downing Street – is that this *splendid* operation will play a vital rôle in the task of bringing Europe and the United States closer together in our unipolar world. They regard your mission as absolutely –' he searches in vain for an adequate superlative.

'Alpha double plus?' Mundy suggests.

'Thank you. And if you play your part to the hilt – which I'm sure you will – there'll be no limit to their bounty. *Huge* cash prizes just waiting for the lucky winner. Medals, titles, directorships. You have but to ask. As one long familiar with your mercenary streak, I feel I must make this clear to you.'

'Rourke's offered me a pretty good package too, actually.'

'Of course he has! And so he should! What more could you ask? A double whammy. Go for it. And talking of double whammies' – Amory drops his voice. They are standing shoulder to shoulder before Ritter's Hotel, studying its superb baroque façade. Rain is falling, and other pedestrians have taken to the doorways – 'consider *this* possibility, Edward, while we're about it. Suppose Brother Jay and Dimitri Who Has No Other Name, instead of being at each other's throats, which ideologically they plainly are –' he breaks off, waits for a group of nuns to pass. 'Are you hearing me?'

'Trying to.'

'Suppose Dimitri and Jay, instead of being deadly enemies, were two horses from the same stable. Would that make any sense to you?'

'No.'

'Well, think about it, Edward. Exert your under-used grey cells. Your guess is quite as good as mine, probably better. Lying for one's country is a noble profession as long as one knows what the truth is, but alas I don't any more. So let us echo our masters and agree that this conversation never took place. And let us both blindly serve our Queen and country, notwithstanding the fact that both are wholly owned subsidiaries of the one great Hyperpower in the Sky. Agreed?'

Mundy neither agrees nor disagrees. They are approaching the Universitätsplatz, where Amory parked his BMW.

'However,' Amory resumes, 'just in *case* you should decide to get as far away from here as you can in the shortest possible time, I've brought you a couple of fake passports. One is for you and one is for our chum, in recognition of services rendered by the little bastard. I'm sorry I couldn't do Zara as well, but at least she's out of the way. You'll find them in the door pocket of the BMW on the passenger side, wrapped in a copy of the *Süddeutsche*. There's a bit of money, not a great deal. I had to steal it from the reptile fund.' Amory's face falls and becomes its age. 'I'm very, very sorry,' he says simply. 'For myself as well as you. Divided loyalty was never my thing. Don't tell our chum where you got them from, will you? You never know who he may fall for next.'

As they reach the BMW the rain stops, so Amory puts on his cap.

He has walked and drunk a bit, not a lot, just taken the edge off his nerves. He has tried to connect himself with the man he used to be, looked up a couple of old haunts but the faces have changed and so have the haunts. From a park bench in the Old City he has tried to phone Zara in Ankara and got no reply. But then he doesn't really expect one, does he? They're having a welcome-back knees-up at one of the other farms, of course they are! They'll be getting her to dance, not that she'll need any encouragement. Makes you wonder, when a girl who can dance like that falls for a giraffe like me.

All the same, from the same park bench, he has rung the airline and established that their plane landed safely at its destination three hours late.

Just odd her cellphone doesn't work. But then didn't I read somewhere that the Americans have depleted the satellites – something to do with Saddam's world-menacing strike power that mysteriously didn't show up on the day?

He walks again. Anywhere but across the bridge and up the hill and back to the school. With a child's wonder, he examines the eternal spire of the Church of the Holy Ghost carved against the evening sky. What would it be like really and absolutely to *believe*? Like Zara. Like Mustafa. Like Jay Rourke's chums. To *know*, really and absolutely *know*, that there's a Divine Being not set in time or space who reads your thoughts better than you ever did, and probably before you even have them? To believe that *God* sends you to war, *God* bends the path of bullets, decides which of his children will die, or have their legs blown off, or make a few hundred million on Wall Street, depending on today's Grand Design?

He is climbing the hill after all. No excuses: there was nowhere else to go. If he knew how Sasha was getting back from Hamburg, that would be another matter. He might try to head him off, go to the airport, the railway station, the terminal and say: Sasha, sport, we've got to elope. But Sasha doesn't need to know. He just needs to do what he's told.

Elope, Teddy? I think you are being a little bit ridiculous, actually. We have a great mission to fulfil. Are you losing heart again already? Maybe I should find you a replacement.

He goes on climbing. Perhaps the Lord will provide after all. Or Rourke will. Or Dimitri will, now that we suspect they come from the same stable. In the meantime my job is to get back to the school and wait till Sasha shows up. Then we'll discuss who elopes when and who with and why. The *Süddeutsche* is folded longways inside his jacket. One corner prods his neck. It's been a bloody long day, Edward, dear boy. What time did you get up? I didn't. In the small hours I was driving Zara and Mustafa to Munich airport and I haven't put my head down since. Then maybe you're too tired to face the microphones tonight, Edward. Maybe give yourself a break, dear boy, and pin a note on the school door: 'Gone to the Blue Boar for the night. Join me there. *Tschüss*, Teddy.'

The false passports inside the *Süddeutsche* are really weighing him down. So is that little extra bit of money stolen from the reptile fund – except that if Mundy knows anything about Amory, he stole it from himself and not the reptiles. The Amorys of this world don't steal. They serve their country right or wrong. Or they do until the day when they come face to face with real life and their warped rectitude deserts them and their faces unlock and become real, puzzled faces like everybody else's. So there's another god for you that's passed its sell-by date: enlightened patriotism, until this afternoon Nick Amory's religion.

No lights are burning in the windows, but that's not surprising since Mundy didn't leave any burning. On the other hand, those young surveyors might have decided to drop by and do some more surveying. But they've got hand torches. The gates squeak. Must oil. Tell old Stefan. In the darkness, the brick path weaves around and his big feet keep wandering off it into the long grass. I shouldn't have had that last one. Mistake. Very quiet up here. Always was, come to think of it. But not as quiet as this, surely. Not on a Saturday night. Must be a big football match on television, except that I can't hear anybody's television set playing, or see any blue lights flickering in windows.

He finds the lock first time and stands in the darkness of the hall trying to fathom where the electricians put the new switches. Worse than Trotsky, I am with my geography, ask Sasha. Under the glow from the skylight, the shrouded pile of books looms over him like a spectral Grand Inquisitor at the centre of the hall. *Lot of interesting books there, by the way, Edward. You should take a look at them sometime.* Good idea, Nick. Come to think of it, I've got a lot of reading to catch up with. He pats the walls, finds the switches but they're not switches, they're dials. Nothing's simple any more. The new lights dazzle him. He sits down on the stair, tries calling Zara again. Still no answer. Pouring himself a Scotch and water he moves to an old leather sofa in a corner of the hall and scrolls through his cellphone in search of her uncle's farm, but fails to find it. Neither for the life of him can he remember the old boy's name, nor the name of his farm. Too many C-cedillas and unintelligible spellings.

Take another pull of scotch. Reflect. Ten-thirty-five by the Major's tin wristwatch. In Ankara it's one hour later. Mustafa will be having the time of his life in that flash blue jacket. Wonder what old Jake's up to. Bringing the rafters down at Bristol University Union. Last heard of, he was running for Treasurer. Kate said she'd send me his cellphone number. Didn't. Must have got stuck in the Ministry's mail room. Maybe if she'd marked it secret they'd have sent it quicker. Cheers.

'And cheers to all our listeners tonight,' he adds aloud, and raises his glass in tribute to the walls. 'Marvellous chaps,' he adds. 'And chapesses, naturally. Bless you all.'

This room would make a pretty decent mosque, he decides, remembering his instruction at the hands of Mustafa. It's entry-free, it has a wall that faces east. So it qualifies. Put a little basin over there in the corner for our ritual cleansing, your *mihrab* where the fireplace is, make sure it points to Mecca, portico there, pulpit here, get some tiles with geometric designs and beautiful calligraphy and a carpet with prayer mats drawn on it, put some kids' rucksacks along the wall and we're home free – how am I doing, Mustafa?

Never took him swimming. Damn. Promised we'd go before they left, and we both forgot. Note to self: swim the moment we get back.

He scrolls up Dina's number in Munich and calls her. How's old Mo doing, Dina? *Pining, Ted*. And no, Dina hasn't heard from Zara either. But then she wouldn't expect to, not unless something had gone wrong. They're probably having a big party over at the farm, she says. Probably they are, he agrees, and transfers his thoughts to Sasha. So where the hell are you, you shit-faced poison dwarf? Late, Teddy. I shall be late. I have many fine academics to interview.

Well, what sort of late, for Christ's sake? Late like midnight? Late like three in the morning? Why should Sasha care? How's he supposed to know I'm sitting here like an anxious mother waiting for her fifteen-year-old daughter to come back from her first date? *Hurry*, you little bastard. I've got the passports. *Hurry*.

He gets up and glass in hand climbs the two flights to the attic just in case, by some miracle, Sasha has come back early after all and gone to sleep on his pile of improvised bedding, but no Sasha is secreted among the cushions.

He descends the curved staircase, very sober now, one hand for his whisky, one for the boat. The shrouded heap of boxes observes his cautious descent. *You should take a look at them sometime*. Reaching ground level he continues to the library. Amid ladders, dust-sheets and paint pots, he locates a carpenter's box. No padlock. A trusting fellow carpenter. Good chap. He selects a hammer and what Des called his Winston Churchill: a wrench with two fingers in a V. He returns to the hall and sets his whisky on the floor beside the leather sofa. He removes his jacket but is careful to lay it sideways on the sofa so that the *Süddeutsche* doesn't undress itself by mistake in front of the cameras.

Purposefully, almost vengefully, he drags the dust-sheets from the shrouded pyramid, rolls them up and slings them into a corner of the room. Take that. With the hammer in one hand and the Winston Churchill in the other, he selects a crate and begins prising apart the battens. As he does so, it is his fantasy that he hears a gasp of alarm from his unseen audience. Or perhaps it's a kiddies' matinée he's imagining, and they're all yelling, 'Don't do it!' or 'Look behind you!'

And he does indeed look behind him – but only at the window, in case Sasha's taxi has pulled up. No such luck.

He has ripped apart the battens on two sides. Des would suggest a bit more science, please, Ted, but Mundy isn't interested in science. Next comes a skin of thick brown paper joined with masking tape. The snarl it makes when he tears it off takes him by surprise. Inside it twelve cardboard boxes are stacked like bricks. Each crate has twelve boxes, each box has twelve books, he thinks facetiously: so how many boxes are going to St Ives?

Consult the inventory, Sasha advised. Box One, *Network Society*, Manuel Castells. Box Two, the same in German. Box Three, the same in French. He labours through each box. He labours through all the boxes. He selects another crate, smashes it apart. And a third. Our front-runner tonight is Frantz Fanon's *The Wretched of the Earth* in nine languages, so let's give a big hand to our Brother Frantz who's come all the way from Berlin to be with us here tonight.

He takes another look at the Major's watch. Midnight. The football match must be running into a lot of extra time, because in three years of living in this place Mundy has never known a silence like it.

But perhaps that's just fantasy too: when all your nerves are jangling, when one part of you is dog-tired and the other part is witless with worry, when you're sitting in a bugged house with a pair of fake passports and waiting for your infuriating friend to show up so that you can get him as far away as possible in the shortest possible time, it is only natural that noises – or more accurately the strident absence of them – should take on a supernatural quality.

At first he assumes it's just a book packer's stupid mistake.

He's come across a few of those by now: a couple of Adam Smiths that found their way into the wrong box, a half-set of Thoreau squeezed in with Thorwald, and Doris Lessing mixed up with Gotthold Ephraim Lessing.

Then his head goes a bit furry and he thinks he must be dealing with some sort of throwback of Sasha's, even a joke of some sort, because he's remembering how, long ago, when Sasha liberated his subminiature camera from the Stasi operational stores, he also helped himself to an urban guerilla's handbook that told him to put his exposed film in a condom and store it in ice cream.

But this isn't the same handbook.

And it's not just one random copy either.

Books that we anticipate will be heavily in demand are supplied in multiples, he hears Sasha intoning in his Party voice.

Well, this is sixty copies if it's a day. And they're not talking about ice cream either – not even about photography, miniature or subminiature. Their preferred subjects are how to make bombs out of weedkiller and how to kill your best friend with a knitting needle, or booby-trap his car or lavatory, or garrotte him in his bed, or drown him in his bath, or smash the horns of his larynx, or send a fireball up the liftshaft at his workplace.

Selecting his next box comes really hard to Mundy. He has a feeling that he mustn't get it wrong in front of his many fans; of being a contender in a high-profile quiz programme: screw this one up and you're out of the running.

But when he looks more closely at himself he realises he's already doing the wise thing and ripping open the boxes one after another without being concerned whether they contain core works of counter-culture or handbooks for aspiring terrorists or snug rows of grey-green hand-grenades the size of elongated cricket balls, with puckered casings so that you can grip them in sweaty conditions, or what he assumes are timers for homemade bombs, because that's what the enclosed instructions say they are.

So it's not all that long before he's sitting alone on the floor of the hall with every crate and box opened if not unpacked, and wrapping paper and straw all around him, and Mundy himself looking as bereft as any child on his birthday when there are no more presents to open.

And all he can hear in the unearthly silence is the sound of his own heart going whack, thump, whack, and Sasha's absent voice pontificating at him through the throbbing of his eardrums. *They are trying to put us into one bed. Liberals, socialists, Trotskyists, Communists, anarchists, anti-globalists, peace protesters: we are all* Sympis, *all pinkos. We all hate Jews and America and we are the secret admirers of Osama.*

And after Sasha's done lecturing him, he gets Rourke extolling the beauties of Heidelberg. *If you want to blow America and Germany apart, Heidelberg's not a bad place to make your point.*

But then it's Sasha's turn to come back with an even better point:

The liberal left will be exposed as the closet fascist bastards they've always been, and the petit bourgeoisie of Europe will go crawling to its American Big Brother, begging it to come to its protection.

But the final word and the most authoritative must come

416

from the savagely indignant Nick Amory this very afternoon. And when all these sibyls have said their lines and
faded backstage, that's Sasha's cue to make one of his own
inimitable appearances.

It can never be certain what prompted Mundy to go
charging up the stairs to the attic again. After all, he'd been
up there only an hour ago. Was it the rattle of automatic
gunfire in the street? Or the mayhem inside the house that
immediately followed it: the stun grenades, the smoke and
smashing glass as a dozen men at least stormed through
every door and window screaming at him in American,
German and Arabic, ordering him to freeze, lie down, back
up against the wall, show us your fucking hands and all
the rest of it?

It's generally accepted that people under this sort of attack
go upstairs rather than down, so perhaps Mundy was simply
behaving according to the standard pattern. Or was it some
sort of homing instinct that caused him to rush up there? —
his memories of the Berlin squat, and the random impulse
to return to it — perhaps in the confused expectation that
Sasha will be there ahead of him, or at least know where to
find him when he comes back from visiting his latest guru
in Frankfurt or wherever, only this time it's Hamburg?

Or was it merely to get a glimpse of what was going on
outside?

Nor could Mundy be sure how long he'd been sitting on
the floor surrounded by his toys before the shooting sounded
and he started his ascent. It could have been minutes, could
have been a couple of hours. Time, when you're stringing
together the net that has snared you, doesn't count for much.
Thinking is far more important. Comfortable ignorance, as

Dr Mandelbaum liked to say, is no longer the acceptable solution, however hard it is to face reality.

He hears the shooting, he sits up in slow motion and he says to himself, drowsily almost: Sasha, you're out there and it's dangerous. But when he thinks more about it, he decides that the car was starting to pull up before the shooting began. It was more like this: car, shooting, screech of tyres. On the other hand, it could have been: shooting, car pulls up, screech of tyres. Either way, he must obviously take a look.

The inside of the house is by now a deafening inferno of smoke and flashes and explosions and abusive screaming. Mundy's own name, coupled with Sasha's, is on the lips of every intruder. And what is remarkable to Mundy's ears, and worth a moment's thought outside the conventional borders of time, is that he's heard a couple of these voices before, when not very friendly hands were loading him blindfolded into the van, and reloading him into the helicopter, and slamming him face down onto the iron deck, before they took on human form and appeared tenderly before him bringing cups of hot coffee and Camel cigarettes and cookies and abject apologies, and calling themselves Hank, Jeff, Art and the like.

And is Mundy *totally* insane, or does he hear Jay Rourke's voice screaming above the rest? It's hard to tell because Mundy never heard Jay scream before, but he'd lay good money that inside that space-invader costume of his, it's the selfsame Jay Rourke whose dear father's birthplace was just sixteen miles from my mother's as the crow flies, if Irish crows fly straight, which Jay begs serious leave to doubt.

And on the subject of voices in the storm that all drowning sailors are supposed to hear as they go down, Mundy hears another familiar voice from his recent past that to begin with, for the life of him, he just can't place at all, until after a mental stretch he gets it: *Richard*. Blond Richard, with the blue blazer and airline steward's tie. Dimitri's Richard, who gives a thousand dollars in cash as an appearance fee to all potential employees, whether or not the interview has a successful outcome. Who wonders aloud what money is beside a great ideal.

So there we have it, Mundy tells himself, falling back on Amory's cumbersome dictum of this afternoon: two horses from the same stable, except that now they're beating down the door. However, he has not been idle while he is having these thoughts. Somehow or other the erstwhile second-row forward with long legs is making his way up the wide oak staircase that he always loved, paddling himself Sasha-like in unequal bounds because one of the legs is acting up and he's got a ton weight on his left shoulder where the ceiling hit it, but perhaps it was a flying object or one of those bullets they told him about in Edinburgh that are recommended for use on aeroplanes and in similarly delicate situations. They knock you for six and spread a pancake of molten lead on you, but they hardly penetrate the skin of a grape.

He makes it up the first flight and through the door to the old servants' staircase leading to the attic. A shower of bullets and plaster and smoke and invective comes up after him, but he has his wits about him, he is climbing, and when he gets to the attic and discovers he is on his knees mosque-style with his arse in the air and his face in his blood-caked hands, he can still crawl to the dormer window and crank himself up high enough to see over the sill.

And what he sees is truly amazing, the sort of *son et lumière* show you'd travel miles for. He remembers very well taking Jake to one in Caernarvon – or was it Carlisle? They had cannon and pikemen and halberdiers and siege towers and chaps pouring very lifelike boiling oil from the battlements, and Jake had a whale of a time: a divorced father's half-term to remember, for once.

But in its own way, this show is just as impressive: spotlights and floodlights and arc lights and searchlights, lights stuck up on cherry-pickers and flashing lights on the police vans and *grüne Minnas* and ambulances drawn up at each entrance to the little grass square below the front gate: lights everywhere except in the blackened windows of the surrounding houses, because marksmen like their privacy.

And costumes? Well, if you don't mind mixing ancient with modern, unsurpassed: frogmen rubbing shoulders with King Richard Crusaders in balaclava helmets, blackamoors with battleaxes, maces and witches' boxes lashed to their belts, West Berlin police in Prussian-style helmets, firemen dressed like Nazi storm-troopers, paramedics in tin hats and laundered white coats with red crosses on, and any number of mischievous black elves and hobgoblins flitting from doorway to doorway looking to stir up trouble.

And for your sound effects, instead of the usual tattoo music and spotty rumble of cannon-fire, we have the sergeant major from the parade ground at Murree, no less, barking unintelligible orders in English, German or, for all Mundy can hear, Punjabi. And at one side of the little square where the road goes by stands a brilliantly lit white taxi with all five doors open, and the driver kneeling next to it with two fellows in gas masks pointing guns at him – the driver being the same Herr Knau who delivered Sasha to the school a couple of days ago. Mundy remembered him as thin. Tied up he looks much fatter.

But the unquestioned star of the show, the man everybody

has come from miles around to see, is Sasha without his *Tarnkappe* but carrying his Party briefcase, skipping down the cobbled road with one sneaker missing and waving his free hand in the air saying, 'No, no,' the way a film star tells the paparazzi, please boys, not today, I haven't got my make-up on.

The loss of one shoe, paradoxically, has evened him out. You'd hardly know he had a limp from the way he skips from side to side like a Kreuzberg kid in the last throes of a game of hopscotch. Are the cobbles red hot? It's probably part of the game to pretend they are. Then suddenly he's outrun himself or he's missed his footing, because the champion's down, and rolling like a rag doll with no Mundy around to pick him up, and his arms and legs are rolling with him but it's probably the bullets that are keeping him going rather than his own efforts, because the bullets are tearing round him as well as into him, they're mauling him and disfiguring him, and even when he's well and truly dead, they seem unwilling to believe him, but give him one last all-together-now-boys salvo, just for safety's sake.

Mundy meanwhile is clinging to the window sill with both bloody hands, but unfortunately he hasn't got the attic to himself any more. There are two frogmen standing behind him, loosing off burst after burst of sub-machine-gun fire through the open window at the blacked-out neighbouring houses, just as coolly as if they were on the range at Edinburgh. And though they are patently over-supplied with weapons, they seem keen to use them all, no sooner firing one gun than dropping it, picking up another and firing with that.

And there's a third, tall fellow joined the party who, for

all the tack he's wearing, can't disguise his lazy Bostonian walk. He's backing away from Mundy as if he's scared of him, and he's putting his pistol back in his belt. But make no mistake: this is not the gesture of someone preparing to talk sweet reason with a wounded man lying on the ground. What this masked, languid anti-terrorist needs is something heavier to shoot with, which turns out to be some sort of sophisticated rifle with sights so big that an uninformed and recumbent person at the receiving end – such as Mundy – might not know which hole to watch when he is being shot. But this is not something that bothers the shooter, clearly, because when he's got himself as far away from Mundy as the room allows – until he's right up against the wall, in fact – he puts this same rifle to his shoulder and, with studied deliberation, fires three high-velocity sniper bullets into Mundy, one straight through the centre of his brow and two more at leisure into the upper body, one to the abdomen and the other to the heart, though neither can have been strictly necessary.

But not before Mundy has filled his lungs for one last intended yell of *Hang on, it's all right, I'm coming*, to his dead friend lying in the square.

15

The Siege of Heidelberg, as it immediately became known to the world's media, sent shock waves through the courts of Old Europe and Washington, and a clear signal to all critics of America's policy of conservative democratic imperialism.

For five full days, press and television were forced to observe something close to a puzzled silence. There were headlines – sensational ones – but there was no hard news, for the good reason that the security forces had operated the equivalent of a closed film set.

An entire sector of the city had been cordoned off, and its perplexed inhabitants evacuated to specially staffed hostels, and held incommunicado throughout the operation.

No photographers, print or television journalists were admitted to the scene of the outrage until the authorities were satisfied that every last shred of potential intelligence had been removed for analysis.

When a television news company's helicopter attempted

to overfly the area, it was seen off by American gunships and the pilot was arrested on landing. When the journalists complained, they were reminded that similar reporting restrictions had operated in Iraq. 'And what goes for the terrorists in Iraq sure as hell goes for terrorists in Heidelberg,' said a senior US defence official, on condition he not be named.

The involvement of American special forces in the siege was celebrated rather than denied, though it was the cause of some anger to the more liberal German constitutionalists. Journalists, however, were blandly reminded that the United States reserved to itself the right to 'hunt down its enemies at any time in any place with or without the cooperation of its friends and allies'.

In confirmation, German officials would only speak uncomfortably of 'ignoring artificial national barriers in the greater interest of the common struggle'. By common struggle was understood the war on terrorism.

One sceptical German commentator referred to the rôle of the German security services as a 'coalition of the belatedly almost willing'.

By the time the schoolhouse was finally opened to the press, there had obviously been a fair amount of cleaning-up, but what remained to be photographed was still rewarding. A total of two hundred-and-seven bullets fired from the terrorists' hideaway had spattered against empty neighbouring buildings. The absence of casualties among security forces was regarded as providential. A commentator for Fox News spoke of the Hand of God.

'This time we got lucky,' said the same senior Washington defence official who wished to remain anonymous. 'We went in there and we did what we had to do, and we came out without a nick on our finger. Unfortunately, there's always a next time. Nobody around here is crowing too loud.'

In addition to the bullet holes there were photo opportunities for bloodstains on the cobbles that had either escaped the cleaners' attentions or been left out of consideration for the press. By following their path it was easy to reconstruct the last moments of Terrorist A, now unmasked as a former Baader-Meinhof sympathiser in middle age known as Sasha, the son of a respected Lutheran pastor.

Sasha, it was revealed by unnamed sources close to the US Intelligence community, had worked in some of the darkest corners of East German Intelligence during the Cold War. His spying activities for the Communists had included the provision of training and other facilities to Arab terror groups.

When the Berlin Wall came down, Sasha exploited his old connections by signing up with a hitherto unknown splinter group of Arab militants believed to have links with Al Qaeda. This information was fed to the press piecemeal over several days, allowing ample time for journalistic licence.

Details of Sasha's twilit career, and his close contacts with members of the German and French radical establishment, were also emerging. Documents discovered in a briefcase he was carrying at the time of his attempted escape were being examined by forensic experts and intelligence analysts.

But it was of course the so-called 'Academy of Professional English' that provided the most blood-chilling insight into the terrorists' intentions. For weeks – until it was ruled unsafe and summarily closed on the orders of the city authorities – the devastated schoolhouse offered all the attractions of Scotland Yard's Black Museum. Television teams gorged themselves and came back for more. No newsflash was complete without the public's favourite images being replayed. And where the cameras went, the print media dutifully followed.

Some classrooms were so perforated by gunfire that, to quote one journalist, they resembled cheese-graters. The main staircase looked as though it had been torpedoed in shallow water. The library, which at the time of the battle was in the throes of being restored, had been blown to pieces, its marble fireplace pulverised, its moulded ceilings torn open and blackened by blast.

'When bad guys shoot first, it's true we get kind of testy,' the same anonymous Washington defence official conceded.

The testiness showed. Doors and windows were eyeless voids. The art nouveau skylight, point of entry for one team of invaders, was reduced to a rubble of coloured glass.

From these scenes of havoc the cameras turned lovingly to the prize exhibits: the bomb-making factory, the arsenal of small arms, sub-machine-guns and hand-grenades, the boxes of commercial chemicals, the urban guerilla's handbooks, the crates of inflammatory literature, the fake passports and the wad of loose cash for two terrorists who wouldn't be going anywhere any more. And best of all, the detailed maps of American military and civilian installations in Germany and France, some ominously ringed in red, the prize exhibit being a ground plan of US military headquarters, Heidelberg, together with covertly taken photographs of the entrance and perimeter.

Estimates of how many terrorists had been inside the school when it was attacked varied between eight and six. Ballistics experts found evidence of six separate weapons firing into the square. Yet only two men were accounted for and one of them never reached the building. So where were the rest?

Townspeople living close to the evacuated area testified to *grüne Minnas* tearing past their windows with lights flashing and sirens going. Others spoke of ambulances escorted by police cars and armoured personnel carriers. Yet no local hospital reported receiving any VIP casualties, no local mortuary or prison could boast a new inmate. On the other hand, the concentration of US military facilities and personnel stationed in the area – since Nine Eleven protected by electronically enhanced high wire – left open the possibility that casualties and prisoners had found their way there.

The devastation inside the school building made it nigh impossible to reconstruct the scene. The builders, questioned by journalists and police, recalled no visitors except for tradesmen and the tall Englishman since identified as Mundy. Bits of crockery and food found scattered around the rubble provided no hard evidence. Builders also have to eat. Terrorists, it is well known, are capable of sharing cups.

The official answer provided little comfort: 'To divulge further details at this time could endanger vital ongoing operations. Other persons found on the premises are in custody.'

What kind of persons? What age? What nationality, sex, race? What custody? Are they in Guantanamo already?

We have nothing further to add at this time.

One mystery figure who appeared to offer the chance of a breakthrough was the driver of a tan-coloured BMW hire car who had collected Mundy from the house on the day of the raid and was said by witnesses to have visited several of the city's historical attractions in his company. The unknown man was described as *fesch* – well-dressed, fit-looking, aged fifty-five to sixty.

The BMW was swiftly traced. The hirer was one Hans Leppink, a resident of Delft in Holland. Credit card, passport and driving licence confirmed this, but the Dutch authorities denied any knowledge of him, and offered no explanation of how he might have obtained such plausible Dutch identity documents. There was nothing for it but to go back to the two dead desperadoes, both in their fifties.

Sasha was clearly the easier of the two to categorise. A flock of terror-psychologists from obscure universities descended from their academic perches to do just that.

He was a German archetype, a child of Nazidom, a seeker after absolutes, the poor man's shrill philosopher, now anarchist, now Communist, now homeless radical visionary in search of ever more extreme ways of subjecting society to his will.

His physical disability, and the sense of inferiority it engendered, drew comparison with Hitler's propaganda minister, Dr Joseph Goebbels. It was common ground, on evidence nobody could afterwards remember, that he hated Jews.

His estrangement from his pious father, his mother's dementia and the prolonged, now suspicious, death of an elder brother while Sasha looked on callously from the boy's bedside, were awarded their proper significance.

So was there a particular moment in Sasha's life – these wise men and women speculated – was there some kind of epiphany, when Sasha saw the path of violence, the *black road*, open up before him and took it?

One writer, from the *New York Times*, knew above all others that there was. Under a sworn oath of secrecy, she said, she had received her story straight from the horse's mouth: an American Intelligence professional as modest as he is elusive, the acknowledged mastermind who had single-handedly brought Sasha and his British accomplice to justice. No physical or other description of this fine operative was vouchsafed by the gushing journalist, beyond the revelation that he was tall, rather formal in his manner and 'the kind of man I just *dream* of being taken out to dinner by, and never am'.

Sasha habitually spoke of the desert as his *wilderness*, this superhero had confided to her: 'You may think I'm crazy, Sally, but I personally am convinced that while Sasha was out there in what he called his *wilderness*, he underwent some kind of very yucky, self-induced religious conversion. Okay, he was an atheist. But he was a reverend's son and he hallucinated. Maybe he used drugs, though I have no direct evidence of that,' he added, speaking as a man who takes the truth seriously.

But it was Ted Mundy who put their penetrative powers to the test. It was the Pakistan-born public-school cricketer, son of a soldier, Oxford drop-out, Berlin anarchist, British Council flunkey, failed teacher and Muslim sympathiser, who received the full benefit of the dissectors' knives. One tabloid even went in pursuit of the dog called Mo. MO – or MAO? it screamed, and for a couple of issues Mo became the canine equivalent of Citizen Kane's 'Rosebud'.

Much quiet compassion was lavished on Mundy's ex-wife Kate, New Labour's ambitious Member for Doncaster Trent, now happily wedded to one of the Party's leading back-room policy-makers, but with her shining future suddenly uncertain.

'Though our marriage lasted eleven years, it was in reality short-lived,' said Kate, reluctantly facing the cameras on her second husband's arm to read a prepared statement. 'There was never any overt friction. Ted was a loving man in his way, but very secretive. For most of the time we were together his thoughts were a complete mystery to me, as I am afraid they will be today to many people round the world. I cannot begin to explain how he became what he apparently became. I never heard him speak of Sasha. I was totally unaware of his political activities while he was studying in Berlin.'

Jake, standing at her other side, was even briefer. 'My mother and I are extremely distressed and confused,' he declared through his tears. 'We ask you to respect our grief as we struggle to come to terms with this tragedy.' And in a grammatical solecism that must have had Mundy spinning in his grave: 'As my natural father, I shall always feel there is a hole in my life I can never fill.'

Gradually, however, under the intense scrutiny of commentators, Mundy the closet terrorist was winkled out of his shell.

His early obsession with Islam was confirmed by school contemporaries: *Mundy insisted on referring to school chapel as the mosque*, said one.

So was his angry nature. One former schoolmate referred to the near-manic ferocity of his fast bowling: *He was just so f***ing aggressive (Daily Mail)*.

Another shed light on his unhealthy preoccupation with anything German. *There was an old chap who taught cello and German. He called himself Mallory. Some of the boys reckoned he was a Nazi in hiding. Ted made an absolute beeline for him. He used to spout German poetry at us until we told him to belt up.*

A leaked American Intelligence report revealed that, during an unexplained period of residence in Taos, New Mexico, Mundy had formed a relationship with two Soviet agents presently serving prison sentences: the notorious

Bernie Luger who used his cover as a painter to obtain photographs of US defence facilities in the Nevada desert, and his Cuban accomplice, Nita.

Speculation about how the British Council had come to employ someone with a West Berlin police record of mob violence and no university degree led to calls for a public enquiry.

Murmurings that Mundy had maintained secret contact with 'cultural attachés' from Communist embassies in London were not directly denied by the Council's spokesman. WHY THE HELL DIDN'T THEY SACK HIM? a tabloid demanded, over a disturbing statement from one of Mundy's former colleagues:

Ted was a total drone. None of us understood how he survived. All he did was work the Commie arts circuit and sit about drinking coffee in the canteen.

The bouncer of a Soho strip club claimed to recognise his photograph. *I'd know him anywhere. Big, gangly bloke, one of the over-friendly ones. Give me the grubby mackintosh brigade any time.*

But for the final clue to this complex man, it was widely agreed, the world would have to wait until the woman Zara, a retired prostitute and Mundy's common-law wife in Munich, could be persuaded to reveal her story. British chequebook journalists were already storming the prison outside Ankara.

Zara, who significantly had fled to Turkey with her eleven-year-old son on the very day of the siege, was arrested on arrival and was presently being questioned. There was speculation that the Americans had only allowed her to return to her homeland because Turkish interrogation methods were known to be robust. She had arrived in Germany as the bride of a Turkish labourer now in a Berlin jail serving a seven-year sentence for aggravated assault. Zara herself was described as religiously observant, intelligent, near-silent and strong-willed. The imam of her mosque in Munich, who was being held indefinitely under investigative detention, insisted that she was 'no sort of fanatic', but this view was challenged by one of her co-religionists, who refused to be named: *She's the type we must purge from our community as we progress into the twenty-first century*. It was later learned that Zara had borrowed a coat from her, and failed to return it before she left for Turkey.

Recent reports from Turkish police sources indicated that Zara, though a tough nut to crack, was beginning to see the wisdom of cooperating with the forces of justice.

So it was inevitable, once the mainstream media on both sides of the Atlantic had beaten their brains out solving the question of how Britain and Germany could have spawned two such heinous characters, that the usual Alternative Voices should have their irritating day.

The most prominent was to be found on a not-for-profit website pledged to transparency in politics. The offending article was entitled THE SECOND BURNING OF THE REICHSTAG — THE AMERICAN RIGHTISTS' CONSPIRACY AGAINST DEMOCRACY and its author was described as a long-serving field operative of British Intelligence who had recently resigned his post and was writing 'at risk of his pension and even prosecution'. The main plank of the article was that the entire siege, like Hitler's notorious burning of the Reichstag, was a sham, perpetrated by what he termed 'agents of a self-elected junta of Washington neo-conservative theologians close to the presidential throne'. The two dead men were as innocent of their trumped-up crimes as was poor Van der Lubbe, the Reichstag's alleged arsonist.

Signing himself ARNOLD – whether as a surname, first name or cover-name was not vouchsafed, though the use of capitals suggested the last – the writer identified 'a shadowy former operative of the CIA' as the creator of the deception, and Sasha and Mundy as his sacrificial victims. The accused man, referred to by ARNOLD with the letter J and described as a 'latter-day Born-Again Christian of Irish-American descent', was regarded by the orthodox intelligence community as a dangerous maverick.

J's unholy accomplice in the 'Second Burning' was an equally unsavoury Georgian-Russian known only as DIMITRI, a professional *agent provocateur* and intelligence pedlar with pretensions as a poet and failed actor. Having worked – sometimes concurrently – for the KGB, the CIA and the Deuxième Bureau, he was presently living in Montana under the Witness Protection Act as a reward for providing details of a bomb attack on an American air-force base which he himself had inspired.

The same ARNOLD further claimed that while Downing Street officials had refused to be party to advance details of the 'Second Burning', they had made clear in off-the-record conversations with their Washington partners that they would welcome any initiative that silenced once and for all Franco-German carping at America's conduct of the War against Terrorism, not to mention Britain's.

As evidence of this he pointed to the so-called 'Heidelberg-Sorbonne Axis of Evil' so beloved of the British right-wing press, and the witch-hunt mounted by those who wished to name and shame the 'freethinking' French and German intellectuals featured in Sasha's now notorious lists of 'mind poisoners' (*Daily Telegraph*) who had willingly signed up, according to the same newspaper, to 'indoctrinate impressionable minds in the three Rs of pseudo-liberalism: Radicalism, Revolution and Revenge'.

ARNOLD's fulminations became wilder as his article ran on. Ted Mundy may have looked like an ex-British Council deadbeat, he wrote, but he was an unsung hero of the Cold War, and his friend Sasha was another. Together, the two men had over a number of years supplied the Western Alliance with priceless intelligence on the Communist threat. ARNOLD even maintained that Mundy was the holder of a secretly awarded British gallantry medal, a claim promptly denied by Palace sources.

And as a *bonne bouche*, ARNOLD alleged that J, by means of a sophisticated smokescreen of proxies, was the sole shareholder of a security company specialising in bulletproof cars, personal protection and survival counselling for prominent Americans in the corporate and entertainment fields who were contemplating a trip to terrorist-stricken Europe. The same company owned the copyright in the only piece of video footage of the siege ever to appear. This showed a posse of unidentifiable heroes in full anti-terror rig storming through clouds of Hollywood smoke across the roof of the school building. In the background, just distinguishable between the chimney pots, lies the body of the Euro-terrorist Sasha, shot dead in the very act of flight. Medics are running over the cobbles towards him; a battered briefcase lies beside him. The clip, run and rerun on every television station in the world, had earned millions of dollars for its owner.

*   *   *

Downing Street's reaction to the ARNOLD piece was appropriately contemptuous. If ARNOLD exists, let him come forward and his allegations will be looked into. More likely, the offending article was the work of rogue elements of British Intelligence whose evident aim was to discredit New Labour and undermine Britain's Special Relationship with the United States. The Downing Street spokesman urged his audience to address larger issues such as real world outcomes, step-changes and effectuality indicators. The *Daily Mail* carried a searing attack on the 'latest whistle-blower to emerge from the shadows of the secret world' and pondered darkly on the hidden agenda of 'closet saboteurs of our nation's good name, masquerading as its protectors'.

Summing up the whole tawdry affair, a well-placed and reliable senior official with access to the highest levels of government was reported as saying that some people these days were getting a bit too George Orwell for their own health. He was referring, of course, not to Downing Street or Washington, but to the spies.

The political consequences of the siege were not slow to manifest themselves. Sasha's prediction that an Islamist-inspired Euro-anarchist outrage on German soil would have its citizens rushing to the shelter of their American Big Brother was no exaggeration. At first, the Social Democratic German Chancellor evinced a churlish reluctance to take the point. An early statement actually contested the *tendentious and premature conclusions* of the German right, which since the night of the siege had assumed a substantial lead in the polls. Realising that he was running counter to popular opinion, he was, however, forced to change tack, first by announcing an independent investigation by German agencies, then by lamenting that his country, having played unwitting host to several of the perpetrators of Nine Eleven, should *apparently have been selected as the showplace for further senseless acts of violence against our American friends.*

For his conservative critics the statement was insufficiently abject. Why wait a full week before speaking out? they demanded to know. Why bother with an independent investigation when the evidence is there for every idiot to see? And what's this weaselly *apparently* that has crept into the text? Go down on your knees, Mr Chancellor! Grovel! Have you looked at Germany's bank statements recently? Don't you know that America will only do business with its *friends*? Don't you realise they still hate us for siding with the French and Russians over Iraq? And now *this*, for God's sake!

But in the end, all was well. The Chancellor did everything short of sending Washington his head on a charger. The Bundestag's opposition parties joined the chorus. The dire fiscal punishments threatened by the US administration were deferred on the understanding that the Federal Government would adopt a more helpful attitude in 'the next stage of the war on terror', by which was clearly meant Iran. A further understanding – implicit if not stated – was that the Federal Government, God willing, would by that time be a conservative one.

Sasha was right too about the Frankfurt stock exchange, which after a period in the doldrums recovered its spirits. A gleeful columnist of Germany's powerful right-wing press boasted that Günter Grass was more prescient than he knew when he declared that we are all Americans now.

Only France, truculent as ever, refused to be moved by her neighbour's display of self-flagellation. An unnamed spokesman for French Intelligence pronounced the list of French left-wing academics supposedly linked to 'the Heidelberg school of Euro-terror' to be 'an Anglo-Saxon phantasm'. The integrity of France's fabled thinkers and academics would remain unscathed. A statement by a French presidential spokeswoman to the effect that 'the entire episode reeked of news manipulation of the most amateurish kind' was dismissed as particularly arrogant. More bottles of French wine were poured down American drains, French fries became Freedom Fries, and the Tricolour was ceremoniously burned in the streets of Washington.

Ingenious Russia, though worn down by economic cares, achieved a double benefit: the silencing of the last remaining voices of 'antisocial' opposition to the government, whether in the media or Parliament, on the grounds that irresponsible protest was the basis of all terror; and Washington's unstinted encouragement to pursue, with even greater vigour than hitherto, its murderous war on the people of Chechnya.

A final postscript was provided by the two dead terrorists themselves. Both men, it transpired, had made a will. Perhaps all terrorists do that. Both had expressed a wish to be buried alongside their respective mothers: Sasha the German in Neubrandenburg, and Mundy the Englishman on a sunbaked plateau near Lahore with views to the world's end in every direction. An intrepid journalist tracked down Mundy's final resting-place. His was the only fresh grave, she reported, but the broken Christian masonry makes it a popular place for children to stage their mock battles.

Cornwall, 9th June 2003

Acknowledgements

My sincere thanks to Sandy Lean, Ann Martin, Tony McClenaghan and Raleigh Trevelyan for their British India and Pakistan, to Imama Halima Krausen for her generous instruction in Islamic practices, to Anthony Barnett of openDemocracy.net and Judith Herrin for their radical Britain in the sixties and seventies, to Timothy Garton Ash, Gunnar Schweer and Stephan Strobel for historical and editorial advice far beyond the call of friendship, to Konrad Paul for his Weimar and Lothar Menne for his Berlin and much more, to Michael Buselmeier for his Heidelberg and John Pilger for his words of wisdom over dinner. I must also confess my indebtedness to the superb *Plain Tales From the Raj* by Charles Allen.

My apologies to the peerless administrators of King Ludwig's Linderhof, who in real life employ none but the best-informed guides, have no plant room in their basement, and whose only visitors are of the highest discernment and sobriety.